# PRAISE FOR
# LACUNA'S POINT

"Tim Meyer gets under your skin and simply no amount of scratching will ever extract him. Lacuna's Point is a rest area rendered by M.C. Escher and Lovecraft on a road trip straight to hell."

**- Clay McLeod Chapman, author of Ghost Eaters**

"Meyer has written yet another page turner. It's not just the plot that exudes a sense of urgency but the fact he is so damn good at writing compelling characters. You believe in them, feel for them and hours fly by as you yearn to discover more. Lacuna's Point yet again cements Meyer as a Must Read author."

**- Janine Pipe, author of Sausages: The Making of Dog Soldiers**

"Twin Peaks has a new home, and it's called Lacuna's Point - a distressing, horrifying and anxiety inducing read. A book which at points made me question my own sanity, and that my friends is the mark of a good book, and a masterful storyteller!"

**- Ross Jeffery, Bram Stoker Award-nominated author of Tome, The Devil's Pocketbook and I Died Too, But They Haven't Buried Me Yet**

"With Lacuna's Point, Tim Meyer delivers a tense and terrifying cosmic horror that focuses on the grief, pathos, and desperation of broken families and the characters who'd do anything to fix them. Even when he's letting his monsters run wild. With that as his baseline, the fear gets under your skin, and the tension builds and builds into an explosive climax. Highly recommended."

**- Zachary Ashford, author of Polyphemus and When the Cicadas Stop Singing**

# BOOKS BY
# TIM MEYER

PTERANODON CANYON

PARADISE CLUB

MALIGNANT SUMMER

THE SWITCH HOUSE

BLACK STAR

IN THE HOUSE OF MIRRORS

PRIMAL TERRA

THE THIN VEIL

69

# LACUNA'S
# POINT

## TIM MEYER

**DARKLIT**
PRESS

# CONTENT WARNING

The story that follows may contain graphic violence and gore.

Please go to the very back of the book for more detailed content warnings.

**Beware of spoilers.**

*For those waiting to be found...*

# CONTENTS

**PART ONE**

CHAPTER 1 ................................................ 15
CHAPTER 2 ................................................ 29
CHAPTER 3 ................................................ 39
CHAPTER 4 ................................................ 59
CHAPTER 5 ................................................ 73
CHAPTER 6 ................................................ 85

**PART TWO**

CHAPTER 7 ................................................ 109
CHAPTER 8 ................................................ 129
CHAPTER 9 ................................................ 153
CHAPTER 10 ............................................... 167

**PART THREE**

CHAPTER 11 ............................................... 191
CHAPTER 12 ............................................... 217
CHAPTER 13 ............................................... 227
CHAPTER 14 ............................................... 241

**PART FOUR**

CHAPTER 15 ............................................... 257
CHAPTER 16 ............................................... 269
CHAPTER 17 ............................................... 285
CHAPTER 18 ............................................... 301
CHAPTER 19 ............................................... 313
CHAPTER 20 ............................................... 327
CHAPTER 21 ............................................... 343
CHAPTER 22 ............................................... 355
CHAPTER 23 ............................................... 363
CHAPTER 24 ............................................... 375

# A TRIP TO LACUNA'S POINT

*(Or what happens to the blood in the heart of the American Dream)*

They say the heartland of America lies somewhere in the Midwest, but don't tell that to the good people of Lacuna's Point, for the good people of Lacuna's Point believe their town is not only the heart but the soul, the mind, the lungs, and the blood of our beloved country.

Sunshine sparkles on the mountains across the way, over the rolling hills of lush woodland. From the town's center, the majestic peaks are candy for any artist's eye, every shadowy, pale-violet stroke and frosted point, the way they stand tall and proud and confident in the backdrop like parents peering into their newborn's crib. The air is cleaner here, crisper, healthier. Not tainted by industrial pollution or car-cluttered highways. There is room out here in Lacuna's Point. Lots of sky, lots of space.

Lots of freedom.

Nature isn't the town's only attraction, mind you. There are other reasons to visit and stay for a while. The beautiful sights are only but a bonus. There is plenty to do, plenty to see, plenty to experience. Take, for example, the museum on the corner of South and Main, a place that offers not just a historical chronicling of Lacuna's Point but the Virginian coastline itself. The museum's a lovely place that's much bigger on the inside than the outside suggests, a fairly common theme you'll find during your stay. Things run roomier in the interiors.

All good towns have a library, and Lacuna's Point is no different. A wide selection of books and audio cassettes/compact discs can be checked in and out, and the best part—the librarians are very lenient when it comes to late fees. It's not uncommon to check out a new hardback, keep it for two weeks past the due date, and return the borrowed merchandise without being charged a dime. Isn't that nice?

There's a diner—ACE'S PLACE—but the doors only open for breakfast (the best diners are, forget that twenty-four-seven nonsense), a world-famous ice cream parlor that whips up the creamy good stuff right on site, a two-theater cineplex that plays contemporary and classic films alike and only charges a measly five bucks per ticket, and antique shops aplenty, perfect places to find that rare home accessory you've been looking for—you know the one, that piece that really finishes off that living room, giving it that special touch, that *je ne sais quoi* you haven't been able to find anywhere else.

But you can find it here. In Lacuna's Point. Here, you can find pretty much anything and everything your mind dreams of.

But only if you look. That's the important part—*the looking*.

Yes, the town itself sits in a time that has long since passed, crawled up into a ball and died, and in its slow death has given birth to a new age crippled by major technological advances and detrimental shifts in the political climate, molded by good old fashioned American greed and the harsh desire to speed things up, make things cheaper, and take advantage of hard-working people, all for the greater good of...

...well, we're not quite sure really who this illusionary beneficiary is. But he's out there. Somewhere. Lurking behind the curtain. Eating from the plate of the American Dream, licking the star-spangled banner clean. Devouring time and space and everything in between.

But this story isn't about that. Not now. Later maybe. Okay, so, this story *is* about that—but it's also about something else.

It's about two girls and their incidental arrival at Lacuna's Point.

It's about the dark side of the American Dream.

"That shit was delicious," Dawn said, pushing through the diner's double doors and out into the open air, a fresh blast of untamed wind blowing against her cheeks. Her hair went wild with the gust's direction, throwing dark-brown curls across her eyes. "I mean, the diners in Jersey have nothing on this place."

Sunlight warmed her skin, her soul. The day was perfect, not a cloud in sight. She hadn't felt this alive since graduation.

Kya Green, her best friend since the second grade, sipped from her to-go latte and smiled around the straw. "Girl, I feel five pounds heavier. If this is how we're eating at Georgetown every day, the freshman fifteen might become the freshman fifty, really fucking fast."

"For real, though."

The girls made their way from the diner and traveled across the quad, toward a small row of shops that ran parallel with Main Street. They had parked in front of Butch's Antiques and it wasn't lost on Dawn that her silver Honda Accord was the only vehicle occupying the street. Hell, now that she thought of it, since pulling into town, she hadn't seen another car or truck. Pedestrians traveled by sidewalk, stopped to take a rest on the park's benches, some of them scurrying across the quad, following signs that gave directional arrows, pointing toward LACUNA'S POINT'S 72nd ANNUAL ARTS FESTIVAL.

"Don't try to hide it," Kya said, tugging on her arm, pulling her in a new direction, the way the arrows suggested. "Dawn Brower never met an arts festival she couldn't avoid. Was this intentional? Drag me down here under the guise of meeting some boy, but really, you wanted to check out this artsy-fartsy festival, instead? Totally cool with it, D. Just, you know, you don't have to trick me with this whole, *I-met-this-guy-on-OK-Cupid* bullshit."

"No," Dawn said, almost resisting her friend's pull. *Almost.* "No, I had no idea this would be here. Honest."

"I don't believe you, sweet cheeks."

"Don't call me 'sweet cheeks.' It's weird."

Kya blew her a kiss, making sure the sound of her lips smacking was extraordinarily loud. "You know I love you, D."

"I love you, too. And I love that you want to take me to this festival because you know how much I love arts festivals…but…."

"Oh God. But what?"

Dawn shot her innocent puppy eyes. "But I promised Todd I'd meet him near the shore, on the boardwalk, underneath the Ferris wheel. We have fifteen minutes to get there, and you know how being late sets a bad first impression. You *know* this."

Kya broke her grip of Dawn's arm. She spun around and faced her bestie, slapped her hands to her cheeks, dropped her jaw, and mimicked, *"Oh, I promised Todd I'd meet him underneath the Ferris wheel. I don't want to be late. Ohhhhh."* She dropped the act and rolled her eyes. "Come on, D. Don't give me that shit. You know there're a thousand Tims or Todds out there surfing the Internet's free dating sites, and they're all the same, and they all want the same one thing, and you can pull one of these scrubs any time you want to."

"Hey, that's not true…"

"Girl. It's true. Open your eyes. Smart as you are, you sure think up some dumb shit."

Kya led her up the small grassy hill, and when they reached the top, Dawn could see the entire arts festival, or at least, a good portion of what was on display. Paintings, sculptures, musicians playing exotic instruments, small clusters of guests listening to poetry and literary readings, and there was even a stage where a trio was dancing to some ambient rock music, the echoes from the speakers extending across the field, reaching out to their ears.

"Wow," was all Dawn had to say, and she couldn't hide her appreciation even if she wanted to.

"Yeahhhh…" Kya said in her ear, "told you there was no arts festival you could refuse."

She was right. Dawn couldn't deny it; her best friend knew her, and that was all there was to it.

But as impressive as the arts festival was on the surface, her attention was drawn elsewhere, like a magnetic lure. Behind the open field packed with enough displays and performances to last them into the late hours of the afternoon, stood a magnificent structure, one she hadn't seen in real life until this moment. Only in textbooks had she examined this type of architectural beauty.

Behind them, a towering clock tower was positioned on the town's outskirt.

"D?" Kya said. She didn't even realize her best friend had wandered off ahead of her, at least ten feet separating them now. "You coming?"

"Yeah…"

"What is it?" Kya asked, but Dawn had tuned her out. Tuned everything out. The only thing she could concentrate on was that clock tower, its face's perfect circle, the bold-black Roman numerals that gathered around the hands' golden fulcrum like cult members during some sacred worship. She wasn't sure why, but she pictured each numeral as a robed guardian joining hands with the neighboring numeral. Praying. Whispering secrets. Chanting at unseen spirits awaiting their corporeal births. "Dawn!" Kya shouted, and this time she snapped free from the hold the clock tower had placed on her.

"Yeah?" Dawn said, blinking the same way she would as if she stared at the sun for too long. Bright spots dominated her vision, and for a brief moment she was petrified the effect would remain everlasting.

Quickly, she discovered it wasn't. Those spots faded as Kya approached her, and by the time she was in her face, they had vanished.

"What's up?" Her friend looked over her shoulder, at the clock tower. "You all right?"

"Yeah. Just. That clock tower…it sure is something, isn't it?"

Kya faced her again, and this time she looked concerned. Dawn couldn't tell if she was intentionally overreacting (as Kya was known to do) or if she was indeed terrified by her spacey moment. "Um, yeah," Kya said, "it's a clock tower. Do I need to take you to the medical tent or something? You're acting weird as fuck right now."

"No," Dawn said, stifling a laugh. "I'm fine."

"Well, come on, space cadet. Let's go experience some of that shitty art you love so much."

Kya led them to the small festival's entrance, a gated area where one older woman stood guard with a clipboard in one hand and a silver Thermos in the other.

"Two please," Kya said, and then dug a ten out of her pocket, the exact cost for two entries as listed on the "Welcome" board.

The woman set down her cup and took Kya's money, immediately placing the bill in the small register resting on the white folding table to her right. "Good to see folks like you out here enjoying the show," the older woman said, and the second the words left her mouth, Kya felt a flare burn up her insides. As if someone opened her up and threw a torch on her exposed innards.

"Folks like us?" Kya flared her nostrils. She tilted her head to the side like a puppy trying to understand some new human quirk. "Like, you mean, 'Black folks?' "

"Jesus," she heard Dawn whisper. A nervous laugh followed.

"I-I…" the woman stuttered, and a pained expression dropped down over her features like a window shade. "No, I d-didn't mean—"

"I'm just fucking with ya, granny," Kya said. "Know you didn't mean it like that."

*But did she?*

A look of relief washed over the woman's face, and she put her hand over her chest as if Kya had just relieved her of heart attack symptoms, some intense bout of squeezing. "Good Lord, you had me going."

"Apologies," Kya said through her teeth. She flashed the woman a smile and batted her lashes. Then she nodded at the sign. "73$^{rd}$, huh? Say, that's a lot of arts festivals."

The woman handed over the ticket stubs and stepped aside, allowing them access past the guard rails. "Yes! Lacuna's Point has a rich history. We're very cultured in the arts."

Kya scanned the faces of the attendees and exhibitors alike, all of them white. "Yeah, I see that." She stepped past the woman, but not without making sure she rolled her eyes and that the woman saw it.

A few paces later, Dawn caught up with her. "Thought you actually gave that woman a heart attack for a sec."

Kya shrugged. "Me too. But you can't say she didn't deserve it. At least a little. Maybe."

Dawn grumbled some half-hearted agreement. She loved her best friend, but there were just some things she would never understand.

For the next hour, they walked around the arts festival, stopping to glance at different paintings and sculptures, listen to people recite their terrible poetry and read from messy works of unpublishable fiction. The more they walked, the more she got the sense Dawn wasn't enjoying their stroll. It was the way she spoke with the artists, how she asked them about their work that clued Kya in. No energy emanated from her curiosity. It was all so very…routine. By the end of their tour, Dawn was nodding along with their answers, not even bothering to follow up her initial questions.

She'd seen her friend at arts festivals before. Normally, Kya would have to drag her away from the exhibits. *Literally* pull her along. Otherwise there was no shutting her up once she got going, speaking to the artists and sculptors, asking them about their materials, their processes—specifics Kya cared very little about but tagged along anyway because—hell—how many concerts and football games had she forced Dawn to endure? It was a solid trade-off.

"What's the matter?" Kya asked as they bypassed the final exhibit, a man with a fedora sitting behind his collection of water-color self-portraits. Kya couldn't blame her for skipping that one; they were dreadful depictions she wished she could scrub from her memory.

"Nothing." Head down, Dawn walked another few feet before announcing, "I gotta use the bathroom. Diner coffee…"

"Gross. There's a Porta-Potty over there." Kya pointed to the green, plastic rectangle that housed a toilet. "Remember to hover. You don't want any germs climbing up into any crevices."

Dawn flashed her a squinty smile and then made for the portable restroom. While she was gone, Kya faced the last artist and his awful collection of self-portraits. The man who'd crafted them grinned at her, clearly an invitation to come and chat, and Kya was disgusted to see he only had about five teeth left in his mouth.

"Ugh," she said, turning away from his display.

"You need to leave," said a voice to her left.

Kya spun and saw a young boy standing there, glancing around the area nervously, bouncing on his heels as if he was ready to sprint off at the first sign of trouble.

"Like, now," he said, his beady eyes darting from place to place, like he'd just escaped some parental stranglehold and whatever adult responsible for this little cretin was on the way to come claim him. After a brief delay, he leaned in and whispered, "You're new here. Right?"

"What the hell are you talking about, you little creep-O?" His hair was sandy-yellow and shaggy, and he wore a plaid button-down with clean jeans, no wrinkles in them. Not a single one.

She looked him over, up and down, and then decided she hated the town of Lacuna's Point, and wished Dawn hadn't forced her to come here at all, regardless of whether she was meeting some hot stud named Todd. The more she scanned the festival, the dopes walking like zombies from exhibit to exhibit, the more she despised it.

"You need to *leave.*" This time, he sounded like he meant it. Like it wasn't a joke.

She stared at the boy and took an offensive stance, like she meant to cream the little butterball if he didn't scram. "Look, kid, if you don't get the hell—"

"*It* will take you."

At this, she balked. "What?"

"Just take your friend and leave. Before it's too late."

Before she could question (threaten) him, the boy took off, speeding away from the festival and back toward town where pedestrians strolled the sidewalks at their Sunday pace.

*Fucking weirdo,* she thought, shaking her head. She glanced back at the redneck hocking his shitty wares, and he was still grinning away like he was trying to impress the purdiest thang he'd ever seen. Kya's stomach roiled. *Jesus, get me outta here. This was a mistake. A big mistake. Let me get back to Georgetown in one piece, and—*

Luckily, Dawn was emerging from the portable toilet. Kya had never been so happy to see her fair complexion, even if her face was currently held hostage by some unbecoming mood. The girl just looked…sour.

Kya ran to her. Once by her side, she hooked her arm around her best friend's waist and marched her away from the arts festival, back toward town, back toward their car.

For some reason, Kya felt every eye that occupied the open field fix on them. Watch them. Study them. Plot ways to keep them from leaving.

*It will take you,* the kid's words echoed in her mind, again and again, until that was all she could think about.

Dawn felt ill. She had wanted to puke inside the portable toilet but couldn't expunge the sick feeling that was coating her insides, clinging to her like honey to a comb, thick and sticky.

It was this place, she thought.

It was Lacuna's Point *doing* something to her.

"You wouldn't believe what happened," Kya said, gripping her tightly and ushering her toward the entrance/exit. "Some little twerp started getting in my face, talking all sorts of weird shit. Almost punched him in his little pre-pubescent ball bag, but I feel like that probably woulda been a bad move, considering the company and all..."

Dawn was hardly listening. She'd heard her friend's voice but absorbed none of the content. The words floated through her like a vague childhood memory she could only recall bits from.

The clock tower stood in her way, intruding on her thoughts. Her eyes were inexplicably drawn to it once again.

"Hey," Kya said, getting in front of her, stopping her from walking another step. "Hey, talk to me. What's wrong?"

"I don't know...I feel...*off*."

Kya licked her lips, then checked over her shoulder, eyeing the only viable exit. "Okay, look. I don't like this place either. It's creeping me the fuck out in a *my-dead-grandma's-funeral* sorta way."

"It's the clock tower," Dawn admitted, and she felt so stupid speaking those words aloud, even though they were true words. "It's watching us."

"What?" Kya shook her head. "Look. Never mind. It doesn't matter. Let's just go, D. Get your keys, where're your keys?"

Dawn went for her pockets, rummaged around, and withdrew her keys. She dangled them like doggy biscuits.

Kya snatched them. "Good. That's good. Let's walk. Now."

Dawn walked. She couldn't escape the lure of the clock tower, and every time she focused on the festival's exit, she found herself turning her head to the side, glancing up at the towering presence, that obelisk that, now, seemed to have grown and become one with the sky. Impossibly tall, the structure stretched the confines of what Dawn understood to be reality. Next to the hands that counted time, on a ledge beneath the ivory faceplate where the numerals were inscribed, a figure shrouded in daytime shadows introduced itself, identifying factors obscured by dark clothing and a black hood. In its hand, the figure held a rope attached to the inner workings of the clock. It pulled. Hard. With force.

A bell sounded, echoing across Lacuna's Point, bouncing off the mountain range, passing through the swaying clusters of greens, dying somewhere between them, and entering the canals of Dawn's ears all at once.

It was a bell that sounded like the kick-off to *the end.*

*The end of time, the end of everything.*

"We have to leave," Dawn said, picking up the pace. Kya was right there with her, step-by-step until they were through the gate. Dawn ignored the eyes of the old woman Kya had messed with. Her heart spiraled. In the near distance, members of the community left their shops, dropping what they were doing and shambling out toward the field, forming a formidable circle around them, a blockade between them and their only way out of here—the Honda. They were drawn to the toll like a night critter lured by the scents of an overfilled, overstuffed garbage pail.

The bell struck again, a long, drawn-out sound that sank into Dawn's body like liquid lead.

The people came forth, gaping at the clock tower as if an angel had lowered itself from Heaven before their eyes. The smiles they held, the affection they showed for the ambient tone, sent Dawn's scalp crawling.

There must have been a hundred people, maybe more. Most were still journeying over, some embarking on their pilgrimage from across the street. Dawn looked behind her and saw that the festival had more-or-less ended, and the attendees and exhibitors had abandoned their positions and were shuffling toward them. A wall of people marched forth, each of their faces blank, wiped clean by the sound the clock tower introduced. That consistent toll kept filling the silence, and each time it sounded off, Dawn felt weaker and weaker, as if the noise were vampiric in nature and her energy was the blood it feasted on.

The people flocked like moths to a lantern, bright and inspiring. There were so many now that Dawn couldn't see a clear path back to the car.

She gripped Kya's arm, perhaps too hard, but she didn't care. The clutch was comforting. "Kya, I don't like this. We need to leave or something bad is going to—"

But Kya wasn't listening. She was already facing the clock tower, inspecting its beauty, combing over its lavish features. Kya came off starstruck, a silly grin pooling across her face. "Isn't it beautiful, D? It's so…gorgeous, isn't it?"

Dawn gripped her friend's shoulders. Shook her. Too hard maybe. Enough force to dislodge her from whatever captivity this magical structure placed on her. "Kya, what—no. Look at me. LOOK AT ME!"

But Kya didn't look at her. Her eyelids fluttered as she tried peeking around her best friend, trying to glimpse the glorious shape, just one last fulfilling glance. It was like watching a desperate groupie trying to catch a clear view of a famous rock star through a sea of other potential groupies.

"Don't you hear it?" Kya asked, her eyes starry and distant. "The beautiful music?"

Dawn heard nothing but the heavy sound of metal on metal, the reverb of the toll rocking her bones to the marrow.

"Stop this," Dawn said. "I'm serious. If this is a joke, I swear—"

"The music," Kya said, her eyes rolling back, revealing whites. "It speaks to me. Don't you hear it?"

Dawn slapped her. Hard. Across the cheek. "Snap out of it!"

But she didn't. Kya reacted as if nothing had happened at all, and those all-white eyes sparkled, a magical shine that continued to radiate with the heavenly glow of the bright afternoon.

"Beautiful," Kya said. "It's the most beautiful sound I've ever heard. Oh, the music."

All at once, the entire town of Lacuna's Point opened their mouths simultaneously with a new sound that dominated the airwaves. This was worse than the tolling bell. It was loud, obnoxious, like one of those old Viking war horns, long and deafening, but with a touch of incessant static. The harsh sound dropped Dawn to her knees. She covered her ears to block out the intruding noise, but her hands did nothing to shield herself from this demonic frequency.

The sound was inside her now, working its way into her brain. Things fuzzed, the world growing grainier by the second. That spell of lightheadedness intensified, dropping over her like a dark veil, and she found herself crawling on her knees as the townspeople marched toward the tower, their eyes and mouths open wide, testing the elasticity of the tendons in their jaws, seeing something she couldn't, something that sat on the edge between her reality and theirs. She could almost see it, though. If she concentrated hard enough, she thought she *could* make out what they were witnessing. If she listened, zeroed in, she could almost hear it. The music, the beautiful sounds Kya had briefly mentioned before she was lost and carried away by them.

The sounds.

They echoed through her.

Everything was a blur now. The people before her pushed through her unfocused reality, stealing her view. Dawn's heart stopped. Their faces were horrid masks of melted flesh, partially revealing the inhuman qualities beneath, moving things that looked like claws and pincers and black ocular bulbs resting on long stems—

She felt hands on her, an impossible number to calculate in this dreamy state, lifting her up as the town and everything she once knew faded into a perfect, white oblivion.

# PART ONE

## THE PAST SENDS A SIGN

# CHAPTER ONE
## THREE YEARS LATER

The house is dark, full of late-afternoon shadows, and Ellie Brower still hasn't left the couch. She's awake, barely, floundering back and forth, tangled in the web of thoughts that surround this particular day. Flipping over, she faces the dark rectangle of the television, the black mirror displaying her shrouded reflection like an alien world projecting a blurry, dim copy of the reality she knows and lives in.

*Get up.*

*[Don't get up. Lie down. Die here.]*

*Get up now.*

*[Die as she died.]*

*Be strong. You're better than this.*

Conflicting words of self-encouragement and self-harm are traded between her, and once the inner dialogue is reduced to vague whispers, she feels something invisible yet heavy, like a wet blanket, press down on her. Every fiber of her soul melts into the sofa, the cushions absorbing her every morsel. This liquid morning is killing her, and she blinks at the shadows, waiting for the inevitable end to drink her down into some dark abyss.

Finally, something gives—she's not sure what—and she summons enough energy to sit up. Grabbing her mug—the one that proudly shouts "NUMBER ONE MOM"—off the coffee table, she takes a sip, feels the sting of the whiskey-laden dark roast, and winces. Over her shoulder the sun peeks through the blinds in slits, causing her untrained eyes to squint. Inside, the shadows protect her from the day, and she loves her shadows, the company they keep.

Especially today. This, the day of days. The very worst date circled on the calendar.

Wrapped in her afghan, she stands, her legs protesting the movement, her knee joints swiveling on what feels like rusty, corroded pins. She's only forty-five and sometimes her body betrays her, not working the way it used to, an icy reminder that she isn't getting any younger. An ache here, a shooting pain here, an occasional cascading ball of fire that rides her spine. Little tributes the body gifts to reaffirm your existence. She's not the twenty-seven-year-old version of herself anymore, the fresh one, so full of life, living out her tiny version of the American Dream with a husband and newborn daughter, feeling like she could take on the entire world, whatever the stars threw her way. Now she's husbandless and daughterless, and her body is failing, falling apart bit by bit, a little more each day.

*You're depressed,* Maura tells her every time she calls. But her sister doesn't understand. Maura has two beautiful daughters—one at college, one graduated and living in New York City working for some haughty fashion rag—and doesn't have the slightest clue what it's like to lose someone. Maura hasn't lost anything. She has her husband, her daughters, her pets.

Maura has everything and Ellie has nothing, and that's just life, the way it is.

As if the universe could follow her thoughts, the doorbell rings, breaking Ellie's concentration on these harsh reflections. She moves through the living room shadows and peeks around the corner, eyeing the foyer. A silhouette occupies the daylight in the door's left sidelight, and for the briefest of moments, she imagines it's her; her Dawn, her beautiful baby, three years older than Ellie last saw her before that fateful visit to Georgetown University. Her gorgeous daughter appearing in the open doorway, tears in her eyes, shoulders shaking, arms opening as she's ready to embrace her mother once

again, bringing a close to the nightmare three years running.

"Ellie?" the voice calls through the door. "I know you're there."

It's not her. Not her Dawn.

"I have wine," Maura says.

Ellie hikes up the afghan over her shoulders, hoping to erase the bold chill burrowing into her bones. She heads for the door, preparing to greet her sister, the only person in the world brave enough to face her today, the day of days. The day, three years ago, when her life began its perpetual downward spiral.

"How are you holding up?" Maura asks, the trivial and obligatory question she always asks when they sit down like this. Ellie doesn't blame her; it's what most people would say to begin these awkward talks. "I'm sorry, El. It's a stupid question, I know."

Ellie sips her wine. "No, it's not. I'm…you know. Doing all right, I guess."

"I know it's hard."

She wants to tell her sister that she doesn't have a goddamn clue how hard it is, but she bites her tongue knowing Maura's words come from an innocent place. A *good* place.

"I just wish I knew, that's all," Ellie admits. "I wish she didn't vanish into thin air and leave us all…wondering." She hates what comes next, but it's the cold truth: "I wish they found her body."

"Aww," Maura says, her lower lip protruding as she touches the small layer of fat clinging to Ellie's triceps. The warm gesture meant to soothe is nothing more than a reminder that she's let herself go. "Honey," Maura continues in her sticky-sweet voice. "It's tough, but today is the toughest. Tomorrow is always better, isn't it? Each day gets a little better, brighter."

She wants to believe that, but honestly, each year has been worse. There have been more good days overall, that's true—but the anniversary is always a hot hell. Today has been the hardest yet, and it's been a struggle to keep herself from opening the medicine cabinet and taking those blood pressure pills (the ones she's pretty sure she doesn't need but her doctor prescribes anyway) and swallowing the whole damn bottle, washing it down with one liter of Jack.

"Have you talked to Dan today?"

Ellie shakes her head. "No, and I probably won't."

Maura shrugs. "Maybe he's hurting too."

"And what—we're going to commiserate?" She laughs at the notion and laughing hurts. "Nah, no. Thanks but no thanks. We split for a reason. Dawn was the only reason we talked at all after the divorce, but…"

"So, you haven't talked to him at all then?"

Ellie tries to recall. She glances up at the ceiling and pinches her lower lip between her teeth. "There was a time, maybe a year after it happened, when he messaged me pictures he had from when she was little. Pretty sure he was drunk and feeling nostalgic. Not sure I ever messaged him back come to think of it."

Maura smiles playfully, huffs. "You bitch."

"I know, Maur. But you know me—I don't handle that stuff well. I'm...awkward, I guess. I never know what to say, and whenever I do say something, I end up spending the rest of the day thinking I should have said something else or nothing at all." She shivers, the thought of communicating with her ex applying cold pressure to her neck. "Plus...there are just too many wounds there...and not all of them have healed."

Maura nods as if she agrees, but something about her face suggests she has no fucking clue, despite being there for it. Through the rough times, she'd been an ear for Ellie whenever Ellie had something to talk about. Arms for whenever Ellie needed a hug. Dan had never been abusive, but he'd been a casual drunk, and his struggle with borderline alcoholism led to arguments, which boiled over and resulted in insults, which led to many nights spent apart, furthering this great divide between them. Eventually everything became a problem, even the simple, silly arguments like "what are we eating for dinner?" became screaming matches, and the marriage inevitably crumbled beneath them. Ellie—for the sake of her sanity—had no choice but to leave. The everyday fights, the broken doors, the smashed picture frames, all the anger that coalesced between them—it all became too much. And once she was free from it, Maura had been the first one there for her. With her sister's encouragement and legal resources, a divorce was finalized within three months of their official separation.

"You've been through a lot, hon," Maura says. "You're the strongest person I know."

Ellie flashes her a smile, and her lips ache from the subtle movement. "Thanks, sis."

"What are you up to the rest of the day?"

Ellie holds up the near-empty wine glass. "You're looking at it. Maybe I'll have another one of these. Maybe five. Then go to bed. What time is it?"

"Eleven."

"Really?" Ellie peeks through the blinds. Sunlight floods her eyes.

"Yeah." Maura takes the glass from her hands and Ellie doesn't fight to keep it. "Maybe slow down just a tad."

Ellie nods. "You're such a good big sis."

She lowers her head on Maura's lap, the way she used to when they were kids listening to *their* parents' screaming matches. Maura saved her then and she's saving her now. Maura Coughlin-Banks, big-sis extraordinaire, a superhero, even if she doesn't know it.

She closes her eyes, and the darkness becomes a relief from the cold reality that surrounds her, the emptiness of the house, the emptiness that fills her like helium in a floating balloon, invisible but present.

"Sssh," Maura says, brushing her cheek with the back of her hand, combing away the loose strands of hair. "Just think happy thoughts."

She does.

She thinks of Dawn.

Her daughter.

And then the tears come, fast and unrestrained.

He sits down in front of the laptop, cracks his knuckles, and starts to type. One word. Two. *He walks...* No, that's not right. *You can't start with 'He walks.' Start over.* He highlights the entire document including the title of the manuscript, his name and his contact information (as if anyone will ever read this), and presses DELETE.

"Damn it," says Mitchell Green, looking to the left corner of his desk where the Miller High-Life rests on the coaster. He picks up the 24 oz. can and goes to take a sip even though he knows it's empty. The few drops left taste like dry piss. Backwash, probably. Nothing left but his DNA.

Tossing the can in the trash basket to his right, he returns to the blank screen. Other hobbies call to him. Chores too. There's an old Mustang in the garage. For years he's been telling Angie his plans to fix it up. Those years have come and gone, and the damn thing still doesn't have wheels on it. So many other things he could be doing instead of wasting his time with something that will never become anything.

He sighs, looks out the window. He sees Misha Johnson on her morning jog, bouncing up the street, her ponytail swaying. Seeing Misha is probably the worst thing that could have happened just then. The girl is Kya's age, the age Kya would have been today, if she was still alive. Misha jogging brings back a rush of memories, all of them good, all of them of his youngest daughter and the times they spent together, the summer morning jogs *they* shared, the times they went fishing off the docks near the bay, the times she went golfing with him (a sport she hated passionately but still attempted because it was quality daddy-daughter time), the hours they spent shooting hoops in the driveway. The last memory causes him to look down on the basketball hoop bolted over the open garage door. Rust coats the once-orange rim, and the net is ripped, torn beyond the capability of handling another swish. He knows he certainly won't hear that crisp snap ever again, that joyous sound when hitting nothing but nylon. That sound reminds him of Kya, how she used to occasionally beat him in H-O-R-S-E, and how proud she was of that accomplishment because he never took it easy on her, never let her win.

Mitch scrubs the memories by rubbing his wrist against his forehead. Behind him, the office door squeaks open, reminding him to locate that can of WD-40 he bought last week and put it to use.

"I know what you're gonna say," Mitch says, spinning back to the blank Word doc. "I hear you, loud and clear."

"Don't see any words on that page," Angie says, swinging the door full open. "And you been up here for two hours."

He rotates to face his wife. To his surprise, she's brought him another Miller. "I know."

Angie strolls across the room like she has nothing better to do. Like *he* has nothing better to do. She sets down the beer and cracks open the can with one pull on the metal tab. The metal-on-metal grinding followed by the wet pop of the released pressure fills him with a familiar comfort. His wife puts one hand on her hip and stands up straight.

"Thought that would come after I wrote a little," he says. "You know, to celebrate."

"Thought it might help get you going. Relax you some. You're wound too tight."

Mitch sighs. He *is* wound too tight; there's no arguing with her there. "I just...I don't know where to start. I have these ideas..."

"Try starting at the beginning," she says, then goes to walk away. He harrumphs. "Now that's funny."

She's at the doorway. Spinning toward him, she flashes a toothy smile. "Wasn't supposed to be."

"Angie," he says, knowing that hearing her name will hold her there, keep her from disappearing, at least for a moment. "I know things haven't been...good, lately."

She loses the smile. Lowers her eyes to the beige and soulless carpet. "Mm-hmm," is her only response, a declaration that makes him shrink inward.

"I've been distant. Cold. And I...I don't want to use today as an excuse, but—"

"Buuuuut you're going to." She snaps her head up, stares at him, and for the first time in forever it's like she understands him again. "Is that right?"

He swallows. He knows what's on the precipice of his thoughts, the things he wants to say but can't. Those words stick like tacks in his throat.

"You know, Mitch," she says, sighing, "after everything we've been through, I really thought you'd turn things around. Know how to fix the things that were broken between us. But it's like..." She's looking past him now. He turns, sees the blank document. "It's like you just don't know what to say anymore."

When he looks back at her, she's gone. He hears footsteps on the carpet, fading, getting farther and farther away. He thinks he should say something, say *any*thing, but there's nothing to say. Whatever he'll utter will surely backfire. Won't be good enough.

Won't fix things.

Mitch stares at the door, noticing Angie left it open a crack. He thinks it's the perfect symbol for something, a metaphor of sorts, but for what, he can't exactly pinpoint.

Later, Mitch sits on the back porch, sipping his beer (fourth of the afternoon) and stares off into the setting sun. Pools of tangerine leak across the horizon. The bruise of night is quickly spreading, pushing orange globs farther down behind the trees to the west. It's a beautiful sight, he thinks, the death of the sun.

Can to his lips, he thinks of Kya again. Their past, their relationship, how perfect everything once was, including the whole family dynamic. Not a day goes by he doesn't think of that, but today, it's practically all he *can* think about, which is why he doesn't beat himself up about only producing a single paragraph in four hours of "writing." The memories consume him. No home project or hobby could have prevented his mind from wandering, and now that the day's chores and the honey-do list are complete, he's sitting there alone with his thoughts, the remaining cans of Miller High Life his sole companions.

He runs through his ideas for the novel again—the very thing that was supposed to distract him from today's anniversary. His idea centers around a Black male protagonist as he experiences life in contemporary America—based loosely on his own thoughts and experiences—and along the way he gets abducted by aliens. Several times, actually. It becomes a regular thing for this main character (Chris, let's call him. Mitch likes the name "Chris" but hasn't settled on it). The aliens want to harvest his memories and experiences for research on the human race. He planned to make the novel more literary and alternate between being serious and humorous in the most Kurt Vonnegut way possible without coming off as a cheap imitation and still giving the story its own voice. *His* voice. He smiles as he thinks about the certain scenes he's lined up. Thinks maybe he should write them as he sees them now, and not wait until he gets to that point in the book. There's no general rule about skipping around, is there? No one says you have to write the story linearly, right? He doesn't think so, but the thought of doing so makes him feel uneasy, as if filling in the blanks between these scenes might prove too difficult. After the first breeze of inspiration, this latter thought brings down a hammer of doubt.

*What am I doing? I can't write a novel.*

He's thinking about that lone paragraph he managed earlier as he realizes his beer is empty.

*One word at a time,* he remembers his college professor telling him. It was that man's teachings that inspired him to write in the first place. *You start with one word, then add another. Before you know it, you have a sentence. Then a paragraph. Then a chapter. Next thing you know, three months later, you have a whole manuscript. A terrible, practically unreadable mess of words* (laughs from the audience, Mitch included), *but hey, at least you will have completed something and that's more than most wannabe writers can say.*

He thinks back to the paragraph he wrote earlier, the struggle that had been. *Won't always be like that,* he coaches himself, but it's his professor's voice that shines through. *Some days will be easier.*

*Most.*

Instead of opening up a Google Doc on his phone where he can assemble his ideas, he hits the Gallery folder where his pictures of Kya remain. He thumbs over to the folder with his daughter's name on it. There's a split second of hesitation but he knows he'll land on it, knows he'll open and peruse the past, the wonderful memories instilled there.

The first picture shows Kya on the Georgetown campus, the day he accompanied her to check out the school two years before her disappearance. She's smiling radiantly. Dawn and her mother, Ellie, are captured in the background. It was a wonderful day for both families, and he remembers having a lot of fun watching the two girls get excited about attending their dream college. Mitch never got that experience himself, being forced to attend community college and having to pay for it himself by working three jobs, ninety-plus hours a week. In the end it was all worth it, so he thinks. That the experience bettered him in a lot of ways.

*Wish it made me a better husband,* he thinks, scrolling through the pictures of his three girls attending a Black Lives Matter march in Asbury Park just three months before his entire life fell apart. Before the panic attacks started. The sleepless nights. The nights that did earn him sleep plagued with terrible nightmares. Horrible images of Kya being brutally murdered, cut to ribbons by some psycho with a machete and a clown mask. One nightmare included a tour through this fictional killer's home, and when Mitch found himself standing in front of the bedroom closet, he saw dozens of skin suits draped on hangers like they were any other article of clothing. He saw one that looked like Kya and vomited. In the dream of course. Not when he woke up. Even though he wanted to. Even though he could still smell the passing-a-landfill stink of dried-out human husks long after the dream was over.

The nightmares came and went; the memories, especially the fond ones, haunted him always and forever.

He scrolls through his texts, wondering if Brianna or Tiana reached out to him earlier that day, if he missed the notifications. He's hoping they did, but when he thumbs through the incoming messages, he sees he hasn't received a single word from either of them. It hurts. A little. Okay...*a lot*. It hurts a lot, like a needle threaded through the center of his chest. He contemplates sending them messages, just to check in and see how they're doing, seeing how they're handling the day and the memories it stirs up. He wishes he could see his other daughters, but with Brianna living out in Chicago with her husband, Derrick, and now that Ti lives in Los Angeles, working in Hollywood as a set designer—he's lucky he sees the girls once a year for Christmas.

But that's just life, he thinks.

That's all it is.

Feeling the tickle of a fresh tear on his cheek, he pockets his phone.

Then his phone buzzes. He dips his hand back in and pulls the Samsung free. His heart leaps with excitement, the prospect of receiving a message from one of his (alive) girls. They're practically the only women in his life who don't hate him—at least to his knowledge.

He opens the text and his heart nosedives.

WE NEED TO TALK.

He reads the rest, the phone shaking unsteadily in a hand that quickly loses the ability to hold things.

IT'S ABOUT KYA.

I THINK I KNOW WHERE SHE IS.

It's hours later when she awakes on her daughter's old bed, the one she hasn't had the heart to throw out, in the room she hasn't had the heart to empty, staring at walls she hasn't had the heart to paint over. With no clear memory of how she got here and how long ago, Ellie lifts her head from the pillow, taking in her bleary surroundings. The wall clock with a hand-painted Mickey Mouse on the ceramic face shows her it's six-forty-two, but it's always six-forty-two because the batteries died a year ago and were never changed. It's still daylight out. The blinds do an adequate job blocking out the sun, but light finds the cracks and spills across her in slits. She shoves off the comforter and swings her feet onto the carpet. Stands. Battles vertigo. The sudden onset of feeling like her body is being flipped plants her back on the edge of the bed.

*Too much wine,* she thinks and then spots the bottle on the nightstand. There's not much left, and she wonders how much of the missing liquid she's responsible for and how much Maura helped.

She picks up her phone and scrolls through it, ignoring messages from a few close friends and colleagues offering up their annual support. The "if you need anything don't hesitate to ask" and "thinking of you today" lines are nice, but they do nothing to smooth over her emotions. She's a wreck, and no number of well-wishes and positive vibes will piece her back together. This is a storm she needs to ride out by herself, alone in this room with a head full of wine and fond memories.

She doesn't know why but she punches Dawn's number into the messages app. A few locked messages appear, communications she's saved for times like this; the most recent, a picture sent from the Georgetown campus, a shot of her and Kya hugging, the Potomac behind them. Smiles. Bright futures full of sunny dreams. She can practically see everything Dawn would have become and more. So much talent sparkling in those eyes. Ellie wonders if her daughter would have become the world-famous artist she always dreamed of, the creator of paintings hanging in every big New York City art gallery. London. Paris. She had the creative appetite to make it, the drive of a true artist.

The same drive Ellie lost years ago, before she got pregnant.

Ellie closes her eyes, begins to cry. Again. So many tears. Her well is endless.

After a few minutes, she gains control of her emotions. In the lull, she taps on the thread's text box, pulling up the keyboard.

I.

MISS.

YOU.

Three words. Three simple words. True words.

She hits send, then lies back down, closing her eyes, fighting off the spins, the rotating spiral the room has become.

Ninety seconds later, she hears a chime and feels a vibration near her feet.

The phone.

Ellie sits up, ignoring the tilt, the hellish carousel dominating her equilibrium. She grabs her phone and checks the messages.

Her heart drops like a busted elevator.

There's a message in her inbox—from Dawn.

Which can't be. Right? Dawn, gone three years now, presumed dead by the York County police, the detectives that promised they had given the case their all and could do nothing more—she couldn't possibly be texting back. Because she was dead. Gone. Lost forever, somewhere south of the nation's capital.

But…here she is. Responding to a text Ellie never should have sent.

HI MOM.

Those five letters turn her marrow to ice. A bed of wriggling worms comes alive under her flesh as she reads and rereads the message a thousand times in about ten seconds.

HI MOM.

HI MOM.

There's a picture above the words. Ellie sees her daughter standing under a bright blue sky, flexing two peace symbols, sporting a slight, *why-did-you-make-me-do-this* smile, a massive clock tower standing behind her, a pillar of time. Ellie doesn't know why but her eyes are drawn to the structure and not her missing—probably dead—daughter.

Something about the towering architecture makes her feel hollow inside.

Finally her eyes break from the impressive structure and concentrate on Dawn, her face, that smile, and Ellie realizes this is probably the last picture she ever took. Then she realizes that the photo was sent from her phone—Dawn's phone—which doesn't make any sense because the phone was disconnected years ago and the number is no longer in service, and, to her knowledge, hasn't been redistributed. She knows the number no longer works because…well, just this past January, she called Dawn's phone—as she did periodically—just to hear her when the voicemail picked up.

That was the last time because instead of hearing her dead daughter's cheery voice asking the caller to leave their name, number, and a brief message, she got a robotic woman telling her the number was no longer in service. That had just about shattered her, and she remembers spending the next few days pretty drunk, waking up in places she probably shouldn't have, in strange bedrooms next to strangers.

Ellie rushes to text back, knowing she shouldn't, that whatever this is, it's a dangerous game she shouldn't play.

But it's of no use. Her mind is a tornado of destructive thoughts, and nothing's stopping them.

WHERE R U?

ARE U OK?

I LOVE YOU

The server denies them. UNDELIVERABLE, reads the notification.

She slumps. Impossible. This is…*impossible.*

Then another message comes through. It's four words that will prevent her from sleeping over the next two days. Her body becomes a statue of ice. Everything she's felt over the past three years, the fear, the exhaustion, the hopelessness—it all comes rushing back to assault her at once, and it merges with a new feeling, one that fills her with incredible light.

That feeling is hope.

HELP ME I'M ALIVE, the message reads, and Ellie's world will never be the same.

# CHAPTER TWO

The coffee is still warm when Mitch brings the mug to his lips. He sips, letting the woman's words digest, sink in. Battle everything he knows to be true. What she's told him doesn't make sense in the slightest. *Can't* make sense. *Can't* be true.

But there's proof. Tangible.

*Real.*

Ellie Coughlin or Brower—whatever she goes by now that the divorce has been finalized—slides the phone in front of him.

"See?" she says, her crow's feet widening, their dark, puffy bottoms stretching. He can tell she hasn't slept a wink all night. He knows the look all too well, having lived through the same bouts of insomnia the first few months after Kya disappeared. "See? I'm not making this up. I...I thought I was dreaming or drunk last night. Maybe both? But I woke up this morning and here it is. The text, the picture, it came from her phone. *Her phone,* Mitch."

"I see it," Mitch says, taking the phone, bringing it closer to his eyes as if that makes the message truer. "It's unbelievable."

"I know. Do you think we can trace it?"

Mitch glances up at her. Stares. There's desperation in her voice, the manic kind. This is a woman teetering on the edge, and if he says the wrong thing, well...she could tumble off. "I don't know."

"What about the cops? We should go to that state detective— what was his name? Stanton? Wally, was it?"

Mitch nods. "Yep. Good ol' Wally Stanton. That was him."

"I think I still have his number in—"

She goes to grab her phone, but Mitch stops her. Puts his hand over hers. It's a gentle touch. Caring.

"What?" she asks. A tear clings to her eyelash, gaining mass and almost ready to fall.

"Is this something you really want to pursue?"

"What are you talking about? It's...it's proof. Proof they're still alive."

"Is it?"

"Mitch," she says, retracting her hand. She rubs her eyes, clearing away the tears. "This came from her phone. It has to…has to mean *some*thing."

"That picture could be three years old. It could be…I dunno, it could be from the day they went missing. I mean, for all we know it could be a glitch in the network. Maybe the text you sent jarred something loose."

"Jarred something loose?"

"Like…" He sighs, nervously rubbing his shoulders. "Like, maybe that message was stuck and when you replied, it came loose and sent."

" 'HELP ME I'M ALIVE?' "

"I dunno, Ellie. I'm trying to think of things rationally. I'm no techie, so I don't know how this stuff works. Can barely get Word to function properly. I manage a beer distribution company. You can talk to someone at Verizon if you want."

"Brian."

"Huh?"

"Brian Reed, the IT guy at my school. He can help."

"Great. Go to Brian. I'm sure he can explain it. But I gotta be honest with you, El—whatever you find…I think you better leave me out of it."

"Are you serious?"

He nods, even though it hurts. There's always been a part of him that believed Kya was still alive. No *body* meant hope. "I'm not over what's happened," he tells Ellie, who's completely ignoring her coffee, the plate of scrambled eggs before her. The waitress comes over and refills their waters with lemons. "But I'm getting there. There's a lot going on at home, between Angie and me—and none of it is very good."

"Sorry to hear that but—"

"I do appreciate you reaching out, though. Telling me about this."

"Mitch, this is a chance to get our girls back."

"Or it's a chance to reopen old wounds and get hurt again."

She shakes her head and looks out the window, staring down the gloom-gray morning. "I can't believe this. We've talked about this moment. The moment we discover that one clue. Remember? That one clue, and…and this is it. I feel it."

Mitch closes his eyes, nods. A persistent sting needles the corners of his eyes. "I get it, El. I do. And I'm happy that you're still hopeful. But…this. This is just a glitch. Nothing about it feels right to me."

"Well, it feels right to me."

"Because you want it to. You're hanging on to the idea that they're still alive, that they're out there somewhere, waiting to be found. I know how you feel, but sooner or later, El, you have to get over it. Move past it, move on."

"You just said you're not over it. Now you're lecturing me about moving on?"

"I'm dealing with things in my own way." He points to the phone that holds the riddle in question. "Whatever that is, it's not healthy."

"Oh, so you're a psychologist now?"

"El, you know what I'm trying to say here."

"Oh, I know. You've given up hope. Nice. It must be awesome to have the ability to let go."

"I'm healing. I'm just not looking to undo what I've spent the last three years doing. This…this right here—this is ripping off scabs and drawing fresh blood again."

"All right. Fine. You don't want to pursue this, *fine*. Fine by me." She gets up and tosses a twenty on the table, then heads for the exit.

"El," he says, the tone lacking any real apology. She doesn't stop, and he watches her leave the diner without looking back.

He sighs and digs a twenty out of his pocket before throwing a finger in the air and asking the waitress for the check.

Ellie shows up to school around noon, scans her faculty card on the device next to the front door, heads inside and down the hall toward the tech room. She passes a few of the newer teachers who've begun to set up their classrooms in preparation of the new year, which starts in three weeks, a fact she's not exactly happy about. The further she gets into her teaching career, the shorter the summers feel.

Making her way to tech support, she passes her art room. Stops on a dime, steps back three paces, and peers inside. It's more or less the same since last week's visit, though there's a noticeable difference.

*It can't be...*

But she saw it. That piece of art hanging on the back wall.

The one she doesn't remember putting there.

She shuffles to the open door, peeks inside, and turns on the lights. When the fluorescent bulbs flicker to life, she sees her mind has played a cruel trick on her, and there is absolutely no difference at all. Everything's exactly as she left it last June.

She shakes her head and laughs off the image she thought she saw, the very last painting Dawn completed before that final summer excursion. The piece currently sitting in her basement with a canvas tarp over it, collecting dust when it should be hanging in some local gallery, because it was the most beautiful thing her daughter ever created.

She's been thinking about the painting all day, the imagery sticking to every thought. Maybe because the abstract piece depicted a giant clock on it, fused with colorful psychedelic smears and misshapen objects that not even Dawn herself had explanations for. The picture Dawn's phone mysteriously sent got her thinking about that painting, the clock tower looming in the background the driving force behind this recent obsession.

Now, she's seeing that image everywhere.

She shuts off the lights to her classroom and continues toward her original destination: the tech room. Once there, Ellie raps her knuckles on the door frame. Brian Reed looks up from his computer station, eyebrows stretching up his wrinkled forehead.

"Hey, El," he says, looking back to the computer immediately, continuing to clack away on the keyboard. "What brings you down here? Issues with the laptop again?"

"No, not today. Brian? I have something I need you to look at."

It must be the wavering sound of her voice, the tonal inconsistencies, *the cracking* that causes him to stop whatever he's working on and focus solely on her.

"What's up?" he asks, pushing his glasses up a sunburnt nose.

"First," she says, stepping inside the room and closing the door behind her. "I need you to promise me you won't say a goddamn thing to anyone."

He holds up two twisted fingers and smiles. "Scout's honor."

She takes a deep breath, steps over to his station, and positions her phone in front of him, the text messages open and waiting for his professional observation. "Okay," she says, "strap in, because this is wild…"

She tells him everything. When it's over, he says, "I can do it."

"You can?"

"Sure. I have some equipment at home. Don't tell the FBI." She can't tell if he's joking or not, but it sounds like he is. "I can get you coordinates. No problema."

She jumps up and kisses the top of his head. "Brian, you're the man."

"Easy there, teach. Don't let my girlfriend hear you say that."

"When can I have it back?"

He shrugs. "I'll do it tonight. Before the lady and I engage in an all-night *Shark Tank* marathon."

"Perfect. I owe you one."

He swats the air. "Think nothing of it. I'll call you later."

Mitch places his beer on the tool cart and closes the Mustang's hood. *For good* this time, or so he thinks. It's not the first time he's given up on the project. He thought it would have been a good change of pace from staring at a blank document all afternoon. It wasn't, and all he can think about is what he wants to write, the story he wants to tell, and how he doesn't believe he has the skills to bring the characters and their world to life. Self-doubt is a motherfucker, and Mitch wants to lay his head on the engine block and slam down the hood.

He wipes his hands on the dirty-white towel until the grease slides off. Then he applies a dab of Gojo and works the abrasive cream into his skin, the grit scratching and cleansing. Next, he washes the stuff off in the sink next to his cabinet of tools.

The door opens slightly. It's Angie in her nightgown, ready for bed. She nods. "You comin' or you gonna play out here all night?"

"Be up in a few."

She looks like she knows he's lying, and he doesn't pretend he isn't.

"In a few," he repeats.

"Okay," she says coldly, then shuts the door. All the way this time, pulling it tight so the wood is resting against the frame's weatherstripping.

He hangs his head and retrieves his phone from his pocket. Every time he looks at the black screen, the dark world it reflects, Ellie's words come echoing between his ears and her tear-ridden eyes fill his visual thoughts. Instinctively he punches Kya's name into the search. Her number still comes up. It's weird he hasn't deleted it after three years, and then he thinks maybe he never will. That deleting the number would feel like deleting *her*.

KYA, MISS YOU BABY

It's a simple text that feels apropos. He hits SEND.

Waits.

Nothing happens. For a solid five minutes, nothing happens. Mitch watches the wall, drifting between more memories of Kya, his baby girl, the good moments they shared, the family outings with all five of them, together, laughing, loving, living. He'd give up anything to spend just one more day with her, to see that smile of hers one last time.

A low tone fills the garage. He looks down and sees a message sitting in his inbox. He's never tapped on the screen so hard before, and for a second he's afraid he's chipped a fingernail.

HI DADDY

His fingers twitch, an unchecked tremor rippling through him. Every part of him tingles with a shocking numbness. He finds himself unable to react, unable to bring his thumb to the screen.

He waits. Watches. Concentrates on the next incoming message, hoping there'll be one.

But there isn't.

Whoever is doing this, the sicko on the other end of this exchange, is waiting for a response, something they can work with.

He obliges.

WHO IS THIS?

He waits again. Swallows. His nerves burn like a four-alarm fire.

IT'S ME. IT'S KYA.

NO IT ISN'T, he responds.

FIND ME DADDY FIND ME

He hesitates. Tears free themselves from their glassy prisons, roll down his face without restraint. His throat releases an involuntary high-pitched whine.

WHERE ARE YOU? he sends back.

Then…there's nothing. Ten minutes pass. Twenty.

The son of a bitch on the other side requires another message. So be it. Mitch fires off another response. IDENTIFY YOURSELF.

Then, one last message arrives in his inbox: <MESSAGE FAILED>

He sits and cries until the sun comes up.

Ellie is making coffee, absentmindedly pouring sugar (way too much) when her landline rings, causing her fragmented reveries to disperse. Peeking over at the display screen, dreading the name that may appear on the caller ID and simultaneously hoping it is her, her Dawn, she sets the sugar dispenser down. But it's not her, and a wave of relief washes over her at once.

It's Brian Reed, calling from her iPhone.

"Yes?" she answers, unable to strip the desperation from her voice.

"Got it," he says, chuckling with a confidence she finds peaceful. "Piece-o-cake."

"Excellent. Well, where was it coming from?"

"Well, I've matched the coordinates and punched them into Google, and…well, it's—uh—weird."

"Weird? I don't like weird. What's weird about it?" Surely, she thinks, it can't be weirder than receiving strange, distressing responses from a daughter who's been missing *(dead)* for three years.

"Well, the coordinates put us somewhere in Virginia, near the shore. But…"

"But what?"

Brian takes his time to respond, and she can hear him clicking away nervously on the top of his pen. "There shouldn't be anything there. There's no town on the map. It's just a beach and some woods."

"Okay, well, what about the number? Is it legit? Did the messages come from Dawn's phone?"

"As far as I can tell…yeah, they did."

"But how is that possible? I mean, her phone was shut off. I verified that with the phone company."

"Don't know. Maybe someone is playing an elaborate prank on you. Some hacker who is using some program to replicate Dawn's phone number. Maybe they duplicated the SIM card?"

"So…some hacker is using her phone number to…what? Fuck with me? Drive me insane?" She touches the pressure building in the center of her forehead, between her eyes. "I don't even know any hackers. Except for you."

"Whoa, not a hacker, lady." He laughs nervously. "I mean, not really. I know a few things. Like, I can do some low-level shit like porn-spam someone's website if—"

"I don't need to know this, Brian."

"Okay, you're right. Sorry. Getting off track." He sighs, loudly. "Look, I wish I had a definite answer for you. From where I'm sitting, the phone was never shut off like the service provider said, and the number is still active. The carrier actually verified they took the number out of service?"

"Yes."

"Damn. They didn't, like, reissue the number?"

"No. Least, they didn't tell me if they did. Do they do that?"

"Oh yeah," Brian said, and now it sounds as if he's eating something crunchy, like popcorn or potato chips. "Totally. Cell phone providers recycle numbers all the time."

"Still doesn't explain how they sent the picture."

"Maybe the message was saved in the cloud and got hung up. Sent by accident when you sent the message."

She hangs her head; it feels bowling-ball heavy.

"I know that's not the answer you were looking for," he says. "I'm sorry. Wish I could give you, uh…you know, the closure you needed."

"It's okay. Hey, can I have those coordinates?"

"What? Why?"

She sniffles, fighting back the surge of rising emotions. "Because Dawn—she was last seen in the Virginia area. The detective working on the case said she was texting some guy she was supposed to meet up with. Near Virginia Beach. She and Kya…they were supposed to be in D.C., but they went to meet this boy instead. That's when they went missing."

"Damn. So you think…"

"I don't know what to think. Honestly. But it's a strange coincidence. Isn't it?"

"I'd say."

"I want to check it out. For myself. *By* myself."

"Don't you think you should call the police? I mean, it might be worth getting them involved, and maybe they can reopen the—"

"No," she says, expecting Brian to convince her that lone-wolfing this investigation is a bad idea, but he doesn't. "They can't help."

"How do you know that?"

"Because…they…they just don't care."

Brian doesn't have a response for this, and if he does, he doesn't speak it aloud.

"I'll be over to grab my phone."

"El, please don't do anything that's—"

She hangs up and immediately heads to the bedroom to start packing.

# CHAPTER THREE

The car is packed with a suitcase that holds enough clothes and supplies for a three-day jaunt. She can stretch it to four if she needs to, but she doesn't want to be gone any longer than that. It'll take about six hours to reach the coordinates Brian gave her, which gives her roughly two-and-a-half days to comb the area, uncover any clues the police may have missed during their initial investigation. Her plan is basic—take the photograph and try to locate the clock tower, maybe interview some locals, ask if they remember seeing that particular eighteen-year-old girl beneath it.

*Wherever this place is, Dawn was there.*

There's something unsettling about the clock tower. Every time she turns her eyes on the picture, an ill feeling invades her stomach, making her want to vomit. Like motion sickness, the kind she gets staring at her phone for too long while in the passenger seat of a moving car.

It's a long shot, her plan. She knows this. The odds are stacked high against her, the possibility she'll find this place and run into someone who remembers seeing Dawn is slim. Even if someone does remember seeing her there, their confirmation won't mean anything unless Dawn's *still* there. She also knows if she doesn't try, the unknown—the potential that could have been—will slowly eat her up like some great cosmic mouth, forever crush her bones between the infinite teeth of time. She'll continue to live out this broken existence, going through the motions, pretending she isn't crumbling from the inside out one day at a time. She knows this, so she has to try.

She also can't help but think her daughter was snatched up by some super-secret sex cult and investigating the coordinates might lead her to uncover some commune in the middle of nowhere, a spot occupied by a bunch of naked hippies whose only interest in life is to share their bodies, minds, and ideas with whoever will allow them to.

*I've been watching too much* Dateline, she thinks, shutting the trunk. Padding up the driveway, she heads for the open driver's door. The car is already running.

"Hey," a voice says from behind her. She thinks it's Brian come to talk her out of it, one last attempt to knock some sense into her, have her reach out to the police and let them explore the new evidence. He almost didn't give her back the phone until she promised she'd alert the authorities. She felt bad lying to him, but not too bad. Not bad enough to actually make the call.

She turns, sees Mitch Green standing on the sidewalk, a camping bag strapped to his back. He looks more fit for a November hike than a Virginian getaway in mid-August; jeans, a long-sleeve plaid button-down made from…is that flannel? Why, yes, it is.

"Hey," she calls back.

"I got your message. I apologize for not getting back to you."

She shrugs off this inconsequential thing.

"Also…I'm sorry."

"For what?" she asks, folding her arms.

"That I didn't believe you."

"Annnnd…you believe me now?"

His audible sigh travels the distance between them. "I got one, too."

Her arms fall immediately to her side, and her whole body tingles with a fresh wave of anxiety. "Holy shit."

He nods. "I don't know if the girls are still alive or if someone is just fucking with us, but I think we should find out."

"Where's Angie?" she asks, looking around, not seeing his wife anywhere. The street is empty save for Mr. Wilson climbing into his Jetta across the street. "She didn't want to come?"

Again, he sighs. Deeper this time. "She doesn't know. About the texts. She doesn't even know I'm here. Told her I was on a writing retreat."

"Excuse me?"

"I know. It's…it's complicated."

"Okay." She bends down, ducks under the roof, and knuckles the button for the trunk. "Throw your stuff in. Let's get going."

Once Mitch's bags are in the trunk and he's seated next to her, she throws the Subaru in reverse. In a blink, they're off down the street, heading toward their destination.

Toward the truth.

And, hopefully, their lost daughters.

For most of their tour through New Jersey, the two talk about the series of texts, what they could mean, and how they'll handle the situation if it turns out to be some Wizard-of-Oz-Man-Behind-the-Curtain scenario. Someone pulling their strings so to speak, some cunning jokester looking for a few cheap, disgusting giggles. Mitch confesses what he'll do when he gets his hands on that person, and Ellie doesn't blame him for exploring those violent fantasies. It would be too sickening to even think about, someone doing that to them. And also unlikely. She hopes that outcome is not the true one, but she can't ignore the possibility that the girls were kidnapped by a couple of psychopaths, murdered, and now the killers are getting their post-slaughter jollies by torturing their victims' parents.

She used to enjoy movies with similar plots, but now she can't stomach them. Real life has become those plots, and any time some crime thriller comes on, she flips to another channel. Even the tamest drama causes her to switch to sports or Comedy Central, anything that doesn't involve killing or kidnappings or death of any kind. Movies in general have become harder and harder to watch—she never realized how many of them (even the funny ones) have some plot thread that deals with death.

*Death is part of life.*

True, but she detests being reminded of the empty casket she was forced to bury.

Once they get through Delaware and cross into Maryland, Mitch has to pee. He asks if she can pull over at the next rest area, and she says, "Absolutely. I could use the stretch."

She parks and gets out. Lengthens her limbs. It feels good to warm up the muscles, to pop the bones. The post-stretch numbness travels her body, and she walks off the pins-and-needles sensation that's stabbing her legs from sitting in one position for too long. Inside the rest stop, she smells Old Bay seasoning and coffee, two odors that don't exactly agree with each other despite her affection for both. She's torn between getting a cup of Starbucks or a crab sandwich from the local fast-food chain.

"Don't even think about it," Mitch says. He must have seen her gravitating toward the crab shack. "A fast-food crab sandwich is probably the worst idea."

"Smells good."

"Tastes good too. Going *down*. Not so much coming out."

"Gross."

"Just warning you. We ate here when I brought Kya down to visit Georgetown for the first time. We both had the runs for days."

"You brought Kya to Georgetown without Dawn?"

He nods. "Yeah, that was before Dawn showed interest. Junior year."

"Huh." She hears the defeat in her voice.

"What's 'huh?' "

"Nothing. Just…Dawn always told me it was her idea to go to Georgetown. Not Kya's."

"I don't…" He stops himself, clears his throat, and starts over. "Doesn't mean anything, El, it was just—"

"No," she says, a tired laugh escaping her. "I know. It's just…the things you learn."

"Right." Mitch motions to the other end of the rest stop with his chin. "I'm gonna run. Nature's calling. Meet back at the car in ten?"

"Yeah, sure thing."

Ellie moves past the snack stand and sunglass hut, toward the back where the women's restroom sits, a constant line of customers filing in and out. She heads in and takes care of business, washes her hands, and doesn't make eye contact with a single soul. There's an invading feeling making its presence known, a sneaking sensation that's zeroing in on her neck.

It feels like…

*I'm being followed.*

She looks up from the sink, has herself a glance around the bathroom. Next to her, a woman is vigorously washing her hands, excessively slathering on soap, but given the recent public health scare, she gives the woman a pass. Then she focuses in on the parade of women coming to and from, heading into the stalls, others making for the exit. There's no glaringly obvious watcher, no one she can peg as a spy. No eyes that fix on her. No evil glare she can pinpoint.

But still…she *senses* it.

Something. Someone.

Close.

Watching.

She turns back to the sink and splashes her face with cool water. Then she faces herself in the mirror, stares down her mess of wrinkly skin, the heavy dark bags beneath her eyes.

That's when she sees her.

*Her.*

Dawn.

Her daughter is standing in the corner of the bathroom, eyes fixed on her, looking drugged, stoned, as if she hasn't slept since she left on that fateful trip three years ago.

Ellie spins, and Dawn is halfway to the exit, following the flow of slow-moving traffic.

Ellie wants to react but she's frozen, fear boxing her into that small space by the sinks. She opens her mouth to say something but her vocal cords lock up like a motor sans oil. A sound comes out like a hiccup, only strained.

Then, her body unlocks. She moves after Dawn, rushing for the exit, scrambling, a frenzied panic propelling her every movement.

When she reaches the mouth of the exit, she hits a human wall. The rest stop is jampacked full of people hustling to and fro, a sea of bodies with conflicting tides. Through the chaos, she spots the familiar head of thick hair, the one she helped comb and straighten before junior prom, the one she might give an arm or a leg in exchange for one more comb-through. Ellie homes in on each dark curl, and she knows her eyes are not deceiving her—it's really her.

It's really her Dawn.

"Dawn!" she shouts, holding up her hand in case Dawn turns and cannot locate her through the parade of travelers.

But she doesn't turn around.

She doesn't even turn slightly.

"Dawn!"

This time, Ellie moves into the crowd and it's like wading into a pool of hard jelly; she wants to move fast but the flow of people bottlenecks, and she stands on her toes just to keep her vision locked on the back of her daughter's head.

The crowd folds in around her. It's getting harder to keep her focus on the hair.

*No.*

She elbows her way ahead of two slowpokes, both of whom grunt and spit a "Hey!" at her. Ignoring them, her sole focus remains on Dawn.

"Dawn!"

She continues to push. Through the people, around them, and, eventually, she gets to a pocket of open floor, dodges past a couple with a stroller who are speeding along horizontally.

Then she stops.

Rotates.

Studies the immediate area.

Dawn's nowhere to be seen. Her familiar tangles of dark hair are gone. Ellie makes two more revolutions before she feels her hope bleed away.

*This…can't…be…*

Mitch is coming toward her. He raises his hand, acknowledging he sees her too, and then his features melt away into a compressed, worried mask.

"What's the matter?" he asks, jogging over to her. She doesn't even realize she's heaving her shoulders and working her hands into tight fists.

She tries to hide it, shake off the notion that anything's wrong. "Nothing."

"Nothing? You look like someone just told you the bad news all over again. What's up? What is it?"

She swallows what feels like an egg. "I thought I saw her."

"Who?" Mitch looks around as if the person is still here and close.

"Dawn."

He stops, turns to her.

"In the bathroom," she says, nodding at the entryway. "I followed her out, and then she just…*disappeared.*"

"Okay," he says, putting a comforting hand on her shoulder, and, to her surprise, the touch actually relaxes her some. It's not much, but it reassures her that she's not alone in this.

"It's okay," he says. "Let's head back to the car, yeah?"

Her body trembles in a way that suggests she's losing her sanity. "Yeah. You want to drive?"

"Sure."

They walk back to the car and Ellie continues to examine the face of everyone she passes. The hairstyles. The clothing. Hoping that one of them is Dawn, *truly her,* and not some figment of her fractured imagination.

She'll do anything for one last look at her beautiful daughter.

She'll kill for it.

They pass the WELCOME TO VIRGINIA roadside sign and Mitch laughs at the VIRGINIA IS FOR LOVERS tagline beneath it. He's not entirely sure that's true—or even partially sure—and wonders about the history behind this interesting claim. *Lovers* brings Angie to the forefront of his thoughts. But not Angie now—no, he thinks back to a time when they were young, when the kids were *kids,* and thinks back to before they had them. That first date. The night he first kissed her, that magical moment in the movie theater parking lot. The amazing sex they'd had later. Then, flash forward to their wedding, how she smiled the entire duration even when she was crying as he recited his vows, even while he shoved a whole fistful of cake into her mouth during the reception. It's weird to think how far they've fallen, how their marriage has crumbled like old, cheap brick under the duress of entire years' worth of nightly storms.

*What happened to our love?*

Was it ever there in the first place?

*Love.*

He knows damn well there was and plenty of it. But whatever magic there was, it's mostly gone now. He hates admitting that, but it's the truth, knowledge he can't deny. He decides when he gets home, he'll finally tell her, let her know what she already knows but has been too afraid to speak herself.

*It's over.*

*We should get divorced.*

The sting in his eyes burns as if he's cleansed his contacts with lemon juice. The interstate before him blurs at the edges.

"When did you know it was over between you and Dan?" he asks, and he knows he shouldn't have, but the words have already left his mouth and there's no taking them back now. "Sorry, that was incredibly random. And really rude. I apologize."

She gives him a sideways look, as if she's possibly offended. But then she shrugs. "I dunno. It was so long ago. When Dawn was little, we fought a lot. Even before we had Dawn. We kinda just held on. Things got better for a little, when Dawn was a baby. Which is weird. Usually that's when couples fight the most. At least…that's what I've heard. Every marriage is different, though. Anyway, by the time she turned five, I knew we couldn't keep on living that way. But we still managed. Didn't want it to affect Dawn. Wanted to wait until she was older, when she'd understand why mommy and daddy weren't living together anymore." A pause. He feels her eyes on him. "Why? You and Angie having major problems?"

A dry swallow instead of an immediate response. He hasn't talked about their issues to anyone, not aloud, not even to his closest friends. The wedge between him and Angie, that invisible gremlin, has been a secret he's been holding in for far too long. Like a deep breath needing release.

"Yeah, things haven't been too good. I…I don't even know why I'm telling you this." An incredulous laugh escapes him. "I haven't told anyone this."

"You don't have to. Just thought, since you brought it up, that you wanted to talk about it."

"Yeah, I know." He debates keeping his mouth shut, but in all honesty—the talking is helping. The pressure in his chest lets up some. "Fuck, I wish things were different. I wish it was the way things used to be. But it's just…not."

Ellie sighs in a been-there-done-that sort of way.

"And I know she feels it too. The emptiness. I feel like we're both holding on, hoping, praying it'll blow over, but…it's like…delaying the inevitable."

He catches Ellie nodding along and wonders if she's truly listening or just being a good sport.

"It's not for the girls," he adds. "They've moved out, moved on. It's just us now. In the house. Alone. And we hardly speak to each other. We should be…I dunno. *Reconnecting.* I just don't know why we haven't called it quits yet. It's the hanging on that's so goddamn odd."

"It's because you're comfortable," Ellie tells him, shifting in her seat, curling up like she wants to take a nap. "Even though you're miserable, you don't want to let go." She shrugs. "At some point, you'll have to." He catches her eyes bulging as if she's come to some great spiritual awakening. "Before you say anything about letting go and Dawn, that's different and you know it."

"Not saying nothing." He tries to smile but it hardly represents his current mood, and the action feels forced.

He doesn't bring up the subject again for the rest of the drive. Instead, they talk about other things—the weather, the trip, what they will do if they find their daughters, how hard they will squeeze them during that first hug.

But the sting behind his eyes is ever-constant, a sharp blade that cuts and cuts, deeper as it goes.

"We're here," Ellie says, "sort of."

Mitch pulls into a gas station. There's a store made to look like a log cabin off to the side of the parking lot. Above its entrance, the sign reads POP'S SHOP. Mitch gets out and stretches his entire body, takes in the surrounding scenery, the long expanse of woods that seems endless and ancient, a space between places where fairy tales could occur. As someone who grew up in cities and suburbias his entire life, Mitch wonders why anyone would want to live out here, so detached from society, so distant from human interaction. There's something refreshing about being amongst nature— certainly the air is easier on the lungs—but in a remote setting such as this, not a building for miles, there has to be that constant sense of feeling lost.

As Mitch heads to the pump to fill the tank, Ellie exits the car.

"I'm getting food," she says. "Want anything?"

"Yeah, I'll poke my head in there once I finish."

She nods, heads for the store.

Mitch looks to his left and sees a man pumping gas, staring at Mitch as if he's walked into a party he wasn't invited to. It doesn't take long for Mitch to recognize why that is—one glance at the black hat with a lime-green forty-two on it, the sleeveless denim shirt that reveals faded Confederate flag tattoos, coupled with the gun rack on the ceiling of the guy's truck, mixed with the loud collection of bumper and window stickers that would make every member of the NRA's boardroom cream their pants, in conjunction with the MAGA decals, and he knows where this is going before it gets there.

He pictures himself raising his hands and saying, *Look, I don't want any trouble.*

But he's not going to do that.

Not today.

Not ever.

"There a problem?" he asks, feigning an amicable smile.

"No problem," the man says, smiling back, his teeth stained from the wad of chew trapped between his gums and cheek. The smile is hardly a smile; looks more like he's just twisted an ankle rather than greeting a stranger with that southern hospitality Mitch has always heard so much about.

"Good," Mitch tells him.

Mr. Gun lover finishes filling his tank, screws the cap back on, and lifts himself into his truck. He gives Mitch one last glance, one Mitch doesn't particularly care for, and then drives off.

Then he sighs, regretting ever leaving his home on the Jersey shore.

His comfortable, miserable life.

"Have you seen her?" Ellie asks, holding out the phone, close enough to the old man behind the counter's face so he can't avoid looking at it. He's not that old but he's old enough that his grayish-white hair and matching stubble are his most prominent features.

He shakes his head. "No, ma'am. When she come through here?"

"About three years ago," Ellie clarifies. "With her friend." She pulls back the phone and then brings up a Facebook photo of the two girls hugging each other at a party.

The store owner—Pop, she thinks—shakes his head. "Nope, haven't seen them. *Three* years ago, you say?"

"Yes."

"Well, sorry, but I hardly remember the faces that came by here yesterday, let alone three years ago." He shrugs. "The memory pools are all dried up, I'm afraid." He taps his temple to punctuate the point.

She returns a wincing smile. "I understand. Sorry to bother you."

"Your daughter's been missing for three years, and you're just coming to look for her now?"

She doesn't think the man intends to insult, but for some reason, his words cause her cheeks to burn ever-so-slightly.

"Well, we just found this photo." She shows him again, Dawn smiling beneath the clock tower. "This was the last time she was seen. We were hoping to find this place."

"Hmm. Looks like the old clock tower in Lacuna's Point." Pop spits his chew into an empty water bottle. The brown gunk travels to the bottom, leaving a muddy trail in its wake. She can smell the heavy odor of the wet tobacco and her stomach tumbles. Suddenly, the pre-made turkey and American cheese sandwich she was eyeing doesn't look so appetizing.

"Lacuna's Point?" Her heart flutters at the prospect of *some* answer, any clue at all.

"Yep. Little town. East a ways, toward the beach. Not too far. No sense going there, though. Wouldn't want to do that, not really." Pop massages his chin, a fun smile resting above his fingers as if this whole situation was a humorous gag on his part. "Not much there, save for a few old buildings. And that clock tower, of course. No one's lived there in…gosh. Fifty years or so."

"Really?" It sounds strange that a place like this still exists. An abandoned town? In America? If it's true, then what the hell was Dawn doing there?

"Really," Pop confirms. "Yep, I imagine the place is overrun with weeds by now. Probably can't even get near it. The road out that way hasn't been maintained. The area's just…well, for the lack of a better term—*dead.*"

"Well, how would I get in? If I wanted to, that is. Could you show me on a map?"

Pop stares at her, his smile losing its stiffness. "You don't want to go there, darling. Ain't nothing there."

"My daughter was there. It's…it's the only clue I have. Please?"

Pop breathes in through his nose, the sound of a man giving up on a debate he knows he'll lose anyway. Then he nods. "Lemme see that again."

She shows him the photo. He leans in and lowers his glasses from the top of his head.

"Well now. Seems I was mistaken. That's not Lacuna's Point after all. Sorry about that."

"Oh, come on. You just said it was."

He shrugs and reiterates, "My mistake."

"You just don't want me to go there."

He hesitates. "Look, you seem nice. You and your…" He nods outside, back near the car. Then glances down at her left hand. "Boyfriend?"

"Friend."

*"Friend."* He chews on his lips. "Just don't want to see you two get lost up there, that's all."

"My daughter is missing. Has been for three years. This is the last known place she was seen."

"I know, I know. But sometimes, looking for lost things, you can get lost yourself. Catch my meaning?"

"No, explain."

" 'Fraid I can't."

"Do you know something?" She shakes the phone, then brings it closer to his face. "About Dawn? About this place she went to?"

"Ma'am, I'm just giving you some friendly local advice, that's all." He pauses, blinks rapidly, then gives her a smile that could pass as the real thing. "Look, you two go up there—can't stop ya. I know that. But you do me a favor, y'hear? You see one thing that don't look right, that looks *off*…you hightail it back here. Got it?"

There's no point arguing with Pop, this man, this stranger. "Yeah…sure." She knows *he knows* something, something more than he's willing to admit, and a part of her wants to call the authorities. But she won't. Can't. This is her opportunity, not theirs.

"Good," Pop says, then nods over to the open fridge where the packaged sandwiches sit on shelves. "Now, I seen you eyeing up that turkey and American. It's yours. On the house. Tell your friend to help himself to one as well. Consider it my good deed for the day."

She pockets the phone and takes the sandwiches.

"We're being followed," Mitch says two miles later.

Ellie looks over her shoulder and sees a single car keeping its distance. It looks like a brand new SUV painted an atrocious burnt-orange color, maybe a Volvo. She can't tell for sure, but the driver appears to be keeping their distance. "How do you know?"

"Saw that couple pull into the parking lot a second after we did. They didn't get out. Just sat there. Now they're following us again."

"Coincidence?"

He scrunches his lips and arches his brow, and she gets it.

"Why would they be following us?" Ellie asks.

"Maybe they don't like me in their neighborhood."

"Are you serious?"

"You missed a small interaction with a good ol' boy while you were inside interrogating the old man." She had told him about the conversation with Pop, his peculiar warning, and the free sandwiches. Mitch opted out of the sandwiches, as a free meal from the pasty old dude didn't sit well with him, but Ellie couldn't ignore the hunger causing her stomach to grumble. "I thought he was going to call a Clan meeting right then and there."

"Jesus," she says, acting more surprised than she ought to have. "I can't believe our country is still like this in some places."

"Well, it ain't exactly *some* places. You just might not have noticed."

She doesn't know how to respond, so she keeps quiet and observes the tail. She can almost make out the driver and the passenger. A man with glasses hunches behind the wheel, a woman with long blonde hair, curly, shoulder-length, sits in the passenger seat. Their faces are stone, lacking any emotion. Corpse-stare eyes beaming straight ahead.

*Might as well be Crash-Test Dummies,*

"I don't like this, Mitch," she says, unable to detach her eyes from the sideview.

"Well, I'm not getting a case of the cozies either." His eyes flick back and forth between the road and the rearview. "We should pull over."

"What?"

"Yeah, confront them. Head on."

"What? Why?"

"Why not?"

"I dunno. What if they have guns or something?"

"You think they do?"

She looks back. She doesn't think so, but you can never know for sure. Not until it's too late, she thinks, not until after she's staring down that lead barrel of death, looking directly into a cylindrical eye of doom.

"I don't know, man," she says, a cold sensation skating over her arms, causing her tiny hairs to rise. "I think that's a bad idea."

"Fuck it," Mitch says, and then throws on the blinker. He drives that way for about fifteen seconds, seeing if the tail will do the same.

They do.

"All right," he says, "so this is happening."

"Shit," Ellie says, undoing her seat belt. She blinks and they're on the side of the road, the burnt-orange SUV parked a solid fifty feet behind them. No movement from within, not a flinch. The dark silhouettes in the front seats sit completely and eerily still. "What do we do?"

"I got this. Follow my lead."

"Okay."

The two figures in the SUV climb out. Mitch opens the door, and Ellie does the same.

She wonders if the same bad feeling that's tearing her stomach apart is doing the same to him.

"We're sorry," is the first thing out of the man's mouth. He's a short guy, the shortest of all four of them, but he's thick in almost every area of his body. A square-jawed face that looks like it could take a punch or two, and it probably has over the years. But not recently—too clean, too smooth. The barroom brawling days seem well over for this guy. Ellie thinks he might have been a bodybuilder in his previous life, possibly a bouncer at some seedy bar, and maybe it's been a decade since he's hit the weight room. "We didn't mean to alarm you."

"You mind telling us why you've been following us?" Mitch asks. Ellie observes his approach, the cool, cautious movement of each step. If he's nervous, Mitch doesn't show it.

"We're sorry," the wife echoes. Ellie doesn't know if they're married for sure, but both are wearing wedding rings and that's enough evidence for her. The wife's a big woman herself and oh-so-tall. Taller than her husband by a solid six inches. "We...oh gosh. This is going to sound nuts."

"Well," Mitch says, "we're all ears."

"My wife and I overheard your exchange back at the Maryland rest stop," Husband says.

Ellie can't keep her jaw from dropping. "You've been following us since Maryland?"

"It's not what you think," he says, raising his palms to them as if Mitch is storming over there with balled fists.

"Please," Mitch says, arching back, folding his arms. "Elaborate."

"We heard you say you were looking for your daughters. We heard you mention Virginia—"

"Our son went missing," Wife blurts out. Her eyes swell with sad tears. "Oh God, about twelve months ago. He was visiting Virginia Tech—the school."

"I know what Virginia Tech is," Mitch says, practically through his teeth.

"He was going to play football there. He was supposed to be visiting with the coaching staff, to go over the playbook or something, about a month before moving into his on-campus apartment."

"After a few days, the coaching staff notified us that Jared never showed," Husband adds. "He...he never made it there. Never made it home, either."

Ellie clears her throat, the similarity of their situations driving cold needles into her nerves. "Did you contact the police?"

Wife lets go of an amused snort. "The police are useless."

"Well, you'll get no argument from us on that subject," Mitch says. "When's the last time you talked to your boy?"

Husband tilts back, looks up as if the sky will help him remember. "Oh, after he left. When he was on his way to..." He trails off, sadness besting his fragile toughness. Lower lip quivering, he runs his knuckles along the bottom rim of his eyes, erasing the loose tears.

"We have this feeling…" Wife says, holding her hands together, fingers interlaced, as if she's about to plead and beg for their help. "…that our Jared is still alive out there, you know?"

Ellie wants to tell them she knows exactly what that feels like, but refrains.

Mitch gestures with his chin. "You got a picture of your boy?"

Husband's left hand dives into his pocket and produces an iPhone, a newer model. Nervously, he taps the screen several times. "Here," he says, walking toward them, holding out the phone. "This was the last picture he sent us."

Ellie leans in, looking at the picture of the eighteen-year-old kid wearing a Virginia Tech cut-sleeve, posing before a—

Her heart leaps when she notices the monumental edifice in the background.

*The clock tower.*

"Keith, tell them the weird thing," Wife urges, her expression changing. She's somber now, clearly touched by something that haunts her. "Tell them."

"Sue, no. They'll think I'm cra—"

*"Tell them."* Sue glares at her husband, and within ten seconds, Keith caves and turns to them, his eyes avoiding their direct gaze.

"All right. It might sound crazy, but…damn, I can't believe I'm actually saying this out loud, but…this photo. It was just sent two days ago."

Cold webs ripple across Ellie's neck. "What?" she asks, the word coming out like a whoosh of air.

"Yeah, I know. Weird. Twelve months—nothing. Two days ago, *this*."

Mitch clears his throat. "We got messages, too."

Keith swallows so hard that Ellie sees his throat bob. "You did?"

"Yes," Ellie confirms.

Keith and Sue exchange glances, both filled with a strange combination of shock and joy.

"That's great," Keith says, and Ellie hates the excitement in his voice. There's nothing to be excited about. This is terrifying and confusing and— "I mean, not *great* great. But great in the sense that this means our kids are still alive!"

Sue rolls her eyes. "Keith, stop. Stop filling your head with false hope." She faces Ellie, then Mitch. "Fact is, we don't know anything yet. We…we haven't found any evidence that our boy is still alive…out there somewhere."

"But this is good, hon. Right? We're not alone, Sue. This means we're not alone. Means Jared might not be alone either."

"I know what it *could* mean," Sue more-or-less snaps. Something about the woman's voice puts Ellie on edge. She can't put her finger on it. "I apologize for my husband. He can get a bit ahead of himself."

"It's just good to find people who can relate to our situation, that's all," Keith says.

Ellie is the first to turn back to them. "We're looking for this place, the clock tower. Do you know where it is? The man at the gas station said it was in some abandoned town, a place called—"

"Lacuna's Point," Keith says, cutting her off. "Yeah, we've been there."

Ellie's heart skips like a stone across smooth waters. "Where is it? We have to—"

"Hold on, El," Mitch says, stepping in front of her, putting his back to the couple and facing her. "Can we talk? Privately?"

Keith and Sue look moderately insulted.

Ellie nods at Mitch. They walk several paces away, around the side of the car, far enough so the two won't hear them whispering.

"What do you think?" Mitch asks. "I mean, for real. Do you trust these people?"

"They seem all right. A little goofy, but…I don't know. I don't get a bad vibe from them or anything. Plus, they have a picture of—"

"I know. I know. But…shit, something feels…off."

"How do you mean?"

"I mean, they followed us from Maryland. Off of a conversation they randomly overheard? You don't think that's a bit suspicious?"

It does sound a bit odd once he lays it out like that, but still—she's willing to believe anything. Explore every possibility, even the ones that don't feel right. *Especially* those. "I don't know."

"And if they've been to this place, what the hell were they doing up in Maryland anyway?"

"God, Mitch, I don't know." She shrugs. "Ask them."

Mitch turns to the couple. "Hey, if you were already down in Virginia poking around, what the hell were you doing up in Maryland?"

Keith responds at once, not wasting a second. "We were returning home."

"And where's that?" Ellie asks.

"New York," Sue answers. "Long Island."

Ellie and Mitch face each other again. She can tell Mitch isn't buying whatever the duo is selling.

*Hope,* Ellie thinks. *They're selling us hope.*

And she wants to buy and hoard it all, every available morsel.

Mitch sighs. He knows Ellie wants to find the town, to find their kids, to give this fucked up three-year-long nightmare a satisfying and rewarding conclusion, but he doesn't trust these people beyond his next step. Still, he finds himself agreeing with her—*We at least need to see Lacuna's Point. We poke around for a day, and if we see anything we don't like, we call the cops or head home, or both. But we need to see, Mitch. For ourselves. We have to go there. We have to see the clock tower.*

Mitch can't argue. The clock tower represented in all three photos has sure piqued his interest, but he doesn't like anything about it, the scenario, what heading to a town they've been previously told is abandoned might award them—he can't possibly subscribe to the idea that this will turn out the way he's dreamed for the past three years; Kya emerging from a building where she's been held captive, her body intact, in relatively in good shape, her mind unbroken from the traumatizing experience, the horrors inflicted; her running toward him, him running toward her, their arms spreading, expecting the biggest embrace two people have ever held.

He's dreamed of that scenario quite a bit, and the farther he gets from home, the deeper into Virginia he heads, the more he doubts that will ever become a reality.

"All right," he says, standing upright, arching his back. The audible pop of his spine brings him comfort. He turns to the couple standing next to their ugly SUV. "So...do we follow you, or..."

Keith smiles at them. "We'll lead the way."

# CHAPTER FOUR

For a few miles they follow the SUV down some back roads, twisting and turning so much that the GPS on Ellie's phone has trouble tracking their location. *Signal lost* has become a consistently frequent announcement, and every thirty seconds or so the lovely voice narrating their travels lets them know the obvious—wherever they are, no satellite can reach them. Green clusters that stretch and extend over the blacktop swallow up the sky. Their drooping collections of leaves are nearing the end of their summer cycle. In a month they'll fall and die and blow away. The woods that surround both sides provide a deep and dark look into an incomplete void, even with daytime sunlight shining down from above. When she was a kid, when her parents took her on road trips and they passed long stretches of woods like this, she couldn't help but wonder what the trees were hiding behind them, back in the farthest reaches, down in the unseen spots, the black hollows and pockets of impenetrable thickets. Now, as an adult, she finds herself returning to these thoughts. The possibilities, like the woods, seem endless.

As they get deeper into the unknown, Ellie notices Mitch gripping the steering wheel harder and tighter with each passing mile. Her nerves fire like the frontline of some aggressive battalion. There's a brief second where she almost tells him to forget it. To pull over, throw the car in reverse, and get out of there. That this whole trip is stupid. Pointless. A waste of time.

*Do you really think you'll find her?* asks some inner demon, and it sounds too close to her sister's voice; Maura, after three glasses of wine, feeling chatty. *After three years? Jesus, after three days, the police assumed the cause is lost.*

*Yes, but there are outliers,* she barks back at the phantom voice. *Some who go missing are found years later. It happens.*

*Outliers. Oh yes. If anyone is an outlier, it is Dawn.*

The voice floods her veins with adrenaline, and she wants to fight something.

"I know you don't like this," Ellie says.

Mitch grunts.

"But thank you."

He throws another glance at the rearview, as if he's expecting someone to pull up on the Subaru's bumper. "Well, we came for answers, right? This is the only clue we got." He winks. "Besides, if they turn out to be murdering psychopaths, I think I stand a pretty good chance against these rich, preppy assholes."

"Maybe we *should* call the police."

"Yeah?"

"I don't know. I'm so confused. I have this feeling…well, two feelings, really. One, I want to see this through, see what this place looks like and just…see if we can find anything, anything at all. On the other hand…I would feel safer with a cop with us."

"Hmm. Interesting."

"It's the clock tower. Something about it seems…*off.* You didn't, like, feel anything when you first saw it, did you?"

His eyes shift. "It's strange for sure. Showing up in all three pictures."

"What do you think it means?"

"Nothing to me."

She gnaws on her fingernail. "I should call the cops. The detective assigned to the girls' case. He still works there." She glances over at Mitch, to see if she's giving him a weird look. "I stalked him on Facebook."

He smirks.

She goes through her phone, searching for his number. Then she deliberates, finger hovering over the green phone graphic. Finally, she says, "Shit," and pockets the phone.

"What happened?"

"Can't do it."

Ellie uses the next few moments to think long and hard about her life, the last few days, her future beyond them if this mission ends up being a complete failure. If she returns home with no more answers than she left with. She figures life won't be any different, that she'll return to that repetitive daily grind; getting by but just barely. There will be days and bad days, none of them good or even close to it. Everything will remain flavorless, pointless, lacking any real enjoyment.

Her insipid life. That's all that awaits her.

"Well, look at this," Mitch says, tearing her away from her thoughts, which is a godsend because she hates those thoughts, vehemently. "We're here."

Ellie glances up and spots a sign that welcomes her to LACUNA'S POINT, POPULATION 743. The blue letters and numbers appear freshly painted, the grass around the bottom of the metal pole recently cut and maintained, looking green and healthy. Not the first impression she expected from a town that's been abandoned for fifty-plus years. She suspects Pop lied to her, or maybe the old man was misinformed. Either way, she hates him.

They drive a little farther down the road, following the Campbells' SUV. The narrow lane takes them in serpentine patterns. Through the open window, fresh wind pelts her face. Ellie breathes in and can't remember ever taking in a lungful so pure, so revitalizing. There's an odd comfort in that simple act of taking in the country air. The wind sinks deep within, filling her nerves with a cozy warmth she hasn't known in years.

The small town gets closer, and the layout appears much like any suburban neighborhood; there's the main street (unsurprisingly labeled Main Street) that divides the town in half, a network of cross streets dissecting the opposite way, the stretch of town about the length of two football fields. Instead of houses, the town is filled with shoppes and businesses, the storefronts facing each other, all done up and decorated with a flair for 1950's Americana. None of it looks abandoned. None of it looks derelict. The grass is short and the window signs are sparkly clean, proudly displaying the names of the businesses inside. In the backdrop, the opposite end of town, she sees a patch of woods and a giant Ferris wheel peeking over them. There's also a coaster of some kind, red and twisting at its highest point. Farther to the right, there're streets and streets of neighborhood homes, ranches mostly, all seemingly modeled after one another; though the color schemes change, the designs remain the same.

She can't see people but the town appears very much alive. In a minute, she's confident she'll see a face, a wandering body walking down the main boulevard...because she has to; the town is too clean and maintained, and it doesn't get that way by preserving and landscaping itself.

Because that would be insane.

*No, this town is alive.*

Behind the rows of buildings, the clock tower stands watch, its circular face appearing like a great eye in the sky, observing the life resting at its feet. Despite so much to behold, her eyes seem to focus on the clock tower, its magnificence, its dominance over this town trapped in time. She pictures Mitch driving up to it and seeing Dawn standing at the base, posing for a picture, the same still shot Ellie received two days ago. She knows that would be impossible, but she can't stop thinking about it.

*Dawn was here.*

*This is where she disappeared.*

"I don't believe it," she whispers, not meaning to.

"What's that?" Mitch asks, continuing to follow the SUV.

"This is where they went missing. Where someone abducted them."

"We don't know that."

She rotates toward him. "But we do. This is the last place they were. The picture from Dawn's phone—it came from here."

Mitch's tongue moves along the inner surface of his cheek, the information a bitter taste he can't get rid of.

"We need to acquire some facts," he says. "Some actual evidence other than a picture that may have been sent three years ago and not two days ago."

"But Brian said—"

"Don't care what your techie friend said. I care about the truth. The facts. We need to dig without getting ourselves in too deep. Otherwise, we'll be running around in circles like a dog chasing his tail."

She nods. "Okay. You're right. I'm getting caught up in this, I think. I need to relax. Stay calm and focused. Go in with no expectations."

"I know it's not easy, but high expectations are bound to crush you."

They pull into a small parking lot off to the side, located halfway between the town's entrance and the clock tower, which seems to rest at the town's farthest point. Ellie practically jumps out of the car before Mitch can bring the Subaru to a complete stop. She doesn't allow him the opportunity to tell her to wait or lecture her about staying sharp, focused, and aware of anything that could lead them into trouble. She slams the door shut and walks away before he can speak a word.

She puts a hand over her eyes, shielding herself from the bright sun. Behind the clock tower, a mountain range sits on the horizon, a blend of purple and pale blue shadows coloring in the craggy surface, the apexes capped with snowy white hats. They're beautiful, she thinks, but it's the clock tower that continues to capture her attention. It's hard for her to look away, and she wonders if the pic message with Dawn beneath it has something to do with its allure, or if the clock tower itself is the source of the attraction.

She shakes her head.

"Well," says Keith Campbell, almost underwhelmingly as he tucks his hands in his pockets and scans the length of the small town. "Eerie, isn't it?"

*Eerie*, she thinks, is an understatement. Still no signs of life, not a sense that the town is truly alive other than the clean streets and well-maintained storefronts. Everything looks recently painted, the sidewalks power-washed and pebble-white. The town practically glimmers in the stark sunshine.

"Have you seen anyone?" Mitch asks.

"Yeah," Sue Campbell says. "Some of the stores keep strange hours, limited, but the diner—it's just next to the clock tower and city hall—always seems to be open."

"How long did you stay here?"

"Couple of days," Keith tells them. Again, Ellie notices his throat bob as he swallows hard. There's something he's not telling them, but she doesn't press the issue. Not while he's volunteering information. "There's a hotel up near those trees over there."

She follows his finger past the town, where the trees cover most of what looks like a tall building that rests between the town and the woods before the amusement park. She can make out the brick façade through the branches and roadside powerlines.

"We stayed there," Keith elaborates. "The rates were... reasonable."

"Why do I get the sense you're not telling us the whole truth?" Mitch turns, leering at them. "You mind telling me what this is? Is it a ghost town, is it not a ghost town? Just what the hell is it?"

Keith and Sue exchange glances.

"We don't really know," Sue says. "We searched the place for days. Interviewed everyone who would talk to us. No one seems to know anything about anything."

"Damn it," Mitch mutters.

"Maybe our kids are here," Keith says, swallowing hard again. He's sweating now, tiny beads rolling down his temples, which isn't exactly a tell—the August heat is brutally oppressive. "But then again—maybe not. Maybe they're just... *gone*."

"No one ever ends up *gone*," Ellie says, spitting the words. "Everyone is somewhere."

Keith nods like he understands. "Maybe that's true for some places. But this place—it's different."

"How do you mean?" Mitch asks, and Ellie can hear his frustration seeping through.

"I can't describe it. It's just something you have to experience yourself."

Mitch shoots Ellie a glance. Ellie just shrugs.

Mitch raises his brow. "There's a diner?"

"Just beyond those shoppes," Sue confirms.

"Well, I am hungry."

"Let's go," Ellie says, and starts walking across the street, hoping two lost girls are waiting for them somewhere in the depths of this mysterious labyrinth of shoppes and buildings drenched in old-time American charm.

From the outside, the diner looks like it was transplanted here in a time machine, plucked out of the 1950s and dropped on the edge of Lacuna's Point. Much of the town appears that way, but the diner is different—its shiny chrome shell of an exterior is fronted by a long row of individual picture windows, ruby-red aluminum siding panels nailed in below them. American-blue trims out the windows. On its roof, a metal rod extends from the center, displaying a gleaming silver statue of a rocket ship, erected like a weathervane rooster. A big billboard-looking sign alerts the town that this is ACE'S PLACE, with the slogan, "TASTES LIKE HEAVEN" written beneath it in perfect, antiquated cursive.

Mitch thinks the slogan should read something like, "THE FOOD IS CHEAP BUT THE HEART ATTACKS ARE FREE!"

"Well," he says to Ellie, who stands next to him, marveling over the authenticity of the place. Even the diners back on the Jersey shore aren't able to capture this kind of charm, and some of them try pretty damn hard to mimic the 50s aesthetic. "What are we waiting for?"

Ellie takes the first step, and Mitch follows.

Inside, it smells like fried grease and vanilla bean ice cream. The first thing Mitch notices is the checkered flag floor tiles, the tubes of fluorescent lighting above gleaming in the white and black squares with crystal clarity. He thinks the floors might be clean enough to eat off of. Next, his eyes settle on the leather barstools, their cherry-red color nearly blinding. There's a framed picture of Elvis over the coffee bar. It's signed and Mitch automatically doubts the signature's authenticity, but still considers the possibility that it's real. His attention then swings to the old cash register that looks more like a giant typewriter, its impeccably clean and dust-free shape.

Not a single soul sits in the row of cushioned booths, nor is there anyone behind the counter. No waitresses hustling about, no noise from the kitchen, no banging of pots and pans or the scraping of metal spatulas flipping over mounds of scrambled eggs on the flat grill. The place just seems…*frozen*. Open for business, but also—not.

*Abandoned.*

"Okay, I'm officially freaked out," Ellie says, moving toward the counter. "Hello? Anyone here?"

No answer, not that Mitch expects one.

A second later, the bell dangling from the front door's handle rings, and in steps a man with a newspaper tucked under his arm. He's wearing a long trench coat and a short-brimmed fedora. He notices Mitch and Ellie, and without missing a beat, the man smiles at them, tips his cap, and says, "Howdy, folks."

Mitch and Ellie just stare as he turns and heads for a booth farther down the aisle. He sets his newspaper on the table and shrugs off his coat, throwing it on the seat across from where he'll sit.

Mitch can't help but utter, *"What the hell?"* under his breath.

Ellie opens her mouth but before she can answer Mitch's rhetorical question, a waitress pops through the double doors with a pot of coffee in one hand and a white ceramic mug in the other.

"Hey there, Dave!" she practically shouts between the cow-like chewing of her bubblegum. "Didn't think I'd see you this morning!"

Dave wraps his knuckles on the table. "Well, gee—I wouldn't miss my daily cup of coffee for anything, Darla. You know that."

"Aw, you're a sweetie," Darla says back, then turns her attention on her other guests, flashing them a welcoming smile. "You folks can sit anywhere you like. Coffee?"

Ellie swallows whatever words were previously trapped in her throat. "Yeah…yeah, I'd love some."

"Perfect. You, fella?"

Mitch doesn't like the feel of this place—not just the diner, but the entire town. The eeriness that Keith Campbell described is coming in large, dizzying doses. But still…the coffee smells good, and coffee is coffee. "Sure thing."

"Coming right up," Darla says, finishing her pour. She heads around the counter, still smiling at them. Ellie and Mitch still haven't found the nerve to sit down. "Sit anywhere," Darla tells them. "The cushions don't have teeth, y'all." This information comes with a side of giggling laughter.

An invisible brush combs the nerves up his arm. Everything within him says to get out—of this diner, of this place. But there's another something that tells him Kya is here, somewhere, that the answers of where she went, where she disappeared to, is right here in front of them. In the heart of this time-trapped town. If he can find out what happened to her, if he can get closure, then maybe he can heal. Maybe he and Angie can heal too.

Maybe this place is the answer to all of his problems.

Mitch sits.

Ellie follows.

They turn and stare at each other. A dubious look circles Ellie's eyes, and Mitch returns an expression of equal caution. The waitress comes over and sets down two mugs, begins pouring their coffee immediately, smiling as she works, nodding along to the rockabilly tunes coming through the radio behind the counter. Mitch lets the bold aroma fill his nose and he breathes it deep into his lungs. It's intoxicating.

"Can I get you folks anything else?" Darla asks. "Or do you need a minute to look over the menus?"

"I'm good with the coffee for now," Ellie says. "Darla, is it?"

Darla points to her name tag, which reads, DARLA. "That's the name my momma gave me," she says, giggling again, a cute sound Mitch thinks could get old quickly.

He forces a smile.

"Darla," Ellie continues, digging her phone out of her pocket. "I was wondering if you could help us out?"

Darla puts a hand on her hip and strikes a pose. "Well, sure, darling. I'd love to help. What can I do you for?"

Ellie pulls up the pic and slides the phone in front of Darla. The woman looks down at it, the sparkle in her smile seeming to dim some as she scans over the image.

"Well, gosh, that sure is a lovely snapshot of Mr. Quincy's clock tower."

Mitch studies her reaction. The cheer hasn't been stripped from her voice, but something about the image is disturbing to her. Her eyebrows betray her. The way they dip too close to her eyes.

"The girl," Ellie says, pointing at Dawn. "Have you seen her?"

Darla puts a hand on the table and leans over. She gives the picture a good look, one that Mitch almost believes to be sincere.

"Nope!" Darla perks up, flashing her a smile. "Can't say I have. Lots of people come through here, though. Especially to see Mr. Quincy's tower. It's quite famous around these parts."

"Is it?" Mitch asks.

"Oh, yes. Ever since he built it, the people just come. It's a marvel."

"And who is this Mr. Quincy?"

She stares at him as if he's from another planet, and honestly, Mitch feels like he's just landed on Mars. "Well, he's the mayor of Lacuna's Point."

"The mayor, huh?"

She squints, then points at them, one finger that toggles between parties. "Gee-gosh, y'all really ain't from around here, are you?"

"What gave it away?"

She giggles at this. "Oh, man. You're gonna love it here. Both y'all. It's so quaint. Every day here is like a bucket of sunshine being poured all over your soul."

Mitch wants to respond to that, but he almost laughs instead.

Ellie clears her throat. "Ma'am. Please. The girl in the picture. Have you seen her? Anywhere? She was here. Three years ago. Then she went missing. She's...she's my daughter and I love her, and I think if you or someone you know can help, then—"

"Three years ago?" The waitress's brow flexes.

"Yes."

"No, no—that can't be."

"What do you mean?"

Darla backs away from the table. "Mr. Quincy's clock tower..." The girl's voice trembles. "...it was only built just last year."

Ellie shakes her head, unable to believe what she's just heard. "Last year?" Her heart flutters as her mind races with impossible possibilities. "Last year?" She turns to Mitch. "That means..."

"We don't know that it means anything," Mitch tells her. The way he speaks, she can tell he's not allowing himself to get caught up in any wild speculations. She wishes she could do the same.

"She was here, within the last year. The girls were—"

Mitch shifts uncomfortably, as if he's embarrassed. "We don't know anything yet, El. Let's not jump to any conclusions."

"Can I—" Darla starts, but then stops. Her features grow concerned. "Can I help y'all in any way? I can get Officer Foley over here to help you out? He's a nice man. Great police officer. I'm sure he'll be much obliged to help you find the missing girl...or girls."

"No," Mitch says. "We're fine, thank you. We just need a minute. Um, I'll take an omelet, please. Extra cheese."

"American?"

"Yes, ma'am."

"Coming right up!" She turns to Ellie. "Anything for you, darlin'?"

Ellie shakes her head sheepishly.

Darla winks, smiles, and then bounces off toward the back.

Once she's gone, Ellie leans over the table. "A year ago?"

"It doesn't make sense."

"Yes, it does."

"She's mistaken, El. Can't possibly have been built a year ago. That would mean Kya and Dawn passed through here within the last twelve months, which would mean they've been alive for the last two years. You don't think someone would have found them by now? The police? That detective? The private dick we hired when the police stopped searching?" He shakes his head. "If they were in plain sight, someone would have found them. *Someone.*"

"So…what?" Ellie huffs incredulously. "This girl just doesn't know when the clock tower was built? She seemed pretty convinced when I hinted the picture was taken three years ago."

"I don't know. Something isn't adding up. This town…it doesn't make sense. That guy back at the gas station—"

"Pop?"

"Yeah, him. He said this place was abandoned. A ghost town, right?"

"That's what he said."

"So… are these people ghosts?"

She looks around. Outside, a few more people have wandered out and about, at least a dozen traveling along the sidewalk in front of the row of shoppes. "Don't look like ghosts to me."

"Yeah, me neither. Unless we're dead, too. Unless this is some Bruce-Willis-is-dead-at-the-end-of-this-movie bullshit."

"I don't feel dead. The opposite, in fact. I feel alive. More than I've been in ages."

Mitch takes another sip of coffee.

"We need a plan," she suggests. "We're here now, might as well make the most of it."

"We spending the night here?"

She shrugs. "Got any brighter ideas?"

He doesn't.

"There's a hotel, right up the road there. The one the Campbells pointed out."

"Okay, okay. Maybe we should check in there first. Maybe…maybe the girls stayed there too."

She snaps her fingers. "Great idea."

"We'll leave after I finish my om—"

Ellie and Mitch turn, expecting to see their waitress, but instead they see Dave, the only other patron in the place. His smile looks sponsored by the cups of coffee he's already sucked down.

"Hey there, folks," he says, flashing a sales-pitch grin. "Couldn't help but overhear your predicament and I just wanted to say—if there is anything, and I do mean *anything*, that ol' Dave Fester can do for you, well, don't hesitate to ask."

Mitch nods. "That's mighty nice of you, Mr. Fester, but—"

"Oh, please! Call me Dave, buddy!"

Without asking for permission, Dave takes the seat next to Mitch.

Ellie raises her brow, shifts uncomfortably. Mitch doesn't budge, not giving the man much extra room.

"I know what it's like to lose someone you love," he says, almost whispering, his face losing some of the joy it displayed only seconds ago.

"Do you?" Mitch asks.

"Yep! When I was six, I lost my puppy. Little poodle we named Tommy. Yep, Tommy was good and lost all right. Never found the little bugger. Always wondered what happened to him. It was like—he was here one day, and poof!" Dave snaps his fingers. "Gone the next!"

"That's what usually happens when you lose something, yes."

Ellie and Mitch exchange glances. In a *get-me-out-of-here* way, she expands her eyes.

"Yeah, I suppose so," Dave says, picking up a sugar packet, staring at it, frozen, as if he's trapped in some reverie, perhaps of Tommy the dog and what could have been. "Gosh!" he nearly shouts, perking up, removing himself from his thoughts. "I am so rude!" He stands up immediately, turns to them, and places his hands on his hips, throwing a glance at his toes. "I just inserted myself into your conversation without even asking. How rude. My wife would be hella-upset with me!"

Mitch bites his lower lip. "I'm sorry, did you just say *hella-*upset?"

"Oh, yeah! It's just a little thing we do, my wife and I. A little Fester family catchphrase, if you will. Hella-this and hella-that. It's fun, more of an inside joke. Sometimes I can't stop myself from using it in everyday conversation."

"Interesting," Mitch says, facing Ellie and shaking his head.

"Gosh, well, I've been a bother enough. You folks enjoy your food and remember—my offer remains. You need help, I'm there for you! I may sell insurance, but that's not the only thing I'm good at. Huh?" His smile is wider than ever, and he turns his hands into pistols, starts cranking his thumbs. "Huh?"

"Yeah, *gosh,* Dave," Mitch says, "thanks for the hospitable introduction. We really appreciate it."

"No pro-blame-o!"

With that, Dave turns and exits right.

"What the fuck was that?" Mitch asks.

"Your guess is as good as mine." Chills drape over Ellie's shoulders like a heavy towel. "You better get your omelet soon, because this place and these people are officially getting to me."

# CHAPTER FIVE

The arctic blast of air conditioning cools her off immediately, and Ellie stops inside the door, closes her eyes, and lets the frigid moment pass until the chill is old news. Then she blinks, opens her eyes, and takes in the hotel lobby that's set to mimic some 70's billionaire playboy's manor. There's a fireplace directly across the way, a buck's head mounted above it on a cherrywood plaque. In front of the fireplace sits a coffee table. Around it, four puffy leather chairs form a square. The carpet below her feet that extends throughout the entire lobby is near-ancient, something akin to her grandparents' tastes, diamond patterns of varying differences, autumn-brown and dead-carrot orange. Above them, in the dim lighting, dark mahogany ceiling beams run the length of the lobby, crisscrossing every eight feet or so.

"Cozy," says Mitch, stepping inside behind her. "But where's the bear rug?"

She ignores the joke and allows him to pass her since she's not ready to step away from the slim space where the air vent's concentrated. Once she sees the woman behind the check-in counter, her motivation changes. She drags herself away from the cold spot and over to the counter.

"Hello," Ellie says before the woman has a chance to greet her.

"Oh, hi there," the woman says back, perking up as if she's been caught daydreaming. "Welcome to the Pine Meadow Hotel. Checking in?"

"Yes." Ellie slips two fingers in her back pocket and removes the credit card. Slapping it down on the counter, she studies the woman's eyes. Amiable. Calm. Doesn't seem to be anything to suggest she's unusual. But then again, there were no precursors when it came to the waitress or Dave being weird, not until they opened their mouths. "We'll need two rooms."

"Very well." The woman, whose name tag isn't clearly visible, partially veiled behind a wool scarf (somewhat odd considering the season), accepts the card and begins to clack away on the keyboard. The monitor is the size of a king pillow and has lost its natural white plastic shine to some dull urine color. As the woman zips along with her task, Ellie studies her. Streaks of gray are woven into her natural dark color. Blood-red nails tap away on the keys. No wedding ring, though. Her face doesn't move, as if her skin is plastic. Each movement is calculated, rehearsed, as if she's not a woman at all, but some machine encased in human flesh.

Though Ellie expects two old-school skeleton keys, the woman places two keycards on the counter before her.

"Two rooms," the woman confirms with a smile, finally breaking her stiff exterior. For a second, Ellie thinks her skin might split, revealing her for the cyborg she truly is.

"Thank you...Nina, is it?"

"Yes."

"Nina," Ellie repeats like she knows someone else by that name, even though she doesn't. "I like that name."

"Thank you."

"Nina, I need your help."

"Oh?"

She brings out the phone, the gallery app already open, the picture already present. "Have you seen this girl?"

Nina takes a close look, her brow bent as she absorbs the picture before her. Her lips squiggle. "Mm, can't say I have. Who is she?"

"My daughter."

"Oh."

"She's missing."

"Oh my," Nina says, putting a hand over her heart. "That's awful."

"It is. And we have reason to believe she passed through here, possibly..." Her voice cracks. "Possibly within the last year. At least, according to the waitress at the diner—she said this clock tower was built just last year, and..."

At this information, Nina tilts her head. Her forehead gathers a collection of wrinkles.

"What is it?" Ellie asks.

"Last year? She said that?"

"Yes."

Nina shakes her head. "No...no, that's not right. The clock tower has been here longer than that. At least five years. Maybe even longer." She winces like pinning down an estimated date is a skewer through her frontal lobe. "Good grief, I can't remember." A not-so-humorous laugh breaks free from her.

"But longer than a year?"

"Yes."

"Why would the waitress lie to us?"

Nina shrugs. "Dunno. But it's Lacuna's Point—time works differently here for some folks."

"What?" Ellie hates the worry in her voice. It makes her seem weak. *That's because you are weak.* Maura's voice again, and how good it is for her to show up at a time like this. "What are you talking about? What do you mean time works *differently?*"

Nina hikes up her shoulders again. "Just an expression we have around here."

"That's an expression around here? Time works differently?" Anger swells up inside her, and though she doesn't think the woman means to fuck with her, that's exactly what she's doing.

*Fucking with her.*

Playing a game.

"Listen to me," Ellie says, smacking the counter with an open hand. It's loud enough to make Nina jump. "I came here for answers, and I'm not leaving until I find out what happened to my daughter. Understand?"

Nina raises her hands. "Ma'am, I'm sorry. But I have no clue what happened to your girl."

Ellie is about to scream when Mitch puts a hand on her shoulder.

"Excuse my friend here," he says, gently pulling her away from the counter, extracting her from the altercation. She steps aside with no resistance. "But she's had a long day." He shoots Ellie a look, and if there was any ambition to speak out, it's gone now. "What she's trying to say is…we're both worried."

Nina shifts uncomfortably like she's being forced to endure this interrogation against her will. "I understand."

"We just need to make sense of some things. Was hoping you could help."

"I can try."

"Good." Mitch nods to the side, back in the direction of the town's center. "Interesting place…Lacuna's Point. We heard this whole town was abandoned some odd years ago."

Nina smirks. "Abandoned? Who said that?"

"Some guy."

"Well, that guy is mistaken. Certainly not abandoned. Lived here my whole life."

Mitch sighs. "That so?"

"Yes. It's so."

He looks to Ellie. Ellie can only shrug.

"Well, look," Mitch says, his voice silky smooth. The more he talks, the more Nina seems to ease up. Her shoulders have slumped some, and her eyes are no longer darting, searching for an easy exit. "We don't want to bother you. Certainly don't want to cause a ruckus." Ellie knows that last part was for her. "Just…if you think of anything, anything at all—could you let us know?"

Nina's quiet for a beat, but then nods.

"Thank you." Mitch grabs the keycards. "Come on, El. Let's check out the digs."

"Well, that was fucking weird," Ellie says, unable to shake the chilly combination of the cranked-up air conditioning and the creeps the hotel clerk has given her. "I mean, what the hell, Mitch? How do these people not know when the clock tower was built? One year? Five? Which is it?"

"Relax," he says, keeping calm. She's not sure how he's doing it, but if he's been popping Valium behind her back, she wants some. "I don't think we should start freaking out yet. Do you know when every building or monument in Red River went up?"

She swallows. "No."

"Exactly. No one remembers dumb shit like that. One year, five years? People can get confused pretty easily."

She paces the hotel room, which is—quite honestly—classier than expected. "This place doesn't add up. Maybe we should…fuck, maybe we should leave."

Mitch chews on the suggestion. He glances about the room, examining the various décor. The bronze lamp on the dark oak nightstand. The small reading light clipped to the table. The coffee bar. The television set that is as deep as it is wide. Scenic paintings of different seasons, a piece for each of the four walls. "We're here now," Mitch finally says. "We might as well check it out. I mean, that's why we came."

"Feels wrong, this place."

"Yes, it does."

"We can go. The car is just on the other side of town."

His cheeks push out a deep sigh. "We're here, El."

It takes a second, but she realizes he's right. They are here. They found the last known place the girls were before they disappeared. Why leave now?

*Because you could go missing too.*

*You could get lost.*

She scrubs these thoughts with a long breath. "Okay, you're right. Let's do this. Let's…go back into town. Interview some folks. Figure this thing out."

"If we don't like what we see, we can always call the cops. We can leave anytime we want. But we might as well do what we came here to do."

"Okay," she says, her brain lingering in these thoughts, overstaying its welcome. "Okay…let's do this."

They hustle across the road, down the hilly incline and back into town. Moving down Main Street, they pass shoppes hosting one or two people. A few pedestrians stroll the sidewalks, heading into the various establishments. Ellie notices a man sitting behind the counter in a bookstore, his face parked behind a thick leatherbound novel, something classic she assumes, Dickens or Melville. She can't make out which, but the gold foil lettering is stamped down the spine, unreadable from her vantage point.

Next, the pair pass a clothing boutique; two women are shopping for a wedding dress, their hands combing over the frills and lacy patterns that run the length of the skirt. Then they speed by a flower shop that has some inventory displayed out front, blooms of creamy oranges and timid pinks. An elderly couple stops to literally smell the roses.

Ellie brakes when she passes the art gallery and catches a brief glimpse of something in her periphery.

A painting.

A familiar one.

The mere prospect of seeing this particular piece sends her heart spiraling. "Holy shit," she says, doubling back.

Mitch stops. "What is it?"

"Holy fucking shit," she says, turning and facing the window, peering into the back of the art gallery and focusing on the 24x36 canvas that she's seen before.

The one currently stored in her basement.

"What the…" she says but loses her breath due to the sheer shock of it all.

"El, talk to me."

"It's…" Her emotional dam breaks. Tears soak her eyes, and a great sadness strains her voice. "It's Dawn."

"What?" He rushes forward to take a look in the window. "Where?"

She points to the back of the gallery where the painting hangs by itself in innocent glory. "That's hers. Dawn painted that."

Mitch can't stop her from running inside even if he wanted to. She rushes the door, barreling like a bull seeing red. He opens his mouth but the words are lost in the town's sacred silence. Following her inside, as he crosses the gallery's threshold, a wave of trepidation slams into him, holding him in place. It's like his heart and mind know he's not supposed to be here.

He spots Ellie heading directly for the painting, no anxiety stopping her.

"Can I help you?" asks the woman working the floor. Her vibrant blouse draws his gaze; there's no tag announcing her name, but the splash of colors decorating her clothing is too loud to ignore. It's like a liquified rainbow splashed against her blouse, left there to dry that way.

"My friend," he says, nodding over at Ellie as she runs her fingers along the painting, tracing every brushstroke as if this gives her insight into her daughter's disappearance. "She says she knows the person who painted that."

"Oh really?"

"Yes. Do you..." Mitch puts on his best smile. "Do you know who the artist is?"

"I can find out," the woman says. "I'm Danielle, by the way. I run the art gallery here in Lacuna's Point. Curator and owner."

"Danielle," he repeats, taking her extended hand, gently of course. "Mitch."

"Mitch," she says, sounding surprised. "You don't look like a Mitch."

"I'm sorry?"

Her cheeks immediately grow pink. "Oh...oh no, I didn't mean—"

Mitch waves off the misunderstanding, a move he's perfected over the years. "No, no. Don't worry about it."

"I just meant, you look more like a...I don't know...a Michael."

"A Michael?"

"Yeah. You know, like *Michael.*"

"Like Michael Jordan, or..."

She rolls her eyes. "I was thinking more like Michael, the archangel."

"What? Like that movie with that white dude from *Saturday Night Fever*?"

She barks with laughter. "No, no. I mean, *yes*, I guess. But, you know—the *real* story."

"The *real* story? Stories about angels are real now?"

"I like to think so. Michael, the archangel who defeated Satan in the War for Heaven, who banished the Morning Star and sent him to the underworld. Michael's a hero's name."

"And I look like a hero?"

Smiling faintly, she nods and says, "Yeah. You do."

An incredulous laugh leaves him, and he can't believe the turn this conversation has taken. He almost forgets Ellie, her eyes glued on a painting that can't possibly be Dawn's. "Are you putting me on? You fucking with me?"

She giggles. "Maybe."

*Flirting,* he thinks, *this is flirting.* It's been so long since he's been flirted with that he can't remember how the song and dance goes. Since meeting Angie, even in the three years before they were married, he never once flirted with another woman, never even entertained the thought. He's been a loyal husband through and through, and even at their worst, he never once thought about stepping foot outside their vows.

*You're a hero.*

What a crock of shit.

"Okay, Danielle," he says, getting back to business, "I appreciate the niceties, but my friend there—she really needs help, needs to know where that painting came from. Think you can help her out?"

She closes one eye in a *meet-me-out-back-in-five* sorta way, then slowly turns toward the back right corner of the gallery. "Sure thing. I think Mayor Quincy brought in that piece."

"Mayor Quincy?" Mitch rubs his chin at the mention of the mysterious mayor. "I've heard of him."

"Yes. He's the mayor of Lacuna's Point."

"Yeah, kinda gathered that when you called him Mayor Quincy."

"Right," she says, continuing to stare at the painting. "It's an interesting piece, for sure. I've always loved abstract art, ever since I was a child. Oh gosh, I could just stare at them for hours, trying to get inside the mind of the creative, see what they saw when they were painting it."

Mitch stares at the painting. At least, what he can see of it because Ellie's head blocks most of it. Ellie continues to obsess over the details, caressing every stroke. He's starting to wonder if she's okay, or if the very sight of this thing has driven her to madness.

"Right," he says. "Well, we'd like to know where or how Mayor Quincy acquired it."

"Oh, may I ask why? You said your friend there knows the artist?"

"Yes."

Mitch sighs, knowing he shouldn't tell the curator the truth, that a lie would serve him better. The people here—on top of being no help—are just weird, and Danielle seems like no exception. But Mitch has trouble with lying. Good at keeping secrets, bad at lying. *I don't love my wife anymore, I don't love my wife anymore, I don't love—*

"Her daughter."

"Oh? Really?"

"Yeah."

"Is she, like, a famous artist or something? Mayor Quincy only has the finest of tastes, so something about this piece must have spoken to him."

"Yeah, I bet. Listen, Danielle, if you could help us out, I'd be eternally grateful."

"Eternally?"

"Forever."

"Hmm, I'll hold you to that, Michael." He lets the nickname that makes him feel uncomfortable slip. Danielle backs away from him and heads behind the counter.

"What are you doing?" he asks.

"Um, checking the logs, to see when and where the piece came from. Who the artist is."

"I told you who the artist is. Can't you look it up that way? I mean, don't you guys have a computer system or something?"

Danielle looks up from the stack of papers. "I don't believe in computers. Everything is old school. Physical records only."

"What?"

"Yeah. It's how I prefer to do things." Danielle runs her finger along the papers that look like dot matrix paper from the 80s, longer and wider than the printing paper of today. "I don't see anything on the logs."

"How do you know what you're looking for? I haven't even told you her daughter's name."

Danielle looks up. Stares. "Mayor Quincy doesn't bring in too many pieces, so I thought I could look it up that way."

He nods. "Sorry. Not telling you how to do your job or anything."

She manufactures a smile and then returns to her chore, combing over the names, flipping through each page.

"It would probably be within the last three years, if that helps," Mitch adds. He looks over and Ellie is resting her head against the painting, whispering something to it.

*This is bad,* he thinks. *She's losing it, big time.*

He's been worried about her sanity ever since she showed him the picture, worried she's one more slice of bad news away from a complete meltdown. The fact she's held it together this long, he thinks, is somewhat of a miracle. But now, observing her reaction to her daughter's (supposed) painting—things are starting to break.

"Nothing," Danielle says, poking her head up. "Not in the log."

"Are you sure?"

"Checked it twice."

Looking around the art gallery, scanning the pieces, Mitch sets his jaw. "Where is this Mayor Quincy?"

"I'm sorry?"

"Mayor Quincy. You said he brought in the piece?"

"I mean...I think so. He must have. I've never even noticed it before, until just now."

"You run the art gallery and you've never seen this piece before? What, did it just magically appear?"

She shrugs like this is common procedure. "Mayor Quincy sneaks things by me sometimes. He's very active in the community. Cares very deeply about Lacuna's Point, especially when it comes to the arts. He's very smart. Some might call him a genius. Have you seen the signs for the annual art festival?"

Mitch tries to recall. "I don't remember."

"It's in nineteen days. Mayor Quincy runs it. It's a big thing around here. Mayor Quincy...he loves his art."

"I'd like to speak with him. Know where I can find him?"

Cocking one eyebrow, her head falls slightly to the right. "I don't understand."

He almost laughs. "I don't know how I can simplify it. I want to see the mayor. This Quincy guy. I'd like to meet him."

"No one *meets* him," she replies, her face rigid now, either from fear or...something else.

"What do you mean?"

She gulps. "I mean no one really sees him. He's kind of like...I don't know—this mythical figure. I mean, sure, we *see* him. But not often. He's like...more of a celebrity, you know?" Her rhetoric draws a smile.

"Ma'am. Cut the shit. I want to see the mayor, this Mayor Quincy, and I'd like to see him now. So, I want you to tell me where—"

"No one sees the mayor, sir," she says with a dab of venom. "It's impossible. Especially for...for people who don't live here. Besides, he's...on vacation."

"Well, when's he coming back?"

"Don't know." She shrugs, uncaring. "He comes and goes as he pleases. He's an adult. He does as he wants."

"That's ridic—"

"Are you raising your voice at me?" Danielle shrinks back as if Mitch has raised his fist instead. "Are you...*threatening* me?"

"What? God, *no*. I just..."

He sees that twinkle in her eyes.

He knows the one.

"Do I..." she says, a glimmer of joy sparkling through her words, "...do I have to call the police?"

"I'm not threat—you...you know what? Call them. Right now. I'll wait."

"What's going on?" Ellie says, drifting back over, clearing the residual teardrops from her lashes.

"This lady wants to call the cops on us," he says.

"Not *us,*" she says. "*You.*"

"Apparently asking questions is illegal in this town."

A snake's smile stretches across Danielle's face. Her hand is on the phone ready to make the ultimate Karen call.

"What's wrong with you?" Ellie asks. "We just want to know where my daughter is."

"Ma'am, I don't know nothing about that." Her fingers grip the landline like it's the only thing keeping her alive. Like letting go will cause her to drop into the chasm that rests below Lacuna's Point, some infinite space that could gobble her right up.

Mitch shakes his head. "Maybe we should just leave."

"I think that's a good idea," Danielle says, and her grip loosens, but not by much.

Ellie strolls over to the counter and rests her knuckles on the laminated surface. "I don't know what the hell is happening in this town, but we're going to find out."

Danielle purses her lips, showing just enough teeth for Mitch to tell how clean and sparkly white they are. Her eyes bounce between Mitch and Ellie.

Mitch swallows. "El, come on. Let's go."

"I want my daughter back, you hear me?" Snarling, she leans even closer, forcing Danielle to back away. The woman's fingers leave the landline and now she truly does look threatened. Ellie practically growls. *"I want her back!"*

Danielle flattens her spine against the wall, the phone now out of reach. Fear etches lines in her face, but there's something else too, something lasting—anger? Pain? Mitch can almost see the truth buried there, somewhere behind the skin, deep inside near the bone.

*It's a mask,* he thinks. *Her face is a mask and it's hiding something. Something hideous. Something that wants to remain unseen.*

He doesn't want to know what sleeps beneath her skin because he has a terrible feeling about what that might be. But at the same time, he craves the truth. Whatever is wrong with Lacuna's Point, he has to know.

"Come on," he says. "Let's go. Let's stick to the plan."

Danielle is frozen against the wall, clutching her heart, waiting for the moment to pass. Mitch wonders if she'll call the cops the second they leave, or if she'll let the confrontation slide.

Ellie peels herself away, refusing to avert her eyes from the woman. Mitch grips her shoulder, and she spins toward him with the quickness of an Oklahoma twister. Mitch braces for her instinctive swat, but it never comes. Her anger suddenly melts away and tears spring forth from their glassy cages, rolling down her face in crystalline rivulets.

He hugs her, pulls her close.

"We're going," Mitch says, and it seems more like an announcement to the entire town than Danielle specifically.

The woman behind the counter doesn't move.

Just watches.

He feels her creepy, soulless gaze follow him the entire way out. And beyond.

# CHAPTER SIX

Making their way down the street, Ellie remains cautious. She keeps an eye on the pedestrians as they pass by, the eyes that watch them from the windows of the shoppes, the apartments and living spaces above them. It seems like every window has a face, staring, empty eyes that examine Ellie and Mitch's every step. She's acutely aware of small-town gossip, and how two strangers showing up in town to ask peculiar questions might draw attention. But this seems like a bit much, above the average curiosity.

*This is fucking creepy.*

Even though they decided to explore the town, Ellie suspects it's time to leave. The painting was too much for her, and Mitch agreed to seek outside help, citing that "something is definitely going on here." After leaving the art gallery, they head straight for the parking lot across town.

They're halfway to the Subaru now. Ellie feels the pull, the magnetic attraction of this place, holding her back, begging her to stay. It's like having weights around her ankles, leaden manacles anchoring her to the sidewalk. Despite its weirdness, despite the strange impression the interactions with the residents have given her, this place feels homey. Like a town she wouldn't mind buying property in, or at the very least, a summer home nearby. Heck, a part of her thinks one of these storefronts would be a great place to sell her daughter's art, the stuff Dawn left behind, the canvas paintings currently taking up way too much space in the cellar. She could open her own gallery. Right here in Lacuna's Point.

Fuck Danielle and hers, those *stolen* pieces.

Ellie can't believe one of Dawn's is just hanging on that wall in plain sight. It was like she was supposed to find it. Like it was put there on purpose with the foreknowledge that she would be walking by.

*Maybe it was,* she thinks. *Maybe it goddamn was.*

No, that's crazy and makes no sense. How would someone—this mayor—get ahold of one of Dawn's pieces, one of her *originals,* and know ahead of time that Ellie was coming? Someone would have had to sneak into her basement and stolen the piece, and that doesn't make sense. None of this does.

*This place...*

*It defies sense.*

"Hey," Mitch says, chopping through her thoughts. "You still with me?"

"Yeah," Ellie says, picking up the pace, not realizing she was lagging behind. "Yeah, can we just get the hell out of here? I feel so..." *Cold?* That's what she wants to say, but that doesn't sound right. It's still about ninety-plus and the sun's arched high in a cloudless spread of pure blue. She settles on, "I feel so uncomfortable here."

They can see the end of the street from here, the road that separates the town from the secluded lot where they parked the Subaru. She wonders if the Campbells are still there, parked in their ugly-as-fuck SUV, waiting for Ellie and Mitch, waiting to see how they fared in the ass-backward place, this town swept away by the slow hands of time.

But, as they reach the end, the opening, and look past it, toward the parking lot, they see the SUV isn't there. And not just the SUV—but the Subaru too.

It's gone.

Missing.

*Just like the girls.*

Ellie blinks, thinking the town is just playing tricks, like, there's another parking lot just around the corner of the closest building and that's where she's parked. She rubs her eyes.

"What the fuck?" Mitch asks, his words breathy, heavy.

"Where's the car?"

"They tow it?" Mitch asks.

"Fuckers," Ellie says, as reality settles in—there is only one parking lot, this is it, and the car is fucking gone.

Mitch grimaces. "What the hell are we supposed to do now?"

A shadow approaches them from behind, and Ellie doesn't know why but she feels threatened, attacked, like the person has come wielding a hammer and is ready to knock them on the head, take them out.

She spins, hands ready, prepared to fight.

"Whoa!" the voice says. A gold badge twinkles in the afternoon sunlight, and it's the only thing she can focus on. Eventually her eyes migrate up the big man's chest, his broad shoulders, and she meets his powdery-blue gaze. "Easy there, cowgirl," the cop says, flashing a Big Texas grin, though this ain't Texas and those sugary-white teeth look less genuine than a politician's promise. "Didn't mean to spook y'all."

"Our car," Ellie blurts out. "Where is it?"

"Now, now," the cop says, putting up his hands. "Not sure what you mean."

"Our car," Mitch repeats, as if that brings clarity to the situation.

The cop shoots him a sideways glance. "I heard your lady friend just fine, friend. I ain't got wax in my ears, boy."

Mitch opens his mouth like that wasn't the last thought on his mind, then shuts it. He throws his hands in the air, a frustrated breath blowing out of him like a slashed tire.

"Sir," Ellie says, drawing the cop's attention back to her. "We're very confused." She hates how he's looking at them, hates the attitude he's given them—Mitch in particular—before she even has time to explain.

"Ma'am, I've been keeping an eye on the parking lot all day. Haven't seen any cars pull up in here."

"What're you talking about? We just—"

"Now, look. We get a lot of you folks around this time of year and—"

"*Us* folks?" Mitch asks.

"Yes, visitors who come in from all over to check out the big art festival. It's a special time of year and we—"

"We're not here for some *fucking* art festival," Ellie snaps.

The cop looks down at her, over his glasses. "Ma'am, you best watch your tone with me."

"We parked there no less than two hours ago. Maybe three." She checks her phone and sees the screen has frozen. Or at least…the time has. She can still navigate the menu and slide through her apps but the time is stuck on 11:30 a.m., when they cruised into town.

*How…?*

"Ma'am," the cop says, looking frustrated himself. "Are you calling me a liar? Wouldn't be doing that, now would you?"

She wants to scream, yell, let out about three years of pent frustration, but there is a gathering now; people have wandered out from the shoppes, curious and nosy onlookers who want nothing more than to watch this cop exercise his ability to "keep the peace."

"No, I'm not," she says. "But is there another parking lot?"

His face doesn't move, doesn't twitch a millimeter. "Not to my knowledge. And I have a lot of knowledge."

"Well, good." She hates how lost and pathetic she sounds, and then she realizes that she *is* lost and pathetic. "Then maybe you can help us. Our girls—they're missing."

"Missing?" The cop rubs his chin, then scratches the white stubble in the same area. "Missing?"

"Yes, *missing*. My daughter and his."

He shifts his focus from Ellie to Mitch. "The two of y'all's daughter?"

"No," Mitch says. "My daughter and hers. Two daughters."

"Two daughters. Got it. And, uh, when exactly they go missing?"

Ellie hesitates, knowing how crazy the answer will sound, knows exactly how the cop will respond before the words are out there.

"Three years ago," she tells him.

"Three years ago," the cop says with mild amusement. "Well, gee darn it, that's a long time."

"Yeah, it is."

"Suppose you got some proof?"

"That she went missing?"

"That she went missing *here*." The cop jerks his thumb over his right shoulder, referencing the labyrinth-like layout of Lacuna's Point. "I mean, something brought you here. No?"

*It's like he knows,* she thinks. "I got a text. A picture." She pulls out the phone, a charade she's used to.

"Ah, fancy mobile device. Not too many people have those 'round these parts."

"Good. Then that should narrow down who sent me this." Ellie shows him the picture. The cop hunches so he can have a closer look.

"Well, golly be. That's the old clock tower."

"Old?" Mitch asks.

"Yeah, old Eddy."

"Eddie?" Ellie asks.

"Eddy with y. You know what an Eddy is?"

Ellie knows but isn't sure what he's asking exactly, so she keeps her mouth shut.

"How long has Eddy been here?" Mitch questions him.

Ellie despises the cop's face when he turns to Mitch. Like Mitch's mere existence is some personal annoyance.

"Well, shoot, son. Twenty years. Maybe more."

Mitch shakes his head, actually laughs at the response. "Twenty years?"

"That funny to you?"

"Well, the waitress at the diner told us it's only been up for about a year. So, we're just a little confused, that's all."

The cop smiles like it's a joke only he gets. "Oh, Darla?"

"That's her."

"Darla's pretty new around here. She wouldn't know the difference. Got her facts screwed up, that's all. Cute girl, though. Nice girl. Pours one helluva cuppa coffee."

"One year and twenty is a hell of a difference."

"Sure is," the cop agrees. "But...one year can feel like twenty to some folks."

"That doesn't even make any sense," Mitch tells him.

"Lots of things don't make sense, son."

"I'm not your son."

A hearty chuckle, and the laugh sounds like shaking a bag of broken Christmas ornaments. "Well, you sure ain't."

"Please," Ellie says, waving the phone urgently. "My daughter. *Our* daughters."

"Haven't seen them. And if it's been three years, it's likely they ain't here anymore."

She lowers the phone, her hand shaking erratically. Eyeing the cop, she grinds her teeth. "We know what's happening here."

The cop only stares at her, allowing a brief moment to pass, the opportunity for Ellie to further explain herself. Then he looks to Mitch. "What in the devil she talkin' about?"

Mitch doesn't answer but keeps his pose and leers at the cop. His nostrils flare.

The cop snorts. "Y'all's pretty funny."

Ellie steps to him.

He doesn't back away.

"Are you going to make me say it?" she asks.

The cop glances around as if he's searching for the hidden cameras of some unfunny prank show. "Say what now, missy?"

Ellie takes another step, practically nose-to-nose with him. "I've seen a ton of Netflix documentaries, pal. This place...it's a cult. Isn't it?" She looks past the cop and surveys the people congregating in the streets. The gatherers face them now, waiting to see some action, eagerly expecting to see the cop bust a head or two. As if the violent display will satiate some primal need within.

"A cult?" The officer bends over and slaps his knee, a burst of hee-haw laughter tumbling out of his mouth. "Well, ain't you just adorable. That's a good one. Cult! Whoo-doggy! That's about the funniest thing I think I've ever—"

"I'm not laughing, asshole," Ellie tells him. Her sharp tongue severs his jolly-good roar. "I know my daughter is here and I know you've...you've brainwashed her or something. Just like everyone else we've met. Everyone here is a fucking weirdo, and they don't know simple *fucking* answers like when the goddamn clock tower was built!"

The officer puts on his enough-is-enough face and raises his finger. "Now listen. You better calm down and—"

"No, I'm not calming—"

"El," Mitch says, reaching out for her.

"NO!"

"Son," the cop tells Mitch, "better control her ass, or I will."

"El," Mitch repeats.

"NO!" she screams again. Her hands are up, ready to punch, and she's prepared to fight for the truth, whoever stands in her way of it. Her breath gets away from her, and she begins to feel lightheaded. Dizzy. Like she might faint. The world before her posts a grainy filter, gets bright for a second, and then dims.

And that's when the bell tolls.

All across town, the sound carries. A single tone. It cuts through her. She feels the noise drum against her bones.

The cop loses his smile. Every visible head turns toward the clock tower.

They begin to walk.

And that's when it all goes to hell.

The bell tolling hits Mitch's ears like a sonic boom. Instinctively, he ducks down as if a literal bomb has dropped nearby and the next one might fall squarely on his head. He's almost to his knees when he looks up and sees the cop's attention shift from Ellie to the direction of the clock tower, old Eddy. The man's mouth is slightly open as if an epiphanous thought has come and gone in the same instant. Ellie continues to jaw at him, asking him questions, questions he'll never answer because he's gone, gone away. Questions that die before they even hit the airwaves, never reaching the cop's ears.

Then he moves, the pig, away from her, without speaking a single word, his focus now solely on the noise, the bell, the anchor of this bizarre town. The others follow, moving like a wave behind him, almost in unison, almost every movement synchronized. Their feet hit the pavement at the same time. It's a march, and the parade moves toward old Eddy, the finish line. Every single eye is focused on that direction, gazing upward at the structure standing over the other buildings, drawing everyone in with its pull.

*Magnets. They're like magnets,* he thinks. The bell collides again, and it sounds like the world's been cracked in half, shattered from pole to pole.

"What's happening?" Ellie asks, and Mitch wishes he could respond with something, anything besides that dumb frozen look. "Mitch—what do we do?"

He watches the townsfolk move like slaughterhouse cattle.

"I dunno. It's..." So many words come to mind—weird, impossible, *freaky.* But no word can truly capture the bizarre scene unfolding before him. He thinks there might be, but his brain fails to find its creative stride.

*And you're supposed to be a writer,* he scolds himself. *How the hell are you going to write that damn novel if you can't think of a single stupid word. Just one goddamn word.* It's a stupid thought to have at the moment with so much going on, but the interaction with the cop has jarred loose an idea, the beginning of his story. His main character will meet a cop, much like the jerkoff officer he's just encountered, and the MC will have a problem, one that requires an immediate solution, and the cop won't help him, won't lift a single goddamn finger because it's too inconvenient or maybe because the MC has the wrong skin color or maybe both. Yes, that's how it starts, and it will only get worse from there, and the MC will—

A few people drift by, continuing toward the end of town, in their listless stride.

"What do we do?" Ellie asks again, and then Mitch has a new thought that cancels his inspirational flow: *Follow them.*

He gets in line behind them, a white granny with a pink sweater and a purple scarf wrapped around her neck—which he thinks is quite weird considering the temperature's definitely over ninety degrees and just standing is enough to break a sweat.

"Mitch," Ellie calls, and one of the townspeople—an old white dude in a Yankees ball cap—shoots her a menacing glare, *how-dare-you-speak-during-the-sermon* eyes that fix.

Mitch turns, rests his forefinger against his lips. Then waves her on.

She falls in line with the others, and he's never seen another person so scared, not even his wife when the doctors told them Kya might be born early, might come into this world a little sooner than expected. Not even when they were performing an emergency C-section on her two weeks before the due date. Ellie looks more scared than that. Ellie looks like her face is about to be C-sectioned by the town of Lacuna's Point.

Mitch follows the peculiar parade and thinks they all must look like ants from above, a whole colony marching up the hill, toward the black centers of their sandy hill homes.

He wonders if today he'll meet the Queen.

Or maybe the Mayor.

The Mayor of Ant-town.

It's true—Ellie hasn't felt this panicked since the day Dawn disappeared. She's experienced a few panic attacks since then, nightmares that leave her stirring awake in a cold sweat, but this is something completely different. This newfound fear melts through her muscles and turns her bones to watery soup. The closer she gets to old Eddy, the further detached she feels from her soul.

She follows the old man in the Yankees cap fairly close; he smells like Barbasol and peppermint. Maybe something her dad would have worn back in the day. The scent conjures up memories of the old man wearing a tweed jacket to school, sporting that hard look that always kept the kids in line. She remembers the stories the older teachers used to tell—how much of a "gentle hard-ass" he was, the kind of teacher that always made the students learn, even if it was painful. The type of educator the kids might not have thought highly of during their school years but would look back on later in life and cherish those times spent in Mr. Coughlin's classroom.

Thoughts of her father make her run through the memories of her own teaching career, wonders how she stacks up.

*Not even close to Dad. Not even in the same universe.*

Her mind quickly swallows those thoughts; there's no time to live in the past when so much is happening in the present.

*This is like the Twilight Zone,* she thinks, continuing to move with the herd. They pass side streets, gaining more followers as they trek toward the tower. In the middle of the crosswalk, she catches a glimpse of the Campbells. The couple merges with the crowd, and Ellie's mind races with questions that dizzy her.

The most terrifying question conquers all others: *Where does this walk end?*

But she knows that. It ends at the clock tower, old Eddy, the same place it began.

"Mitch!" she half-yells, half-whispers, being careful not to draw too much attention to herself. The look Yankee-Cap gave her is enough to make her think twice about riling up the locals. "Mitch!"

A slight turn of his shoulder. He tilts his ear in her direction.

"Look," she says, nodding.

He sees them. Hard not to. They're entranced like the rest of the town, walking like hungry zombies driven to reach their meaty human meals. The clock tower is that meal.

*It starts and ends there.*

That unknown. That eye of time that looks down on her, them, the entire town, watching, waiting, an invisible mouth with sharp teeth resting somewhere beneath the nucleus of time kept. Ready to eat, gobble her up in a few quick bites. The unknown is ravenous.

She shakes these notions as Mitch breaks from the parade and heads over to the Campbells.

"Shit," Ellie says, breaking too. She runs up behind Mitch, keeping her eye on the nearby faces; they're so many of them now, more than she expected considering how dead the town looked earlier.

*Where are they coming from?*

It's like they materialized from nothing.

"What are you going to do?" Ellie asks.

"Gonna get some answers, right fucking now." Mitch doesn't hide his intentions. His brash approach earns him some looks, the kind Ellie hoped to avoid.

"Mitch, think about this. They're like...fucking zombies or something. Don't provoke them."

"Well, I'm gonna wake their zombie asses up to answer some fucking questions." When he's about twenty feet away, he shouts, addressing Mr. Campbell directly. "Hey, you!"

Ellie sees the man's eyes shift. It's slight but noticeable, and she knows the look is far different from what Yankees-Cap directed at her.

*He's not one of them.*

*But he knows the drill.*

*He's done this before.*

"Yeah, I'm talking to you," Mitch says, stomping toward him. "Keith, right? You want to tell me what the fuck is going on or do you want to keep playing games with me?"

Keith breaks his stride and puts his fingers over his lips. "Sssh!" he hisses. "Quiet!"

The man's reaction stops Mitch the same way a thrown punch would. Mitch stares him down. Keith hesitates for a second, then continues, merging with the crowd and his wife who hardly misses a step.

"Walk with me!" Keith says, returning the whisper yell.

From across the street, Ellie sees Yankees-Cap watching them. Spying. Taking mental notes, even though his eyes appear to lack any cognitive thought behind them.

"What is this?" Mitch asks, listening to Keith's advice and trailing closely behind.

Ellie follows. She tries to peek and gain a sense of how the procession is accepting their intrusive presence. She feels their eyes on her, but when she looks, their focus is on the clock tower and the clock tower alone.

Eyes. Everywhere.

*Inside her.*

"What is this?" Mitch repeats, and Keith makes a face, a pained look, like Mitch's words are tiny razor blades cutting the webbing between his fingers.

"Just play along," Keith says. "They like it when you play along."

"And what happens if I don't?" Mitch asks.

Still walking. Toward Eddy. He's getting close. Ellie can see it now, the base, the buildings, the quad, the diner next door. The grand scope of the town fills her vision, consumes her entire view of the world.

Keith and Susan exchange looks.

Then Keith says, "You really don't want to know the answer to that question."

And Ellie believes him.

She really doesn't want to know.

"Where's the car?" Ellie asks, the first thing she can think of.

"Don't worry about that now," Sue says, rushing to get the words out, practically scolding her. Ellie's cheeks burn with an even mixture of anger and embarrassment, and part of her wants to throat-punch this bitch.

"I am worried," she snaps back, grabbing the woman by the shoulder. "I'm worried about a lot. Hey, I'm talking to you, will you just—"

Sue spins, and for a split second, she looks like she might slug Ellie one, a right hook squared up, a real first-round knockout. But she pulls back before her arm gains any momentum. Sue's eyes are alive with simple fury; it's as if Ellie has admitted to killing her pet and handed over the bloody body as evidence.

"Just walk," Sue growls. "Just do it and shut up."

A few people turn their attention toward them, languid gazes that have no staying power. Sue's eyes flick back and forth between Ellie and the town, the people sticking them with their seedy eyes, dull, hateful glares. The soulless spectators convince Ellie that maybe she should listen, shut up and walk.

Mitch seems to have given up on his pursuit of answers. He's following Keith, the flow of traffic funneling into the streets, taking over the blacktop belonging to Main Street. They cross the sidewalks and assemble in the quad, standing before the magnificent clock tower. That cyclopean metal giant of wood, bolts and screws, motors and gears.

*Gears that run time itself.*

She trails the group to the outskirts of the quad. The entire town stands, stops, faces Eddy, looking up as the hands click toward three o'clock. She wonders what will happen at three as she scans the faces before her, around her, their captivated looks. It's as if God himself is about to appear before them in an explosion of golden light, as if the Man Behind the Curtain is about to reveal the true meaning of life, expose the purpose of their very existence.

They are statues, the people of Lacuna's Point.

Frozen in time.

Like the town itself.

Ellie doesn't want to, but she glances up at the tower, its face, the hands that move with the seconds, the minutes, the hours.

There's a robed guardian standing on the ledge next to the town's all-watching cyclopean eye. He's pulling on a long piece of manilla rope, and the bell goes off once again, sending a sturdy vibration throughout the entire world. The ground beneath her trembles as if the Earth's core is afraid of what's to come.

Whatever happens at three.

*The world will end,* she thinks. *This is how I die. This is how it all ends.*

In many ways, she is right.

Mitch can hardly believe what his eyes are showing him. The man on the ledge sounds the bell, and the bell carries a sound across town, the deep toll penetrating his skin, his bones, every single molecule his body contains. He feels ripped apart by the sound and pieced back together by the silent aftermath. He drops to his knees, the carrying tone splitting his brain in half like a hot knife through warm cream cheese. Nausea sets in and he sticks his head in a nearby trashcan, unloads the diner's omelet into the black plastic abyss. His vision is shifting, sliding, and he suddenly feels like he's been drinking all afternoon and evening, and this is just an ordinary case of the "night spins." Only it's daylight and he isn't drunk. Not even a little bit.

He glances over at Ellie. She's on her knees now, a string of vomit stretching from her lips, a small pile of whatever she grabbed back at the gas station before her. She didn't make it to a garbage can; the grassy surface of the quad was her landing spot.

Another toll. Another harsh cringe. Mitch feels like his whole body might split in half.

No one else reacts this way. Not even the Campbells. They're standing, facing the clock tower, their backs to him, their heads cocked back, getting a nice long look at the robed figure, the faceless person whose purpose is to control the clock tower. Mitch wants to climb the damned thing and hang the figure with the rope. Anything to make him stop.

He doesn't think he'll survive another pull.

A harsh wind blows in from the coast, and a paper flyer smacks Mitch in the face like an unexpected slap. He peels away the 9x11 sheet and, even though there are more important matters at hand, he glances down at the advertisement. It's for the art festival a little over two weeks away. *Nineteen days,* just like Danielle said. COME ONE, COME ALL, the flyer shouts. LACUNA'S POINT 75th ANNUAL ART FESTIVAL. He notices the special message down there at the bottom: OUTSIDERS WELCOME! The strange notation that seems like it was left for his eyes alone has a signature beneath it. It reads: Mayor Quincy Black.

Mitch looks up from the flyer, watches as the townspeople open their mouths, conform to a collective gasp. Their eyes roll back, exposing pure white ovals like small eggs turned on their side, heavenly orbs that erase the identities of the souls behind them. And it feels like that—doesn't it? Like…they're being erased. The cosmic clang crushing them into oblivion, destroying them from the inside out.

This is their undoing.

This is their demise.

Mitch waits for death to crawl over him, that sound to come back and pulverize him, melt his brain to nothing.

He waits to be erased like them.

And then he sees *her* in the crowd, standing amongst the gathered like she's one of them. Because she *is* one of them.

It's Kya. Her mouth is open. She's singing, he thinks. The most beautiful song. He can almost hear it.

Then the crash comes from above, blowing out his ears and everything he knows of the real world. Sunlight plummets into a dark world, and darkness, Mitch thinks, going forward, is all he will ever know of this vacant reality.

# LONG WAY FROM HOME
## (2 WEEKS AGO)

The public bus smells like cabbage and farts, and even though Joshua Davis has spent a solid three hours sitting in the back, away from almost everybody, he still hasn't gotten used to the smell. The awful culmination of two unpleasant scents seems to have taken permanent refuge in this cabin on wheels. The foul odor reminds him of Seymore Langley, the dopey, husky kid who sits behind him in science class. Kid's always farting something fierce, and they always smell like different vegetables.

When he thinks of school, he thinks of home, and when he thinks of home, he thinks of his parents and the last blowout fight, which wasn't that long ago. Three hours old to be exact. He swears his father was this close to hitting his mom. That's how angry he was. They both were, shouting at the top of their lungs, so loud he could hear their argument with crystal clarity from his room, even with his door shut and his head buried under heavy blankets. Nothing muffled their fury; nothing muted the constant flow of obscenities and phrases, harsh insults that couldn't be taken back; nothing silenced the bony knuckles cracking the drywall.

*If only I had a T.V. in my room,* he thinks, and maybe if he did have a T.V., he wouldn't be here.

He watches the people exit the bus for three hours straight, wondering when the bus driver will pull back around and drop him off near his house in Stockton, Delaware. It's been a while since he's recognized the streets, the landmarks. He got nervous when the bus turned onto the highway, but since then, he's been so active in his thoughts that he hasn't paid attention to the course of travel.

Now, looking out the window, the view doesn't register. The last person to get off got off twenty minutes ago, and now it's just Josh and the bus driver.

Ten minutes later, the driver pulls into a parking lot. The bus rolls to a squeaky stop. The driver opens the door, gets up, arches his back, and then locks eyes with Josh. He stares at him like he's never seen a kid before.

"Hey, kid," the driver says, nodding. "You by yourself?"

Josh swallows. He feels the need to lie, but there's no fibbing his way out of this one. "Yes. Sort of."

"Sort of?"

*Think of something, think of something—*

"What do you mean 'sort of?' " the driver asks, leaning on the first seat's backrest.

Josh knows something bad will come of this. Something he could've prevented by just sucking it up and dealing with his parents' incessant arguing. Just go for a bike ride like he always does when they're going at it. But no—he had to do things differently. Get daring. Push the boundaries. He thought taking his allowance and disappearing for longer than usual would punish his parents. Scare them. Make them *think* he's lost, and maybe once they're scared enough, they'll stop. The fighting, the yelling and screaming and punching holes in the walls. Maybe they'll get it, finally understand him.

*Maybe they'll love each other again.*

"I mean..." Josh says, looking out the window, inspecting the beautiful small town before him. In the backdrop, he sees a Ferris wheel rising over a tree-cluttered horizon. The farty aroma gives way to salty scents that clear up his allergies. "No, I'm...I was just taking a ride."

"When'd you get on?"

"Stockton?"

"Delaware?" the man says, sounding alarmed.

Josh nods sheepishly.

"Well, hot dog. That's a long way from here."

"Is it?"

"Yes, sir. We're in Virginia now."

*Virginia! What!?*

His stomach tries to leave his body through his butthole, gets stuck somewhere along the way.

"That's right, kid," the driver says, obviously noticing Josh's reaction to the news. He nods and then removes a white cloth from his pocket, begins wiping away dribbles of sweat from his brow. "Though I'm not exactly sure where in Virginia we are. Can't get a damn signal, and my GPS has gone all screwy. No matter, once we get back on the road, we'll head north and keep going until it starts to work again." He gives Josh a reassuring smile, and honestly—it helps. He feels better already. "Say, I'm gonna head into town and grab something to eat before we head back. Wanna come with? I smell bacon in the air."

Josh doesn't smell bacon. Just the strange miasma of those leafy farts and the salt of the ocean.

"No," Josh says. Although he trusts the driver, he doesn't want to go anywhere with him except for home. "I'm not hungry."

The driver pauses, stares, then nods. "Suit yourself. Hey, shut the door behind me, will ya?" He quickly illustrates how to do so by pulling the lever toward the driver's seat. "Don't let anyone else on until I come back. Got it?"

Josh gets it.

"And I know how much is in the cash box, every cent, so don't go thinking you'll get away with pinching some change. We understand each other, kid?"

Josh agrees, bobbing his head.

"Good. What's your name?"

"Josh—Joshua Davis."

The driver knocks his knuckles on the backrest and then heads out.

For twenty minutes Josh sits there alone. He thinks the driver should be back by now, but he tells himself not to worry, to give it another ten. Fifteen, maybe. Give him some time. Maybe he got held up talking to one of the townsfolk, asking directions back to the main highway.

Another thirty goes by and Josh starts to sweat a little—partially because the driver turned off the engine and the air conditioning, but mostly because he's starting to sense the driver's not coming back. He has no hard evidence to support this theory, but to his ten-year-old-mind, the man is gone. Not coming back, not ever.

Josh gets up, leaves the bus, and it feels good to stretch the bones, the muscles. He doesn't remember seeing what direction the bus driver bounded off to, but Josh takes one quick look to the left and right, assessing the best course of travel. More buildings and stores sit to his left. Over them, a giant clock tower stands tall, and he doesn't know why but the towering edifice sends a shivering bolt through him. It's a weird thing to find himself afraid of, but now that he's alone and lost and so far from home—everything's a potential threat. To the right lies more buildings and shoppes, and beyond them, houses that look almost identical to their neighbor save for different color schemes.

And then, he looks straight ahead. Where the Ferris wheel sticks up from the trees. He begins walking toward it with no clear destination in mind, though, deep down, on some level, he thinks he'll see the Ferris wheel up close and personal before he leaves this place. This town.

*Where am I?* he thinks. *Just where the heck am I?*

The closer he gets to the opposite end of town, the more he can smell of the shore. Hints of fried dough populate, and he breathes in the sweet, savory scents. The cinnamon and sugary aromas lure him in like a fish to a hooked worm, and Josh finds himself strolling through the patch of woods, taking the trail through the trees, all the way to the coast.

When he reaches the beach, he turns to his left and spots the amusement park. It's a dinky one, not like the kind they have in Maryland, nor like the attractions at the Jersey shore. His parents took him to Point Pleasant, New Jersey just last summer and that had one of the better seaside amusement parks he'd ever been to. The one before him now is a fraction of those other places.

And furthermore—it looks dead, the aromatic promises of zeppole and cotton candy and frosty sugar drinks a clear ruse. He doesn't see a single attendee or ride operator, and he thinks that's an awfully strange sight considering the season, a weekend no less. The place should be thriving, packed with people, crowds that could hardly move due to the tight traffic.

The only soul he sees is near the water, standing where the small waves crash against the shore. A man faces the ocean, his back to Josh, and it seems like he's just enjoying the way the saltwater laps at his toes, how it pools around his ankles. The man is still, frozen, statuesque for every moment. For a second Josh thinks the man truly is a statue, a mannequin left behind to give the appearance that the beach is populated—but that's a dumb notion, and even in his worried and slightly disoriented state of mind, he knows this.

Josh moves toward the amusement park, hustling as if the mannequin man might come to life and chase after him. He reaches the boardwalk, ascends the ramp, and enters the park. It's truly dead—no people, no one working the rides. Everything looks shut down, nonoperational, or out of order. There's an arcade with the interior lights off. The sign out front, which should have blinking bulbs to attract the eye, is dim and full of empty promises—FOOD, GAMES, FUN! Disappointment fills him, as he suddenly has the childish need to partake in all three of these proclamations.

He's about to leave, shuffle back toward town in the direction of the bus when something flashes in his periphery. A tall something— well, taller than him, which is practically everyone who's older than him. The shape is a shadow at first, but when he spins on it, he sees the shape materialize into a woman his mother's age, maybe younger.

Instinctively, Josh shrinks away.

The woman puts out a hand, an act meant to instill calmness, assuring him she means him no harm. Still, he can't prevent the spike of fear from driving through him.

"Hey," she says, "I'm not going to hurt you."

Josh—who thinks that's exactly what someone who *is* going to hurt him would say—doesn't back down from his defensive position behind the metal barricades that would ordinarily help organize the Ferris wheel's waiting line.

"Seriously, kid," the woman says, crouching, as if getting on his level will prove her good intentions.

Josh is smarter than that. Knows better than to trust a stranger of any kind.

*But not smart enough to* not *get on a bus and end up three hours from home?*

*I'm not lost,* he tells that other voice. *There's a bus waiting to take me home.*

He doesn't know why that sounds like a lie, but it does.

"What do you want?" he asks the woman, getting ready to sprint in case she advances.

"I just want to talk," she says, breathing much heavier for someone who isn't running. "Ask you a couple of questions."

"Okay…" he says, eyeing the best path out of here. "What?"

The woman smiles and then goes for her pocket. He's seen way too many movies and television shows he shouldn't, and thinks she's pulling out a gun, that she's going to shoot him or rob him or both. But she doesn't do that. Instead, she pulls out a phone. She faces him again and then steps closer. He doesn't shrink away.

"Here," she says, holding out the phone. "Look at the picture."

He doesn't get closer, but he's gaining a sense that the woman is harmless. A little upset, sure, but she doesn't mean any threat. But then again—maybe that's the point. Maybe that's what she wants him to think.

"What is it?" he asks, fighting the tremble in his soft voice.

"A picture of my sister," the woman says. "She went missing around here. About three years ago." The woman looks at the picture, tears swelling in her eyes. "I think...I think she still might be here. I suspect anyway. Look. There's this picture of her next to the clock tower—"

"Clock tower?" Josh asks, gulping.

"Yes...the clock tower."

He swallows, looking elsewhere for an escape from this awkward exchange, and then slides his vision back on the worried woman.

"Look," she says, flustered, "maybe your parents can help me out. Where are they—"

"My parents aren't here, okay?"

She recoils. "Okay, gosh. Look, her name is Rosetta. My name is Marissa. My parents," she says fondly, and Josh wishes he could utter the word "parents" with that kind of smirk/smile. "My parents, they had this thing for names that end in 'a.' Kinda funny when you think about it."

Josh doesn't find it funny at all—except his full name ends in one, which is more ironic than funny—and he doesn't ask for her to explain herself.

"Five of us," she says. "All of us end in 'a.' " She continues to smirk and look elsewhere, the past maybe.

Meanwhile, Josh plans his escape. "Wish I could help, but...I must get going."

"Wait!" Marissa says, stopping him by the sheer urgency in her voice. "Please. I'm not from around here. We actually live in Arizona, and my sister was...she was traveling up the coast when she went missing. Following some band around, you know. Going to shows? Look, I just need some direction, that's all. Someone to talk to. Someone who can help me."

"I wish I could," he says, backing away from her, leaving the safety of the barricades. "But I'm not from around here either."

"Really?" she says, interested. "Where you from?"

"Delaware."

"Delaware?" She looks over her shoulder, back down the shore. "Parents somewhere around here? Are you on vacation?"

That's too many questions he doesn't have time to answer or explain, so, instead, he says, "I gotta run!" And then he does. He runs as fast as his legs can carry him—which is pretty quick now that he's been in soccer for the last two years—and heads around the Ferris Wheel, back down the ramp and across the beach, seeking that path that cut through the woods. He hears Marissa calling after him, begging for him to wait up, but he pays her absolutely no attention, doesn't dream of getting caught up in her family drama. He has enough of his own, and besides—he can't help her.

He can't even help himself.

When he's back on the beach, he sees the man near the shore again, and this time he's bending forward, digging in the shallows for something. His hands splash around and when the water retracts, the tide withdrawing, Josh sees the man wrist-deep in the sand, wrestling around with something beneath the surface.

*Mole crabs,* he thinks. He remembers the trip to the Jersey shore last year when his dad taught him about mole crabs (sometimes called sand crabs) and how to catch them for fun. When the water leaves and retreats back into the ocean, *look for the bubbles in the sand.* Sure enough, Josh had done exactly that and dug where the dimples showed in the wet sand, and he found the little creatures burrowed beneath the surface. They kicked their little arms and legs and rolled on his palm, over and on their barrel-shaped shells.

*Cool!* he remembers saying. *Can we keep him?*

*No,* his father said, rubbing Josh's longish hair. *We have to put him back. They live there. That's their home. They'll die anywhere else.*

It was a good memory, the kind he has a short supply of these days. His attention turns back to the man and his pursuit for whatever lies beneath the surface of the wet sand. An instant later, the man yanks upward, excavating an object that looks similar to the mole crab, only much larger, the size of a rabbit. The man looks at the beetle-shaped crustacean head-on, an awe-inspired grin spreading rapidly. It's the same way Josh's parents used to look at him when they told him they loved him.

Josh wipes a tear from his eye as the man cradles the crab like a baby. He doesn't think this is as strange as it appears, but when he starts to analyze what's happening, he realizes this is not normal, that nothing about what he's seeing is typical, and he suddenly wants to be very far from this place.

That's when the mole crab starts to dig. Into the man's stomach, using its furry claws to peddle its way inside him, burrowing into the stranger's gut. The creature shovels aside blood and looping innards that look like red-painted sausage links. Before he can blink, Josh loses sight of the oversized crab in the furious arcs of blood and internal matter. Organs slop onto the wet beach, making room for the creature's new home. Josh looks on in horror as the man's eyes shift and locate his. He expects this man to call for help, to plea for his life, but no—the man continues to grin as if this is not only normal...but enjoyable.

Josh hears him laughing.

Then Josh runs in the opposite direction, his curiosity-driven paralysis breaking. Sprinting the path, he doesn't look back. He puts every drop of strength into the dash, and even when he reaches the town, he does not stop or even slow down. The streets have filled with more people since the stroll out to the shore, and he dodges them with ease. A couple of them beg him to slow down—some demanding it—but he listens to no one and keeps running like he had when Mrs. Jacobson's snippy toy poodle chased him down the sidewalk when he was six. He weaves through traffic, cutting through the town's center, back to the parking lot where the bus is waiting for him.

Only when he gets there...it isn't.

*No...*

He's so terrified his strength flees the lower half of his body, and he pisses himself while he sinks to his knees. An uncontrollable wave crashes over him, and without warning, he's sobbing into the palms of his hands.

No one comes over to help him.

No one offers to console him.

No one pays him any attention at all.

*(just like home)*

He's lost in a town he does not know the name of, and there is something very wrong with this place.

As he contemplates his next move, the clock tower sounds off, ringing its massive bell, hammering his eardrums and hitting him with a world-spinning spell of nausea that does not fade with the lengthening seconds.

# PART TWO

## STUCK ON THE POINT

# CHAPTER SEVEN

*It's Christmastime and there's snow falling outside, a thin layer of sugary-white dust accumulating on the exterior window grilles. The house smells like cooked ham, the air sour with hints of pineapple. She looks down and sees a plate being shoved in front of her, her husband's smile as he delivers his favorite meal, the one he always cooks on Christmas Day. Dawn is sitting next to her, playing with the new Barbies she got from Santa. This memory is from a time when she used to play with such things, when Barbies and My Little Ponies took precedence over everything else, way before they were replaced by an obsession with art and the thrill of chasing boys.*

*"Here you go, madam," Dan says in that faux butler voice, the one she finds annoying, though it's certainly not his most irritating habit. Since it's Christmas she lets it go. Though, how much control she currently has over her actions, she doesn't know. Still—it's annoying and it bothers her, even if it's a fun kind of annoying and not the you-left-your-disgusting-pube-shavings-on-the-toilet-seat-again kind of annoying. Tolerable. For now.*

*"Thanks, dear," she says, feeling quite hungry. She wants to dive in. It's been so long since she's eaten a good meal—the last thing she ate was back on the road, at that crummy rest stop, and that sandwich was hardly satisfying.*

*Wait, no. That's not right. Can't be. How could she remember the rest stop in the dream? Dream logic doesn't work that way—at least not to her knowledge. It's like this dream is connected to her reality, a psychedelic extension of the real world she was just living in.*

*And furthermore—she shouldn't know she's dreaming. A dreamer should never know when they're dreaming—that realization is an instant ticket back to reality.*

*She glances up from the slice of ham. "Am I...dreaming?"*

*Dan smirks, tilting his head this and that way. "More or less."*

*"Well, which is it?" she asks hastily.*

*"Mom," Dawn says, putting a hand on her wrist, a gentle, concerned touch. "Just go with it. Stop asking so many questions, gosh. Being a real downer."*

"This is wrong," Ellie says, and then goes to stand.

But she can't.

She's glued to the seat. She looks down and sees nothing keeping her in place, no physical apparatus that binds her to the chair, no adhesive, no tether, no nothing. Just her and the chair. It's too ordinary what she finds there, and this fuels her dread even further.

"I can't move," she speaks, and the words come out like a frog's ribbit.

"Why would you want to?" Dan asks. "It's nice here." He licks his finger, another habit Ellie hates and could never get him to stop. Nothing ever worked. Oh, the fights they used to have over it. Something as silly as finger-licking.

But that was them, wasn't it? Big fights over small things. It was a tagline that should have been stamped on their divorce papers.

"Germs," he says. "I know. Germs get under the nails, they get everywhere. You know—that school nurse friend of yours really has gotten in your head."

She glares at him. It's Dan, all right. It's him. An accurate replica of her ex-husband. His lips move like Dan's. He walks like Dan. He has Dan's flat ass and noticeable spinal curve. He even has the finger-licking down pat, sucks his thumb with that kissing pop sound that sends icy tendrils down her back.

"Are you going to yell at me, Ellie?" he asks, plopping a few slabs of ham down on his plate. After, he puts down the tray and rests his knuckles on the table. "Are you?"

"No," she says, nearly voiceless.

"Good!" He springs up, puffing out his chest, filling his lungs with fresh air, like an opera singer about to belt out the big notes. "I don't like being yelled at, Ellie. Loud noises are bad for the soul, don't you know."

Ellie studies him. He's perfect. Almost too perfect. Then she glances at Dawn, the young twinkle in this replica's eyes.

It's not them, she thinks. They're doppelgangers built by her dreaming mind.

None of this is real.

"But it feels real, doesn't it?" Dan asks, closing his eyes, inhaling every fictitious breath this mirage offers. "It feels…invigorating. No?"

"Where am I?"

Dan shrugs. *"You're in a safe place."*

*"What does that mean?"*

*"Means...you're safe."*

Dawn's head falls crooked on her shoulder. *"Mommy, calm down and eat—"*

*"Shut up,"* Ellie snaps. *"You're not her, you're not my daughter. You're nothing."*

*"Well now,"* Dan says, shaking his finger. *"Everything is something."*

*"I want to know where I am and where my daughter is."*

*"She's right here,"* Dan says, presenting the smiling demon child with a magical wave of his arm, like this is some crappy game show and the thing sitting in the chair next to her is just the first of many prizes. Only...

...she isn't a child anymore. Ellie blinks and Dawn's older now, the same age when she left for that secret getaway three years ago. Ellie gasps when she sees the top of her daughter's head missing, sliced cleanly off like the top of some spherical fruit. An empty crater takes up the space where a brain should be. Blood seeps down from where the scalp was peeled back, where the cranium was sawed through. Despite the butchery, Dawn is looking at her, blinking and smiling as if nothing bad ever happened or has ever happened to her, ever.

*"This is Dawn,"* Dan says with a harsh laugh, a smoker's har-har. He takes the bowl to his left, and Ellie sees it's overflowing with moving things. Upon closer inspection, she realizes the moving things are crabs, small football-shaped creatures that refuse to stay put. Some of them fall over the rim, onto the table, and scurry off the edge, hitting the floor with soft thuds. Dan uses the tongs to pick up the crabs and place them on his plate. Cruelly, he sets them on their dome-like shells so they can't flip over and escape. Once he finishes stocking his platter, Dan picks up a live crab and bites into its crunchy carapace, ignoring the kicking legs and wavering claws. A burst of bright yellow juice that reminds her of energy drinks runs down his chin.

*"Oh Jesus,"* Ellie says, feeling something break in her throat. A teary burn fills her eyes. The once-sweet smell of ham and pineapple is now replaced with the fetid stink of rotting seafood and death.

"Yeah, Jesus ain't gonna do a whole lot of helping here, hon," he says, crunching the raw crab between his teeth—shell, belly, leg and all.

Ellie tries to move again but her muscles are rigid, rock hard, and she's not going anywhere until the dream is done with her. "I want to go back."

"Back?" Dan nods over his shoulder as if reality is just beyond the front door. "Back to Lacuna's Point?"

"Back home."

"Home-home?" Dan shakes his head as if he's never heard of the place and rapidly clicks his tongue several times. He sets down what's left of the crab, which isn't much. Some legs and a few mushy internal organs. "This is home now."

"Don't play games with me."

"Don't like games?"

"Not particularly. If you were truly Daniel Brower, you'd know that."

He shrugs like he's been caught in a small, humorous lie.

"TAKE ME BACK!" The words explode from her mouth like a shotgun blast. Both of the human copies jump, their knees hitting the table, causing the silverware to jingle and the water inside the pitcher to ripple.

Dan puts a hand over his heart as if he's measuring the beats. "My, my, the lungs on you."

"I'll scream louder."

"Please don't. Loud sounds do not agree with us."

"Who are you? What is this?"

"Questions are so repetitive, aren't they? Who? What? When? Why? These are things that shouldn't concern you, hon."

"What should concern me?"

At this, the Dan-Thing smiles, exposing the perfect pearly whites of his teeth, showing no evidence of Real-Dan's three-cups-of-black-coffee-a-day habit and the pack of smokes he burns through every two. "Nothing. You don't have to be concerned with anything. Lacuna's Point is a place you can just...exist. It's perfect. Like us."

"I want to go back. I want to find my daughter. Take me back right now. I'll scream again, I swear to god, I'll scream. As loud as I can, as long as I can. I'll—"

*She sees the Dan-Thing's face twist with immediate concern. Below her topless head, Dawn's expression sours as she frowns through the dark streaks of old blood.*

*Then...Ellie lets loose and screams, the pitch impossibly shrill. The feral call for help pierces her ears as it strips her throat raw.*

*Both the Dawn-Thing and the Dan-Thing open their mouths, much like the people of Lacuna's Point had when the clock tower was sounding its alarm, when the white light fell over them all like a great blanket of doom.*

*And then there is darkness.*

*She blinks.*

*Still dark.*

*Blinks again.*

*And then, finally, there's a light.*

*A frail, flickering light, and a trail of smoke lifting toward something real.*

Ellie wakes up in a candlelit room feeling like victim number one in a sledgehammer massacre. Victim number one gets it the worst, she muses, because that's when the attacker has their full strength and is most motivated. Head pounding, she uses her weakened core to crunch to a sitting position. The bed below her is made, the comforter showing no signs of wrinkles. She assumes she was dumped here, having no memory beyond hearing the clock tower and seeing the white light that knocked her into a dreamy state. No memory of getting here at all. Everything that happened since they arrived in Lacuna's Point is unclear and fuzzy, *real* and *present* but illusionary like a dream itself.

The alarm clock on the nightstand blinks, the digital numbers flashing like the one back home after a power outage. For a split second she thinks she might actually be home, that she never left her house that day and everything she's experienced since has been, in fact, a terrible dream, a wild vision, a fever-induced hallucination stoked by the stress and pain of losing her daughter, the whirlwind aftermath of that dark, dark anniversary when she'd learned that terrible knowledge.

But as the world materializes and the shadows clear, as the last twenty-four to forty-eight hours begin to take shape in her mind, the candlelight doing its best to push back the dim folds, she realizes that not one aspect of her theory is correct—no, this is real; every breath, every second. She wakes up alone, like always.

Alone.

*Mitch.*

She wonders where he's been stashed and who did the stashing. Maybe he's still back near the quad, kneeling before the clock tower like when everything fell apart. Or maybe he's in his room. Maybe he's just waking up, confused like she was and still is.

Feet swinging onto the floor, Ellie gathers herself, the wobble in her knees a reaction to the horrible dream she just stepped out of, and maybe she's experiencing some aftereffects of whatever sleeping aide they dosed her up with.

*They.*

*The people of Lacuna's Point.*

Psychos. Every one of them.

Certainly they gave her something because she feels drugged, lagging behind how her body ordinarily responds to mornings. It wouldn't be the first time someone's slipped something into her system unknowingly. Like that one time in college, at a bar with some friends, when some scumbag weirdo slipped a powder into her martini. She hadn't noticed but someone else at the bar had, but only after she sipped some of the poison down. Her friends were able to collect her and get her back to the dorm, into bed, safely and without a hassle. Even though not every memory of that night is tangible, she'll never forget the in-and-out feeling, the drifting between having control of her actions and being a mere passenger in her own body. She also remembers what she can only describe as *weird sleep.* Waking up from it. Much like she woke up now, with the kind of hangover that feels like someone is smothering you with a wet, heavy blanket and every muscle, every joint feels corroded.

Thunder pounds in her temples. Feet heavy like concrete blocks. An empty belly croaks, requiring something greasy to fill the void. Overwhelmingly awful, this whole experience.

After the delay, she stumbles across the room, where her phone is resting on a small table. She's surprised to see it, thinking whoever took her, whoever knocked her out probably would have stolen it.

Dumped it somewhere. Ejected the SIM card and stomped the thing to pieces. Disposed of the evidence.

But no.

It's still here.

And...

There's even a full charge.

*How's that for service?*

At least her kidnappers are generous. She wonders if they did the same thing for Dawn and Kya, how they were able to send a text.

*HELP ME I'M ALIVE.*

She scrolls through her phone, the collection of names and numbers, and stops when she reaches *his* name.

DAN.

Over the years she's thought several times about deleting the number. Early on, when Dawn first went missing, there were lots of calls back and forth, text threads that ran throughout the night. But since—squat. Not a single message. A part of her thought she would text him once in a while, check in and see how things were going, and that he'd do the same, but alas—it just wasn't in the cards.

She hovers over his name and taps the message icon.

HEY, she writes, and that seems so insignificant to everything she wants to tell him. *Needs* to tell him. After all, he's Dawn's parent too; it would be unfair to hide this little adventure from him. But it's also too late, too late for him to come along. Isn't it? Even if she gets in touch, he's back in Jersey, two hours north of the shore, living near the town he grew up in, the place he returned to after the divorce. He wouldn't come down to Virginia, a place he believes his daughter *died* in. No way.

*He will if Dawn's alive,* she thinks, and she believes that—the *Dawn being alive* part, not the *Dan coming to save her* part. She's not sure if there's anything she can do or say to convince him that she *is* alive, other than forwarding the few texts, but that's hardly evidence, hardly any proof at all. Dan's the kind of guy who will make up something to rationalize why it can't be possible—the way most humans would react to something as unnatural as your presumably dead daughter sending you text messages from beyond the grave.

Dan was never a believer.

She deletes HEY and writes I NEED HELP instead.

Hits send.

*Whatever happens happens,* she thinks, drifting across the room, over to the window. She looks outside and sees a view into town obscured by naked tree branches, as if winter has taken over in the last four hours. The sky is a shimmering steel lake, the threat of inclement weather looming over. Her eyes migrate from the endless silvery body to the town itself, and she can't help but notice the difference. Different *how* exactly, she can't pinpoint, but *different.* She's sure of it. She doesn't remember the clock tower being the centerpiece of town, and seems to remember it being up front, next to the diner and another small stretch of buildings. She remembers the town itself, the streets running front to back, like rows of classroom desks and chairs; if old Eddy was the teacher's desk, then the stores and shoppes were the students'.

But it's not that way anymore.

Now Eddy sits in the center, much like the nut and bolt that holds the hands of time on the clock's dial, and the storefronts face it, but not in rows. They form a spiral effect, the clock tower centered, the *eye* of the town so to speak, and the town coils around it like a resting python.

She blinks, hardly able to buy into this new perception.

Then, something moves below her. Leaving the hotel. Hustling quickly across the street, making for the naked trees, and snow-spotted dirt below them.

It's Mitch.

*Shit!*

He must have woken up around the same time she had, and instead of trying to understand what was happening, instead of trying to make sense of it all, he just left.

*Shit!*

Before she shoves her phone in her pocket, she checks her inbox. Zero messages. She makes sure the message to Dan went through, and it did, but he hasn't looked at it yet. She backs out and clicks down to Dawn's last transmission.

HELP ME I'M ALIVE.

*I'm coming, baby,* Ellie thinks, and heads for the door, thinking maybe she shouldn't. That maybe she should stay here until the town goes back to normal, whatever—*wherever*—normal is.

If such a concept still exists.

Mitch hustles down the slope, feeling the frost in his shoes, winter biting his toes (insane considering how hot it was…how long ago exactly, he doesn't know). His head hurts, throwing off his equilibrium, making his body feel like he's just survived a serious traffic accident. A part of him firmly believes he's still dreaming, that he'll wake up soon, same as last time, only this time the hotel and the world outside will be real. Not this illusion he's found himself stumbling around in.

The chilly air clears his nasal passages, perhaps the only good thing about this colorless, winter setting. He makes for the town, pushing through the dead branches that block the way. Once through, he glances up for an unobstructed view of the clock tower—the very sight of old Eddy chilling him to the core, more so than the frigid mountain air. He remembers pretty much everything that's happened now, though, that wasn't the case twenty minutes ago when he was lying in bed, trying to figure out how the hell he got there. The memories of before were foggy at best, but now, the past is clear.

The bell tolling. The people gathering. The way their mouths opened wide as the brightest light Mitch has ever seen spread over them. *Filled* them. He remembers the sick feeling that rose in his throat, the sudden illness that preyed upon his nerves, dropping him to the ground. And he remembers...

*Kya?*

For some reason he recalls seeing her face among the gathered. It's hazy and he thinks maybe his memories are faulty, not one-hundred percent accurate, but also—*no*, he remembers. She was there. Standing with the crowd. Looking up at the clock tower and being blinded by its all-encompassing wash of light.

*Where is she now?*

It's a question that deserves an answer. But, as Mitch makes his way into town, noticing the new layout, the changes that transpired when the bell of doom struck the world, another question begs to be answered—where did all the people go?

The streets are vacant and so are the shops. The town looks like an apocalyptic version of what it was, a husk of its former self. It could be the gloom-ridden skies that cap the town now, that endless silver stretch, Mitch supposes, but there's something else, a feeling that digs into his nerves—something bad is happening to this place, something that's sucking the energy right out of its center. What that something is, Mitch has no clue, though a part of him wants to unveil this great mystery. Expose it.

*Forget the town and fuck these people,* he thinks, *you're here for Kya and that's it.*

Mitch approaches the town from the rear, heading around the side of the last building in the spiral-shaped layout. He approaches what would be the end of the snake's tail, if indeed the position of the shoppes were a python's coiled body. He looks down the street that now bends to the right instead of offering a straight view to the next street over.

*How is this possible? How can a town change its layout like this?*

Searching for logical explanations inspires another disorienting wave to come crashing over him. It's best not to think about it, and he understands this now. It's best just to explore, find his missing daughter and get the fuck out of there.

He takes to the sidewalk, keeping a brisk pace, peeking inside shoppes, the menacing bulk of shadows trapped within. There's no movement, no signs of life, and he's not sure if that should ease his mind or put him on high alert.

Something skitters across the road behind him and it sounds like coarse sandpaper brushing across the smooth edge of a two-by-four. He spins, his eyes zooming in on the source of the noise.

A newspaper tumbles across the street, carried off by soft, autumnal winds.

"Jesus," he says, putting his hand over his heart. "Goddamn."

He silently prays for forgiveness for using the Lord's name in vain—*Sorry, Ma,* he thinks, signing the Stations of the Cross.

Then he concentrates on the task at hand. The town. The spiral before him. More darkness waits up ahead, shadows and secrecy, and he wants to peel back those dim spaces and get to the root of this mess, discover the truth of it.

*Are you sure that's what you want?*

That's Angie's voice and he can picture her—arms folded, that *you're-gonna-regret-this* smirk resting below her slightly crooked nose, the one she broke during a college lacrosse game in what seems like another lifetime ago. Despite all the troubles and fights they've gotten into over the years, he kinda wishes she was here, now, beside him, holding his hand, the two of them heading toward those countless shadows armed with uncertainty.

His lips burn and he wants to kiss his wife again.

Wants to hold her.

He needs *someone* to hold.

"I wouldn't go down there if I were you."

A cold touch presses down on Mitch's neck. He turns, slowly, toward the voice, balling his fists. He scans the area for a weapon, something blunt he can use in case the situation calls for it.

But there's nothing available along the sidewalk.

He relaxes when he sees a small, skinny white boy wearing plaid shorts and a *Minecraft* T-shirt. The kid can't be more than twelve years old and Mitch wonders why he's not shivering his balls off.

"Where'd you come from?" Mitch asks, squinting, immediately not trusting the only human he's had contact with since waking up.

"That's…." the kid says, holding up a finger. "…a complicated answer."

"Well, uncomplicate it for me."

The kid winces like Mitch's request can't exactly be processed. "I don't think we have time for that."

"Oh no? Why's that?"

Eyes shifting right and left, the kid says, "It's not safe here. Not when the town is…is like this." He looks to the sky, surveying that vast gray coating, cloudless and promising nasty weather.

"Do you know what's happening?"

The kid shakes his head. "No, but I have theories. Skelly's told me some things, but he's an old crackpot who speaks in riddles. Can hardly make sense of him half the time."

"Who's Skelly?" None of this is making sense, but Mitch knows one thing—this is a dream. It has to be. It's the only way this adds up. All of it. He's sleeping somewhere. Drunk. Not working on his novel, not working on his marriage, but sleeping this one off. And dreaming oh-so-interestingly.

"He plays the banjo. You can meet him if you want. Marissa, too. She's cool. We got here around the same time, so we stick together." The kid's eyes slim. "You're not one of *them*…are you?"

"One of who?"

"*Them.* You know? The people who live here? I suppose if you were, you might not tell me. And—shit," the kid says, looking scared. "I probably shouldn't be talking to you."

Mitch gulps. What the hell is going on, he doesn't know, doesn't have the slightest inkling, but he knows he wants out of it, whatever it is.

The kid moves to leave, and Mitch stops him. "No. Wait." He shakes his head. "I'm not one of them. I'm not from here."

The kid halts, relief flushing away the ill-natured panic that had rendered him stiff. "Good," he says, finding a slice of cheeriness. "You're like me then. Like Marissa. And Skelly, mostly. Although I think he's one of them, too. Just…not all the way."

"Kid, I have no idea what you're talking about."

The kid smirks, understanding that he's talking in riddles. "I know. But you will. Seriously—don't head that way."

Mitch peers over his shoulder, looking down the street, the way it curves to a sinister bend, like anything and everything could be hiding just yonder. "I'm looking for my daughter."

"Yeah," the kid says, scratching his head. "Everyone's looking for someone it seems. Marissa's looking for her sister. That goofy couple's looking for their kid…what was his name?" He taps his chin, trying to recall. "Jorgen? Jackson?"

Mitch helps him out. "Jared?"

The kid's eyes shoot open and he snaps his fingers. "Boom! That's it. Jared. You met them, I guess?"

"Yeah, we met them."

"We?" The kid looks around, staying in place but rotating in every direction. "Someone with you?"

Mitch nods. He almost forgot about Ellie. He was so occupied by seeing Kya's face before the light hit, he hadn't even considered grabbing Ellie before venturing out and exploring the town's new alignment. "Yes. My friend, Ellie. She's looking for her daughter too. Her daughter and my daughter were best friends. Went missing three years ago. Then we got these texts…" He reaches into his pocket to grab his phone, but the kid stops him with a wave.

"Save your energy," he says. "I've seen and heard it before. Seems to be this town's MO. Takes people and then sends messages out to their loved ones."

"Have you seen her?" Mitch pulls out the phone and shows him anyway.

The kid creeps forward as if he expects Mitch to reach out and snatch him. Then he allows his guard to drop and takes a glance at the photo. "Nope, haven't seen her. But that's normal, I guess."

"Normal?"

"It's like they hide them until they become them."

"I don't understand." He pleads with his eyes. But he can tell from the way the kid looks that he doesn't have all the answers. Or even some of them. Just speculations.

"What's your name?"

"Mitch."

"Mitch," he says, nodding. "I'm Josh."

"Josh. Pleasure to meet you."

"Likewise."

"Josh," Mitch says, clearing his throat. "Do you have any idea what this town is and what it could possibly want with us?"

Josh's lips twist like pretzel dough. "I can't say for sure...but I get the feeling it's hungry...and we're on the menu."

Ellie runs down the small cliff, ignoring the frosty conditions, the slippery, snow-slicked mud below her feet. It doesn't come as a shock when her foot slides out beneath her, and she's planted on her bottom. Her jeans immediately absorb the arctic moisture, stinging her left butt cheek. Fighting the snowy touch, she gets up, keeps moving down the hill, toward the empty and dead town. It's like a gray filter has been stamped over Lacuna's Point. The vague sky has begun pushing storm clouds eastward, and Ellie wonders how long she has until snow or rain begins to fall on her.

She reaches the bottom of the hill and heads toward the beginning of town, unable to get over how much the layout has changed in mere hours. The dreamlike realization that this place certainly doesn't compliment the confines of reality she's accustomed to hits her with a dizzying rush. Her stomach flips and she ignores the bout of nausea, willing it to go away.

She moves along the sidewalk now, taking in the empty shoppes with her curious eyes, looking for any signs of Mitch. He couldn't have gotten too far ahead, but she sees no signs of him. No signs of anyone, really. The term "ghost town" comes to mind, and she can't fight off the notion that maybe she's truly dead. That they had an accident sometime after crossing the Virginia border, and that this is now their permanent residence—a town that can change from summer to winter like someone changes a pair of shorts, a place that's the home of hundreds of people one minute and an abandoned purgatory the next.

*There's a logical explanation for this,* debates Ellie's rational side. *Global warming or something. The weather is always whacky when the seasons change nowadays.*

But snow in August? In Virginia? On the coast? Where it probably flurries once every five years? No, not even the educator in her can believe that.

*You're dead. You're in Hell now. Welcome to the afterlife, hon.*

That last bit of wisdom sounds like it could have come from Dan's mouth and she hates that he's still there, lurking in the depths of her thoughts. Dan coming up again reminds her to check her messages.

She pulls out her phone, looks down, and sees no new messages in the inbox. No signal either, which doesn't surprise her much. This town doesn't look like it provides much reception, and honestly, she's surprised her outgoing message went through without kicking back.

Pocketing the phone, she continues to hurry down the sidewalk, taking the bend, following the spiral. "Mitch? Hello?" She cups her hands over her mouth and shouts louder. "Mitch!"

Still nothing. The town responds with a little wind in her ear. A rattle, balled pages of newspaper tumbling across the blacktop, scrapes her eardrums. She turns to the noise, half-expecting to see some animal, some scavenger waiting for her body to drop dead so it can feed on her carcass, appear from the shadows that fill in the edges of this place.

But there's nothing. Empty streets, empty buildings. Beyond them, in the distance, empty homes.

She follows the bend until she can't see the last shoppes behind her. Then she glances at the clock tower, the face of Lacuna's Point, and watches it count the minutes and hours, which are virtually useless here. Time seems like a nonexistent piece to this complex puzzle. Or is it? She's not sure. Maybe time is everything here. Or maybe time doesn't exist at all, and the clock tower is an illusionary symbol of something this place will never know.

She forces herself to look away from Eddy as if—in staring too long—she might lose a piece of herself. The skyward eye continues to leer at her, examining her every movement. She can't help but feel like the hobbits, Frodo and Sam, from *Lord of the Rings* as they got closer to Mordor. The lure of that awful center pulling her, infiltrating her brain and accessing her thoughts without permission. Rearranging things.

She snaps her head to the side, refusing the hypnotic appeal a pathway to her thoughts.

Another five minutes and she finds herself deeper into the coil of shoppes and establishments. Still no sign of Mitch. It's like the man has disappeared. She's surveying the street before her, the one that only travels in one direction, when she notices the art gallery across the way. The same one from earlier except now the lights are off and, like most of the storefronts, no one seems to be working inside. She wonders if the Dawn Brower original is still hanging on the gallery's farthest wall.

She wonders...

Ellie licks her lips. She looks both ways before crossing the street as if some car will come barreling out of nowhere and plow into her. Which is ridiculous because of how silent the world has become— she'd hear the motor coming from a mile away.

Once in front of the store, she hustles over to the glass window. Shadows cover the interior, making it impossible to see past the curator's welcome desk. There's no one inside unless they're sitting in complete darkness, which wouldn't be the craziest or creepiest thing that's happened today.

She tries the front door just in case someone forgot to do their job the night before and left it unlocked. But it is locked, the thumb lever above the ornate curve of the handle refusing to budge.

Fuck.

She backs up, peeks down the street, both ways, and decides she's getting into this closed art gallery one way or another. Maybe the back door is open? But she doesn't even try for it, doesn't want to waste time checking it out. The time to break in is now, when no one is watching.

She looks around for something heavy, solid, something that will shatter the glass window. There's a tree, not more than twenty feet from her, anchored to the sidewalk. A collection of stones the size of ostrich eggs rests at the base where the tree's trunk meets the shallow soil. She picks one up, softly lobs it to herself in her right hand, and then heads back to the gallery. She stands before her reflection, barely recognizing the woman staring back at her, and for a split second, she wonders if this is another dream-like consequence of spending too much time in Lacuna's Point. Upon closer inspection, she realizes it is her staring back and that it's the visage of a tired woman not cut out for this kind of adventure.

She takes the rock and throws it, putting her entire spirit into the launch, and watches the stone crash through the center of her image. The glass shrieks and comes apart in pebbles, crumbling to the sidewalk below. Ellie takes another gander at the vacant streets of Lacuna's Point, expecting *someone* to come running, if for nothing more than to see what all the fuss is about.

But there's no one.

Nothing.

The town is as dead as she feels.

Ellie swallows her reluctance and heads inside.

"Where the hell are we going?"

The question stops the boy in his tracks. He glances over his shoulder, his brow furrowing, suggesting he isn't sure what to make of Mitch's question. "I'm taking you to see someone."

"Who? The Mayor?"

The kid shakes his head. "No. No, God no. No one sees the Mayor. I mean, at least not us. Not until…the arts festival, I hear."

"What the hell is with the arts festival?"

The kid shrugs. "Big deal around here, I guess. Something happens on that day. Can't really tell for sure. Skelly won't tell us. He's very cryptic about these sorts of things. It's like if he tells us too much, the town will somehow learn about it and he'll be punished. Never tells it to us straight."

"Guess we're heading to meet this Skelly dude?"

"Yep. Marissa too. They're at the house." The kid points to the development resting just beyond the spiraling center of town. A few hundred homes are tucked back there, each looking similar, reminding him of the little houses in Monopoly if they were all lined up in a row with even space between them. About a dozen or so streets from front to back, a perfect square block of housing development. It has this *Edward Scissorhands* vibe that Mitch can't shake.

"Let's go," the kid says. "Walk and talk. Don't stand in one place for too-too long."

The kid speed-walks down the street, leaving the safety of the sidewalk and heading toward the gap between two buildings that offers passage to the residential development. Mitch jogs to catch up.

"And why's that?"

"Gee, man. You ask a lot of questions." Mitch hears the amusement in the kid's voice.

"Oh, I'm sorry. Am I bothering you?"

"No." The kid scratches his neck. "No. Sorry—geez, look, it's like this—I've been here for two weeks and I barely understand what's going on myself. We're in the same boat, you and me—you see? I want to get out of here just as much as you do."

"I want to find my daughter first."

"And you will—probably." The kid relaxes his shoulders as he begins to trespass the area behind the shoppes, that grassy divider between the spiraling layout and the first block. "If she isn't...you know...dead."

"You said you feel like this town wants to eat you. What did you mean by that?"

At first the kid doesn't respond, and Mitch wonders if he heard him. But before Mitch can ask again, Josh says, "It's a feeling I get. Skelly can probably help explain a little more. But I gotta warn you. The guy...he isn't all there."

"I don't understand this place. The weather—how can it change like this?"

At this, Josh stops. Again. Mitch slows to a halt just before they reach the sidewalk of the first street. Mitch can see the cross streets are closer to double from his original estimate.

"It does this sometimes," Josh says, like he's admitting something he's done and not proud of. "The weather gets weird. Goes from summer to winter like that." *Like that* is uttered with a finger snap. "It happens when new people come here. It happened the day I got here."

"And why does it happen?"

Josh rolls his eyes. "I mean, again, I don't really know. I'm just speculating."

Mitch bends over as if looking at the kid on his level will summon some sort of magical truth. "Why do you *think* it happens? Gut feeling."

Josh's eyes sweep right to left and back again. "I think we're dreaming, but...not."

Mitch quickly shakes his head. "Huh?"

"It's like a dream when it does this. But...like a lucid one? Is that the right word?"

Mitch shrugs. "Sure."

"Like everything that's happening inside this dream space is actually happening to us, but it's still not 100% real. Does that make sense?"

"Nope. Sounds like nonsense to me."

"Sounds like nonsense to me too, but I think it makes more sense when you've experienced it a few times. And you've seen the things that I've seen while we're here. In the dream, that is."

"How do I know you're real then, you know, if this is a dream?" Mitch stands back up, arching his spine, relieving some of the pressure on his lower back.

"I guess you don't. Same way I don't know that you're real. But it feels real, doesn't it?"

"It does feel real." He shivers. "Except the fact it's forty below in August, it feels pretty damn real, man."

"Exactly. I think..." Josh leans in as if the houses have ears. "I think we *are* dreaming. Together. But it's not our dream."

As if he isn't cold enough, Mitch's veins flush with an arctic blast. "Whose dream is it?"

Josh gulps, looks upward. "I dunno…but sometimes, during the dream, if I look up…I can see its eyes."

# CHAPTER EIGHT

Ellie makes her way through the unlit lobby, accessing the shadows behind the curator's desk, searching, her eyes bouncing between dim pieces of art, *stolen* art, she thinks, art that shouldn't be here, shouldn't be trapped in the hell hole that is Lacuna's Point. She moves around some boxes, dilapidated cardboard squares that contain random canvas paintings and floral knickknacks, as her eyes slowly adjust to the darkened state of things. After nearly tripping, she concentrates where she plants each foot, mindful of the hazards the studio is offering, thinking it would be unwise to twist an ankle here where no one can save her.

Once she makes her way to the back, she retrieves her phone from her pocket and offers the blue square of light to the shadows. The light does little to combat the dark, but it does help. It prevents her from tripping over another box.

She pushes to the back of the gallery where Dawn's last piece was mounted. That abstract canvas painting that should still be sitting in the corner of Ellie's basement, not on display for some weirdo town that doesn't seem to follow the same rules of reality the universe put forth at the dawn of time. As she peels away the layers of shadows with her phone, the gallery's back wall slowly reveals itself. She sees a different piece in place of the one before. Inching closer, her eyes take in the replacement, the details. As her heart sinks into a pool of icy dread, she can tell that the new piece also was done by Dawn's hand. Ellie can tell by the color choices, the acrylics used. The subdued glaze that coats the surface, keeping the sheen to a minimum but still giving the piece enough shine that Ellie's iPhone LED picks up on it. And there's the content itself. It isn't one of Dawn's usual creations; lacks the abstract elements her paintings typically include. No, this one is different. It's a self-portrait of sorts—being that Dawn herself is the focal point. Her back is to the spectator and she's looking out into a dreamy void, full dark spirals and misshapen entities floating among a dark and cavernous abyss, a twisted vortex of scraggly lines and smudged brushstrokes, lacking a true definite shape as well as color and tone. Very different from the usually bright and cheerful vibe that Dawn Brower was always so proud of.

Ellie brings her eyes closer to the surface, her vision battling the dark. She wants to see what Dawn saw, this chaotic spiral she clearly stood before, looked into, *examined* with her artist's eye.

*What did you see, baby? What was this?*

Possible answers haunt her. For a split second Ellie thinks she sees it, that undefinable shape lurking in the darkness, swimming through the shadowy gyres. Eyes and teeth and distorted appendages stretching the confines of rational thought. A beast floating in this colorless, colossal realm. A monster, an unspeakable—

"Well, well," a voice says from behind her, and she spins around so quickly she almost twists her ankle. "Looks like we got ourselves a little B and E, huh?"

A flashlight's beam catches her eyes, forcing her to shield them with her arm. Looking away, she says, "Please, I can't see."

"*Ohhhh*, you can't *seeee*…" A throaty giggle accompanies the sarcasm. Glass crunches beneath the man's heavy feet, the broken pebbles skittering across the sidewalk as he drags his boots, their scraping filling the dead silence of this gray afternoon. "What a shame. Wouldn't dare want you to miss out on *seeing*."

"Wh-who are you?"

"Me?" The man titters. "Just a man trying to do his job and keep the peace. Protect and serve, all that bullshit. But you— you…*interlopers*…just want to make it goddamn hard on me, don't you?"

She attempts to steal a peek but the light's still too raw. Shrinking away like a vampire beneath the rising sun, she moves to the opposite end of the gallery, feeling the wall, seeking an open door to sneak through.

"See, you just made me take the Lord's name in vain." The man clicks his tongue against the back of his teeth. "I don't like that, Miss. I don't like that one bit."

"Please," Ellie says, knocking into a box. Whatever's inside spills out across the floor, clattering as it goes.

"Clumsy, aren't you? Bad enough you have to break into private property, now you gotta follow it up by destroying the joint. And in front of the arresting officer no less." More laughing. He's enjoying this game. "Stand still."

His approach sounds closer, boots stamping on the floor. She shrinks, looks around, and although she's partially blinded by the light, an opening that separates two walls appears in the dim haze, giving way to a potential hallway she can escape down. Or, maybe the hallway leads to another dead end. Like this town.

*Full of dead ends, roads that take us nowhere.*

He steps into a patch of light coming in through the shattered window, and she sees it's the policeman from earlier, the one who got in her face and was most uncooperative in helping them locate her car.

"Officer," she pleads. "I don't think you—"

"Shut up." He makes a sound with his throat, like he's coughing up phlegm. A disgusting sound that lets her know that he's disgusted by her. "You people are like mice. You come here, think you can just take over, like we're supposed to cater to you and your needs, leave your little droppings here and there, and then you know what you do? You multiply." He clicks his tongue and the sound echoes. "Such filth."

"I don't understand—what is this place? What is happening here? I don't under—"

"Hey!" he snaps. "Didn't I tell you to shut up?"

Deciding she only has one chance and that chance is now, she makes for the hallway. A turn and a single step forward; that's how far she gets before she's yanked back by her hair. Her neck muscles pull and strain under the forceful guide.

*"Ugh!"* Her hands collapse on the pressure, feeling around for the source. A calloused hand is gripping her ponytail, pulling her in the opposite direction with so much force she's now on her heels, tipping away from her destination, the shadows down the hall. *"Get off of me, you bastard!"*

With more ferocity than the first yank, the second one causes her to lose her already-teetering balance, and she goes to the floor, hard.

"You trying to run from me?" the officer asks, pulling her through the gallery now, dragging her as she kicks and screams and curses. She pedals in a fury, trying to grip the floor and boost herself back up to her feet while twisting her body, trying to break the man's bullish grip. But all actions are useless; he's too strong and she's too weak. She screams but no one is around to save her. After a few seconds, she realizes there's no point and gives up, deciding to save her breath and throat for when she'll need it.

*And you will need it,* pipes the voice within.

"Really? Ain't nowhere to run to, darling. Should know that by now."

Her shirt is lifted slightly from being dragged, and she feels the glass pebbles scraping her raw skin, cutting, slicing the flesh.

"You're hurting me!" she shouts, and by the time she gets the words out, she's outside of the gallery, on the sidewalk, sitting in a small collection of shattered window fragments. "Fucking asshole!"

He lets go and backs away, crossing his arms, a proud smile across his...

...face?

In the gloomy shadows hanging over Lacuna's Point, she can see his features with perfect clarity. And he's...well, he's in rough shape. Cut. Scratched. Like someone locked him in a linen closet with a small pack of aggressive feral felines. The wounds are open, not actively bleeding, but definitely open and definitely raw. Criss-crossed lines of darkening scarlet show in patches. He's sweaty, beads clinging to the space below his receding hairline. She stares at that dark mustache (too dark to be natural at his age), the wolf-like lips below it. The cop is smiling, proud of his accomplishment, the way he handled Ellie and her attempted escape, how rough he was with her.

"Why you running, darling?" the cop asks, his upper lip twitching.

Ellie swallows, afraid to rise from her position on the sidewalk. The dragging, she thinks, is only the opening act of what the man can do, *wants to do,* and she doesn't want to give him a reason to put on the whole show.

Her eyes find the revolver holstered to his hip.

"I asked you a question, sweetheart. Do your best to answer it now, y'hear?"

The pain near her hair tie pulses. She looks right and left, sees nothing but the empty streets and the empty shoppes. No help coming. Nowhere to go. Running won't get her anywhere because Ellie Brower can't outrun bullets.

Tears leak from her eyes, tears she cannot control.

"Now, now. No sense in crying. Teardrops ain't never had much effect on me. Might work on some cops, but not me, darling." He holds out his hands, an impatient twirl of both forefingers. "Still waiting on that answer, girl."

She dips her head to the right and left, drying both eyes on her T-shirt. "What was the question again…officer?"

He glares at her, his happy elastic smile fading into something not-so-happy. "It's Foley—Officer Foley. And the question was— Why. You. Running?"

"I thought I was in danger. I was…scared."

"Scared of me?" he asks incredulously.

She only returns his gaze.

"Gosh, girl. You ain't gotta be scared of me. I'm just doing my job. And my job is to arrest people like you."

"People like me?"

"Criminals."

"I'm not…a criminal." Following the cop's eyes as they shift ever-so-slightly above her right shoulder, she sees the full scope of the damage done to the front of the art gallery. It looks much worse now that the cop has called attention to it. Really bad, in fact. She feels a deep embarrassment bloom on her cheeks and can only imagine the rosy pink splotches that appear there, furthering her guilty campaign. "That I can explain, actually."

"Oh, boy!" He whistles, matching the inflection of his previous sentence. "I'd actually love to hear it."

"Officer Foley, there's something *really* messed up going on here. With this town. My daughter, she went—"

His smile widens, and he reminds her of a carnival clown putting on a good act despite the children before him cowering in fear.

"What?" she asks. "What is it?"

"You people never get it."

"Get what? Officer, you don't understand. This town is…I don't even know how to explain it. It's like…the fucking *Twilight Zone* or something. I mean…man, look around you. It snowed. In August. That doesn't clue you in that something's royally *fucked* here?"

"This town, missy," he says, hands on his hips and puffing his chest. "Is a big ol' slice of American pie. That's what this town is, what it represents. And I will not have you badmouth Lacuna's Point. Not on my watch. Now there are good people here, the best kind of people, and we don't need you or any other interlopers coming here and mucking things up for us. We won't have it!"

The increased volume causes her to shrink.

"Sorry about that," he says, shaking his head. "Didn't mean to get my Irish up. Just…y'all test my patience is all."

"I think someone in this town kidnapped my daughter. I need help finding her. *Please*."

An exaggerated sigh. "Ma'am, I doubt someone from town kidnapped your daughter. All right? I lived here my whole life, and nothing ever bad has ever happened in Lacuna's Point."

"Nothing bad?" She swallows what feels like one of those glass pebbles that tore up her back. "Then what the hell is with that clock tower? The blinding light? The fact that this town has changed its entire layout in one day?"

"The what now?"

She shakes her head. "You know what—you were there. When the clock tower went off, when the light came, and then everything…changed?"

Foley's eyes dart back and forth. "Girl, what in the hell are you babbling about?"

A rush of anger flashes through her, and she feels like she might combust from the spell of rage. "That clock tower started to ring at three o'clock. There was a blinding light. And now…I mean, Jesus Christ, look around you, man."

"Hey! Don't you say Jesus's name in vain. Don't you dare!"

She raises her hands like he's going to shoot. "Sorry."

He pauses to look her over, and she senses a morsel of pity in those dark eyes of his. "You off your meds, lady, or what?"

She blinks several times. "Look around you. You don't see anything…off?"

He gives the town a look, but she thinks it's more for show than a genuine examination of the gathering storm clouds hovering above, the abandoned shoppes and lifeless streets.

"No, not really. It's always like this on Sundays. Town closes for religious reasons. We sure love our religion in Lacuna's Point."

She doesn't argue. She nods, slowly, her eyes unable to focus on the cop's face, the split skin, for too long. "Oh, well, I guess that explains it."

"All right, stand up."

She pushes herself to her knees, then her feet. Every muscle feels like a pinata at a six-year-old's birthday party after the drunk dad got his whacks in. "You're letting me go?"

His harsh, inhuman smile returns. Lifting his arm, he reveals a pair of handcuffs, dangling them as if they're a treat and she's been a good puppy. "Turn around."

Her heart nosedives. "Please…"

"Don't make this harder than it has to be," he says, though what he means to say, she thinks, is, *Don't make me hurt you.*

Rolling her eyes, she turns. Puts her hands behind her back. He isn't gentle when he clamps the metal around her wrists.

He isn't gentle at all.

Mitch follows Josh as he weaves through the residential district of Lacuna's Point, taking the sidewalks and the little narrow paths between the alike housing units. They're about halfway through the neighborhood when Josh veers off, walking directly through the front yard of one house in particular, passing a small Japanese maple (that looks strangely alive and in bloom despite the wintery atmosphere) and a bed of lilies and wild orchids. Mitch can't believe the plant life survived this setting, but considering the impossibilities his mind has accepted since coming to Lacuna's Point, the flowers prospering and looking quite healthy are just more *strange pills* he has to swallow.

He clears his mind and follows Josh up the yard, to the front door of a house painted the color of an aged tangerine. The louvered shutters are white and perfectly aligned with the windows.

Mitch goes to follow him to the door when he's overcome with the feeling of being watched. *If I look up…I can see its eyes.* The kid said that, *actually* said that. Mitch wishes he asked Josh to elaborate, but he was too scared to hear the explanation—the statement was enough to work his skin into that creeping, crawling state.

As Josh jogs up the stoop and pushes through the front door of the house, Mitch thinks this might be a trap. It's a fleeting thought, but the fact remains—he doesn't know this kid, and he could be easily lying to him. Mitch doesn't stop though, following his instincts. If there's one thing Mitch is certain about, it's that his instincts are on point and always have been throughout his life. It's kept him out of a lot bad social situations, kept him from ever hanging out with the wrong crowd, kept him from getting arrested in his formative years—something his two brothers could not say. Mitchell Green was born with all the good instincts, while Darius and Darrel got all the bad ones. The fact Mitch's brothers were still alive and doing well was somewhat of a miracle considering all the bad shit they'd gotten into. Mitch partly blames their mother's early departure from this world on their early shenanigans, but there were probably other, indeterminable factors.

"Come on in," Josh says, standing in the doorway, looking behind Mitch, at the street, as if he's expecting spies. Mitch can't help but feel like he's entering a speakeasy during the prohibition days. "Seems clear!" Josh calls over his shoulder.

Mitch hustles in and Josh closes the door behind him.

There are two other people in the room. One is sitting on the couch; an old Black man wearing a leather-brown fedora with a red feather sticking out of the band, and a white, untucked dress shirt with a bow tie, crisp suspenders to match. The fedora is tipped back, revealing the patchy fuzz of his hairline, little curls of white peppered in with the clinging dark. His beard, however, is completely white and grown in, neatly trimmed and tight against his face. Aftershave dominates the stagnant air around him, and Mitch's nose becomes overpowered with the smell, tickled. The other person in the room is a young woman with long, curly black hair, pulled back in a sizable bun. She flashes Mitch a nervous smile. Her expression is a good representation of how Mitch feels.

"Here he is," Josh says, presenting the man on the couch as if he's a celebrity, like Mitch is here to grab a quick pic and an autograph. "Skelly, meet Mitch."

Skelly doesn't say a word—instead, he picks up the acoustic guitar that has been on his lap since Mitch entered the living room. The sharply-clad man doesn't lift his eyes to meet him, his sole focus concentrated on the instrument. He gently strokes the strings with his thumb, playing a mellow, quiet chord while humming along in perfect harmony. Mitch gains a sense that the man is a musical talent (maybe even a great one at that) based off that one strum.

Mitch clears his throat. "Excuse me."

The old guitarist slaps the strings with an open palm, striking a messy, discordant chord. The abrupt ending hits Mitch's ears like knives down a chalkboard. The man doesn't look up.

"I was told by Josh here," Mitch says, "that you could help me find my daughter."

Now he looks up and Mitch sees two eyes, both of them completely whited out. It's freaky at first, and a series of cold bumps populate across Mitch's arms, and that's only because he wasn't expecting that. Mitch feels bad that the man's visual impairment elicits that kind of response from his body, but he quickly adjusts.

"Help, help, everybody lookin' for help here nowadays," the man says, and then continues to allow his fingers to dance up and down the neck of the guitar, playing some folksy blues riff. The riff sounds familiar, but Mitch's ears can't place it. "Help, help, help. Help me, help you, help yourselves."

Mitch looks to Josh who only puts on that *yeah-this-is-normal* face. The girl—Marissa, Mitch assumes—just shrugs.

"Mr. Skelly, I—"

"Just Skelly, no mister," the man snaps, not missing a single note on whatever song he's strumming. "Ain't no mister, mister's for making mist."

Mitch nods like he understands but he doesn't have a fucking clue, and all he wants to do is get the hell out of there and go find his daughter. This...this is just a waste of time.

He turns to Josh. "What is this, man?"

Josh rocks himself on his heels. "Yeah, I did warn you."

"Skelly is different," Marissa adds. "He might speak in riddles sometimes, but he has his moments of clarity." She turns to Josh. "Josh, who is this man?"

"He's like us, don't worry."

"I am worried. I'm worried a lot."

"Hey," Mitch says, "I'm cool."

Marissa glares at him. Studies him like she's not so sure he is cool. "I'll be the judge of that."

"Look, I get it." Mitch nods over his shoulder. "It's fucked up out there."

Marissa scoffs. "That's the understatement of a lifetime."

"Help me understand. I'm looking for my daughter and—"

"We're all searching for someone, okay?" Marissa's breathing heavily, this tiring conversation vacuuming the wind from her lungs. "We've all lost someone here."

"I actually haven't lost anyone," Josh says in a way that's designed to lighten the growing tension.

"You've lost yourself, short stuff," Marissa tells him, and Josh rolls his eyes. "This place," she continues, focusing on Mitch, "it's like a Venus Flytrap but for people. How long have you been here?"

Mitch looks to the kid as if he might know the answer; certainly, Mitch only has a vague idea. The concept of time is pretty much lost on him. "Yesterday? I don't know, really. Was only here a few hours before the clock tower thing happened."

"The Light," Marissa says, nodding, looking at Josh, then to Skelly. "You caused the Light."

"Whoa, I didn't cause anything. I was just—"

"Not your fault, man," she shot back. "It wasn't an accusation. It was an observation. Seems that when someone new comes to town, that clock tower goes off at three o'clock and then…well, we all go to sleep. Wake up like this."

"Where's everyone else? The rest of the town?"

She shrugs. "Assume they're in their homes, waiting it out."

"Does…is everyone in on this?"

Josh and Marissa share a glance.

"It's hard to say," Josh says first. "We think most of the town is in on it. Our working theory is the longer someone stays, the more influenced they become. At least, that's what we've found while interviewing the townsfolk."

Mitch feels dizzy. "I need to sit down, man. I'm spinning." He wanders over to the couch and plops down on the end opposite of Skelly. The old man continues to play his songs, shifting from one chord to the next, seamless transitions that eke out beautiful tunes.

"It's a lot to digest," Marissa says. "But we stick together, and I think we'll find a way out of here."

"How long you been here?" Mitch asks.

Marissa seems to roll the numbers in her head. "Two weeks, best we figure it."

"Yeah," Josh confirms. "Two weeks."

"You find who you're looking for?" Mitch asks Marissa.

She pauses. Shakes her head. "No. But I'm not gonna stop looking."

"You'll stop," Skelly interrupts, breaking his bout of silence, but continuing to play and pick away at the strings. "They all stop, they all give up. Ain't no shame in it. Ain't no shame in letting it take you. Letting you take it."

"I'm tired of these riddles," Mitch says, trying to mask the anger in his voice, the frustration, but failing on both fronts. "I'm tired of this place. I just want my daughter back and I want to go home."

"We all want that," Marissa says. "Which is why we need to stick together and—"

Skelly laughs, his wheezy interjection bringing Marissa's statement to an immediate stop. "Tired? You tired?"

Mitch swings his head toward him.

"Well, shit. Boy is tired. Let's all drop everything because the boy is tired." He glares at Mitch and Mitch finds it difficult to stare back, the all-white gaze leaving him a bit unnerved. He gets the sense that the old man can see just fine, maybe even better than the rest of them, despite the apparent blindness. "Long you been here? A day? Shit, you ain't even begun to feel tired yet."

Mitch saves his breath.

"Boy is tired, someone get him a nap." Skelly laughs again and Mitch wonders how the man is even able to breathe with that much wheezing going on. "What's the Lacuna want with your raggedy-ass?"

The question surprises him on more than one level. So much so, the only way he can respond is with, "What? Me?"

"Yeah *you*. Who else I be talking to?"

Mitch grinds his teeth. "How the hell am I supposed to know the answer to that question? And what do you mean 'Lacuna?' You mean the town? Lacuna's Point?"

"Lacuna, lacuna. The. Lacuna. You know the Lacuna. La. Coo. Na."

Mitch looks to the others for support, but he gets none.

"I don't know. You tell me what it wants."

"The hell am I supposed to know what's in your heart, boy. You got a piece in there, a part of your soul you holding onto, the Lacuna wants it. Damn right it does. Wants a piece, it wants the whole thing. The Point don't hold onto the worthless, so you worth something to it, the Lacuna. Worth a whole lot, I gather. You got a radiance to you, a certain kinda—shit, what we call it?" He breaks from playing guitar to snap his fingers in rapid succession, as if in doing so someone will feed him the answer. "Glow! That's it! Heh-heh, you got yourself a glow about you!"

"I do?" Mitch feels like whatever glow he once had has long since gone dim.

"You got a glow, and the Lacuna wants it. Sure, sure. You a musician? Can you strum a tune for us?"

He shakes his head. "No."

"Then what is it? What's your poison?"

He shrugs. "Don't have one. I'm...I'm nothing. I manage a delivery warehouse. We deliver, distribute...beer."

Skelly swats the air and smacks his lips. "That's what you do. Ain't what you are. What are you? An actor? An artist? You paint? Sculpt? Spit poetry?"

Mitch swallows. "I...uh, write. Sometimes. I guess."

No one says anything. Even Skelly stops playing the guitar. A second later, he sits back against the couch cushion.

"Welllll, there we go. You a writer. What you written?"

"Well, uh," Mitch says, laughing, chuckling through a fractured smile. "Nothing yet. I'm working on a novel. Well, I'm *working on* working on a novel, if that makes sense." He glances up and sees on their faces that it doesn't make sense at all. "I'm planning on writing a novel. Got started on it, but then...I dunno. Stuff happens."

"Stuff happens," Skelly says, nodding. "Sure, sure. Stuff happens. Happens here, happens there, stuff happens all over the place. But none of that stuff is preventing you from writing that novel, no?"

Mitch shrugs. "No, it has. I just...can't concentrate."

"Try harder then."

"Look, not to be rude, but what the hell does that have to do with getting my damn daughter back?"

Josh is the first to answer. "We have a theory."

"Lay it on me then," says Mitch, throwing his hands up.

"This town seems to take people with talent. Specifically those with artistic tastes."

*Art.* Kya wasn't much of an artist, could barely string together a couple of lines for stick figures growing up, but she was a damn good poet. After she was gone and he and Angie were going through her room, they stumbled upon a box of poems, some recent, some that dated back to her tween years. That afternoon, they read every single one out loud and laughed and cried and broke their hearts over and over again. Kya was a poet all right, an artist with words, whereas Dawn was the painter. The two of them together, youth teeming with so much talent. If what Josh is saying is true, then it's no wonder the town abducted them.

But why? For what purpose?

"And why's that?" he blurts out.

Josh sighs. "Well, again—we don't really know. But we think it has something to do with the arts festival."

"The arts festival?"

"The arts festival," Josh confirms.

"The goddamn arts festival," Marissa piles on.

"Won't know for a good two and a half weeks." Josh's shoulder shrug says, *Eh, what can you really do about it?*

"I can't be stuck here for two and a half weeks," Mitch says. Two and a half weeks in a place like Lacuna's Point, a place where reality itself is the missing component and not the people—well, a two-and-a-half-week sentence seems like an eternity. "I have to get back to my wife—"

"Two weeks!" croaks the old guitar player. "Two weeks! Two weeks! No, no, you gonna last two weeks—you gotta last a lot longer than that. Try…oh, Jesus, try about forty-seven years. Try that and come back to me with your two weeks bit."

Mitch stares at the man, then at the others. *Forty-seven years,* he thinks. *Forty-seven years?*

He doesn't ask the question, ask if it's true or question the logic of Skelly's claim, but he doesn't need to.

Josh and Marissa staring away, at the ground, the ceiling, is all the proof needed.

She looks around but doesn't see the squad car. Officer Foley clicks on the shoulder speaker and barks into it: "Two-nine, I just stopped a ten-sixty-two and I'm bringing the suspect in for questioning, over."

"I can explain," Ellie pleads, one last attempt to exploit whatever shred of humanity this cop still has. Not that she thinks she'll be successful—the man seems determined to bring her in.

"Explain to the Mayor." He pushes her along, shoving her in the back, harder than Ellie feels she deserves, even if she's guilty. Which she is. But she has reasons, *good* reasons, and if the cop would just slow the hell down for a minute and listen, all can be smoothed over. She thinks so anyway.

But Foley doesn't slow down. He parades her down the street like she's some common criminal.

"You mean, a judge?" Ellie asks.

"Mayor is the judge, darlin'."

At this, her skin crawls. As they walk, her eyes find the shoppes and she sees how desolate and derelict everything appears, how dead and apocalyptic and gray the world's become. Where was the vibrant town, so full of life? Full of people? Even if they were strange, somewhat robotic and inconsistently aware of their environment, at least there was human interaction. There's nothing now, and Ellie isn't buying the whole "it's closed for Sunday" excuse. No, she can smell that bullshit from a mile off.

Her thoughts turn back to her sole purpose, Dawn, and she hopes she's still alive, and that she can find her and soon. She wonders if she's hiding in one of those houses, lying low until someone (her mother) comes and saves her.

Hiding from whatever this place is.

*Hiding from the stars.*

She glances up and sees starlight twinkling behind the blanket of gray clouds.

*Three years. Do you really think she's still alive after three years?*

The question summons a falling teardrop.

"What's the matter?" Foley asks, hearing her sniffle. "You done this to yourself. Ain't nobody to blame but you."

"You don't understand."

"Oh, I understand alright. Thought you could take advantage of a town during the celebration of their religious freedoms. A day of rest for us means a day of looting for you. That's what I understand.

Wait until the good people are gone, enjoying their quiet times of solitude and prayer, and then you come along, sneak in here like a wolf in sheep's clothing, ready to steal and take what isn't yours, what these people have worked so damn hard for. You should really be ashamed of yourself, missy."

"I…" Ellie has the words to explain, but she knows they're useless. Now. Maybe later when she's in front of the Mayor (Judge). Maybe he has some common fucking sense Officer Foley apparently lacks.

It's a long shot, but it's her only shot.

"Come on, girl. Keep walking." The cop shoves her forward again. This time she trips, stumbles ahead, her knees knocking against one another. Her strength fails her and she's unable to catch herself. Within a blink she's on the ground, rolling over to face her attacker. "Oh come on, woman. I didn't even push you that hard. Enough with the theatrics. You want the Taser?"

She winces from the shot of pain injected into her right shoulder. "You asshole. Don't fucking touch me."

"Get up."

"Fuck you."

"Oh! We're gonna start with the mouth now. I've Tasered people for less, you know." He takes great admiration in this claim. "Now get up. I ain't playing games today, sweetheart. It's Sunday and I'm late for kickoff."

"Get your hands off me!"

He bends over to pick her up, and she lashes out with her right foot, aiming for the man's ball bank. She hits the desired target, though it's not enough force to send him reeling, which is a problem because all it does is piss him off. His eyes shoot wide open with the quickness of a hornet's stinger, and the cuts in his face morph, mutate with the rippling of flesh. As if there's something below the surface moving around the skin, reshaping it, reforming it, molding it into its own mask of mindless fury.

Her bones absorb a series of winter chills.

"You little cunt," he says, anger reducing his voice to a gruff grunt. "I oughta blow yer fuckin' brains out for that."

She pushes herself across the pavement, kicking her feet. She's able to put a couple yards between them, though it's not enough. The next town over wouldn't be far enough away from this monster. As she kicks, he lumbers toward her, his face moving, writhing like a thousand worms partying beneath the wet soil after a good rain.

"Where do you think you're going, huh?"

Ellie thought the kick in the nuts would have, at least, caused him to stop or slow him down some. But no. It's like she didn't kick him at all.

"You assault an officer of the law and you think I'm just going to let you run away?" He throws his head back and cackles. "Good Lordy, you're an interesting one."

"Back up! Stay the fuck away from me!"

"You know, girl. You're starting to get my Irish up." His massive boots tramp forward and close the gap between them, and she continues to pedal herself away, kicking her feet like she's swimming across the concrete, floundering like a land-stuck fish inching its way back to its watery domain. "Stay put now," he demands.

"Fuck your face!"

He snarls, a bestial sound that emanates from the bottom of his throat, a noise that Ellie will debate later whether or not the sound was human. In any case, it gets her moving even faster. Then Foley pounces, a cat-like leap, and grabs her ankles, trying to pull her back toward him. She kicks her legs furiously, trying to shed his grip. But it's no use. His fingers sink so far into her muscles that the pain almost numbs her.

She screams out.

Then she screams again when his face starts to change, when the slits in his face open, and little insect-like appendages poke through the fleshy cavities, wiggling in the air, making themselves known to this new, strange habitat.

That scream almost breaks her throat.

He's on the porch with Marissa. She's smoking a cigarette. He's drinking from a cold bottle of water Josh offered him. The kid's inside with Skelly, who remains on the couch strumming away on the guitar, the delightful tunes carrying their way through the walls.

Mitch looks out across the gray neighborhood. Still no visible life to assure him they're not alone in this place. It's weird, but everything's been weird here. He fights the incredible urge to start knocking on every damn door until Kya answers. But he promised Josh he wouldn't do that because the kid said they'd look for Kya together, as a group. And that they needed to stay together because they were outnumbered here.

*Outnumbered.*

Mitch doesn't like the sound of that.

"So," he says to Marissa, who continues to puff away on her smoke. "You're looking for your sister Josh says?"

"That's right."

"Been here two weeks and you haven't seen her?"

"Nope." She seems more interested in her thoughts than a conversation, but he can't help himself. He needs to know more about the town, and since Skelly seems a bit whacked out of his mind, and the kid is—well, a kid—he looks at Marissa as the only other adult he can talk to.

"Can I ask how she went missing?" Mitch feels a bit bad for prying, but maybe hearing the story will provide some answers. Something they can use to help find their loved ones. It's a Hail Mary but until this bizarre sky passes and the town returns to normal again (both Josh and Marissa agree it will), there's not much else to do but talk.

"You're asking a lot of questions there, newcomer," she says, finally looking him in the eye. She leans against the porch post and smokes.

"Sorry. Just figure it might help to know how we all got here. I told you guys about Kya, just thought it'd be cool to know your story."

She studies him. When she realizes that he's acting genuine, she flicks her cigarette on the front lawn and straightens up. "Her name's Rosetta."

"Rosetta," Mitch says. "Nice name."

"She was out on the east coast following around some hardcore band. Going to shows in various small towns. Helping them with promotion and selling T-shirts at their merch stand. You know," she says, like Mitch should know these things. He gets the picture and nods along. "She designed most of the logos and T-shirts herself, printed them up and everything. She was talented that way. Always wanted to be a fashion designer. Anyway, the band was playing some VFW in Virginia Beach and then that was it—no more contact with her, the band. No more posts to her Instagram account or the band's, which she used to update at least twice a day, and post about a bajillion stories there. She was one of those big social media types, but when you're nineteen and grew up on the shit, I guess that's pretty normal." She rubs her nose and looks down as if the story is making her admit things she doesn't want to. Mitch considers making her stop, telling her 'that's enough' and 'please don't continue if this is upsetting you,' but he doesn't. The beast of curiosity has sunk its claws into him. "Anyway, she went missing that night after the show."

"What about the band?"

"Two of them were found dead on the beach, underneath the boardwalk. Died of heroin overdoses, the needles still stuck in their arms. Rosetta never fucked with drugs, she didn't even smoke cigarettes, so I knew she couldn't have been a part of that. And those two deaths never added up to me, even though the cops were pretty satisfied with the thing, a true 'open and shut case' they called it. I thought that was just a term they used in T.V. shows, but it turns out they really say that shit, cops.

"Anyway, they never found Rosetta, or the two other remaining members of the band. Found their van and all their equipment, but no bodies. The three were missing persons. That was a year and a half ago. Then…I got a text about three weeks ago. Of Rosetta. Standing in front of a clock tower." She motions with the crown of her head toward the center of town, where the towering structure sits like some temple of worship. "Next thing you know, I'm on a plane from Tempe to Richmond. My parents didn't want me to come— said to let the past die, which, I thought was a shitty thing to say, you know? Let the past die? Fuck's that?" She shakes her head like she's just swallowed a mouthful of mushy vegetables, the texture disagreeing with her throat. "We fought a lot over that text message. How they could say it was a mistake, that there must be some mix-up, and that they knew in their hearts that Rosetta was gone forever…I'll never know." Her eyes find Mitch's. "I know she's alive and that she's here, and I will find her. After all, it's kind of my fault."

"How so?"

She shrugs. "My sister is ten years younger than me. When I was her age, all I listened to was hardcore music and was really into the 'scene.' My tastes became her tastes. She never would have found that band, got in touch with them, become their number one fan without me introducing her to the music." Marissa sniffles, and Mitch watches a crystalline sparkle appear in both eyes. "It's my fault she's gone."

Mitch shakes his head. "Not your fault at all. Can't think like that."

"It's weird when you think about choice and the past. Isn't it?"

Mitch feels this in every fiber of his being. "Yes, it is."

"Imagine yourself doing one small thing differently, and then watch your whole future change. Choice...is a motherfucker, you know."

"Yeah, I know."

Before Mitch can think about his choices, his missteps and mistakes, situations he wishes he could get do-overs on, a scream rips across the town, and as soon as he hears it, his senses are jolted alive as if they were previously dormant and suddenly zapped back into existence.

"Ellie?" He goes to the porch railing and tries to see his way into town, but too many houses block a clear view. He can only make out some of the back alley behind the outer layer of shoppes. "Shit."

"You recognize that scream, stranger?" Marissa asks him, her voice unsteady.

"Sounded like Ellie—my friend. The one I came here with, looking for her daughter too."

"Well," she says, "I don't think we want to be anywhere near her judging from that shriek. I think we should—"

"Fuck it," Mitch says as he puts his hands on the railing and hops over, clearing the bushes on the other side.

"Hey! Wait!" Marissa calls after him, but he doesn't wait.

He sprints through the residential district, all the way back to the center of Lacuna's Point.

Ellie kicks and kicks, but the angry cop does not retreat. It keeps him at bay, but she realizes this distance is temporary. She's handcuffed, he's a cop, the stronger of the two of them, and he has weapons at his disposal—resistance is just delaying the inevitable. And probably making things worse on herself. Because he's being "nice" now, and he's warning her that things are about to get "nasty."

"Real nasty," he repeats, struggling to corral her.

When she doesn't listen, he lets go of her legs, allowing them to fall back on the concrete. Then, he lifts a boot and brings it down on her left ankle. Hard. There's a *crunch* and an incredible injection of pain, and immediately she thinks the bone's broken, cracked in half. Pain zips up her leg, into her hip, and the aftermath of the agonizing explosion is filled with a tingly numbness that strengthens with the passing moments.

She shrieks again, both hands collapsing on the boot's point of impact. "MotherFUCKER!" she screams between short sucks of wind and throat-tearing grunts.

"Shit, girl," Foley says, backing up, distancing himself from the violent result. "Didn't mean to do that, but you made me."

"Fuck you, you fucking pig!"

"Now that's not nice, not nice one bit." She can't believe there's a trace of humor in his voice, not after he's just ruined her ankle in such a savage manner. As if he's somewhat proud of the act itself. A job well done. "You don't stop fuckin' around, things might get a lot worse for you. Just a friendly warning. I don't want to have to—"

*"Hey!"*

Ellie turns toward the new voice and sees Mitch across the street, emerging from an alley between two shoppes. Two shadows materialize from the darkness behind him, one small, one about Ellie's height. She sees the small shadow is just a kid, no older than thirteen or fourteen. The other is a young woman, maybe a little older than Dawn should be now. But it's not Dawn, and her heart rises and drops all at once.

Mitch looks worn from his journey over here, out of breath and struggling to catch it again. "What the hell is this?" he asks, braving the distance between them and crossing the street.

In a quick, robotic response, the cop goes for his gun. Doesn't pull it, but his right hand is stationed on the cool metal grip, ready to free the beast if the situation calls for it, and Ellie sees that inhuman glare in the man's eyes that makes her think the situation will call for it whether it actually does or not. There's a murderous quality to his eyes that wasn't there a moment ago. A temper better suited for a bloodthirsty mercenary than a public servant. He trains his vision on the approaching man, staring, lips quivering with anger.

"Stop right there, boy," the cop says, holding out one hand, the other still gripping the gun.

Ellie squints, faces Mitch, and pleads with her eyes. Pleads for him to walk away. Not that she doesn't want help—she absolutely does—but because she doesn't want to see Mitch hurt for intervening.

"What happened here?" Mitch asks.

"You friends with this woman?" The cop freezes in that pose, one hand pressed against an invisible wall.

"Yeah, she's with me," Mitch says. "You saw us together before the clock tower did its thing. What are you doing to her?"

"I'm not *doing* anything to her. She broke into Miss Danielle's art gallery and started destroying private property. Probably would have stolen a few things had I not intervened."

"Officer," Mitch says, putting his hands up to show he doesn't want anything bad to happen here, no mistakes of any kind. "I implore you to look around."

The cop doesn't take his eyes off him. "Boy, I will do no such thing. I suggest you back away, slowly, and let me do my goddamn job." He winces. "Ah, there you go, making me use blasphemous swear words again."

"Sir," Mitch says, his brow lifting with concern. "Please. There is something mighty wrong happening here, and we could really use your help."

The cop growls.

And then Mitch's expression suddenly changes. "What's...what's with your face, officer? You alright?"

"My face?" The cop shakes his head. "What in God's name you blathering on about, boy?"

Mitch shrinks back, clearly not wanting to be the bearer of bad news.

"Mitch, he's..." Ellie says, scooting farther away, putting a few more feet between them, dragging her busted ankle along. If it's not broken, it's damn close. "There's something wrong with him."

"That's it," Foley says, unleashing his weapon. He points it directly at Mitch's chest. "I've had enough of this nonsense. Sir," he says to Mitch, aiming true. "Put your hands on your head and get down on the ground."

Mitch doesn't move.

"Oh fuck," Ellie says, closing her eyes, waiting for the moment to pass, wishing she could speed through time so she didn't have to watch the following situation unfold.

"What'd I do, officer?" Mitch asks, holding out his hands, not putting them on his head like the cop demanded. "I literally just asked a question."

"You're meddling and obstructing justice."

"That's such bullshit and you know it."

"Hey! Did I stutter, asshole? I said hands on your head, get on the ground. *Now*. I ain't fucking around here today."

Mitch's eyes flick over to Ellie, and she feels hers fill with tears, the well within overflowing again.

Reluctantly, Mitch does what he's told. Biting his lower lip, he puts his hands on his head and kneels.

"Good boy," Foley says, creeping toward him, gun still drawn.

Mitch can hardly look at him.

Ellie sneaks back, dragging her foot, not wanting to add any additional pressure.

*"Psst,"* she hears from somewhere close. *"Psst, over here."*

Ellie turns her head toward the noise, sees two familiar faces staring back at her, both with great lines of worry etched in their pale expressions.

The Campbells.

"Can you get to us?" Sue asks, waving her on, mindful that the cop is only about fifteen, twenty yards away and could easily hear her in the town's spell of dead silence.

"I think so," Ellie says back, quietly. She takes one last look at Mitch, debating whether she should stay and help him—though, what could she really do except get both of them arrested or killed or both—and apologizes with a soft stare that reaches him. He doesn't react, and she assumes that's because he doesn't want to tip off the cop who's too busy fiddling with his cuffs to notice her great escape in progress.

Speaking of cuffs, the ones around Ellie's wrist make it hard to scoot backward. She manages though, and, impressively, does so without making too much noise. She gets to the space where the Campbells are parked, between a soup kitchen and a used record store, and they take her in, help her to her feet and down the alleyway. Pain shoots up her leg and nests in her hip but she ignores it, does her best to, and concentrates on her freedom, being away from the psychotic cop and his fucked-up face.

*What were those things? Those...worms?*

She doesn't want to know. Lacuna's Point has left her with that walk-through-spider-webs sensation that's clinging to every inch of her, and she thinks she'll never be clean of this feeling even after a thousand showers and rigorous body scrubbing.

This place will always cling to her.

It's inside her now. Working its magic. The dark kind.

The kind that hates.

# CHAPTER NINE

The cell stinks like rotten meat and animal piss, and Mitch can't think of a worse combination to sit in. A candle sits on the desk outside the cell, lit, the flame wavering, sending tendrils of black smoke toward the ceiling. Shadows cover the walls, the places the lone light source does not reach. Subdued daylight provides a visibility boost, but not much.

"What's with the lights?" he asks the cop, who has finished putting him inside the holding cell and has now turned toward the front door. "Forget to pay the electric?"

The cop half-turns, speaks from the side of his mouth. "We save electricity on Sundays. It's a time for quiet and personal reflection." A wicked smile. " 'Cept football—get that on the battery radio."

Everything about the man's claim seems like a lie, but Mitch doesn't want to push him too far. He's obviously unstable—arresting Mitch for doing absolutely nothing and leaving Ellie (who looked pretty guilty of the accusation) to go free pretty much proves it, among other clues—and he's carrying a loaded weapon. It doesn't take much for Mitch to realize that he needs to play it cool if he wants to see the sun come up tomorrow.

The cop turns all the way around now, and Mitch finally gets a decent, up-close look at his face, the deep scratches trenched in his flesh. The activity that was once there—that *squirming*—is no longer visible, but Mitch knows that whatever was there is still present, living beneath the surface, waiting for the right opportunity to reveal itself once again. "You know, you were pretty quiet on our way over here. Now that there's some bars between us, you're getting all mouthy again. Bars are only temporary, son. And I got the key."

"And you got the gun," Mitch says, as if the man needs a reminder.

The cop throws a glance at his holster. "That's right, hoss. I got the gun."

"You ever shoot a man?"

His eyes slim, his tongue pushing the question's bitter taste along his inner cheek. "What's it to you? Think I'll shoot you?"

"You were pretty quick out there to unleash that demon. Just wondering if you ever pulled the trigger before."

A big boot forward and the cop leans toward the cell. "I don't have to answer to you." He looks him over. "Or anyone like you."

"Fuck's that supposed to mean?" Mitch asks with an incredulous laugh.

Lines of humorous amusement carve a path across his face, merging with the deep lacerations. "Criminals. What'd you think I meant?"

Mitch's eyes slim because he knows exactly what he meant, and the cop does too, even if he remains cryptic. "Still like to know what I'm being accused of, *sir*. I don't believe you've told me or read me my rights. Isn't that against the law?"

"Oh, you a lawyer now?" Foley waits for an answer, even cups his hand over his ear and leans in a little. "No? Didn't think so. Why don't you shut the fuck up then and think about what you *did* do. You meddled with police business, and now I gotta go back out and find that little thief, that little fucking *cunt thief* and bring her in."

"Weird you let her go just so you can arrest an innocent Black man. How's that work?"

"You..." At this, the jelly in the man's cheeks trembles. "You shut the fuck up with that shit. You know that's not what this is about. You *know it.*"

"Oh fuck off, man. You're delusional."

"I'm going out there. To find that woman, bring her back, and the both of you are spending a night in the slammer. Until the mayor gets in tomorrow, when he can sort this mess out. This...*interloper* bullshit."

"You do that, man. I hope you find her. I'll be right here in case you need me."

"You think about your life, boy. You *think* about it."

"Will do."

Foley leaves the room, slamming the door on his way out.

"Racist asshole," Mitch mutters, and then debates whether he wants to sit down or spend the night standing. He figures standing might be the best option. The floor is coated with some sticky residue, its origin unknown, and so is the bench.

They drive for about three minutes in silence, and then Ellie can't take it anymore. "What is this place? And no more bullshit—I swear to God, just tell me." She hates the fear in her voice, that out-of-breath pressure that feels like a belt strapped around her vocal cords.

Keith and Sue look at each other once again, the stare lingering, and Ellie wants to slam their heads together like two coconuts.

"Stop that," she says. "Stop looking at each other like you don't know whether or not I can handle the truth—I can. I can handle it. I've seen..." She hangs her head, the migraine returning, kicking against her skull like a horse taking its rage out on a barn door. "I've seen the weirdest *shit* here, and I just want to know. The truth."

"The truth," Sue says, collecting her thoughts, scratching her cheek, "is we don't really know what this place is."

Not the answer she wants. Not good enough. The Campbells know something, something they aren't telling her. "Don't lie to me."

"Honest," Keith chimes in. "We've been looking for our son for six months—*six* months—and we haven't found a single clue. Only thing that's here are people, and they are...well, you've seen them. They're strange."

"Really strange. Like, you wouldn't believe how strange they are."

"What about the clock tower?" Ellie asks. "The thing that happened with the bell and the light? What the hell was that? What did it...*do* to this place?"

At this, Keith balks, but Sue is there for him. "It happens when they introduce someone new to the..." She swallows what looks like a grape. "...to the town. We don't know why. The people here aren't very talkative or willing to say much about what goes on here."

That invisible belt tightens around Ellie's throat.

"We're sleeping," Keith adds, and this really throws Ellie off. The sheer lunacy of this statement causes her neck to spasm.

"What?" she asks in a breathless whisper. "What the hell does that mean?"

"I think," Sue says, "what my husband is trying to say is...that it feels like we're dreaming."

But Keith is adamant, sticking to his claim. "No, no, hon. You're wrong. This…this is a dream. You know it is. Everything that happens inside the…*this*," he says, pointing up at the ceiling, though Ellie knows he means the sky, "is a goddamn illusion. We've talked about this a dozen times and—"

"I'm trying not to freak the woman out," Sue snaps back, whispering as if Ellie can't hear her from an arm's length away.

Their bickering isn't helping Ellie forget about the pain in her ankle. She looks down and sees the swollen skin has ballooned to twice its usual size.

*Definitely broken,* she thinks.

"Please," Ellie says, "I don't understand. None of this is making any goddamn sense, and I just want my daughter and I just want to go home. Will you help me?" she asks, even though it's clear they can't help themselves.

No one can.

They're lost. Here. Now. They'll never see the real world again.

*Just like Dawn.*

"What do we do?" Keith asks, completely ignoring Ellie's begging. Honestly, she can't blame them.

"Just keep driving," Sue says, nodding up ahead. "We should show her. She should know the truth."

"Where are we going?" Ellie asks, feeling drowsy, drained, like someone stuck tubes into her veins and is draining her vitality bit by fucking bit. She tries to shift, taking pressure off her hands, which are still cuffed behind her back. The metal has rubbed her wrists raw, and the burn intensifies with the movement. "Where are you taking me?"

"We're going to show you something, dear," Sue says. She speaks to her husband next. "Turn left here."

"Are we going somewhere…safe?"

A slight hesitation. "Not exactly."

"Then where?"

At this, Sue turns to her, and there is pure fear entrenched in her, a deep-seated terror that has stolen the woman's soul and refuses to let go. "Just promise me that when we get there," she says, "you won't scream too loud. It doesn't like the noise."

The derelict stationhouse's walls are covered in knuckle-sized holes and growthy filth, dark patches that could be mold—is probably mold—and Mitch wonders how he'll survive five minutes without contracting some sort of deadly disease. He paces the small cell which is about the size of the master bathroom back home, counting the seconds until he can get the hell out of there—not that he knows when that'll be exactly, but he figures it won't take the cop long to track down Ellie and haul her in, especially considering the condition of her leg. Even from his vantage point, he saw how swollen the area was. How she dragged it behind her as she was crawling away from Foley.

His mind gravitates toward the guy, that prick and his fucked-up face. He didn't have those lacerations before the ringing of the bell, and whatever had gotten hold of him had gotten some good licks in, that's for sure.

Mitch stews in the cell for about an hour before he hears footsteps outside. Light footsteps, footsteps that definitely do not want to be overheard. Just outside the door. The stationhouse is one giant room, and the holding cells are across the way from the front door, but he can still hear the pattering, the scraping of rubber hitting the concrete stoop, faint but there. Too timid to belong to Foley, so that must mean—

"Mitch?" he hears a small voice call his name, and his heart blooms with gratitude.

"Yes, I'm here!" He goes and grabs the bars, puts his mouth between them as he focuses on the door where his rescue will bust through at any moment. "Josh?"

"Yeah, it's me! Are you…" A pause. A scared pause, and the longer the silence drags, the more Mitch begins to worry. "Alone?"

"Yeah, he's gone. The cop. He went to get my friend. Did you see her?"

The door squeaks open and Josh hurries inside. "She got picked up."

"Shit. By him?"

Josh shakes his head, then holds open the door before it can close. Marissa enters next, pushing back her hood as soon as she crosses the threshold. The last one to appear is Skelly, and the old man limps his way into the room, his trusty guitar strapped to his back. He admires the cell as if he's been there before, many times, and he's just looking back on some fond memories.

*Nothing fond about this shithole,* Mitch thinks.

"No," Josh says. "She was taken by that couple from New York."

"Shit. The Campbells?"

"That's them."

He's glad she's out of the cop's clutches, at least for now, but how much better she is in the hands of those two, he can't say.

"Got any idea where we can find the key to spring you loose?" Josh asks.

"I think that racist piece of garbage took the key with him."

"Well, that sucks."

"You ain't kidding."

"He'll be looking for your friend for a while, so he won't be back anytime soon." Josh grabs his chin. "We can try to pick the lock?"

"You ever pick a lock?" Mitch asks.

"I have," Marissa says. She stands over the huge desk in the corner of the room, rummaging through the effects scattered across the top. Grabbing a box the size of a pack of cigarettes and tearing into it, she turns to them with a smile.

She digs out a silvery object and discards the rest, tossing them aside. The contents scatter across the floor. When she's ready, she reveals a paper clip. As she walks over to the cell, she bends and twists the thin wire to her exact specifications.

Mitch rolls his eyes. "I don't think that works in real life. Movies, maybe. But not in—"

She sticks the clip into the back of the padlock and in two attempts, the lock releases with a sweet cracking sound Mitch thought he'd never hear.

"Well, I'll be damned," he says, unable to conceal his amusement.

"Yes," Marissa says with a wink, "you probably will be." She turns to the other two. "We all will be if we don't get the hell out of here."

Mitch glances over at Josh. "You got a plan, big guy?"

Josh slumps his shoulders. "We need to lie low. Keep out of Foley's sight. That guy's bad news, man. No matter what version of the town we're in, he's a guy we want to avoid, whatever the cost."

"Yeah, no kidding," Mitch says, moving toward one of the windows. It's hard to see through the layers of dust and grime coating the glass, so he smears away some of it with his palm, but it does nothing except smudge it up. "Is there a safe place we can get to until, you know, this whole thing blows over?"

Marissa shrugs. "Boardwalk?"

"We're not going to the boardwalk," Josh says. "You know what happens at the boardwalk."

"What happens at the boardwalk?" Mitch asks.

"Nothing good," Josh says. "I'll just say, you'll never want to eat crab legs again."

Mitch has no clue what that means, but he doesn't like crab legs anyway, so he lets it go. "Well, where to then?"

Before anyone can answer, Skelly thrusts his head forward as if someone has sucker-punched his pecker. He holds his lower stomach, gripping himself so tightly the veins on his scrawny arms stand out. The guitar flips over, falls to the ground beside him with a hollow thud, the strings drawing out deep, discordant sounds, which feels like the perfect score for the unexpected chain of events. Skelly sheds the guitar before it has a chance to wrap around his neck, slipping off the nylon accessory with a simple shoulder shrug. Then he sinks to his knees, grasping his belly as he groans from whatever intense agony is being driven through him.

"Skelly!" Josh shouts, backing away.

Mitch's instinct is to rush forward, but Marissa stops him.

"Don't touch him," she says. "Just don't."

Mitch tries to make his way around her, but she puts her hands on his shirt, grabs fistfuls of the fabric. "He's—"

"I know, I know. We can't help him."

Josh stamps his foot on the floor. "No, not Skelly!"

"It's just a dream, Josh!" Marissa says. "Remember, this isn't real." And then: "Not completely."

But it doesn't feel like a dream. Not even close to one. It feels real as all hell, and Mitch Green wants nothing to do with what's about to take place. He can sense that much.

"What's happening to him?" Mitch asks, dreading the answer.

She looks at him sharply, and Skelly continues to deal with the internal torment, holding himself, the cords in his neck standing out like a network of elevator cables, and letting a high-pitched wail escape past his lips, which surprises Mitch because the man's voice had been deep and dark, giving no inclination that he could produce such a sound.

"He's changing," Marissa says.

*Changing?*

"Into what?"

Marissa gulps. "Something that definitely shouldn't fucking exist. Not even in dreams."

The Campbells' SUV rips down the stretch of road, dense forests flanking each side. Ellie stares off into them, wondering what kind of evil lies dormant there, waiting to make its move, to let itself be known. To peel back the layers of shadows and lies, reveal itself to the town of Lacuna's Point.

She looks over her shoulder—the town now gone from their view—and ponders the nature of Lacuna's Point, what it is exactly. She comes up empty on answers, and she believes it's a question that will go unanswered, even if she makes it through this. At its core, the place is evil, and she can feel that evil penetrating every square inch of the region. Even now, on the road out, she can sense it lurking there, hidden behind the gray skies and towering pines, a thing that's just sitting there, watching, waiting, reveling in all the terrible events that have unfolded and will unfold, then, now, and forever.

"Are we there yet?" Ellie asks, the sound of her voice reminding her of Dawn when they used to take long trips. Like the time they drove to Disney World, straight through, no stops save for running into a welcome center to use the toilet.

"Almost," Keith confirms. "But...just don't get too excited."

She hates the sound of that, but the prospect of answers, some form of them, excites her. Fills her with some sense of progress toward the truth, like when the photo unexpectedly showed up on her phone. She feels like she's on the right path again.

"I'm not feeling so hot," she admits, looking down at her busted ankle. The bruise is already shining through the skin, a swollen purple mark exactly where the asshole cop brought his boot down. A feverish fog envelops her, leaving her hot and shaky and cool all at the same time.

"We call it *The Pull*," Sue Campbell says plainly. "The farther you get from Lacuna's Point, the sicker it makes you. The Pull, you know—because that's sorta what it does—pulls you back."

A raging headache now, all-encompassing, like tiny hammers taking shots across her cranium, working behind the temples, her eyes, behind her ears. A sharp spike penetrates her cerebral cortex, the core of her thoughts, skewering her ideas, hopes and dreams. Next comes the fire, a thousand matches scraping against the inner lining of her scalp, tiny combustions spreading from hair follicle to hair follicle. Burning. Raging. Invisible destructions making their way.

"I feel like I'm going to puke," she says, hunching over.

"Well, feel free to unload back there," Keith says humorously. "Won't matter in about ten minutes anyway."

At this, Sue's lips break with a brief chuckle. She puts a hand on her husband's shoulder in that *oh-you're-so-funny-darling* way.

"What are..." Words hurt coming up, and opening her mouth feels like she's aiding the sick filth bottled in her throat. "Whatdoyoumean?" She burps. *Oh shit.* "Ohfuck."

Then she hurls, unloading chunky bile and other odorous fluids onto the Campbells' backseat. Some of the splatter hits the floormats.

"Whoa!" Sue says, peeking over her shoulder and checking the yellowish-vanilla explosion that sprayed past Ellie's lips. "That was...not as impressive as I thought it would be. I puked much more my first time."

*"Wha's happening?"* Ellie asks, the acidic flavor burning her throat, her tongue.

"Better to keep quiet from here on out. Just go with it, dear." Sue rubs her shoulder, and although it's meant to soothe, she hates the way the woman's touch feels, and she shrugs her off. "My, my. Frisky, aren't we?"

Ellie vomits again, less than before. Her stomach is empty, and all that comes out is a long string of drool-like bile.

"You'll get used to it. After six months, we've built up a tolerance to The Pull. Hell, we made it all the way to Maryland without puking once. Though, we did get a little queasy at the rest stop. Right, hon?"

"That's right, darling," Keith confirms.

"Are we..." Sue squints at the road past the windshield. "Goodness, are we here?"

Keith slows down. "I think this might be it." His tone is confident but fragile—like he knows what he's doing, has done it before, maybe too much. He parks the SUV in the middle of the road. "Get out," he tells no one, everyone.

Sue leaves the safety of the vehicle first, realizes Ellie isn't leaving at all, that she's too lethargic and ill to stand. She opens the door and extends her hand, but Ellie barely recognizes the help that's been offered. "Come on, princess," the woman says. "I got you."

Ellie's reluctant to touch her, "the spins" being the main contributing factor, but also—she doesn't trust the bitch. Not a bit, not now, not when she's feeling so horrible, and not when Sue Campbell is looking fine and ordinary.

"Come on," Sue says, her fingers dancing in a wave. "Trust me."

Ellie, despite her reluctance, gives the woman her hand and allows Sue to pull her out of the car. Making sure Ellie is safe indeed, Sue wraps her arms around her body and sets her on her feet as if she's some human-sized bowling pin. Then, Sue looks ahead to where her husband is standing in the middle of the road, about forty feet from the SUV's front bumper.

"Should be about here, I gather," Keith says, and then feels the air with one hand the same way he would seeking the light switch in a dark room.

"Come on, hon," Sue says, assisting Ellie toward Keith like she's some feeble old person.

Ellie can't shake the feeling that she's being fed to something, has a quick vision of the world opening up and swallowing her while Sue and Keith stand back and watch with morbid amusement as the world chomps her up in its great cosmic mouth. The vision is fleeting but oh-so-vivid. She can almost feel the teeth on her bones.

Ellie starts to retreat. "No...Idon'twanto."

"*Ssh, ssh, dear,*" Sue whispers in her ear as she stops Ellie from backpedaling, gripping her arm. "It's okay. I won't let it hurt you."

*It?*

Now she starts to panic, her chest building up that familiar fluttering feeling, a butterfly army flapping their wings at once, heading into battle. "No, you can't make—"

And then she loses her stomach again, but this time there's absolutely nothing left, not even the lining of bile. She gags, heaves, but not a drop of acid exits her mouth. A burn rises up her throat but that's the only thing to come of it.

"Help me, dear," Sue tells her husband, and he hustles over to grab Ellie's other side.

"NO," she bleats out, but it's no use—she doesn't have the strength to resist one of them, let alone both.

They help her over to the spot where Keith was standing, that invisible wall he picked out of the nothingness, the ordinary section of nature where the man-made road meets the God-made forest.

"Here you go, dear," Sue says. "You need to see this. It will free you. Your mind."

They let her go and she drops to her knees.

"Look at it," Sue says. "Go on. Look."

Ellie glances up at the road and the forest, the swerve ahead and the clusters of trees to the left and right, the ashen-gray sky above looking like it might drop a dusting of snow on them at any given moment. "What am I looking for?" she asks, and then her eyes go heavy, too heavy, like someone has stitched the skin around her eyes and is pulling on the threads.

*Endless black stretches across her vision and the obsidian depths become a wall of eyes, open eyes staring at who? Staring at her, looking, not at her, through her, into her mind*

—and then she opens her peepers, stares down the road, that twisting walk of cracked blacktop, the forests that eat it, and she wants to keep looking, staying conscious, but her eyes are heavy, oh-so-heavy, and she has to close them, has to, promises it's just for a second, just one sweet second, just to rest, just to get some relief, some temporary release from the world and everything in it, a break from the problems, the issues, the past, her life, the clusterfuck it's been the past three years, and then she opens her eyes again and it's—

*nothing but black, a curtain that goes on forever, reaches through time and pulls her through, eyes floating in the abyss, blinking orbs, a billion little seers, ocular devices from time itself, looking, peeking, penetrating, absorbing her past, her future, everything time holds near and dear, and she's falling into it now, that dark, that endless night, the eyes that blink staring and eating and twitching in the ink*

—hell, that place is pure hell, wherever it is, and she hates the way it makes her feel, like every time she has a look into that dark place, this netherworld, this place between places, it's like she brings a piece of it back with her, a darkness that her eyes drink in, absorb, and that she leaves a little piece of herself in there, and she hates that, *hates* it, and suddenly she wants to die, wants this to end, wants this suffering, this painful loss, this aching that's been infecting her for the last three years to just fucking end already, and if she had a gun or a knife she'd use it, kill herself without giving it a second thought because she'll never see Dawn again, never see her face, feel her touch, and it's over that life, the one she had, her life as a mother, and she never wants to go back to that distant reality, that cold place at home, that empty nest, empty for all the wrong reasons and she can't—

*it's watching her, this wall, this beast, this great big endless black meadow with eyes that see, see far beyond, and she thinks that even if she can escape this place (can she? will she? she doesn't think so), even if she manages to get away, she never will because those eyes will follow her, watch her from all angles, hover over this great beyond that lingers over her world, her universe, her reality, and nothing will ever be the same because she knows what exists there now, the place between places, the darkness between worlds, between distant realities and it's a cold feeling, an endless feeling, a feeling that sinks into the marrow of her bones and sucks, drains, depletes everything, slowly and quickly all at once, leaving her with nothing, nothing, not a thing and she can't—*

—keep her goddamn eyes open, because they're so heavy and she—

"Get her out," Keith says, and suddenly there are two arms under hers, pulling her away, dragging her backward, away from the invisible barrier, away from that impossible truth.

Within thirty seconds, she's sitting in the backseat of the SUV, her face a wet mask of tears, and though she feels no sadness, no real feelings whatsoever, she can't stop crying.

"Did you see it?" Sue asks.

She doesn't move. Can't.

"She saw it," Keith says, nodding, examining her tears.

"Good," Sue says, and she can't help but crack a faint smile. "Then now she knows she can never leave this place."

# CHAPTER TEN

Officer Elroy Foley has an ache in his chest as he storms down the sidewalk, wondering how long on God's Green Earth he has left before the big one comes along and sweeps him off his mortal feet, when that ache becomes a full-blown bite that sends him to the high heavens and places him in front of those pearly gates. Not soon, he hopes, not when he has so many things left to accomplish, tasks given to him by the sole man who makes Lacuna's Point exactly what it is today—Heaven on Earth. A premium slice of American pie.

Foley scans the empty streets, sees a newspaper page blowing in the soft, wintery winds that carry with it a biting frost. Whatever dirt-burger was uncaring enough to litter, well, Elroy Foley sure hopes he never runs into the shitkicker, no sir, because if he does, he'll teach the fucker a lesson or two. Or three.

He can't see any movement down the street, so he turns to the shoppes and peers through each darkened glass, hoping to catch a glimmer of motion. Something, the slightest movement, the faintest signal of life inside. He knows the woman is here, somewhere, hiding, probably crying and regretting the crimes she *obviously* committed. Breaking and entering, destruction of public property— naughty little things that interlopers do until they are converted to the traditional ways of Lacuna's Point. Until they start acting civilized, shedding their animalistic instincts and abiding by the laws set forth by the good ol' Mayor.

*If it were up to me,* Foley thinks, *interlopers wouldn't even be allowed. Nope, I'd shoot 'em on sight. This place is perfect just the way it is, and we don't need them always creating havoc.*

Havoc. It happens every year, around this time, just before the greatest Arts Festival known to mankind. But it's the Mayor's wish, and that's what Elroy Foley is here to do—carry out the Mayor's wishes and keep the peace, whatever the cost.

He moves down the sidewalk like he's got a firecracker in his shorts and the only way to stop it from popping off is to find the goddamn woman whose ankle he probably broke. He feels bad for handling that situation so aggressively, so *violently*—but...on the other hand…she was asking for it. All she had to do was comply and the whole thing never would have happened. So, in reality, Elroy Foley doesn't feel *too* bad, not really, not when it wasn't his fault, *not really*, not when the woman could have cooperated, not really at all.

His brain's attuned to any movement that shouldn't be happening, and he catches the slightest motion off to his left. Whipping his entire body around, fast enough to where a less coordinated individual might twist an ankle or rip a tendon, he focuses on the object that zipped into his periphery. But nothing's there. Just the empty road, the gray skies, and the whispering winds that supply his face with cool strokes of air.

He thinks he's hit a dead end when he remembers that he tucked the woman's driver's license in his front pocket. Fishing it out, he makes sure to keep his eyes on the scenery, the town, to make sure there are no other interlopers running amok, creating chaos while Lacuna's Point *(dreams)* rests. Taking his eyes off the town, he scans the woman's information—Ellie Brower, 1416 Winchester Road in Red River, New Jersey. *Hmm*, he thinks, so familiar that name, that information, but he doesn't give it much thought. His brain certainly isn't what it used to be, but that could be said about a lot of aspects of Elroy Foley. *Not what I used to be* is practically his life in a nutshell. He's far from the football star he was in high school and two years of college, his bulky six-pack of abs now covered with a few layers of flab—mostly due to excessive binging on heavy beers and fried foods. One day, he thinks, he'll return to the form of his former self, those glory years where he could walk into any bar and end up going to bed with any single chick (married ones too) that he set his good looks on. At least, that's the way he remembers it, but then again, the memory isn't what it used to be. He doesn't think about it much, doesn't think about the pockets missing from his past, certain omissions of memory that he can't recall, even when he tries really hard. Most of the time when he tries to access his memories, severe headaches stampede him, forcing him to abandon his pursuit to remember the chain of events that made him *him*. The events that led him to Lacuna's Point.

But he doesn't want to think about that now, and he wonders what the Mayor would say if he caught him daydreaming again, living inside the world his head has built rather than the outside world the Mayor has. *Thinking (dreaming)* instead of working, carrying out the Mayor's good work, keeping the town in order. Finding interlopers like Ellie Brower and making them understand the importance of toeing the line, walking straight, obeying the laws set forth by the lone lawmaker—The Mayor.

He's pissed at himself. One, for allowing his mind to stray from the task at hand. Two, for allowing the woman to escape. He thinks it's impossible. How could she disappear like that, on a bum ankle no less? It doesn't add up unless she had help, help from other interlopers. The Mayor has invited a decent amount this year, more than the last few years combined, which, if Elroy's being honest, had him on edge since the beginning of the season when they started to show up. He knew then he was in over his head, and now, now that it's happening, now that they're here and running rampant through the streets, taking refuge in the residential area like cockroaches behind a stove in a city apartment, he feels deep beneath the surface of his capabilities.

Frustrated, he stomps his foot on the freshly-paved street top and faces the clock tower standing like a totem for the town itself, an idol to gather and worship around. He watches the big hand make its revolutions, and he finds himself unable to guide his eyes elsewhere, completely captivated by the movement of time as a sense of impending annihilation settles into the shallows of his chest. He doesn't know why he feels such a thing, only that something bad will happen and happen soon, and there will be nothing he can do about it. A part of him believes that whatever destruction will come will be the interlopers' fault, in some direct or indirect way, that whatever ruin will come won't be his fault at all. This appointment with the great unknown is happening soon, and he throws his hands up in an *Oh, well, shit happens* motion before finally breaking eye contact with the tower's cyclopean façade. A low, growling thunder sounds across the colorless skies like a dragon waking from centuries of deep slumber and letting the lands know that a storm of fire is on the way. Foley feels the earth's bones shaking beneath his feet.

A storm is undoubtedly approaching.

And whatever climate Lacuna's Point wills forth, Elroy Foley will welcome it with open arms. Because whatever future the Mayor has planned for him is far better than the past he can't remember.

They drive with the windows down, and Ellie smells the rain in the air. A bolt of lightning zigs across the silver dome overhead, pressing down on the horizon. She stares down the passing trees, wishing she was somewhere else, somewhere beyond the towering pines, somewhere beyond this place that can't be real, that feels like a bad dream, a nightmare her brain refuses to wake from. The farther they drive away from that bad place in the middle of the road, the better she feels. Nausea abates, crawling back into the filthy sewers of her gut from whence it came. A few minutes later, she feels like she can breathe again without the risk of dry heaving.

"I know that was hard on you, sweetheart," Sue says, half-turning, peering into the backseat with her left eye only. Her husband is concentrating on the road ahead. They pass a sign that says Lacuna's Point is only two miles away. "It was hard on us the first time."

"I want to go home," Ellie says, and she means it, truly means it, even if it's without her daughter. "I just want to go home. Can you take me home? Please? I'll pay you, I'll…give you money, all the money I have, just take me…back, take me home. Please?"

The Campbells behold each other. Keith grimaces, then says, "She'll be fine."

"I feel so bad for her, though," Sue says, shifting in her seat, staring at Ellie like she's a lost puppy in a cage, beyond filthy and infested with fleas.

Ellie hates her.

"She'll calm down once we get back to the Point," Keith explains. "We'll take her back to the hotel and—"

"No," Ellie mutters, a low sound, her voice practically failing her. "No, don't take me back, don't you dare take me back there."

"Now, now," Sue says, "it'll be good for you. You'll get your bearings right. You'll see. Tomorrow you'll wake up feeling good as new, and the town won't…it won't be like this anymore."

"Pull over," Ellie says, sounding feral, barely recognizing her own tone. "Pull over, right the fuck now."

"I'm afraid we can't," Keith says, and he actually sounds like he feels badly about it. "See, we have a meeting with the Mayor, and you wouldn't believe how much he values punctuality. He's a real stickler for it. Now, he's the only one that can help, and he doesn't see just anybody, so, you know, we can't exactly miss it."

"I don't give a fuck about your goddamn meeting," Ellie says, the words like razor blades, scratching up her throat. "Let me out."

"You're gonna want to sit back and relax, dear," Sue says, her lip twitching now, like a hooked worm squirming, trying to stay alive.

In the distance, Ellie hears the sound. A horrible, wretched sound; the bell as it bangs against metal, a great clang that vibrates through her, thrashing her soul.

"No…" she says, leaning back. "No…make it stop."

"We're losing her."

"Damn it," Keith says, pounding the steering wheel. "Well, hopefully we'll make it back in time."

"She's passing out, Keith."

"Let her. We're almost there anyhow."

Ellie feels the pace of her breathing pick up, her heart hitting her chest like a woodpecker's knock. Sweat forms on her brow and begins its slow descent down the slopes of her face. The world turns a fuzzy gray color, muted, lacking any vibrancy at all, like an old television set on the brink of its eternal demise. She concentrates on staying awake, staying lucid, but the world—the goddamn clock tower—has other plans. Each sound is a hammer against her head, each strike driving deeper down into the dark world, the place below this one, as if she could feel any lower.

"That's good, dear," Sue adds, reaching out, taking her hands. Ellie's too sleepy to take them back, and she feels the pressure of Sue's skin, her cold-corpse touch, squeezing her, breaking her down. "That's good. Shut those peepers. It'll all be over soon. And when you wake up, it will all feel like a dream that never was."

She does as she's instructed and closes her eyes, not because she wants to, but because the world has become all-too heavy and she can no longer bear its tremendous weight.

Ellie slips from her conscious soul and trespasses into a dark, dreamless landscape, filled with ambient transmissions from a world she doesn't want to know.

Mitch hears the gong and his heart springs like a frog from a lily pad. The lasting ring drives deep into his ears, forcing its way into the core of his brain, leaving him temporarily stunned, speechless and dumb. After the moment passes, he waits for the next strike, that hypnotic sound that brings with it the sweet, distant music that replaces something inside of him. It's his fear, he thinks. The sounds of the clock tower submerge his fears, smother his pain and memories, the things that make him incredibly human, and fill in the gaps of his emotions and sensory balances with something else. A hollow something. A *nothing* something.

The second clang hit the airwaves, and his paralysis comes undone. The bell, along with Skelly's painful sobs, gets him moving.

"Do we help him?" asks Mitch as he hustles around to the other side of the stationhouse, where Josh has pinned himself against the wall.

"No," Josh tells him. "You can't, not now."

"Is he sick?"

Josh seems to lob the concept back and forth. "You can say that."

"Well, if he's not sick, then what the fuck is wrong with him?"

Marissa, standing between Skelly and the others, shoots Mitch a sharp glance, one that tells him to lay off. "Just relax. It can't hurt you in here."

"In where?"

"In the dreamworld." She faces Skelly. The man is hunched over, grabbing his belly as if he's got the world's worst case of food poisoning. "They can't physically hurt us here."

One look at Skelly and Mitch begs to fucking differ. "We need to leave, get out of here."

Josh grabs his wrist as Mitch tries to make for the door. "You really don't want to go out there, man. Not now. We wait it out. Here. Until it's over."

"What happens when it's over?"

"We wake up," he says, as if the answer is obvious.

"Then what?"

"Then we find each other. In the town. We meet up."

"Okay," Mitch says, going along with the plan despite the sense it lacks—but he guesses that's what dreams are for. The illogical becomes logical, the insane becomes commonplace, and everything mad makes perfect fucking sense. "We meet up."

"The diner," Josh says. "The waitress—Darla—she isn't one of them, at least I don't think. Maybe she can help."

Marissa wrinkles her face at this statement. "I don't know if I trust that bitch."

"She's the only other person who can help."

Before Josh can explain, Skelly bellows a loud roar of agony and begins ripping at his shirt, tearing the buttons right off their stitches and exposing his smooth, hairless belly and chest. "IT EATS IT EATS IT EATS," he screams. "YOWWWW!"

Mitch gets a good look at the man's stomach and realizes it's pulsing, contracting like there's a heartbeat beyond the small layer of pudge the man has accumulated in the past seventy-something years. Splits have appeared on his flesh, open lines that leak tears of blood. The man shudders as he weeps, unable to bear any more of the internal torment. The cuts show on his face as well—under his eyes, on his cheeks, across his forehead—and Mitch swears he sees something poking through the tiny gaps where his flesh should be. It's like something is stretching the skin, testing the elasticity of human flesh, and Skelly's earthly encasement is not up to the challenge. The more Mitch stares, the more grotesque his appearance becomes. Blood begins to spill from the man's eyes, his mouth, red rivulets that pour from every facial orifice and collect in small puddles on the stationhouse's linoleum floor. The man's eyes bug, the realization of whatever is happening—dream or not—won't end well for him.

"Skelly," Josh says, gulping. "Your face…"

The man replies with another strained grunt, clutching his stomach as if doing so is the only way to prevent his insides from spilling out. The slits in his face widen, exposing more of the sinister qualities beneath, little antennas that pierce the skin, splitting open his face wider now, exposing big gaps of raw, bleeding pink.

Eddy clangs. The subtle music grows louder, less sweet and accessible, darker and foreboding now, the melancholic turn of a simple change in key.

Mitch's veins flood with icy panic; it feels like he's slowly suffocating, unable to catch a complete breath.

Those antennas poke out of the loose skin of Skelly's face, and, next, Mitch sees something else exit the widening slices—claws. *Crab claws* to be specific. Serrated pinchers that break through the skin, snapping and writhing in the air as they seek things to grab hold of, and from the furious behavior exhibited upon its initial introduction to the world, it doesn't look like they are particular as to what they get ahold of.

*As long as it's human,* Mitch thinks.

The small mole crabs the size of a baby's fist begin to spill from the man's face, his stomach, as if a fisherman has dumped a bushel of fresh catch onto the trawler's deck. The old man's skin breaks apart, revealing more red than flesh, and he drops to his knees, screaming and hugging his body all over, the parts that hurt the most, torrents of blood splashing out of him now, slicking the dirty floor with a spreading gory mess. After a moment of enduring the crabs' collective exit from his body, Skelly rolls around the blood-slicked ground like a muddy pig trying to relieve an itchy back. Mitch can't look away, though he wants desperately to release these nightmarish images from his mind, wishing he could hear the soft music again instead, the beautiful sounds offered to his senses, the calming nature of the great toll.

The bell sounds again, sending an electric shock through Mitch's body. He collapses onto the floor, his eyes stuck on the old man, the harsh dealings inside his face and body, and he sees the man's flesh and bone break apart, crack like the earth in a Hollywood earthquake. The top of his head fissures, the sizable split breaking his skull, offering a perfect view into the red, jellied chasm within. A burst of chunky crimson sprays out, splattering against the nearby desk, and the emergence of this stock gore causes Mitch to take a giant step away, pinning his back against the far wall. Strength leaves Mitch's knees and he sinks to his butt, using the wall to guide him. As he does this, Skelly's entire body cracks in half, a vertical split that zigs and zags from the top of his cranium down to the end of his tailbone, a jagged fracture of skin and bone. He lets out one last wet plea before the words are lost in a scarlet gurgle that explodes from his opened throat. Crabs teem out of him, and Mitch can see the colony of crustaceans that were living inside the man this whole time.

Before Mitch can debate the human anatomy and how this revelation makes any sense, how it plays by the rules that his previous reality has set forth, Mitch spots a larger object that's been living inside Skelly. It's a gray, dome-shaped object that looks like a football, and it's rising from the sticky mess that used to be the man's heart. As the object stands, he realizes the gray dome is another crab, a larger crab, maybe the mother of all these smaller ones. Its black marble eyes penetrate Mitch down to his core, and he can't help but think the creature wants to find a new host to lie inside and nest in—and he can't shake the feeling that that person is him.

Mitch nearly screams as the crab steps over the splattered remains that used to be an old guitar player named Skelly and begins to journey across the stationhouse. He tries to, but his naked shout is bottled somewhere at the base of his esophagus. He looks over at Josh and Marissa, both of whom have pinned themselves to the far wall as well, and sees that—despite their previous knowledge and experience of the town and the alternate reality they've found themselves in—they're just as terrified and disgusted as he is. Watching the crab emerge from Skelly's violent demise, Mitch cowers from the new sounds that have been introduced to his ears, the growling and hacking as the birthed things glance around, their obsidian eyes searching. Then...the thing skitters away from them. Toward the only exit. Though the door is closed, it proves to be no barrier, and the force the mother crab utilizes—as it barrels its hemispherical body—is enough to crack the jamb, knock the door off the hinges completely, and free itself from the confines of the police station. Doing so allows bright white light to infiltrate the immediate area, the shine too much for Mitch's eyes to absorb without going blind. The tolling grows louder as he looks away. The music fades to static.

Mitch shields his eyes, but that doesn't stave off the invading brightness.

The shine claims his conscious mind. Oblivion calls, and Mitch Green unwillingly answers on the first ring.

# DAN GETS A VISIT

Dan Brower spots them approaching when he cuts the wheel and starts heading back for the farmhouse. He brings the John Deere from a trundle to a neutral roll as he observes three unmarked cruisers casually making their way down Whitmore Lane, the tires against the gravel road kicking up miniature dust storms. The drivers take slow turns onto the property. He can tell it's the cops immediately because of the tinted windows and the black rims, not to mention the visible light rack through the front windshield, the sunlight reflecting off the glass and beaming back into his eyes.

*Ellie,* he thinks. *This is about her.*

He doesn't want to admit she's dead, that she's finally drunk herself over the edge. When Maura called him a couple of weeks back on the anniversary of Dawn's disappearance, she had said her sister was in rough shape and that Dan should reach out to her, maybe talk her down from whatever ledge she was thinking of hopping off. He was hesitant at first, but when he got the text, the I NEED HELP message, he did the good-ex thing and called her the second he got it, which, according to the message's metadata, was a day after she sent it, probably due to the service on the farm being spotty at best. The callback went straight to voicemail and he hadn't heard from her, and so he thought nothing of it—it wasn't the first time he received cryptic messages from her, but it had been some time since the last one. He supposed he should have done something, like tried to call again, but he never got around to it, never even gave the message much thought actually until now, until he sees the cops pulling down the dirt drive, and wonders why that is exactly. He's been busy lately for sure, with Janice being pregnant and taking care of the daily chores, her father's farmhouse, the one he left to them before passing away last summer. He supposes the busy schedule is to blame, but he's also shocked for not remembering to call Ellie back, especially considering the tone of her initial text. As much as his previous marriage pains him to think about, he's not calloused and would never intentionally ignore anyone in need—especially someone he once loved.

Dan hops off the John Deere once it stops dead and takes off his gloves, resting them on the seat. He sees Janice outside now, watching the approaching squad cars. Catching her eye, he knows exactly what she's thinking—it's similar to what he's thinking, the news they are about to receive.

*Someone died.*

*And it's her. It's Ellie.*

He begins the walk back to the farm, and the medium distance feels like a hundred miles.

"Sorry to pop on over here all unexpected like this, Dan," says Sheriff Patrick Gibbs, resting his arm on the roof of his car as he leans against the doorframe. "But we received some news, and, well, we've been asked to deliver it. And, if you wouldn't mind, we've been instructed to ask you a couple-a questions."

"Well sure, Pat," he says, draping an arm around Janice. "Absolutely."

"Would you fellas like to come in?" Janice asks. "I've got a fresh pot of coffee brewing and Dan's already had two cups. Won't be able to drink it all by myself."

"That's a generous offer, Mrs. Brower, but we'll have to decline. Won't take long what I got to say and what I got to ask."

"Okay then..." She shoots her husband a worried look that borders on *unsettled*. The cops never come out here unless the business is important and dire, something that can't be solved with a quick phone call.

"So what's going on, Pat?" Dan asks, not wanting to delay the inevitable any longer.

"Well, it's about Ellie, I'm afraid. Your ex-wife," he adds, as if Dan doesn't already know that particular tidbit. As if there's another Ellie in his life.

"What about her?"

"Well, she's gone missing, I'm afraid."

"Missing?" He takes his arm back from his wife and then folds both across his chest. "That's something, huh?"

"Yeah, it's something, all right. She hasn't reported to work the last two weeks and no one from the school's faculty has heard from her. Local cops did a wellness check and found squat. Just a place that looks like a teenager has been living in it."

*A teenager struggling with borderline alcoholism,* Dan wants to add but doesn't out of respect.

Pat Gibbs winces like he swallowed a thorn bush bud. "You haven't talked to her at all lately, right? Seen her? Heard from her? In any capacity? I only ask because one of her friends, a tech teacher at her school, admitted to helping her trace a strange text message she received. The coordinates, he said, pointed to a place in Virginia. Not far from where they think Dawn went missing."

Dan swallows. "Huh?"

"Yeah. Weird stuff, Dan. I gotta say."

"Well shit, Pat. I did get a text from her a couple weeks back." Dan digs out his phone. Quickly, he pulls up the message and shows it to him. "Didn't think much of it. Tried to call her back when it came through, but her phone was already dead."

Janice rubs his back. "You never told me this." She doesn't use an accusatory tone, instead sounding more concerned, and Dan loves her for it.

"Shit, I know. Must've slipped my mind. You know, with everything going on." He puts a hand on his wife's stomach. "Three months along now," he tells Pat.

"Well, congratulations you two."

"Thank you," Janice says, her mood sunny, not that it ever isn't. She's the sunniest person Dan's ever known. "He's a little on the small side, but the doctors are monitoring him closely. So, it's been on our minds a lot and we have to go see the specialist every week."

"I understand," Pat says, handing back Dan's phone. "Dan, I have a favor to ask. And I hate asking."

"What is it? Anything I can do to help, consider it done."

"The detective from Dawn's case, this, uh..." He checks his notes. "Wally Stanton?"

"Yes. I remember him."

"He's wondering if you don't mind meeting with him. He's in charge of Ellie's disappearance. As well as investigating a missing man named Mitchell Green, and—"

"Wait, Mitch is missing too?" Dan feels a punch in the gut, and he doesn't know why but he hates the way this whole situation sounds. It's kicking up too much dust, too much of the past he thought had settled years ago.

"You know him?"

"Yeah. Kya's father. Dawn's best friend's father. Kya went missing too, along with Dawn. They were together when it happened. Haven't talked to Mitch since...since we buried them. The empty caskets, I mean."

"I see," the sheriff says, head down, watching himself toe the dirt. "Well, it seems like the pair went on a little road trip together. Now they're...you know. Gone."

"Shit."

"Yeah, my sentiments exactly." He glances up, then hangs his head again and sighs. "Look, Dan. I don't like anything about this, but this Wally Stanton guy, he's been calling me every day, asking me to come out here and talk to you, and I've been putting it off, because...well, you and I go way back, to high school, and...shit, buddy—I know how hard that was for you, but...but it does seem like they could really use you down there."

"In Virginia?" An incredulous sound escapes his mouth. "He can't be serious."

"He is. About as serious as I've ever heard another person."

"I can't, Pat. You know that. I have the farm. Janice and her appointments."

"I know it's a tough ask, friend."

Dan turns back, looks over his shoulder at the farmhouse, the silo, the fields beyond it, the endless acres, so vast that not even he knows where the property ends. Probably something he ought to know by now but still hasn't researched. Then he looks to Janice. Her belly, the tiny bump. His future son.

"Go, honey," Janice says. "It'll be all right."

"But...I can't leave you alone with—"

"Derrick can come over and take care of the farm while you're gone for—what?" She looks to Pat. "Two days?"

"Play it safe and make it three."

"Three days." Janice's smile shines at him, filling him with a brightness that he never thought a human being could know. "We don't have another appointment 'til next Thursday."

Dan bites his lip. Everything about it, his intuition, is telling him not to go, that there's nothing left for him down there. That everything in Virginia is in the past, and the past should be left alone, unbothered, not to be tested or messed with. The same way you wouldn't dig up a loved one's corpse just to catch a glimpse of the person you missed, or the same way you wouldn't scratch an old wound to see if it can still bleed. The past is the past for a reason, and it's time to move on.

He doesn't want to go, and he hates that he can't say "No." Was never good at saying *no* to anyone or anything, especially when it came to family.

"All right," he says, facing the sheriff of Warren County. "Three days. You tell them."

Pat Gibbs told them all right, and eight hours later Dan Brower finds himself sitting in Wally Stanton's office, tapping his foot nervously on the floor, two beats per second, waiting for the detective to make his grand entrance. When he finally does amble his way into the office (about twenty-five minutes later than expected), he's holding two steaming cups of coffee. He hands one to Dan, who accepts it, but not without stalling.

"If I remember correctly," Wally says, "you take it black."

"Yes, sir. Good memory."

"Cop's curse, I suppose." He plants himself in the seat behind the desk, takes a sip of coffee, and then begins to shuffle around some paperwork, which Dan thinks is an unnecessary way of showing him that he's somewhat organized and knows what he's doing. It wouldn't surprise him if those papers have zilch to do with Ellie's disappearance, or Dawn's for that matter. "Let's get started, shall we?"

He checks his watch, wondering if he needs to text Janice to remind her to take her prenatal vitamins. She's been oh-so-forgetful lately and he worries about her. "Yeah. Let's."

"How've you been?"

"Been all right, I suppose. You?"

"Can't complain. Wife's good, the kids are good. The older one is getting a little mouthy, but it's probably just a phase."

Dan nods, not really wanting to talk about kids, seeing them growing up. He thinks Wally should know that, but maybe the detective is light on common sense. Or low on plain old empathy.

"So, you and Miss Brower are no longer married, is that correct?"

Dan finds this lead-off question amusing. "Don't you know that already?"

Wally shoots him a hey-you-got-me-there smile, amiable enough. "Well, yeah, I know a lot of things, I guess. Part of the job is asking questions we already know answers to. It's repetitive, sure. But it helps."

"Yeah, we divorced. Not long after you guys stopped looking for our daughter."

Wally squints as if the fact is an insult and not a fact. Dan certainly didn't intend it as such, but the end result brings him a glimmer of satisfaction.

"Ouch," Wally says. "You know, we did all we could to find her. We were out there every day looking. Six weeks straight."

"I understand. You did your best."

Another needle he doesn't mean to thread.

Wally taps his fingers on the desk. "All right. Let's move on."

"Okay."

"Did Ellie contact you in the weeks leading up to her unannounced vacation?"

*Ellie now,* Dan thinks. *Not Miss Brower.* Dan doesn't know why Ellie never changed her last name back to Coughlin after the divorce. Sheer laziness? Hoping to rekindle the love that once was and get back together? Dan would place his chips on laziness or just not caring what her last name was. Then he thinks maybe it's because that's Dawn's last name, and keeping it might make her feel—on some level—more connected to her memory. He likes that notion best.

"A phone call from a different number perhaps?" Wally asks. "A text?"

"Nope. Just the text you already know about. And my call back to her, which she didn't answer, which you also already know about."

"Got it. What about before that? Months ago? Years?"

"We haven't talked much since the divorce. Not at all since I married Janice."

"No contact?"

"That's correct, sir. I mean—first two years, we used to talk on the day she went missing—Dawn, I mean—but that stopped after I remarried."

"So, it's been over a year then?"

"Never been good at math, but yeah, that seems right."

"Good," Wally says, leaning back. "Thank you."

"Can *I* ask a question?"

"Shoot, partner."

"What am I doing down here? What am I really here for?" He bites his tongue, wondering if that's all he should say on the subject. "I mean, I know I'm not a suspect. Wouldn't make any sense. But you didn't bring me down here to ask questions you could have over the phone or on Skype."

The detective takes a longer-than-usual look at him. "That's true. We didn't. Fact is, we're reopening Dawn's investigation as well as Kya Green's. We think Ellie and Mr. Green going missing in the area is too much of a coincidence to be ignored."

"Well, I agree with you there."

"So, I wanted you to hang out for a couple days. Help us look."

"Not much of an investigator. These days, I'm just a farmer."

"I know," Wally says. "But you're still a father, aren't you?"

The question comes as a jolt. He has to think about it for a minute before responding, "Yeah, I guess I still am." *Will be again, soon.*

"Sometimes...parents see things first," Wally says with an innocent shrug.

Later that afternoon Wally drives them to POP'S SHOP, a little gas station and convenience store combo on the outskirts of town. The drive was only twenty minutes, but it still feels good when he gets out to stretch his limbs.

"What are we doing here?" he asks, mid-yawn.

Wally lights a smoke, cocks back his head, and releases a fog that quickly gets lost in the sunshine. "Ellie's service provider told us her GPS pinged a satellite in this location, the last day anyone saw her. Same day Mitchell Green's wife told us he left with her."

"And you haven't checked here yet?"

Wally shrugs. "*We* have. But *you* haven't."

"I don't understand."

Wally squints as he takes another drag. "Owner's kind of a dick. Doesn't like cops."

*Who can blame him?* Dan thinks, but doesn't say. It's not that he's anti-police—far from it—but his experiences with the boys in blue have been less than satisfactory, present company included.

"So what do you want me to do?"

Wally pulls a picture out of his pocket and hands it over. Dan glances down at Ellie's face, a photo from last year's school yearbook, Ms. Brower printed under the black and white copy. The picture feels like a grenade on his fingertips; heavier than it ought to be, ready to blow up in his face.

"Ask the guy if he's seen the woman. If he asks you if you're a cop, you tell him 'fuck no, do I look like a cop?'"

"Can't you just get a warrant?"

"I can."

"So?"

"Filed for one. Hasn't been approved by Judge Morrison yet. That yellow-bellied son of a bitch is really breaking my balls on this one."

Dan pulls down his John Deere hat, shielding more of his face. He rubs the curling stubble of his beard, a few days past when Janice typically likes him to shave. "All right." It's starting to make a tad more sense why Wally asked him along. He still doesn't like it, still wishes he was home with Janice, doting on her every whim, bringing home ice cream from an impromptu QuickChek run, rubbing her feet until she falls asleep, all the things a pregnant wife-o would want from him, things he'd do anyway even if she wasn't carrying his son. "I'll do it."

"Great." Wally reaches into his pocket and grabs a twenty. "Also need to gas up."

Dan accepts the bill and then heads inside. The convenience store smells like someone tried to spray down a skunk with Lysol, the lemon-scented kind. Dan ignores the unpleasant aroma and strolls over to the sodas, grabs himself a glass-bottled Coke, which was always Dawn's favorite, and seeing it reminds him of the trips they used to take when she was little. They'd always stop at some highway rest area, head inside, and get gummy worms and glass Cokes. It was their tradition. Even during their last father-daughter excursion, a trip down to Georgetown, they had stopped along the way, some Maryland rest stop, and, ritualistically, purchased two bags of assorted gummy worms and two glass bottles of their favorite pop.

"Can I help you?" asks the man behind the counter. Tufts of white poke out from under the man's cap. He leans back against the plastic barrier protecting the tobacco products, folds his arms, clearly expecting some sort of immediate answer. A simple nod or shrug won't do, not for this man in the denim overalls. "You been staring at that goddamn Coca-Cola freezer for two minutes now."

"That illegal?" Dan asks, hinting at humor.

The store's sole employee, *Pop* maybe, remains stiff, rigid like a propped corpse. "Nope. Being an asshole isn't illegal. Not one bit."

"Fair enough." Dan grabs two Cokes (out of habit, he thinks) and heads for the register. "Pump two."

Pop dings the register. "Twenty-four, twenty-four."

Dan hands him the twenty and a five he found crumpled in his pocket. As Pop handles the money, Dan slaps the picture of Ellie on the counter. "You seen this woman?"

Pop stops, glances down at the picture, then back up at Dan. "Who's asking?"

"I am."

"And who are you?"

"She's my wife." *Ex,* he thinks, but leaving off the prefix sounds better and will probably get him farther. "She's missing."

"You a cop? I've had an awful lotta cops poking their snouts around these parts lately, infringing on my freedoms, my rights as a warm-blooded American. You wouldn't be of that godless sort, would you?"

"Not a cop."

"And how the hell do I know that?" Pop nods toward the pumps. "That dick-masher outside looks like one big juicy pork chop to me."

Dan bunches his face up to keep from cracking a smile. "He's full of pork, all right. Just ain't no pig cop."

Pop squints, studying him. Dan's played poker enough times to know how to hide a bluff. It's all about relaxing the muscles in the face, keeping them loose, keeping them free. Most people who lie tighten the muscles to keep them from moving, but that causes too much movement, thus giving away the tell.

"Well, shit," Pop says, handing him the change. "I believe you. Now, this young lady here... let me take a look." He picks up the picture and scans the image.

*Tightens his jaw.*

"Nope, haven't seen her."

Dan nods as he takes back the photo. "Sure about that?"

"Pretty sure. I may be old, young fella, but my memory is sharper than a lawnmower blade."

"Well..." He pockets the picture and collects the two bottles off the counter. "I really appreciate you taking a look and all."

"My pleasure. I hope you find her."

"Me too."

Dan leans through the open window and rests the Cokes on the seat. When he looks up, Wally is looking directly at him, arms open, his mouth catching flies. "Well?"

"Said he hasn't seen her."

"And..."

"And he's full of shit."

"How do you know?"

"Know a lot of liars." He opens the door, sticks one leg inside. "And he's fucking lying."

"Well, fuck. Guess I shoulda expected that."

"Wonder why though."

" 'Less he's in on it."

Dan squints. "In on what, exactly?"

"That's what you and I are bound to find out, hoss."

Both men get inside the car and buckle up.

"Hey!" Dan hears the old man calling from the open door of the shop. "Hey! Wait a darn second!" He's waving his arms over his head, and Dan thinks there's a trace of a smile resting on his face, but, in the distance, he can't tell for sure.

"You paid the man for the gas, right?" Wally asks.

"Yes I did."

Pop comes ambling over, a slight limp in his gait. When he reaches the car, he crouches down, and Dan swears he hears something crackle inside the old man's knees. Somehow, the old-timer keeps his balance, and that faint trace of a smile doesn't waver.

"Shit, I just remembered," Pop says, light laughter following the declaration. "I have seen that woman. Yes sir, not more than two, three weeks ago."

Wally beats him to a response: "Did she say anything? Anything at all? Where she was going?"

"Well. She mentioned heading to a place called Lacuna's Point."

"Lacuna's Point?" Wally shakes his head. "Never heard of it, sir. And I've lived out here nearly my whole life, mister."

"Well, shit. That's because Lacuna's Point ain't a place most folks are familiar with. Especially 'round these parts. Kind of a place that sits between places, if you will. You ain't never gonna find it unless you know where to look. Now, ain't no one lived there in almost fifty years. The grass is all grown up 'round the area, doubt you'll get to see very much. Ivy covering up all the buildings, the old shoppes. I think kids go there to drink sometimes, smash bottles all over the grounds. Good spot for the junkies to shoot their smack, *knowwhatImean?* No place for anyone to go really, but this woman—hell, I couldn't stop her."

*Sounds a lot like the woman I married,* Dan muses.

Wally breathes in and his face suggests he doesn't like the stink in the air. "What was she doing there? You recall?"

"Oh, I don't know. She was looking for someone, I think. Had a man with her. Black feller. About ye big."

Drumming his thumbs on the wheel, Wally cocks an eyebrow. "Can you draw us a map to this Lacuna's Point place?"

"Mister," Pop says, with a twinkle in his eye. "It would be my pleasure."

Wally Stanton parks his Land Rover on the outskirts of Lacuna's Point in a parking lot that gives a wide view of the town that once was. Dan sits there as Wally kills the engine, staring across a dead town with a touch of apocalyptic charm. Pop wasn't kidding when he described the place—it looks like no one's called this place home in fifty years. The grass has grown so high it's folded sideways. Ivy has crept up the buildings' exteriors, creating drapes of dead-green latticework. Paint has been stripped and chipped, gone completely in most places, leaving patches of bare wood exposed, knots and black craters of rot peeking through.

"Well," Wally says, popping the door open. "I don't see any sign of them. Was hoping to maybe find a car, or…you know, *something*."

Dan squints, spotting the clock tower behind the rows of derelict buildings. "Is that a clock tower?"

"Yeah, looks like it. Got a huge crack in it."

"I see that." A lightning bolt-like split runs vertically down its center, dividing the clock in half. "Don't think I've ever seen a clock tower in person before."

"Kinda cool, isn't it?" Wally chuckles to himself. "Shit, reminds me of that *Back to the Future* movie, right? Whole town does come to think of it. What was the name of it again? Sweet Valley? Hill Valley? Moon Valley?"

"Never saw it."

"Never saw…wait, what do you mean?"

"Never saw that movie."

Wally cocks his right brow. "You live under a rock or something, amigo?"

"Not a movie guy." Dan can't lift his eyes from the clock tower's face, the ivy that's grown through the damage, the split, and spread around the circular plate, hiding most of the inscribed numbers, coiling around the hands of time like a nest of sleeping snakes. "You've lived down here your whole life?"

"Yeah, that's right. Virginia boy, through and through."

"How come this is the first time you're hearing about this place?"

If Wally has an answer, it gets lost in the labyrinth of his throat.

"Isn't that weird?" Dan shifts in his seat, facing him now.

Wally's tongue probes his inner cheek. "It's a strange circumstance, I give you that."

"Strange doesn't really begin to cover it, though." Dan shakes his head. "I don't like this, Detective Stanton. I ain't no cop, but shit—this gives me the worst feeling. I almost don't want to leave the car."

Wally nods. "Yeah. Thing is, though…we have to."

Dan furrows his brow.

"Because I have that same feeling slithering around my belly," he says, stepping out. "The one that tells me when something is all sorts of fucked up. And you know something?"

Dan waits for it.

Wally grins. "My belly is rarely wrong."

# PART THREE

## ROUND AND ROUND WE GO ON
## THIS OLD-TIME CAROUSEL

# CHAPTER ELEVEN

The musty smell hits her nasal cavities and travels to her brain, rousing her from dreamless slumber, plugging her back into reality.

*Reality.*

Reality is that goddamn hotel room again, the very same one. A crushing *déjà vu* sensation coats her brain like a thick, roaming fog. It's hard for her to shake, even when she lifts her head from the floral-patterned throw pillow.

*Am I drunk?*

Wouldn't be the first time she's lifted her eyelids to find herself somewhere other than her own bed with little memory of how she arrived there. Rarely has she ever found herself in a hotel room— once or twice over the last few years, and only one of those times was there a man lying next to her, naked, snoring, dreaming good dreams and blissfully unaware of her waking presence. After that experience she promised herself she would never drink again, and the promise was made during that shameful scamper back to her car. The promise was broken a few days later when Maura came over with a new bottle of merlot.

But she's not drunk now. She knows the difference between a hangover and…and whatever *this* is. It's like she's stuck somewhere between a dream and the real world, and her mind isn't sure which line to cross and where to remain.

She throws the sheets off her body and looks down at her ankle, expecting to see a swollen knob, blackened and ballooned. She's surprised to uncover a perfectly healthy ankle, no swelling at all. It can't be, *just can't,* so she touches the spot where the cop brought down his boot and feels nothing out of the ordinary. Just regular ol' skin and bones.

A slicing pain runs laterally through her head, and she touches both temples with her fingers, massaging them, hoping to calm the beast spraying fire through her brain's epicenter. Thinking of the cop, the way he'd attempted to crush her ankle, only intensifies the agonizing stretch.

*How am I okay?* she wonders, fighting through the splitting headache, trying to dissect past events and figure out exactly how she ended up back at the hotel room. She figures she can't—the more she thinks about the foggy dreamlike memories that happened (minutes, hours?) earlier, the more her head feels like someone's taking an axe to her skull, cleaving through bone and brain matter, halving her.

She decides to drop it, chalk it up to a terrible nightmare. There's no sense dwelling in the past, not when there's so much work ahead.

*Stop fucking around,* she thinks, *and find your daughter. You know she's here—you know this place has her. Find her. Find her. FIND HER.*

She slides her feet to the floor, which is more of a chore than it sounds in theory. The slightest movement feels like a test of her body's strength—a test she doesn't exactly think she can pass. Afraid to put pressure on the ankle that looks quite all right, she uses her other leg to support herself. Hobbling across the room, she notices a note has been stuck to the television set. For some reason she thinks the T.V. is just for show—a lot of things in Lacuna's Point are—that it doesn't actually have any cable running to it. But the note—written lazily on yellow sticky tab paper—calls to her, captures her attention. She moves to it slowly, cautiously, deciding whether she should trust it. Everything feels like it could be a trap.

Peeling the paper from the black mirror, she quickly reads the message: ACE'S PLACE @11 – MITCH. She checks the clock on the nightstand, sees it's twenty minutes to the proposed time.

She blinks, helping clear the hazy shroud over her mind, her thoughts, and then heads for the door. As she steps through, planting her feet in the empty hallway, a sense of doom falls over her, the kind she will never shake.

"She'll be here," Mitch says, digging into his disco fries.

Across from him, Josh scoops up a spoonful of his hot fudge sundae and fills his mouth with the sweet goodness.

Marissa smokes her cigarette, tapping ash into the plastic tray before her. If there are NO SMOKING signs, Mitch doesn't see them.

"Well," Josh says, swallowing the vanilla ice cream and the dab of whip cream that accompanies it, "if she doesn't show in five, I say we get started without her."

"What are we doing here anyway?" Marissa asks, sucking down a lungful, blowing out a cloud above her, generously avoiding her company. "I mean, what can we possibly do?"

At this, Josh raises his finger. "We need to get out of here."

"We need to find my daughter," Mitch says, dangling a cheesy fry before his open mouth. "Then we get out of here."

"Same with my sis," Marissa tells them. "Not leaving without my Rosetta."

"Okay fine," Josh says, popping the sundae's cherry into his mouth. "We find your loved ones, then we make like a banana and split."

"How do we find them?" Marissa asks. "I haven't seen Rose and it's been two weeks. Who's to say we ever will?"

Josh wrinkles his nose as he swallows the cherry. "I think we'll have an opportunity at the arts festival."

"First off," Mitch says, shaking his head, "that's two more weeks away. With all the whacky shit going on, what's the guarantee we live that long? Plus…" He stares off, thinking of home. Angie. What she would do if he didn't come home for over two weeks. He believes he'd come home to divorce papers. After all, she thinks he's hunkered down in a hotel room for the weekend, working on the novel. Not gallivanting around some town lost in time, lost…well, wandering aimlessly through a place where time doesn't actually exist, not the way it should, not the way time works elsewhere. *Not the way reality works elsewhere.* "I can't be here for two weeks."

"I don't think you have a choice," Josh tells him. "The town isn't going to dangle your loved ones out in front of you like those disco fries. It's much smarter than that. The arts festival…everyone will be there."

"And how do you know that?"

Josh rolls his eyes, reaches into his pocket, and pulls out a crumpled ball of paper. He lays it on the table and irons the creases with a fist, making a wrinkly square, then slides it across the way, pointing to the evidence. EVERYONE WILL BE THERE! is written in bold lettering, encapsulated by a spiky shout balloon. "See?"

Mitch wishes he had a point to argue, but the flyer is pretty clear on the matter.

The bell dangling from the diner's front door rings, and a newcomer enters, looking utterly lost and confused, looking utterly hopeless. It's Ellie, and she looks around like she's just landed on the alien surface of a brand new planet.

Darla greets her, tells her to sit anywhere.

Mitch forms an O with his lips and whistles a low tone, snaps his fingers, and watches Ellie's head dart in his direction. She puts her head down like she's trying to get down the aisle incognito, as if someone from her past—a one night stand perhaps—is sitting in one of the booths behind her. She makes her way to the table and stops when she gets there, noticing Mitch isn't alone. Scanning the new faces, she hesitates—as if she vaguely recognizes them, as if she's run into them before.

"It's okay," he tells her. "Have a seat." He slides out of the booth and offers her the inside spot. She accepts it, not without looking around the immediate area, searching for a quick exit should something bad happen.

Once seated, Mitch makes the introductions. Josh and Marissa introduce themselves to Ellie and the duo quickly relays their stories, how they ended up in the slice of heaven that is Lacuna's Point. Ellie doesn't offer hers, though; Mitch has told them everything already.

After they're acquainted, Darla brings them more coffee, and Ellie orders breakfast.

"Where were we?" Mitch asks them.

"The arts festival," Marissa states. "You were telling us how you didn't want to wait."

Mitch quickly catches Ellie up on the conversation. He shows her the flyer Josh's been carrying around.

"That's…" Ellie says, "crazy."

Josh smirks. "Crazier than having your ankle broken and then waking up fine?"

Ellie's eyes expand, and for a second Mitch thinks she's going to jump up on the table and out the window. "How do you know about that?" she asks.

Mitch answers for him. "We saw you."

"That was a dream."

Josh shakes his head. "That's what it wants you to think."

"It?" She turns her head, finding coffee. "What's *it?*"

Marissa and Josh study each other for a beat. Then Josh says, "We don't have a name for it exactly."

Haunted, Ellie struggles to pick up her coffee. The mug rattles against the saucer plate as her hand trembles.

"It's just the town," Marissa adds. "The town makes us dream, and the dreams are...for the lack of a better term, *real.*"

Ellie swallows down some coffee, but the warm wake-me-up does nothing to change her mood. Mitch feels for her, understands her confusion. Understands that what happened before he woke this morning was a confusing, surreal experience, and he isn't sure he can fully buy into the theory that it all truly happened. The way the guitar player—Skelly—split open, revealing the colony of crablike creatures within—that couldn't have been real. But then again, Josh and Marissa were real—*are* real—and they are sitting across from him just as they had when they broke him out of the holding cell. They communicated in that dream version of Lacuna's Point, made plans to meet up here.

And they showed.

"I don't believe it," Ellie says distantly. She's protecting herself, her mind, Mitch thinks, and he doesn't blame her.

Marissa sighs, clearly frustrated with Ellie's refusal to accept the truth, and then looks to Mitch for some help.

"I think we needn't worry about that stuff now," Mitch tells them. "What we need to do is figure out a plan. How we're getting out of here."

"We'll need to do some research," Josh tells him. "Two weeks gives us plenty of time to explore the town, to discover some possible exits. Cracks in the armor."

"You've already been here for two weeks," Mitch tells him. "You haven't figured that stuff out yet?"

Josh shakes his head. "It's been...difficult. I feel like we're being watched at all time."

"What makes it different now?"

"Well, now there's more of us. Maybe there'll be fewer eyes on us. The town only has so many, right? Can't watch us all the time, at once."

Mitch nods, liking that answer, though he feels like Lacuna's Point has an endless supply of eyes. He thinks back to his first visit to the diner, the way the lone patron—Dave, was it?—watched them, studied them, spied on them.

*Eyes. Everywhere.*

"Maybe," Mitch says. "Do you think there's more like us? You know? Not changed?"

Marissa and Josh glance at each other. Then Marissa nods over her right shoulder. Mitch follows the direction of her motion, sees Darla behind the counter, squeezing out a coil of whip cream on top of another sundae.

Mitch raises his brow. "Darla?"

"If she's not like us, she's definitely not one of them, not all the way," Marissa says, stubbing out her smoke and then reaching for the pack to grab another one.

"I think she's more like Skelly," Josh muses aloud. "One of them, but not totally."

*Skelly. Splitting apart. Halved, those alien creatures pouring out of him like cockroaches from an infested apartment wall.*

"Where is our friend Skelly?" Mitch says, then turns to Ellie, quickly explaining the Skelly portion of the story, what happened during the dream. The tale doesn't seem to have any effect on her, and Ellie continues to sip her coffee and remain silent. He can't help but notice the drastic change in her, and he wishes there was something he could do to break her out of the funk. "Hey," he whispers to her, and she faces him. "You okay?"

She nods and that's all he gets.

"Skelly is resting," Josh says, after a bout of awkward silence. "You know...he's fine. Just...whatever happened to him in the dream really twisted him up."

"This morning," Marissa says, lighting up another smoke, "he was more cryptic than usual. If you can believe that."

Mitch nods as if he understands completely. "So...where does that leave us?"

Josh breathes out his nose, a long drawn release. "I have a plan."

"Lay it on us."

"We need to find their weakness—the people. Whatever's...inside them, it has to have a weakness. All monsters have one, right?"

"Inside them?" Mitch can't keep the nightmarish episode of Skelly cracking in half at bay. "You mean those crab things?"

Josh bobs his head several times. "Mole crabs. They come from the ocean, I think. My first day here, I saw one. It...entered someone."

"Huh?"

"It was really gross. The guy dug through the sand and yanked out this creature, one of the crabs, but a pretty big one, and it was moving, all those little legs, and then he...he put the mole crab inside himself—or, the crab put itself inside him. I don't know. It was weird."

"Well, like you said..." Mitch pours himself a cuppa. "They gotta have a weakness and we gotta find it. You work on that."

"I'll work on finding an exit," Marissa says. "There has to be a way out...somewhere."

Mitch doesn't care for the lack of confidence in her voice, but he understands it. "Okay, okay. You're in charge of breaking us free." He looks to Ellie. "Guess that leaves finding the girls," he points to Marissa, himself, and then Ellie, "all three of them, to us. What do you say?"

Ellie swallows an empty mouthful. "Yeah, sure." No enthusiasm at all. "Whatever you want."

"Okay, okay. We got a plan. Hopefully it doesn't take us two weeks—"

*"Oh no."* Mitch turns his head to the counter where Darla is standing over the completed sundae. At first he thinks she messed it up somehow, that she forgot a step or added the wrong color sprinkles. But then he realizes she's looking straight at him. *Them.* "Quickly," Darla says, and for a second he's not sure if she's addressing him or herself or someone else entirely. Mitch doesn't move. Neither does anyone else at the table. He can't see anyone else in their vicinity—the reason they chose that corner of the diner in the first place—so he just decides to wait, let the interruption play out. *"Quickly,"* she says again, and then bangs her hand on the counter three times.

"You talking to us?" Mitch asks.

Darla swallows as if she feels a ghostly presence running its fingers across her neck. "Yes. The four of you need to leave."

Stunned, Mitch can hardly open his mouth. "But—"

*"Now,"* she repeats. "They're coming for you."

Josh is the first one to ask it: "W-who's coming for us?"

Tears stream from Darla's eyes, and she begins to quiver. "The Mayor. His secret service. *The black hoods.*"

The way she says this turns Mitch's heart into a block of ice.

An hour later, Elroy Foley takes his first sip of fresh coffee—black, always black, and hot but not too hot—and basks in the nutty aroma, breathing in and allowing the steam to travel all the way into his lungs. He breathes out and up so he can pull the second-hand scent back through his nose. After this, he stares down at two eggs over easy, his belly grumbling. He knows he'll pay for eating them, the eggs along with the few slices of bacon and three sticks of sausage, but he hardly cares—the future gas pains and irritable bowel movements will all be worth it. It's the experience of the moment that matters, how it tastes going down. Elroy Foley is a man who lives for the moment, not what comes later. Anyone who lives for later isn't truly living.

*Hell yeah,* he thinks, pinching a fat log of sausage between his teeth.

"That looks mighty good, officer," Darla says, topping off his coffee. She swallows nervously, like she's hiding something or doesn't enjoy interacting with the police. In his career, Foley's seen a lot of both and can usually tell the difference. In Darla's case, he ordinarily thinks it's the latter. But today, she seems even more nervous than usual. It's like…as if she senses something bad is about to happen.

"Sure is, darling," he replies with a mouthful. "Finest sausage this side of the Mason-Dixon." He's not even sure where the Mason-Dixon is exactly but figures he's probably south of it. *Ought to be, out here, in Lacuna's Point. This delightful slice of American Pie.*

About halfway into his second sausage, a sense of unease falls over him, pressing down on his shoulders like a wet cape. He doesn't react, not immediately. He thinks it'll pass like an intermittent toothache, dull and pulsing, but gone after a shot of whiskey and a good night's worth of sweet dreams. But as the seconds stretch on, the feeling only grows stronger, and he knows what it is, what's coming, and that panicky feeling, the one wrapped around a pit of perpetual dread, begins to stick to his bones.

And now he knows why Darla was acting the way she was.

Elroy sets down his fork as the diner's front door swings open, the groaning of those old metal hinges the only thing that can be heard because all conversation inside the place peters out. Heavy boots clap against the checkered tile floor. The jingling of spurs sounds like a pocket full of tokens. Every patron in the place swings their head toward the diner's new guests, and once their eyes settle on the leader of the small pack, they turn away at once as if holding their eyes on him for too long will cause blindness. The diner-goers face their spouses, brothers and sisters, and pick up their now meaningless conversations, wherever they left off. Some forget where they were exactly and begin to blather, speaking nonsense, speaking about anything and everything, and only because the silence needs to be filled.

Anything to keep the man and his men's attention off them.

Darla greets them first. "H-Hello there, Mayor Black. P-pleased to suh-uh-see you."

Mayor Quincy Black stands before her, not moving, just studying her, and the few seconds it takes for him to inspect her feels like several minutes. Foley doesn't want to look at the man—if he's a man at all, and Foley doesn't believe so. But, like a power magnet, the man's appearance draws his eyes and Foley takes in the terrible image of this devil in human flesh. A mask of well-worn, yellowed bandages hides his true face. His eyes, like the eyes of a shark, primal and exuding dominant, predatory inclinations, can be seen through the weaves of medical fabric. Same goes for his mouth, and Foley can see a dark split in the center of his upper lip, as if someone drove their knuckles into his nicotine-yellow teeth at some point in the last twenty-four hours. Below his face, on his body, is a dark suit, a matching tie, looking expensive and much too nice to be wearing out to a place like Ace's. But...isn't that always what the Mayor has worn? Since day one? Foley searches his memory and can't remember seeing the man in anything different—even on the day he'd first arrived at Lacuna's Point, when the Mayor sought him out and offered him the job of the town's only constable.

The three men in tow wear similar suits but have black hoods over their heads, hiding their identities, though, if Foley wants to, he can probably venture a guess who the Mayor's secret service are. He'll hold his speculation for future debates; now, it's time to get through this little emergency, impromptu visit without incident.

Mayor Black doesn't respond to Darla and continues to stare at her, way past the point of awkwardness. His dim gaze wanders over her body, and the look is so predatory that a touch of embarrassment burns Foley's neck, his cheeks. He can't imagine how the girl feels. But, like all moments, it will pass, and then the Mayor's eyes will be on someone else.

*Me,* Foley thinks.

"Puh-please," Darla says, avoiding that awful gaze. "Si-sit anywhere. Wh-wherever."

With that, Black passes her and faces Foley, who pretends he wasn't staring and wipes his mouth on a napkin. He leans back in his seat, no longer hungry, forgetting completely that he has a few sausages to shovel down. Mayor Black invites himself to the table, plopping his bottom on the soft cushion, the sound of air escaping the tiny vacuum between his lumpy, misshapen ass and the vinyl fabric is loud enough for the entire diner to hear. It reminds Elroy of those Whoopee cushions he and his friends used to play with when they were little, sans the funny flatulence that accompanied it. A soft kiss of air, that's all the sound is, but it's enough to remind him of the past, being a child, those simpler times. It's a silly thing to think about now considering the man sitting across from him could conceivably destroy him with just a simple command, but the brain is funny and the mind sometimes protects itself from harmful realizations.

Mayor Black glares into him. Not *at* him. *Into him.* And Foley feels the man inside his head, shuffling through his thoughts and memories like files in a cabinet, each labeled for organizational purposes, and that Black is trying to find the right one to access. When he seemingly finds what he's looking for, he raises his hand and snaps his fingers. The sound carries like a whip cracking against a sturdy specimen of muscle and flesh, and the entire diner— everyone, whether they're eating, drinking coffee, or just plain chitchatting away with friends and family—abandons their meals mid-conversation and makes for the exit in single file in a calm, orderly fashion, and looking nowhere else but the back of the person in the front of them. It's clearly a well-practiced exercise, but Elroy

Foley can't remember ever seeing this evacuation route executed so swiftly.

Once the place is empty, Elroy puts up his hands as if the Mayor is pointing a loaded pistol at his private parts. "Mayor," he says sweetly, "to what do I owe the pleasure of your company?"

Mayor Black squints, holding up a finger, asking for another couple of seconds to formulate a correct response. "You know, Elroy Foley, that is a good question, a great *goddamn* question."

Elroy squints, a spastic jerk twisting his head to one side. "Oof. Mayor. With all due respect, please refrain from blasphemy in my presence. You know me—know I'm a man of Faith and a man of God, and I do take offense to that kind of language."

At first the Mayor gives no response, but a few seconds later, he comes down with a case of giggly trembles, and then a second after that, his lips separate, and he laughs wildly.

Foley feels his face burn, but not with embarrassment this time.

"You got something else you want to say, Elroy? *Officer* Foley? Do you?"

He doesn't, knows it's better to go along with it. He said his piece and that's that.

"Didn't think so." Black reaches out, plucking a fat sausage off Foley's plate. The buttery grease pools near the touch, and Black grips the link so hard that a dribble of heart disease runs down the man's black-leather glove. He bites into the sausage and chews slowly. The sound of the juicy meat swishing around his mouth is hell on Foley's ears, much louder than it should be. Foley watches the bandages covering his face move along with his jaw. "Now," Black continues, still chewing, cow-like chomps that make Elroy thankful his mother had the sense to instill good manners when he was just a pup, how to chew with his mouth closed. "I got a bone to pick with you, Elroy Foley. It seems like we've got a few mice in the cellar, and, well, looks like they're coming for the cheddar."

Foley stares at him blankly.

"Did I fuckin' stutter, Foley?"

"No, sir."

"Then wipe that dumb fuckin' look off your face and tell me what we're going to do about it."

Foley fights the fledging ire within. "We talkin' the interlopers?"

"Oh yes. Oh yes indeed."

Foley nods. "I think we've got that handled."

"Oh? Do you?"

"Yes," he says confidently. He wants to add that they wouldn't have any problems if the Mayor didn't keep bringing them in, but he digresses. Can't say that. Can't be critical of the Mayor's methods. His reasons are his, and though Foley doesn't understand why things are the way they are, he doesn't feel the need to question the traditions of Lacuna's Point. He has a life here, a happy life, and that's that. Anything else does not matter to Elroy Foley, not in this moment, not ever. "Yes, we have that under control."

At this, Black stops chewing and leans back in the booth. "You know, I'd like to believe that. But I hear things, Elroy. Not so good things. Heard you had some problems in the Eddy. That true?"

*The Eddy. The Dream. That Glimpse into the Lacuna's Mind.*

Foley's tongue sours as if someone has spit lemon juice into his mouth. "It was under control. Had some setbacks, but…" He pats the table several times in rapid succession. "We got it now. All good from here on out."

A knowing smile rearranges the Mayor's lips. "You know how important the arts festival is, don't you? You realize we cannot have *any* setbacks, right? Not a single one. We don't want a repeat of what happened three years ago, correct?"

Foley swallows. "No, of course not."

Black leans over, spits the chewed sausage back onto the plate. Then he looks up from the gooey lump of saliva-slicked meat, directly into Foley's eyes. "They're here. Both of them. And they have very different but important roles to play here in Lacuna's Point. You know that as well as I do."

"I understand, but—"

"No *buts*. We've worked very hard to get them here. Very hard indeed. Our benefactor is pleased with our progress and—yes—I do agree that we've taken on more inductees than we ever have in the past, but it's important we carry out the needs of the Lacuna. It's important that the interlopers *make it* to the arts festival. I was hoping that the Eddy would break them down a bit more than it has, making them more susceptible for assimilation, but…that's just the way it goes sometimes. Seems they're determined. Like their daughters."

"I understand."

"Good," Black says, nodding. "Make them comply with these new ways of life. In fact, better yet—bring them to me. I want to speak with them directly and impart the importance of our ways of living. Do you think you can make that happen?"

Foley's eyes dart around the empty diner. "Yeah," he says, almost absentmindedly. "Yeah, of course."

"Today."

"Today?"

"You will bring them to my office beneath the tower today, so we can teach them the importance of compliance. You can take my men, as many as you think you'll need to get the job done, but I want them there, in my office, no later than sundown. Understood?"

"But today is—"

"Today is nothing, Elroy Foley. You will bring them to me. Not more buts. I hear one more *but*, and…gosh, I don't know. I might lose my shit."

Foley understands, gulps down a mouthful of sour air.

"I brought you here, Elroy Foley," the Mayor explains, "to be my right-hand man, and the only thing I had in you was trust. I saw in you what no one else saw. I saw a man who understood the concept of truth, of justice. Of the American Dream. You are the embodiment of the American Dream, Elroy Foley. Don't ever forget that."

"Sir, with all due—"

The Mayor snaps his fingers, silencing Foley mid-sentence. Two more black-hooded men enter the diner, and this time, they have a guest—it's Darla, the waitress. She's struggling in their grasp, trying to break free, but the men are stronger and waste little energy escorting her over to the table. One of them has a hand over her mouth, silencing her pleas.

"Do you remember when you first came here?" Mayor Black glares at Foley, ignoring their new guests. "All those years ago? Do you recall?"

Elroy tries to think back to the early days of his arrival, but the past seems so distant to him. It's like trying to remember a previous life through clouds of déjà vu. It's too hard, impossible. The past is easily forgotten in Lacuna's Point, and maybe that's *the point*, the purpose of this lovely town—live for now, because the past is inconsequential, an unchanging piece of oneself that contributes nothing to the future. The future is what you make it, and the past has no influence on things to come.

*Live for now, not for later.*

Also, he finds it hard to concentrate with Darla whimpering, her muffled screams.

"You remember," Black says with delight, the words slithering from his mouth like a snake through a leaf-infested thicket. "And do you remember what you did before you arrived here?"

Elroy racks his brain. For the life of him, he doesn't know what Black is talking about. But also—if he thinks long and hard enough, he can make out images that seem important to him. Still shots of something that might be worth remembering, worth hanging onto. Like a first kiss or a first dance, a first something. He remembers a city intersection and a blinking traffic light. A car with the driver's side door open. Dark holes on the white door. Whitewall tires. A body inside, eyes closed, blossoms of red in the center of a T-shirt. *Blood blossoms.*

"You remember, Elroy, I know you do, no matter how hard you want to forget." Black's words sink deep inside Foley's brain, and the being's voice nearly hypnotizes him, sends him sideways into a dull, dreamy state. He thinks he could sleep sitting up. "Not all art," Black continues, "can be found in books or magazines, paintings or pictures. Sometimes the world itself is art, and sometimes a gun is a paintbrush or a typewriter. Sometimes stories are told with the pull of a trigger. Sometimes blood is paint, sometimes a wrongful death is the art the world needs to see and hear." Black clicks his tongue, and it sounds like the cylinder of a revolver carrying a round into its rightful place. "You're an artist, Elroy Foley, and the Lacuna needs you. You are on your path of purpose, along with all the other lovelies of Lacuna's Point." The Mayor shrugs. "See, I'm an artist too."

Black jumps up and grips the back of Darla's head, then slams her face into the table, so hard that the ceramics and silverware jump and rattle. The woman lets out an abbreviated cry, and then she looks up at Foley, her eyes weeping, begging for his help, help he cannot give. The Mayor is not to be reasoned with—Foley doesn't even want to try. Instead, he attempts to look away, but the Mayor's soulless eyes are on him, and he knows that if he strays from the woman and whatever's coming to her, the Mayor will just *make* him watch. His men will make him. Or…that other thing that's truly in charge of this place—the *benefactor*—will make him.

"This one," the Mayor spits, "isn't playing by our rules. You know what we do, Elroy, when they don't play by the rules?"

Foley blinks, reluctantly nods.

"Good," he says, grinning, those black eyes shining like smooth obsidian, "then you won't object to a little artwork." Without much of a warning, he takes his gloved thumb and forefinger, and sinks them into Darla's left eye. The girl screams, wails, and the shrill sound of her agonizing outburst pierces Foley's ears. Still, Foley doesn't look away, not even when the Mayor takes one good rip, detaching the eye from the socket, pulling with it a long, sinewy strand of muscle. The wet splashing sound it makes when the eye comes free is almost enough to make Foley lose his breakfast.

Now he looks away. But it's too late—those images will burn through his thoughts forever.

Done with his *art,* the Mayor instructs the black-hooded men to take Darla away and get her "cleaned up." Once they're gone, Black plops the extracted eye down on the table, and it makes a funny splat when it hits the placemat. He sits back down, a sick smile appearing in the opening of his bandaged façade.

"I'm a man of God, sir." Elroy Foley doesn't know why he says it, but he does, and he can't take back the words once they hit the Mayor's ears.

Another sinister smile, those parting lips, the black split threatening to separate flesh and muscle. "Oh, me too. The difference between my god and your God, is that my god is real, he is here, and he is whispering in my ear all the time." Those black beads for eyes twinkle with devilish light. "You know what he's saying?"

Elroy doesn't dare to know the answer, but he knows the Mayor won't keep this awful knowledge to himself.

"He says, 'Go forth and create.' Neat, huh?"

Foley keeps silent. His God is a silent God, and Elroy Foley likes silent Gods best.

"Now go," the Mayor says, instantly losing the joyous smile he displayed only seconds ago. "You have a lot of work to do and our god is waiting."

The four of them hustle down Main Street. Mitch glances over his shoulder at the diner, trying to peek at whatever's going on over there, but in five minutes it doesn't matter—the shoppes swallow the view.

They follow Josh down the street, putting distance between them and Eddy, and Mitch can't stare at the enormous clock tower for very long without having dread and despair press down on him, a suffocating truth that smothers him with the knowledge that he'll never see anything outside the town's limits again. He'll never see home. He'll never see his wife, his daughters. And hell, he'll never get the chance to write that damned novel.

Silly thoughts to have when so much is happening, but he's torn from those notions when what sounds like a scream hits the airwaves. Mitch stops. Turns back. Faces the diner's direction once again.

"What is it?" Ellie asks.

"You didn't hear that?" Mitch tunes out the other people scurrying past them, going about their workday, and listens for another shrill outburst. It doesn't come. "I heard someone scream."

"Let's keep moving," Josh says to them.

"Where're we going?" Mitch asks, abandoning everything behind him, focusing on what lies ahead. "I mean, what the hell are we doing here?"

Josh shrugs in an *Isn't it obvious?* way. "You heard Darla. The Mayor's men are after us."

"How do we know she's telling the truth?"

Marissa steps in. "Darla's different."

"How?" Mitch snorts. "I mean, seriously? How is she different? She's not like us—that's for damn sure."

"She warned us. She's not one of them, trust me." Marissa glances suspiciously at the passerby. "You can almost tell that about people when you meet them."

"We shouldn't be discussing this out in the open," Josh says. "Too many ears."

Mitch has half a mind to turn back and discover what the scream was all about. "This feels wrong."

"We need to hide out somewhere. Until this blows over."

"Blows over?" Mitch can't believe what he's hearing. "This isn't going to blow over."

Ellie steps in. "Mitch is right. We can keep running, but eventually…they'll find us."

"You don't want them to find you," Marissa says. "That's the point."

"So, we what?" Another incredulous laugh escapes him. "Run forever?" He shakes his head. "Nah, fuck that."

"What if they kill you?" Josh asks.

Mitch puts his hands on his hips. "They wanted us dead, don't you think they would have killed us by now?"

"Fair point," Josh says, scratching his head.

"They let us in here for a reason. And I'm going to that clock tower to find out why." He nods over his shoulder, back at Eddy, the towering structure that sits in the same position it had when they first arrived. The sun shines upon it, highlighting the structure in this golden, sparkling glow. Despite this angelic representation, the tower still inspires a nest of anxiety in the center of Mitch's chest. "I'm going there, and I'm going to meet the Mayor."

"Oh Jesus fuck," Marissa says, looking away. "That's…that's like a really bad idea, man."

No one else says anything for a few seconds. Mitch watches the townspeople pass by, sees the sideways glances they throw at them, their unkind eyes. *It's because we're not like them.*

*Not yet.*

A chill licks his neck, and he shivers.

Ellie shrugs. "I just want answers, and I want my Dawn back, and maybe if we meet this *Mayor*…maybe he can help make that happen."

Josh looks to Marissa.

Marissa shakes her head. "You do what you want. I'm not going near that fucking place." And then she takes off, down the street, the way they were headed, opposite the diner and the clock tower and the front part of town where Mitch desires to travel.

"Marissa!" Josh calls after her. But she doesn't listen.

"Let her go, man," Mitch says. "She's made her choice."

"I can't leave her." Josh begins to walk backward. "Sorry!" Then he turns and runs off after her, calling her name. The two of them disappear down the sidewalk beyond the hustle of the day, other pedestrians going about their morning business.

"That leaves us," Mitch says.

"Yes." Ellie straightens her spine, faces him. "Are we off to see the Wizard?"

Mitch bites his lip. "Yeah, I guess we are."

*The Wonderful Wizard of Lacuna's Point.*

"Sorry, Elroy," Danielle says, "haven't seen them since, you know...before Eddy's tune. They were very interested in that piece back there, though. The woman claimed it belonged to her daughter or something." She shakes her head as if the whole situation is confusing, even to her. "I dunno. She was very distraught. Manic. Not making much sense." Danielle shrugs as if to say, *Eh, it happens.*

Foley chomps down on his wad of chew, then spews a brown stream into his empty water bottle. "Well, shit, seems the two of them are on the loose somewhere, tearing through town, really making a mess of things. They have two accomplices—a boy named Joshua Davis and a young woman named Marissa Garcia—seen anyone that might fit those descriptions?"

Danielle bites her lip and leans forward on her desk, making sure not to rest her elbows on the newest piece of art she's received. It's a painting of some woods and Foley sees nothing special about it, except it's arrived in a fancy wooden box. "Well...names are hardly descriptions, Elroy."

Foley smiles. *Of course.* "Well, shoot. Got me there. Just...ain't too many youngins in Lacuna's Point—thought they might stick out like a big pecker."

Danielle giggles. "God, no. Haven't seen any kids lately. We do need some youth around here, though. Don't you think?"

He doesn't think they need youth, quite the opposite. Youths are trouble, and if what the Mayor has described is accurate—then this Joshua Davis character might be the most trouble Lacuna's Point has ever seen.

*Conspirers. Bring them to me.*

"Sure, youth is important. Youth is the future," he adds, though he doesn't believe that, not one bit. If youth is the future, then the future is fucked.

"Precisely," Danielle says, wagging a finger at him.

"Well, the Mayor is on my ass about it. He's got the black hoods after them, so...you know, some shit is going down."

"Gosh, that sounds like a real pickle. Tell you what. I'll keep my eye out for them and spread the word."

"I'd appreciate that, little lady."

"It's the least I can do for the town." She blinks, smiles, tilts her head slightly to the side. "Lacuna's Point has been the best thing that's ever happened to me, so, you know—I'm here to do anything I can to preserve what the Mayor has built here."

Foley tips his hat. "I do appreciate the help there, darlin'. And don't think I'll forget it."

"Anything to keep the town clean and pure...and creating, of course."

"Mighty fine of you, ma'am. Mighty fine."

After leaving Danielle's gallery, Foley makes his way down the street, toward the center of town, toward the main and busiest intersection. He starts to think he should interview every single person he comes in contact with, asking if he's seen the interlopers, asking if he's seen the four people the Mayor is focused on. But if he doesn't want a repeat of three years ago, then why did the son of a bitch over-invite this year's talent? Foley doesn't know; he doesn't question the Mayor's methods—never has and he's not about to start now. All Foley needs to do is what the mysterious fucker tells him, and he'll get through this year's inductions just fine.

He dips into Bob McDonald's gun shop. Bob's an observant citizen, and if anyone's seen the quartet making their way around town recently, Bobby Mac is the guy.

"Hey there, Elroy," says Bobby Mac, stroking his long, white beard from behind the counter. Foley's eyes are immediately drawn to the American flag that's neatly pinned to the back wall, not a wrinkle in that red, white, and blue fabric. Next to it hangs a yellow flag with a coiled snake on it, the infamous phrase, "DONT TREAD ON ME" beneath it. "What brings you in?"

"Hey there, Bobby," Foley says, putting his hands on his hips, surveying the place. The store smells like dry gunpowder and GREY flannel, two smells that don't exactly mix well, but two smells that Foley doesn't exactly hate, either. He takes a good whiff and then begins to circle the shop.

"Looking for ammunition?" Bobby points to a rack with a huge yellow sign over it, shouting out the specials. "Got a two-for-one'er going on."

"Naw, naw," Foley says, peeking at the magazines on the far wall. His eyes can't help but bypass the rows of NRA-sponsored publications and wander to the top rack, specifically the magazines stuffed in the back, the kind with the black plastic slips over them announcing he needs to be 18+ to even touch the things. He shakes his head, moving on to other sinful merchandise. "I was just hoping you could help me out with a little situation, is all."

"Sure," he says. "Anything for the boys in the blue."

"You seen some newcomers hustling through here?"

"You mean…in the shop?"

"Naw. I mean, through town? Lately. Last hour or so."

Bobby Mac scratches his beard. "Ain't seen anyone out of the ordinary. Why? You got yourself a little situation with them? Bad seeds? Shoot—do we got ourselves some wannabe terrorists, Elroy?" Bobby Mac licks his lips like he's been waiting to deal with some 'wannabe terrorists' his entire life. "Got a whole locker of C4 back there. I can really fuck 'em up for you, if you—"

Foley waves his hand like a magic wand. "No, no, nothing like that, you crazy asshole. Just a couple of hoodlums trying to fuck with the peace. You know, always gets a little tense here before the big day."

"Ah. Got some *un*-peaceful protesters?"

"No, look," Foley says, wiping his face with his palm. He leans forward and lowers his glasses, peering at Bobby Mac directly in his squinty eyes. "You remember three years ago? The arts festival, what happened after? Those two girls?"

"Well…shit yeah. I remember. Quite a ruckus they caused us. I remember the Mayor was mighty pissed and…well…you know." Bobby Mac's eyes go to the ceiling, but Foley knows he's referencing something far beyond the twelve-foot distance. "Those were bad times."

"Bad times indeed. Seems our *benefactor* has requested the residence of the two girls' parents. Respectively."

"Is that right?"

"Indeed. And they are here. And...and they've had some help causing a little trouble. During ol' Eddy's song and dance, one of them—the mother of one of them—broke into Danielle's art gallery. Smashed a bunch of stuff. I tried to bring her in but things got hairy—you know how it happens."

"Indeed. You gotta do what you gotta do."

"Indeed is right. Well, that was all well and good, because it happened during the change and all is forgiven when the Lacuna sleeps, but the thing is...they seem to remember it. According to the Mayor, the benefactor isn't happy with the way things are going, and, so, the Mayor wants to sit them down for a little chit-chat, assess the situation and smooth everything over until the big day. So you see? I need to find them."

"Well, sir, you have my eyes. I see something, you'll hear something. That's for damn sure."

"I do appreciate your help, Bobby Mac. And don't think I won't—"

The bell rings as the front door opens. The intruder seems to be in a hurry because the door slams against the wall. Both men look over immediately, and Foley sees Dave Fester standing in the open doorway, huffing, completely out of breath.

"You want to be careful with my door, Fester," Bobby Mac says, glaring at the businessman as if he intends to use him as target practice. "Christ on a cross, Fester!"

Hearing the blasphemy, Foley twitches, but he doesn't correct his friend. Instead, he focuses on Dave Fester and the reason he's barged in here like the hounds of hell are after him. "You gonna stand there with your dick in your hand or you gonna say something?"

Dave swallows. "Elroy...it's the interlopers."

Foley stands up straight. "I'm all ears, boy."

Dave tells him, "They've given themselves up. To the black hoods."

"Huh?" Foley can't believe it, but there's no reason why Dave Fester would lie to him. Fester's a stand-up guy, and he's been part of Lacuna's Point as long as Foley can remember. "Seriously?"

Dave nods. "Yes. They're taking them to the Mayor as we speak."

When the black hoods march Ellie and Mitch into the Mayor's octagonal office, the first eyes she meets belong to Keith and Sue Campbell. At first she thinks they've been captured too, that they've been on the run since the town came back from that awful alternate reality, since they showed her the town's limits and that terrible truth along the highway—but then, as she walks past them, she sees their gazes concentrate somewhere else, *anywhere* else, other than her own. There's no sorrow in them, no sadness or fear—only guilt.

And then it clicks.

"You..." she says, passing them as the black hood pushes her along. "You...it was you..." The rest stop, the convenience store—Pop's Shop—following them. It all makes perfect sense now. "You led us here."

Keith pinches out a tear, but he keeps silent. As does Sue.

"You fuckers, you knew, and you didn't tell us. You knew everything!" Ellie spits and then stops herself from doing something very stupid. The black hood directs her over to one of two chairs. They seat Mitch in the other.

Once planted, the two face a mahogany desk stacked with papers, a typewriter that looks like one of the first ever made, and a tin can containing several writing utensils (one of which is an ink quill). They wait, but not long. After about thirty seconds, the heavy wooden doors behind the desk began to part like elevator doors. A man steps through the opening, but the second Ellie lays eyes on him, she's struck with the notion that this isn't a man at all. Not a human being, but a thing in human disguise. As if the black suit he's wearing is just a cloak concealing some hideous form. The bandaged head reveals no facial features, and she's left to wonder what abnormalities hide beneath the fabric. She can use her imagination, her artist's eye. And what she comes up with injects cool needles into her nervous system.

Behind the man, two black hoods follow.

"Welcome!" shouts the Mayor, throwing his hands up jubilantly, a celebration for all. "I am the Mayor of Lacuna's Point, but you may call me Quincy or Quincy Black or Mayor Quincy or Mayor Black. Names are trivial and I have so many, so let's not fuss, shall we?" His smile stretches in the mask's cutout. "You two," he says, pointing, "have been causing quite a pickle in here lately." Even though this shouldn't be something to celebrate, he dances in place, pumping his fist as if he's in a club, thumping to the beat of some electronic banger. Once he's done, he stops, pantomimes dusting off his chest, and then ambles around to the front of the desk, resting his rump on the edge. "You, Mitchell Green—I am very excited to meet *you*."

Mitch looks around curiously, as if there's been some mistake, that there's no way the Mayor should know who he is. "Me?"

The Mayor nods slowly. "Yeah, I know what you have in that head of yours and I'm very excited to read it." Mitch doesn't look any more enlightened. "Oh, come on, man! Your novel. The very thing you've been working on—or haven't been working on—over the years."

Mitch's throat clicks, jumps. "How…"

"How do I know?" The Mayor snorts, raises his hands like he's just performed a mind-blowing magic trick. "I know a lot of things. A great many things. Let's just say I'm on a higher level, man. You dig?"

Ellie grits her teeth. "Where's my daughter?"

The Mayor shoots her a look, and for the first time she can see into his eyes—and she wishes she couldn't because what is staring back at her is far from human, so far that one single glance sends a rod of instant unease through her sternum. She wants to look away, turn back the hands of time so she could avoid this exchange.

"Ah, yes," the Mayor says, the situation, his position of power, continuing to amuse himself. "Your daughter. The inimitable Dawn Brower."

Her heart wilts at the mere mention of her name.

"She's safe," the Mayor informs her. "In fact, she's just beyond those doors. They both are, both of your daughters. And you know what?" His brow moves beneath the disguise, rapidly, several times. "You can have them. You can be with them again. In fact—I prefer it that way. After all, it's the reason you two were brought to Lacuna's Point."

Speechless, Ellie wants to cry, wants to thank the Mayor, wants to praise him for his kindness, for his generosity, thank him for ending three long years of torment and unknowing. However, she feels a *but* coming, a big one, perhaps the biggest *but* she's ever heard.

"Well, it's *one* of the reasons," he says, turning to one of the black hoods and snapping his fingers. At once, one of them bends down and opens a small cooler behind the desk. Ellie didn't notice it earlier, but now that the hood has opened it, she's surprised she didn't. He pulls out a clear plastic cup with a straw. Some chunky red liquid fills the cup to the brim. The hood hands over the cup and the Mayor accepts it, begins to drink from the straw as soon as it touches his fingers. He sips loudly and obnoxiously, and the sounds of his throat slurping down the thick (*blood?*) liquid is enough to rotate her empty stomach. "Refreshments?"

Ellie shakes her head. Mitch does the same.

"Suit yourselves. Probably wouldn't like this anyway." He puts a hand to the corner of his mouth, about to let them in on some gossip. "You'd probably throw up if I told you what's in it." Ellie might throw up anyway, and upon realizing this, the Mayor giggles mischievously. "Well," he continues. His lips locate the straw once again, like a horse finding its way awkwardly around a carrot, and he resumes sucking down the mysterious smoothie. "All things need to eat. Like this town."

"I don't understand," Mitch says. "We don't care what's happening—honestly, we could care less what you people do here, what kind of...I don't know—*operation* you're running here."

"Operation?" The Mayor looks confused, slightly offended. "Oh...oh no—you misunderstand." He cackles, another amusing outburst, and Ellie thinks it must be so much fun to know all the secrets. "This isn't a...a cult? Is that the term you were looking for?"

Mitch looks like *cult* is as good as any.

"No, Mitchie, my boy. Mitchie-my-bitchie. No, the town is not some cult. We don't worship anything here. People are free to do what they want—well, *mostly*. Obviously there are rules—all places have rules, a series of established guidelines and…laws, I guess, though I'm not a huge fan of the word myself—but laws, yes. However, they are free to worship whatever deity they want—no laws against that. Just…we have to feed the right one."

"You're talking in riddles, man." Mitch leans forward. "Look, we won't tell anyone what's happened here. Honest. You have our daughters? Great. Bring them out here and we'll be on our way. No harm, no foul."

The Mayor shakes his head as if Mitch's suggestion isn't in the cards, and the small hope that Ellie once had regarding a safe, happy ending has all but withered and died.

"Well, Mitchie, I wish I could do that, I really do. But…*Gods*…" he says, the same way an exhausted pet owner would say, *dogs, am I right?* "They need to eat too."

Ellie gulps. Gods? Eat? She has no idea what the hell this crackpot is talking about, but she can't help but ask the question now that the topic's out there. Suddenly, some internal gears click into place, and though she doesn't exactly know what the answers are, she seems like she knows which questions to ask. "And…" The forthcoming words feel like a bitter ale creeping back up her throat. "…what, exactly, are you feeding them?"

Those black eyes shine with a dull glimmer, like moonlight peeking through folds of billowy fog. "In a sense…*you*. We feed them *you*."

# CHAPTER TWELVE

Foley gathers his breath, hikes up his pants so the waistband rests snugly against his hips, and then heads down the long hallway, the narrow space that seems much longer on the inside than the outside of city hall suggests. His eyes don't leave the center of that mahogany barrier, that door that looks like it should never be opened, and he can't shake the feeling that he's voluntarily heading toward his own hanging. Tasting bile on the back of his tongue, he presses forth, knowing that going any other way is only delaying the inevitable. It's best not to keep the Mayor waiting.

Foley already knows he's fucked up, even though the situation wasn't his fault—it wasn't on him that the interlopers decided to give themselves over to the black hoods. In years past the Mayor might not have made note of such a thing. But Foley's been in hot water since the season began and the invitees started making their way into town. He doesn't know why—doesn't understand why the Mayor acts this way or that—but there's a noticeable difference this year.

*The Mayor is spooked* is the best reason he can come up with. *He's scared of something.* And Foley doesn't have the slightest clue as to what that *something* is. A man who seems to wear many faces, who seems to communicate with the residing presence over this town, this *benefactor*, doesn't seem like much should bother him, and the fact that he is scared or worried or *something,* well, that doesn't rest well with Elroy Foley. That *scares* him.

He knocks three times on the door, then enters without waiting for a response. Once the door is open and he can see inside, see the interlopers in their seats before the town's highest government official and his cronies and the Campbells, a heightened tension smacks him in the face like a betrayed lover. Whatever's happening here, it ain't good.

"Elroy Foley!" the Mayor shouts, like Foley's a celebrity walking into a restaurant and ready to receive preferential treatment. "How good of you to join us!"

"Came as soon as I heard," Foley says, closing the door behind him.

"You're just in time to see the show." He snaps his fingers, ordering the hoods around like their only purpose in life is to serve. *Because it is.* "I was just explaining to our new friends what the future has in store for them. I have no doubt that they will be exceptional, productive members of our community. And that they will be reunited with their loved ones, and we can all get along— happy again. Oh, I also have news."

"News?" Foley asks. He's confused, nervous, much like the Campbells appear. The husband and wife shift in place, looking like they'd rather be anywhere else. Foley relates. "What news?"

"Well, you know how it is, Elroy." His finger and hands dance, flap in the air as if that's a signal that should explain everything. "Certain members of our society…let's face it—they get old. Used up. The juice of life, those sparks of creativity, they die after a while. Not in every soul—hell, no. I've seen your kind live nearly a century with their souls teeming with talent and the creative energy that would nourish our benefactor many times over. But, those people are rarities in this world, certainly not the norm, and well—this particular individual was no longer up for the task, I'm afraid."

Foley knows where he's going with this before he gets there. As with every year, a few of the older members of Lacuna's Point need to be *recycled.* It's to help make room for the younger, rawer talents. It's a deed that he's never really had to participate in—thank the *Lord*—as that's usually a chore reserved for the hoods, but Foley wouldn't put it past the Mayor to include him in the grisly festivities going forward as punishment, a way to get back at him for what happened three years ago.

*Those girls, they fucked everything up for me,* he thinks, as a hood brings forth a black plastic bag, holding it the way one would a pumpkin. Foley doesn't want to see what's inside.

The Mayor takes the bag, sets it down on the desk. He teases the top, pulling on it some, allowing the opening at the bottom to lift up, but not enough to reveal the secret inside. Foley watches dark fluids seep out the bottom. The mysterious fluids dribble down the front of the desk.

*"Voila!"* the Mayor shouts, flicking his arm, taking the bag with it, the plastic supplying the airwaves with a sharp and wet crack. Dark flecks, like fine red Bordeaux, pepper the table, some getting

on the Mayor's shirt, staining the white cloth between the jacket and tie. "It's magic!"

Foley doesn't look away, though his brain is begging him to. Dead eyes, open as if the last thing they held was some unspeakable terror, stare back at him, and Foley puts a hand over his mouth like he's about to scream. He won't do that, not unless he wants the Mayor to think even less of him. There's a lot of blood near where the head was severed, and some has matted the man's hair some. It takes Foley three seconds to recognize the victim—it's the old guitarist, the one who used to play sweet acoustic tunes in the center of town for people's pocket change.

*Old.*

*Used up.*

Foley swallows, his throat thick with nausea, and he wonders how many good years he has left before the Mayor decides it's time to take his head.

"This is what happens, ladies and gentlemen, when you A.) don't play by the rules, and B.) no longer provide Lacuna's Point with any flavor." The Mayor dips his forefinger into the pooling red on his desk, then sticks the blood-covered tip in his mouth, rubbing his gums. "Mm. Flavorless," he says, as if this is a cooking competition and he's the celebrity expert judge. "So…" The Mayor once again leans on the desk, holding out his hands like he's asking for criticism. "Do we have an agreement? You play ball and in return—you get your lives back. Sort of. You get to live them here, in Lacuna's Point, until you…" He pats the top of Skelly's severed head like a friendly puppy. "Well, until you can't anymore. Deal?"

"I want to see them," Ellie says, and Foley slides closer, having a look at the woman's ankle. Hard to tell from that distance, but it doesn't look swollen. Looks like she can walk on it just fine, and it seems the little incident that happened during the change was forgiven by the rules of this new reality. It's a load off his conscience—even if it was, deep down, the woman's fault. She just had to protest, challenge his authority, even though she was completely in the wrong. "I want to see our daughters," she tells the Mayor, and the Mayor looks open to it.

Quincy Black cocks his head to the side, delaying his answer. Then, he says, "All right. I think that's fair."

He snaps his fingers, and Foley gulps, knowing damn well that he's about to show the two interlopers nothing they want to see.

Hell, it might not even be their daughters. Might look like them, but the two girls...they won't *be* them.

They most certainly won't be human.

When the door opens and she can see the vague outline of her missing daughter, panic swells up around Ellie's heart as she realizes this is it—three years of build-up and the day is here, the one she's always dreamed of, the one she's begged, pleaded and prayed for. Though the conditions are not ideal (far from it), it's happening.

She's going to see Dawn's face again.

The Mayor waves in the girls, and as soon as she sees Dawn, Ellie springs up from her seat like a punched Sock'em Bopper head. Someone's hands immediately latch onto her shoulders and shove her back down. She doesn't fight it—the hands are strong and relay a sense of imminent danger through every nerve her body has left.

"Stay put," a voice speaks into her left ear and she instantly knows that voice—it belongs to the cop that stomped on her ankle when the town took that scary side trip into that alternate dimension. Ellie thinks the next words out of the cop's mouth will be "or else" but those words never come. She feels his presence towering over her, and that's enough to keep her there.

Several black hoods squeeze through the opening, forming a tight band around the two girls. It's as if they're celebrities pushing through a crowd of fans and paparazzi. Once inside the octagonal office, the hoods spread apart, making a line, four on each side of the girls.

Ellie can't believe it. It's her. It's Dawn. Despite her ragged appearance—hair that looks like it hasn't been washed in months, tangled and gnarled, and the splotches of paint (daffodil yellows and cobalt blues) on her cheeks and forehead, arms and clothing (that looks moth-eaten)—Ellie weeps. Cries because it feels good to see her again. To know that she's alive even if she's been mistreated, mishandled, and abused—it's good to know that she's still breathing and that Ellie was right; above all else, it's good to know her motherly instincts served her well over the years, and that she never gave up hope. Because if she had, then she wouldn't be here. With a chance to save her. With a chance to be family again.

*"Mom,"* Dawn says, her voice fragile. The simple word strikes Ellie's heart like a studded hammer, and she feels her soul unravel. She loses it, begins to sob openly, her body hitching along with each broken breath.

She looks to Mitch and sees tears running freely from his eyes, and he's smiling, overcome with the realization that his daughter is still alive, and—like her—that the rebuilding can begin. The life they once had, that slice of perfection pie, is still a feasible outcome. They can go back and be happy, be free, be—

"What a wonderful reunion!" the Mayor says. "Not ideal, I know, but still—has to feel good, doesn't it? Let's make some memories!"

Ellie looks to Kya. She's dressed in a French maid's outfit, and she's carrying a feather duster. Ellie glances back to Mitch, and the initial elation of seeing his daughter again quickly bleeds away.

"What the fuck is this?" he asks. Thick spittle leaves his lips in haste. "The fuck have you done to my daughter?"

The Mayor asks him to pump the brakes with a quick hand gesture. "Calm down, sir. Your daughter is fine."

"Dad..." she says, and the way she speaks, the subdued tone, it's as if she's drugged. "Dad...what...why are you here?" Kya looks to the Mayor, her fluttering eyelids, the soulless gaze behind them asking for clarification. "This real?"

"It is real, Kya," the Mayor confirms. "You'll have to excuse them. I figured this moment might get a little, uh, *tense*, so we gave them a little something to help ensure things run smoothly." He chuckles insanely as if this is the funniest thing he's heard in life so far. "These girls are a riot. Their more formative years must have been a real treat. No?"

"You stay the fuck away from them!" Mitch shouts.

Ellie pleads with him, silently, shooting him a glare that goes ignored. She can't figure out if that's by design, but it doesn't matter. Mitch is off and running with his anger, and there's nothing Ellie Brower can do to stop it.

"You let them go, right fucking now," Mitch says, his chest heaving. "Or I'll...I'll..."

"You'll what?"

Mitch owns his current defeat, slumps in his seat, hangs his head, and allows the tears to run down their shallow beds of flesh.

"That's what I thought. Here's the deal—and you have to say yes, because it's the only deal you'll ever get—you live here, the four of you, and act like obedient, civilized people, and you get to work on that art of yours. You," he snaps at Ellie. "I know you've got some creative juice in that internal well of yours. You're a teacher, right? You *inspire*. That's good. We'll need that. And you, Mitchie, we're going to need that novel, the one I know you so desperately desire to rip out of your subconscious world and put on paper—the Lacuna is going to need it and in two weeks from now, you're going to read us what you've written—at the talent show, on center stage, in front of the whole damn town. And you're going to allow the benefactor to drink from your fathomless elixir, eat your juicy words, and taste your delicious mind. You will read and the Lacuna will eat, and we can all get along happily for as long as we need to. Understood?"

Mitch says nothing. Ellie follows his lead.

"Silence is agreement, lady and gentleman," the Mayor assures them. When they don't protest, Mayor Black nods. "Silence it is."

Someone clears their throat, and for a second, Ellie thinks the sound came from Mitch. But she glances over at him and his head's still directed at the Mayor's feet.

"I have something," Keith Campbell says, and it's only when he speaks that Ellie remembers the couple is still there with them. He shuffles forward, into the center of the room where Ellie sits, but also far enough away so she can't reach for his face and scratch out his eyes. "Mr. Black, I have something."

The Mayor glances over in the Campbells' direction. "Well, if it isn't the Campbells. Hardly remember you even being present. A delightful surprise," he says, the words slick with sarcasm. "What can I do for you?"

"Well," Sue chirps, "it's just, that, uh, we upheld our end of the bargain—see, we brought them here, made sure they got here safely and kept them, you know—company—and we were wondering if we could, if *you* could, um…" She swallows as if this could be the last time she ever speaks. "…let us go now?"

"Let you go?" The Mayor rotates his head as if his neck isn't working properly, broken in places. "I'm not keeping you here, Campbells. You're free to go about the town as you please."

Keith smiles, laughs humorlessly. "Yes, we know that. But...as part of our agreement, we were told that you would let us *go* go. Home."

"You are home now," The Mayor says dryly.

Sue holds up a finger. "Now wait a moment, you said that—"

"I say a lot of things to get what I want, Sue Campbell."

"What..." Keith shakes his head, an adamant gesture that earns zero reaction from the Mayor. The man in the bandaged mask looks on, seemingly bored of this conversation and the direction it's headed. "You promised. Promised that if we escorted them safely, that you would let us take Jared and leave safe—"

"I SAY A LOT OF THINGS," Black's voice thunders, shaking the ground beneath them. Ellie feels the vibrations all throughout her body. The sound that follows the outburst is hardly a human one, deep and throaty, like a frog singing some nightly hymn in some southern bog's inner darkness. That sound—Ellie never wants to hear it again as long as she lives. Everyone in the room shrinks, recoils, except for the black hoods who stand impossibly still, overseeing this *transaction*.

"Sorry about that," Black apologizes, and the Mayor licks his thumb and attempts to work the droplets of blood out of his silky-white shirt's fabric. "Temper flared. Won't happen again. Unless you make me."

"Mayor Black," Sue says, weeping now, shuddering with each breath, the same way Ellie spent so many nights thinking about Dawn, about losing her. Now, the woman is feeling that pain, knowing she's lost and the fight she's fighting will end in the Mayor's victory. Ellie doesn't feel an ounce of sympathy for her. "You promised," she cries. "What's fair is fair."

The Mayor abandons his shirt and sighs. "Didn't want to have to do this, but...it appears you've left me no choice." He quarter-turns, signaling to his black hoods with a subtle nod.

Ellie catches it, though; so does Sue, because she immediately reverses her course.

"No, Mayor, Mayor Quincy, please—" She puts a hand over her mouth as if that will erase the words she's already spoken. "It wasn't—I wasn't being disrespectful or rude or ungrateful—I just wanted to—"

She doesn't get to finish the feeble apology. From behind her husband, a black hood emerges, swinging an axe into the bulk of muscle where Keith's neck and shoulders meet. The action is too fast for Ellie to look away, and once the sharp end of the blade bites into him, spraying a generous arc of scarlet, dousing Ellie's face in wet droplets, she's frozen and captured by the violent imagery. Keith's eyes roll back and his body crumbles to the floor, like he's a robot and someone's just pulled the plug on his electric consciousness. His weight hits the floor with a sickening slap, and then his body lies still. When the hood pulls the axe free from Keith's neck, fresh crimson dapples the far wall.

Sue's hands collapse over her open, stretched mouth, and the woman screams like a vintage Hollywood horror queen. As her caterwauling drags on, her piercing vocalizations cutting through the center of Ellie's brain, the black hood brings down the axe once again, connecting with the unfinished task of taking off Keith's head. The blade gets through more of the mangled meat, but it gets stuck halfway, and the killer is doomed to repeat the process once more. But…third time's a charm, and Keith's blood-slicked face is finally separated from the rest of him, ending any fantasy Ellie may have had about getting out of Lacuna's Point alive.

Sue sucks in a terrified breath and prepares to release another shrieker upon them all. But before those ear-splitting sounds hit the airwaves, the murderous hood turns and strikes her in the throat with the bloody axe head, cleaving a thick scarlet indent in her doughy flesh. When he removes the blade, the hollow spot wells with fresh blood, spilling down her throat, coating her chest. The trench bleeds more profusely as the seconds pass, and within a few blinks, Sue Campbell is sinking to her knees as her hands go to the wound, trying to do anything and everything she can to stop her vitality from escaping. The killer winds up like a Major League slugger and swings the axe blade into the back of her neck, managing to work the metal four-fifths of the way through. Her head pops off like it wasn't sitting correctly on her shoulders in the first place, and a little shove is all it takes to rid her neck of the burden. A squirt of blood ejects into the air like an angry torrent from some volcanic pit. Her body and head fall to the ground separately.

Ellie can't breathe; every short breath is heavy with the metallic smell that fills the room, and she thinks the sudden change in air quality has the potential to suffocate her.

Mayor Quincy Black smiles, stands up straight, and looks down at the brutal display that rests only a few feet from his cowboy boots. "Now," he says, looking away from the two corpses whose blood is staining the carpet, breathing in that awful blood stench as if it's cleaner than fresh mountain air. "Who's ready for supper?"

When Josh and Marissa step through the front door of the house, their temporary home until they can escape the endless, repeating circles of Lacuna's Point, Skelly is waiting for them, his decapitated body sitting ever-so-still in a chair about twenty feet from the open doorway.

Josh loses it. Feels himself break.

He lands on his knees, screaming out, while Marissa tries to catch him in her arms, whispering in his ear that everything will be all right.

But it won't be.

It really won't.

# CHAPTER THIRTEEN
## TWO WEEKS LATER

The wet mop head hits the floor, smearing a mixture of sticky-dried soda pop residue and slippery butter-flavored topping around the black marble surface. The last movie lets out of theater ten and a dozen people parade past the snack stand, heading for the exit as they discuss the fantastic flick they've just seen (*The Bridges of Madison County*) for probably the hundredth time, since all the movies here are recycled classics, approved by Mr. You-Know-Who. Mitch smiles at them as they pass, leaning on the wooden end of the mop, wishing them a "good night" and that he's looking forward to them coming back to enjoy more of the fine cinema that Lacuna 10 offers the public. The patrons pay him no mind as they pass, treat him like a ghost. He's perfectly okay with it. He gets to hear all their conversations that way, enjoying the menial things people talk about. Town gossip. Who's seeing who. Cheating husbands. Nagging wives. Church talk. Parties and social gatherings. The upcoming arts festival that everyone can't wait to partake in and showcase their talents in front of Mayor Quincy Black. Mitch watches and listens to every one of them, smiling, just smiling.

After they're gone, after the last moviegoer exits the lobby, he locks up the snack stand and counts down his till before handing the bagged money over to the night manager, who accepts the cash-drop sans a single word. In the two weeks he's been employed by the Lacuna 10, the night manager, Robert, has barely said a word to him. And Mitch doesn't mind this either. Robert gives him the creeps, and Mitch knows he's deep in Lacuna's Point's pocket, possibly deeper than that asshole cop, Foley.

After Mitch fakes a smile and the manager scoots off toward the back office, Mitch heads upstairs to the locker room. There, he slips off his uniform and puts on a flannel shirt—it's definitely not summer anymore, and the seasons have changed practically overnight forcing him to bundle up after the sun goes down since the hotel room's heater hardly puts out a single burst of hot air. Funny what a difference two weeks can make in terms of weather, but

Lacuna's Point's weather system is eternally off anyways. At least it's not snowing like it was on the day he first arrived, in that *alternate* place. Luckily the clock tower hasn't signaled once since that first terrible experience, and since then…the town has actually been quite normal. Not *normal* normal. But no one has gotten decapitated, split open, or has been seen sticking mole crabs into their abdomen.

Once dressed to meet the night, Mitch heads out of the locker room and into the projection booth, the shortcut way to the back alley that leads him to the main drag, toward the hotel. The projectors are still running through the last reels, chewing through the credits, their incessant clicking as the film passes through the latch gates over the apertures filling up what could be a dreadful, eerie silence. Mitch is thankful for the noise—nothing could be worse than touring the dark, creepy-ass projection booth with Barry lurking around, doing God-only-knows-what up here. Barry's not a bad guy—in fact, he's one of the nicer people he's interacted with. Mitch isn't sure that he's one of *them,* one of the converted residents, but he's not sure he isn't, either. And since the group has agreed to err on the side of caution when determining the influenced and the non-influenced, Mitch can't exactly hold the kind of conversations he'd like to with Barry. Mitch isn't sure if some of the citizens are acting *un*influenced to gain information, collect some truths for the Mayor. It's a tight rope to walk, and it's better if Mitch just sticks to the plan. Fewer people know about them the better.

He passes the projectors, watching the huge silver platters feed the film through the machines, about empty of their supply as the last reels wind down. He turns a corner, heading toward the back stairwell and spotting Barry as the man watches the end credits of some obscure arthouse pic Mitch has never heard of.

"Good night, Barry," he calls to him, throwing up his hand in a courteous wave. From the porthole's reflection, he can see Barry's eyes shift toward him. The man looks like he's pulled an all-nighter, maybe two. Dark sacks hang under his vacant stare. His pale complexion and sweaty brow are noticeable even in the shadowy images the dark glass throws back at him.

*He looks haunted,* Mitch thinks. *More than usual.*

Barry is ordinarily a sweaty, nervous guy—but this on some other level.

"I had the dream again, Mitch," Barry says. "Last night. They're getting worse lately."

Barry's only been here two years, which is part of the reason Mitch thinks he's not a full convert. No two people react to the power of this place the same, but some can fight off the influence for longer periods of time. The girls, three-year veterans, have done tremendously well in that department. Skelly had done his best, but fighting the powerful energy had taken its toll on the old musician. Fractured his mind, his soul, and there was hardly anything left of the old man's sanity near the end. Which is what will happen to Barry if they can't find a way out in time. Or…if they give up. Stop fighting. Join the cause and give the town, the Mayor, the benefactor, what they want—their art, their souls.

*Never,* Mitch thinks, and realizes this is a fight he's willing to die for.

"I've been having them too, Barry," Mitch tells him, and that part is true. For the last two weeks, he's dreamt about being home with his entire family, Angie and the three girls. His two sons-in-law. They're eating live crabs, *mole* crabs, and then eventually Mitch realizes that he's dreaming and begins to fight back, and then one of his family members changes appearances. Sometimes they turn into the Mayor, sometimes they turn into something else. Huge antennas poke through their craniums, their eyes become these obsidian globs that leak from the sockets, their bodies splintering apart, revealing these membranous strands that reach out of their bodily cavities, leaking out into the dreamworld like ribbons flapping in a soft breeze.

He's had these nightmares every night, and so have the others. Ellie was the first one to confirm this, but Marissa and Josh also admitted to having similar episodes.

"Think they'll stop?" Barry asks. "I can't sleep at night. Feel like I haven't slept in months."

Mitch shrugs, sympathizing. When this is over, *if* it ends, and he's home and safe and Lacuna's Point is nothing but a bad dream itself, he thinks he'll sleep for a month straight. "I think so."

"I think it's the Light."

"The Light?"

"The Light from the tower. When the clock strikes just right, and the music plays..." Barry is smiling now, with childlike wonder. "...and the light hits you. Fills you. You know?"

Mitch nods as if he does. "Yeah, yeah, I do."

"I need the Light again, Mitch. We all do. It...helps."

Mitch checks his watch. He's late. "Absolutely, Barry. Hey, I gotta run."

"The Light is coming, Mitch," Barry says, his eyes turning back to the porthole, the credits on screen. "Two days and we'll have the Light again."

*Two days.*

*The Arts Festival.*

"I can't wait," Mitch says, and truly—he can't.

Because that's the day they fight back.

The day they'll leave Lacuna's Point...

Or die trying.

Mitch wakes up in a hotel room; from the radio on the nightstand, two morning-show hosts jaw on about some political news story through bursts of intermittent static. As he pulls himself up, clearing the foggy sleep from his eyes, there's a faint, lemony-fresh scent in the air, the kind that smells like it's only there to mask some other hideous odor. He slaps the alarm clock, silencing the two idiot pundits at once. It takes him five minutes to wash his face, brush his teeth, throw on some clothes, and head downstairs. He passes the new girl behind the counter, waves and smiles, though she hardly pays any attention to him, too consumed by the old, tattered paperback positioned in front of her face.

Next, Mitch heads over to the diner. When he passes through the doors of Ace's Place, a few eyes in the room migrate toward him, but they don't linger like they would have weeks ago. It seems his "good behavior"—working at the local theater and not causing any trouble (not breaking into places or trying desperately to exit this sealed place) has earned him that much. A little conspiracy here and there, but he and the others have done a good job keeping those meetings few and secret. He'll never shake the Mayor's suspicions completely, considering the hell that Kya and Dawn have caused over the last three years, but he's done enough to keep him off their back. For the first few days, Mitch couldn't take a single step without one of the black hoods lurking around the corner. Now, the last few, he hasn't seen a single one of those faceless, menacing creatures.

He takes the usual booth in the back and is thankful the place isn't too busy. After he checks his watch, seeing that Ellie herself is now five minutes late, Darla brings him his cup of coffee, winking as she sets the ceramic down before him.

"Hey there, darlin'," she says, her gum-stuck teeth on full display. Mitch does his best to look her in the eye and not to stare at the eyepatch. She doesn't speak about it, never has, but Mitch suspects either the cop or the Mayor himself had something to do with it.

*That scream.*

"Hey," he says, then clears his throat. "You got a minute?"

She glances around, keeping her smile where it is, though her eyes glimmer with disquiet. "There're too many people here," she says through her teeth.

Mitch observes the immediate area, seeing a family of four eating their main courses, the man and his son's backs facing him. The wife and daughter are facing Mitch, but paying him zero attention, or so it seems. The rest of the occupants are farther down, engaged in discussions, and there's no way anyone in the place can hear them if they keep their voices low enough.

"I think we're safe," he says.

Darla centers herself, facing Mitch, putting her back to the rest of the patrons. "We're never safe here."

"We need to hash out a few more details."

Darla freezes, looks around like she's being watched, and then sighs. "What is it? I was told by the kid…"

"Josh."

"Yes. Him. I was told to keep my distance until…you know."

Mitch leans forward, tapping the table with the tip of his forefinger. "We can't mess this up. We got one shot. You know what happens at the arts festival—you've seen it."

"I…I can't remember exactly what happens, but it's a spectacle for sure." She eyes the rest of the diner from her periphery, then continues in a low, hushed voice, calm and measured. "It's like my brain is trying to protect me, trying *not* to remember."

"Two days. We have two days to figure it out, and you—you're the only one who's been through it before. You need to remember so we can prepare accordingly."

Darla winces, straining to see the past but the mental fog is too thick. "No...I'm sorry. I can't."

The husband of the family sitting about five booths down looks over his shoulder at them. His eyes linger in a way that makes Mitch want to knock his teeth out. Then the man says, "Hey, honey? How about a little refill?"

"Coming!" Darla says, and before she goes, she whispers to Mitch, "We'll talk later."

As she leaves, the front door opens, and Josh bounces his way inside. Marissa isn't far behind him, and she's looking around the place like cockroaches are littering the counter, belly-up. Then Mitch realizes it's just the people she's looking at.

"Well, well," Mitch says, checking his watch, surprised it's still working. "About time."

"We got a late start," Josh says, nodding over at Marissa. "Someone didn't want to wake up this morning."

"Cram it, shrimp," Marissa tells him. "I need my beauty rest."

"How's it going with Darla?" Josh asks. "She remember anything yet?"

Mitch pushes his cheek around with his tongue. "Not enough."

"I have an idea."

"Great. Can't wait."

From his pocket, Josh pulls out a little brown book, leatherbound. Unearthing the thing gives off a strong aroma, and it takes Mitch back to when he was little, those summers on the shore when his mother used to take him to the county library. Those trips, of course, inspired his love for stories, reading, and eventually, wanting to write that novel.

*The novel you're supposed to be working on.*

"What's that?" he asks. "Mother Goose's nursery rhymes?"

"Not quite. It's a book on hypnotism. Got it from that used bookstore over on 7$^{th}$. Got some wild stuff in there, man."

"Say what?"

"Hypnotism. It's a method of—"

"I know what *hypnotism* is, shortcake, I'm just wondering why you've taken up the sudden interest."

"Well," Josh says, opening the book, snapping the spine with an audible crackle. "I was thinking—a lot of these people don't know what happens during the arts festival, right? Most of them think it's a celebration, a way to give back to the Mayor and the—you know." He nods up at the ceiling. "Some say they're given Light. Right?"

"I've heard the Light mentioned a few times now," Mitch admits.

Marissa starts her chain-smoking habit. "Me too. Some old lady in church said the Lord gives the most Light during the festival—it's her favorite day of the year." She smiles wanly. "Fucking bitch. She was more cracked out of her mind than Skelly was—no offense, Josh."

Mitch watches Josh's face change, his positive attitude taking a noticeable hit. It's clear to Mitch that the kid is still shaken up about the whole Skelly ordeal—and Mitch can't blame him. Seeing a headless corpse at his age would really warp him, too.

"So…" Josh says, trying to recover from the mention of Skelly's name. "Anyway…I think maybe we can try some tricks on Darla? Unlock something that's buried inside her head?"

"Interesting observation, sprout," Mitch says, and he means it. He's willing to try anything to get her to remember everything, to give them more details about the event other than, *Something big happens.* "All right, go for it. But we're going to have to make it quick. Has to happen today."

"I've already convinced Darla to stop by after work," Josh says.

"Good."

"Good."

"That's settled then," Mitch says, looking around the diner, focusing on the door. Still no sign of Ellie and he's starting to freak out a little. Over the last two weeks, she's been absent-minded, clearly not herself, and Mitch is beginning to worry that her heart's not in the plan the four of them have been working so hard on.

And he knows why.

And he can't blame her, not completely.

"Looks like your best friend is a no-call-no-show again," Marissa informs him, tapping ash into the tray.

Mitch shakes his head. "Shit."

"Can't blame her," she adds with a shrug. "I mean, if we got to see our loved ones every day, I can't say we'd be eager to change things."

Mitch tightens his jaw. He can't blame Ellie much either, but she did make a promise—a promise to all of them—and by not being here, she's breaking that promise.

*Shattering it.*

"I'll go get her," Mitch says, and then begins to slide out.

Josh stops him. "We've been thinking…"

From the edge of the cushion, Mitch stops, waits, his eyes flicking between his new friends. "About what?"

"Just…Ellie." Nervously, Josh spins the book around in circles before him. "She's…she's losing herself and…"

Marissa drops her hand down on the spinning book, stopping the tedious rotation. "I'll say it since Josh seems like he wants to dance around it. Your friend—Ellie—she's compromised."

"Compromised?" Mitch asks, snorting. "No, no. She's…she's not."

"She is, dude."

Josh adds, "She doesn't seem like she wants to be here…"

"This is the third time she's ghosted us," Marissa tells him. "*Third.* That's like fifty-fifty whether she'll stand on our side during the arts festival. You don't know what they've done to her daughter, you don't know what's happening other than what you can see with your own eyes. We have to assume she's been compromised."

"No…Ellie—she wouldn't. Besides. That's not how it works— you said," he says, directing his rising anger at Josh, "it takes years for the town to change a person. *Years.* We've been here weeks."

"Affects everyone differently, dude," Marissa answers for Josh. "You know that, too. It's why your girls have been essentially locked up for three years while the others are free to roam as they please. That douchebag cop—he's probably been the law here since the first day he arrived. There's no way to predict how people react to things, react to influences. No human being is the same, and we have to take that into account too. We have to assume that Ellie is—"

"All right, I'll talk to her," Mitch says. "Look, I'm on your side. I am. She's been…not herself lately. I can admit that. So let me talk to her, let me try to get some answers. Let me see what I can find out before we just…I don't even know what you're proposing—we cut her loose?"

Seconds before answering, Josh scrunches his lips into a tight knot. "We just think she shouldn't be trusted with sensitive information is all."

"That's fair," Mitch admits. "But let me talk to her. I'll go to the gallery, I'll find out what we need to know."

Marissa sighs and shoots Josh a look, *that look*. "Your call, kid. I'm just along for the ride at this point since I'm pretty sure my sister is dead and I'll never see her again." She takes a long drag and then releases coiling tendrils of smoke toward the square-tiled ceiling. "Either way, we're already dead and one step closer to Hell."

Josh takes a second to collect his thoughts, and then says, "Fine. Talk to her. But be honest. If you don't think she's going to help or worse—if you think she could be spying for the Mayor—then you need to tell us. It's only fair."

Mitch nods, not exactly happy about taking orders from a twelve-year-old kid, but Josh isn't an ordinary twelve-year-old and Mitch knows it. There's something about him, something that Lacuna's Point wants from him, otherwise, he wouldn't be here. Sure, the kid can doodle some superheroes fairly well, far better than the average Joe-artist, but Mitch believes that's not the real reason for his "invitation." There's something else, something deeper.

Staring the kid in the eyes, he thinks he might know why—the kid's intelligence is off the charts, and he thinks the Mayor might want some of it for himself. Or the thing commonly referred to as the "benefactor."

But Mitch doesn't want to commit to that theory. Doesn't want to commit to anything besides getting beyond the town's limits safely, and with Kya.

"I'll talk to her," Mitch says again. "I'll find out."

"Well," Josh says, "good luck. You'll need it."

The art gallery smells like wine and old lady perfume. Mitch nearly sneezes the second he walks through the door, but he's able to control his sinuses. Slipping past the front counter where the head curator, Danielle, is flipping through a magazine, he heads directly for the back where he knows Ellie will be. He thinks he's home-free but freezes the second he senses Danielle's eyes on him.

"Hi Danielle," he says, flashing his teeth, the ends of his lips pushing his grown-in beard apart.

"Hi, Mitchell," she says back, her suspicious gaze all over him. It's like she knows he's up to no good, that his presence here is a misdemeanor in and of itself. "How are you this morning?"

"I'm doing well. Got a good night's sleep. Feeling pretty refreshed."

"Hmm." She's unimpressed, treating his lines as a story she's not buying. "And how are you settling into Lacuna's Point?" she quizzes, eyebrows flaring. "Good? Heard you're working at the old movie theater on ninth?"

"You know? Gotta be honest with you. Hated this place when I first got here—I mean, *hated* it." He watches her stand there, statue-still, judging his every word. "But it's actually growing on me. I could...I could see myself living here."

She doesn't seem wholly convinced, but it's enough to keep her from prying deeper. Cool relief washes over him and his heartbeat simmers.

"Glad to hear it. Suppose you're looking for your girlfriend?"

"Suppose I am."

"She's in the back. With Dawn. They're unboxing a new piece. The Mayor's newest acquisition. I hear it will appear at the festival."

"Can't wait to see it myself."

At this, Danielle smiles. "You might enjoy it."

He hates the amusement in this statement just as much as he hates everything about this godforsaken shit town and almost everyone in it.

Ellie watches her daughter survey the piece, run her fingers along the canvas surface, tracing the artist's each and every brushstroke. It's as if she's learning about what went through the creative mind as they gave life to this very scene. Ellie smiles, remembering a time when art used to fill her with happiness, when it was *her* world. When she used to lose herself in a painting for an afternoon—or several—working and creating like nothing else mattered. That was before she had Dawn, before she met Dan. Before her life became complicated, when the only thing that mattered was the art.

"What do you think of it?" Dawn asks her.

She studies her daughter, her face, still not convinced this is reality. That she's truly asleep somewhere and this is all one big dream she will eventually wake from. If that's the case, she wants to sleep forever. Because she's here, with Dawn, and the two of them have spent more time together over the last two weeks than they had in the last two years prior to her disappearance—and it's been wonderful.

Well, sort of. Dawn's different now, that's for certain. Ellie hasn't been able to pinpoint what exactly, but *different* is the best way she can describe her. Inconsistent. Somewhat broken. Whatever the Mayor had her doing (she refuses to talk about it) prior to Ellie's arrival has certainly taken its toll on her mind. She's skittish. Like an abused dog, frightened to place a paw outside the lines set forth by its asshole owner.

"I think it's lovely," Ellie says, not looking at the painting at all, but the smoothness of her daughter's skin.

Dawn smiles, continuing to run her fingertips along the painting of an endless field of wildflowers. In the distance, the enormous, familiar clock tower sits alone, a brilliant sun shining glorious streaks of golden light down upon it.

"What do you think it means?" Dawn asks. "What was the artist's intent?"

"I have no idea."

"If you had to guess." Dawn shrugs, alluding to the fact that there is no correct answer, that every opinion is a little bit wrong and a little bit right.

Ellie sighs, finally turning to the piece, taking in the green landscape dotted with colorful flowers, the subtle darkness resting behind the tower, pushing smudges of shadows into the invading golden glow raining down from cobalt skies. "I don't know. There's so much beauty there, but…it ends. When it reaches the clock tower. There's darkness there, behind it, and it's settling in." Ellie touches the tops of the painting, tracing her fingers along the tower's outer walls. "But there's more beauty than darkness. The wildflowers take up most of the painting, so I think that's why."

"I like that," Dawn says, putting the painting down, moving on to the next piece.

Ellie wants to open her mouth and tell her this is meaningless, that she should forget about the art, this place, Danielle, the Mayor, and come home with her. But she can't. There's a fragile balance here, and she doesn't want to compromise the relationship she's reestablished with her daughter.

As Ellie watches Dawn sift through the new merchandise, she senses a presence behind her. Defensively, she turns, almost ready to claw off the face of the intruder. She half-expects Danielle to come pushing through the curtain that stands between the sales floor and the backroom, only emerging to break up their time together—a part of each workday she thinks the owner looks forward to.

Ellie is relieved when it isn't Danielle.

"Hey," she says to Mitch. He's holding out his arms, expecting an immediate explanation. "What? What is it?"

He doesn't answer, but his face melts into that *C'mon, don't give me that* mask, and she immediately realizes what he's referring to.

Ellie's head falls to the side. "Oh shit, is it Tuesday?"

"Yes," Mitch says.

"Shit. Totally lost track of the days."

"We were supposed to meet up at the diner, you know, have *breakfast* together." *Breakfast* is code and Ellie speaks the language of the conspirators. She watches his eyes fall on Dawn; she's still flipping through various prints, half-listening to the conversation.

"I'm so sorry, Mitch. I totally forgot. I was working and—"

"Well, I'd sure like to have breakfast with you sometime soon." Mitch swallows. "Your friends sure would." Then he looks over his shoulder, making sure Danielle hasn't snuck up behind them to listen through the fabric partition. "Josh seems to think that—"

"I don't give a fuck what he thinks," she snaps.

"Mom?" Dawn asks, rising from her position on the floor. She leaves the prints where they are, half gone through. "Is everything okay?"

"Yes, fine," Ellie says, without turning, focusing on Mitch's eyes, staring deep into them, as if she's speaking directly to his soul. "Mr. Green was just leaving."

"El—"

"Now, in fact," Ellie adds, and that's enough to shut him up.

He shakes his head, disappointment blossoming across his features. "Fine. I'm happy you're happy with this...*arrangement.*" He lingers like she's going to explain herself, but she isn't. She lets him know this by directing him to the curtain with her eyes. "You know I can't help you now, right?"

"Just go."

He nods. Turns. Storms through the curtains, pushing past Danielle, who was just entering the back hallway. After Mitch leaves the gallery completely, Danielle rotates toward Ellie, her smile curling to one side of her face.

"You two break up or something?" she asks, unable to keep the joy from her tone.

Ellie doesn't answer. She goes back to spending time with her daughter, absorbing as much as she can before whatever's happened to her happens to Ellie too.

Before she forgets about home and remembers what a lovely place Lacuna's Point truly is.

# CHAPTER FOURTEEN

Elroy Foley strolls down the sidewalk, coffee in one hand, donut in the other, nodding and grinning at the passing people, every step filled with cheerful pride. They return smiles and energetic waves, thanking the cop for his good service and keeping them safe from all the bad things that could potentially happen to them—robberies, murders, violence of any kind. He tells these people that it's no problem, that he loves this job and is happy to serve them. And that they should thank the good Mayor, for he's the real reason he's here, the real force behind Elroy Foley being selected as the sole police presence to watch over their happy town. People continue to shower him with praise despite Foley's humble approach, and he doesn't argue with them any longer on the subject, accepting their compliments and taking them to heart.

*Feels good to be loved,* he thinks. He knows how lucky he is. Not all cops are loved. Not these days. He remembers a time when he was hated for nothing more than putting on that uniform. Those were unfair times, times he wishes he could forget, and thankfully, due to the Mayor and the town of Lacuna's Point, he's been able to forget those times. Start fresh. A true, real do-over.

But sometimes he sees things, and even though the past is behind him and no longer a part of his life, the memories still seek him out like a vengeful spirit, sneaking up on him when he least expects it. The barrier that Lacuna's Point has put between the past and the present is, still, sometimes not enough. Between sleep and lucidity, the dark void will sometimes come for him, and with it, replays of those things he wishes he could bury in perpetuity.

But some things are too big to bury. Some things always find a way to the surface.

He clears his mind, not allowing these painful intrusions to impede on what's been a spectacular morning so far. No calls, no paperwork, nothing that needs to be attended to. That, and the Mayor has been fairly satisfied with what's been going on lately, happy with Foley's upkeep of the peace, especially when it comes to the interlopers and the destructive nature of finding themselves lost in the coils of this inimitable paradise. Lately, surprisingly, things have calmed. They've been integrating, transitioning into their societal roles quite smoothly, and he hasn't heard a single complaint from anyone in town, with the exception of little "meetings", gatherings in public spaces as well as in the privacy of their abodes, but it's not against the law to meet up and shoot the shit. The Mayor agrees they need to lean on each other, be there for one another, get through the *rough patch* that is adjusting to the town's peculiar ways.

The town. *The ways.*

They'll assimilate soon. They have no other choice.

It's that or…well, that *other* option, the one Foley doesn't want to think about. Not today. It's too cheery outside to dwell in negative spaces.

He makes it halfway down the next block when he hears someone whistle, and, instinctively, he turns toward the sound, much the way a loyal dog would to its owner. Across the street, he sees Danielle, the art gallery's owner, a favorite citizen of the Mayor's, waving her hand, summoning him over. She's by herself and looks dissatisfied at something—maybe Foley himself—and the first thing he thinks is, *Oh here we go, the perfect day had to end sometime.* Foley glances around the immediate area as if maybe she was calling someone else. But there's no one around him—just him—and he can't ignore her icy stare.

"Yes?" he asks.

She doesn't speak a word. Instead, she nods and then begins to walk toward the next corner. She turns and then heads up the street, toward the art gallery.

*Gosh dang it,* he thinks, and his mood immediately shrivels up and dies. *What could this possibly be about?*

Foley thinks he can ignore this. Just keep walking the way he was headed. But he can't do that, can he? No, that would not be doing his duty, the job he's sworn to report to, day in and day out, and to do the best dang job he can. Anything else would be a failure. A letdown. Anything less would get the Mayor on his ass, and he's had enough of that to last him a lifetime.

He thinks of Darla's eye, how easily the Mayor stole it from the socket. Thinks how easily that could have been him.

Elroy Foley likes his eyes where they are, so he keeps walking. Follows Danielle to her shop, where two men are waiting inside. He was expecting black hoods, but what he gets is Dave Fester and

Bobby Mac. Two citizens who look very troubled. By what, Foley doesn't have the foggiest, but he's fairly certain the three are about to tell him.

"They're up to something," Danielle says the second Foley is inside the shop, closing the door behind him. "They're plotting. Scheming. Don't know what, but it's big."

Foley blinks. "Sorry?"

"The interlopers. They're plotting against the Mayor."

Foley looks to Dave, then to Bobby Mac. Both men corroborate her allegations with raised brows. "Suppose you have some proof?"

"Well…" Danielle says, looking to the men, her eyes asking for assistance in the convincing department. "Not exactly."

"What then?" Foley waits for an answer that doesn't immediately come. "A hunch?"

Dave clears his throat. "Someone overheard them talking in the diner. The black guy, the kid, and that Mexican chick. At least, I think she's Mexican. Not really sure, but she—"

"I get it, Dave," Foley says, using his palm as a stop sign. "I know who you mean. I ain't stupid, son. Who was it that heard them and what'd they hear?"

"It was Roger Ballard," Bobby Mac says. "He and the wife and kids were having breakfast, minding their own beeswax, when he overheard something that sounded like…conspiracy."

"Conspiracy," Foley says, tasting the word, the sour flavor it leaves on his tongue. "Of what sort?"

"The bad sort," Bobby Mac tells him, as if there's any other kind. "The hell should I know—I ain't the one who heard them."

"Well, why isn't Roger Ballard telling me this? Why you three?"

Danielle holds out her hands like she's praying to Jesus. "He was scared to come to you, Elroy. He didn't…didn't want to be involved. He's a good guy, just looking out for his family. You know these interlopers and what they're capable of—you know—before assimilation. God, you know better than most."

It's true—he knows all too well how the period leading up to the arts festival can bring about tumultuous times.

*All too well.*

"Well, I suppose I can look into it," Foley informs them.

"We would appreciate that," Danielle says. "We love this town, and we will do anything to help it. Anything."

Dave and Bobby Mac mumble in agreement.

Foley tips his hat. "Well, I love it too. So, consider it done." He heads for the door.

"Good. Please make sure you do." Danielle hesitates as if there's one more thing to add. And there is. "Because it would be a shame if you didn't do anything and the Mayor found out."

Foley quarter-turns back to her. "You threatening me?"

She gasps, then laughs out loud, a thunderous noise that causes Foley's heart to skip a few beats. "Gosh, no, Elroy! Not a threat at all. Just…you know. Looking out for you and your best interests, is all."

Foley doesn't tip his cap to her again. Instead, he sees himself out.

Darla gets to the house just after sunset. She steps inside, takes off her winter coat and leaves it hanging on the copper wardrobe tree near the front door. Josh greets her, offering her a bottle of water or coffee, and Darla jokes, asking if he has anything stronger, maybe a bottle of wine or better yet, a shot of whiskey. Josh says they have neither.

"And that's the worst thing about this place," Marissa says, sitting on the couch, looking at the pack of cigarettes next to her, debating whether to light up. "Dry town." Of course, she grabs the smokes and sparks up immediately.

Darla sits down on the couch, a few feet from Marissa. Marissa shifts, scooting away from her, putting a few more inches between them. Mitch can tell Marissa isn't exactly comfortable next to her, the way you wouldn't feel comfortable next to a dog that's been known to bite—and Mitch feels that. Even though she seems nice, there's always something unknown about her, about the people here. He hadn't seen the Campbells' revelation coming, even though he damn well should have. And that situation was reason enough to assume that everyone here is a suspect, everyone could be acting as someone (or something) else.

*Trust no one, not completely,* is the motto Mitchell Green now lives by.

"How's the novel coming?" Darla asks Mitch, a faint smile tracing her lips.

He's not sure if that's a clue, Darla secretly telling him that he should distrust her. "Fine," he says. "You know. Slowly. But I think the Mayor will be happy with the progress."

Darla nods darkly. Then she shifts to Josh. "I'm nervous."

"Don't be," Josh tells her. "I don't even know if it will work."

Josh pulls up a seat across from her, sits with the book on his lap. From his pocket, he pulls out a small box. Mitch knows it's a pocket watch before he reveals it, and it is. Josh takes the watch and lets it dangle from the gold chain out in front of him, setting the box down on the ground at the same time.

"Have you ever hypnotized anyone before?" Marissa asks.

"Hell no," he answers immediately. "But the book made it look easy." He stares at Darla and begins to swing the watch back and forth in perfect rhythm. "Just focus on the watch and nothing else. Try to clear your mind. Think about nothing. In fact…picture a white space. Blank. Like a sheet of paper. Think about that and look at the watch."

Darla seems to do what she's told, her sole eye focused on the watch, the back and forth, that pendulum of time kept. This goes on for a minute or two, and Mitch begins to doubt whether they're working toward a positive outcome or just wasting time, time better spent preparing for the big day.

Just when he thinks he should put a stop to this, Darla's eye flutters like dragonfly wings testing the air before a flight. Josh shoots him a look as if to say, *It's working!*

"Okay, Darla," the kid says, keeping his arm raised and the watch moving. "Your eyes are getting heavy, aren't they?"

Her mouth moves in slow motion: "Yes."

"Good."

Marissa doesn't seem convinced and rolls her eyes so dramatically. Stamping out her smoke, she moves away from the couch and over to the side of the room where Mitch is watching from. "This is bullshit," she whispers to him, and he ignores her.

"You're getting sleepy?" Josh asks.

Barely parting her lips, Darla says, "Yes."

"Good," Josh says dreamily. "Can you focus on something for me, Darla?"

Darla doesn't respond, but her one eye is completely zoned out. Mitch has never stared into the eyes of a dead person before, but looking at Darla, he imagines that's exactly what it looks like. *Vacant* is the only word that seems to do the description any justice. *There's nothing there. She's...lost.*

"Focus on how you got here." Josh leans forward, sticking the watch closer to her eye. "Tell us how you came to Lacuna's Point."

Mitch observes her eye grow slightly larger, wetter than before.

"I..." Darla says, "I came here with my boyfriend. He proposed to me, down by the water. By the Ferris wheel. It was a beautiful day."

"How long ago was that?"

She turns her head, squints, trying to remember. "Five years ago?"

"You tell us, Darla. Was it five years ago?"

Squinting, her eye is nothing more than a slit now. "It won't let me remember completely. Five sounds right."

"What's *it?*"

Darla's eye flicks up to the ceiling, then back to the watch. "The benefactor. The thing that dreams. The thing that eats from us."

"Does the thing have a name?"

She swallows. Beads of sweat dot her hairline. Shaking her head, she says, "It's a nameless thing. Nothing like it exists anywhere else, not in the entire Great Verse. Not even the Mayor knows its true name."

"Who is the Mayor? *What* is he?"

"His name is Quincy Black. I don't know what he is—not exactly. But I know what he's not." Her eye finds Mitch's, and Mitch doesn't know why she's answering him now—he hasn't asked a single question even though Josh is running the interrogation quite well, better than expected. "He's not human."

"What does he want?"

Darla fixes on Josh again, the watch. She leans back, getting more comfortable with the conversation, less teary-eyed. "He wants to please the benefactor, make it happy."

"Why?"

"So it gives him what he desires."

"What does he desire?"

"A power," she tells him, her smile stretching, the answer bringing her great pleasure. "A power beyond human comprehension."

"And he's not human?"

"Certainly not human."

"How can we kill them—the Mayor, the benefactor?"

"These are secrets we don't know. How can you kill a thing that lives in dreams?"

Josh looks to Mitch, and Mitch shrugs. Then he focuses back on Darla. "One more thing, Darla—how do you know these things?" A pause, and for more clarity: "What are you?"

Her tough mask begins to break. Cheeks trembling, she tilts her head to the side, and then a violent shudder runs through her, attacking every nerve. The quick contortion is enough to put Mitch on his heels.

"Darla?" Josh asks, stopping the watch at once. He stands up and the backs of his legs knock the chair back. He doesn't bother with it, his eyes lasering in on Darla, who is now lying on the couch, her limbs moving in wavelike patterns, as if she's putting on some interpretive dance move, stretching and curling her arms to the rhythm of the music inside her head. "Darla, what's happening to you?"

She opens her mouth, letting go of a croaky sound that reminds Mitch of the bullfrog blues sung across the swamplands of south Jersey. Mitch senses everyone in the room's mood instantly change from cautious to on edge, and he can see Josh has been the one most affected by the girl's reaction.

"Darla," Mitch says, trying his hand at breaking the girl from this strange trance. "Darla, can you hear me? It's Mitch. Can you snap out of it?"

In response, Darla opens her mouth, and the sound that comes out causes Mitch to back the fuck up. It's a throaty growl that reminds him of feral wolves. Her spine arches back in a way the spine is not meant to, and she begins to convulse, huge contractions that make her body bounce up and down on the sofa. Her arms and legs continue to move through the air like some rehearsed, ritualistic gyration.

Josh goes to touch her, and Mitch lunges forward, grabs him, hauling him back.

"Hey!" he shouts.

Mitch turns him away from the disturbing scene. "Don't touch her."

"She's in trouble!"

Marissa approaches them cautiously, her hands balled into fists, ready to rumble. Judging from the violent positions Darla's body has taken on, he can't blame the woman for taking any and all precautions. In fact, Mitch begins to survey the room, looking for something to arm himself with.

"You can't help her," Marissa says.

Josh looks on, leaning around Mitch, his eyes filling with tears. "How do you know?"

"Cause—remember when we said she wasn't one of them?" Marissa points to the woman's body, the contortionist going through the cringy motions that shouldn't be possible. "I think we were wrong."

Darla stops as if Marissa's assumption has some magical command over her. Mitch breaks it down to sheer coincidence. Darla rests on the couch, her right arm outstretched, as if she's reaching for something, maybe one of them, the humans, for help. Her mouth remains open, a stiff oval, and the strange sound has ceased. Her eye stares, more vacant now than ever before.

Something moves near her nose, a timid movement, something that seeks exit via her nostril. Mitch blinks, thinking the movement was just a trick of the mind, the way the light from the lamp next to the couch is hitting her face, but after a few seconds, he realizes his eyes were not deceiving him.

There is something inside her nose, and it wants out.

The appendage is thin, wiry, and deep-ocean blue. As it stretches farther from her nose, Mitch can see it's jointed in several spots, and at the end of it rests a small hooked claw, good for gripping the most slippery surfaces. Something moves beneath the girl's eyepatch, wiggling, trying to break through the surface like a hatching chick. In a blink, the eyepatch is lifted, and two more appendages slip over the patch, pushing it down. Once the thing inside the girl's head finds its legs, the creature shoves the eyepatch down her cheek. Something finds an exit, and just before the entity reveals itself, he knows exactly what it is—it's a crab, a *mole* crab, the very same kind the Mayor had been eating in that shared dreamworld, the one that depicted Angie as the Mayor, feeding the entire family platefuls of live crabs.

The crab makes a bloody birth, exiting the eye in a gushy slide of scarlet. It falls to the floor with a gentle splat, and then scurries toward them as if anyone and everyone's eye could be the next entry point for this hungry villain.

Mitch puts a stop to it. He lifts his leg, brings his foot down on the scurrying crab with an impressive, effective stomp. The squashing sound of the crab's shell, along with the squelching juices within, echoes through the house, and the sand crab makes a noise like a dog's squishy toy getting stepped on, a weakish honk. When Mitch removes his foot, he reveals a small collection of puke-green fluids mixed with the shattered remains of the crab's exoskeleton. Two beady eyes stare up at him, completely devoid of life.

Mitch immediately takes off his shoe, as if the clingy crab guts are acid eating through. He wipes the remains on the window curtain, and Marissa and Josh are too stunned about what's just happened to care about the ruined drapery.

Before anyone can take their next breath, Darla launches herself up from the couch, back to a sitting position. Her limbs relax, her entire body released from that peculiar hold, and she gasps for air as if she was being held underwater for far too long and on the verge of drowning. Her whole body hitches with each deep breath. Josh goes to her, sits beside her and puts a comforting hand on her back, tells her it's all right and to breathe slowly.

"It's okay," he says, and repeats the words over and over again like it's some mantra Darla needs to hear to get through this thing. And it works. Within a few moments, she's breathing normally, and better yet—she's mostly herself again.

Darla touches the ruined, raw cavity that used to be her eye. "What happened?"

Josh quickly explains everything, the hypnotism, the chaos that followed. He explains the splotch of green death that's beginning to dry on the carpet.

"It was crazy," he ends with.

"I feel," Darla says, "different." She uses the wet paper towel that Mitch fetched for her, pats the blood away until it's all gone. "Better. More...free."

"That thing was inside you," Josh says.

"Yes. I think…everyone has one."

Mitch's blood runs cold and he can't keep from shivering.

Josh turns to them. "We need to capture Foley," he says.

"What?" Marissa says. "That crazy-ass cop? You've lost it, little dude."

"No," Josh says, in a way that makes him fairly certain he *hasn't* lost it. "No, I haven't. I've never been more sure about something in all my life."

*Great,* Mitch says. *The twelve-year-old has an epiphany.*

"We can capture him," Josh says, "and I have a plan."

Ellie exits the art gallery and Dawn locks the door behind her. Under the guidance of the streetlights, the pair walk down the dark streets of Lacuna's Point. Ellie knows their time together is coming to end; it's only another five minutes or so before she has to say goodbye and see her daughter off. It's the worst part of the day, but hey—at least she got some time with her, and that's more than Mitch can say. Kya's been locked up for the last two weeks, and no one has seen her, not even Dawn, who claims this situation is odd. *Used to see her every day,* Dawn said. *Now, since you're all here—nothing. It's like the Mayor doesn't want us to see each other until…after.*

*After what?*

At that question, Dawn always hangs her head and never answers. Ellie knows something bad is going down, but she doesn't press her daughter. Doesn't shake her, doesn't yell at her, demand an answer to questions that need answers. She doesn't do any of those things because the situation is delicate, and if she presses the issue, this fragile arrangement could crumble apart within a few wrong words. Dawn's not the same Dawn she was when she left for Georgetown three years ago, and not in the *oh my daughter is all grown up!* sort of way.

Once in front of old Eddy, Ellie turns to her daughter.

"Goodbye, Dawn," she says, and gives her daughter a hug, fighting off the burn seeping through her scleras. "I love you so much, baby."

Dawn hugs her back, a weak embrace, like she's afraid of squeezing Ellie too hard, of breaking her.

Ellie ignores this, focuses on the good. The fact they have a relationship again, that they are together. Nothing else matters.

Right?

She lets go, looks her daughter in the eyes. What stares back scares her because the eyes, Dawn's, don't conceal the truth—that she's not her daughter, that she's something else now, something Ellie won't ever understand. Or…maybe she will understand. And soon.

She doesn't know which is more frightening, but at that precise moment, frigid fingers grasp her neck and fill her soul with a deep freeze, one she fears will never thaw.

"Want to come with me?" Ellie asks. "Back to the hotel? We can stay up all night and chat about boys? School? Whatever you want?"

Dawn looks away. "I can't." She throws her head at the clock tower. "The…He won't let me. You know that."

Ellie nods. "Of course."

"Well, good night, Mom."

"Good night, love."

Dawn spins and power-jogs up the steps leading to the tower's entrance. Through the blur dominating her vision, Ellie watches her go. Then, not wanting to linger in front of the clock tower for too long, she heads back to the hotel, feeling the eyes from above, those stars twinkling in a sky that probably isn't real, following her the entire way back.

Twenty minutes later, she finds herself in front of Mitch's door. The hallways are empty; there's not so much as the faint, distant din of a fan motor in the background. Complete silence, which somehow makes everything worse. On a positive note, she'll hear something coming a long way off. Or someone.

She knocks, gently tapping on the wooden shell, making sure to keep it quiet in case others are sleeping. There are only four other rooms on the floor beside theirs, and she can't remember seeing anyone staying there—but still, it's best to play it safe, keep the noise level down.

She knocks again.

This time, the door separates from the jamb, just wide enough for one eyeball. Mitch's right eye glares at her. She expects the door to open wider, but it doesn't.

"Can I help you?"

"Can we talk?" Her voice is small. "I want to apologize. For missing the meeting. Well, all the meetings, really."

He seems to mull it over. Then he opens the door, stepping aside, inviting her in. He's wearing a muscle tee and basketball shorts, nothing else, and she wonders if he was actually sleeping or if he's become an insomniac like her. Either way, she thinks she should apologize for knocking this late, but then decides to forgo those niceties and get to the meat of her arrival.

"First off, I'm sorry I blew you guys off. It was wrong." She leans against the wall opposite his bed, near the television. "Just…it's Dawn, you know." As if that explains everything. And she thinks it might.

Mitch looks like he might rip her a new one, but instead, he backs off, sighs, and says, "I understand."

"You do?"

He nods. "If it were Kya, I'd probably be spending every minute with her too."

She wants to cry but fights off the threat of tears. Then the burn becomes too much and the sadness leaks through. "She's not her, though."

Mitch's eyes slim to almost nothing.

She clears her throat. "She's not my Dawn. I mean, she is. But she's…different. Changed somehow."

"I think I know what you mean."

"You do? How?"

Mitch shakes his head in that *this-is-crazy* way. "You're not going to believe me."

"I'd believe almost anything right now. Christ, the things we've seen, Mitch. This place is…*fucked* up. I tried to fight it, hoping that if I spent a little time with Dawn, that everything would be okay, and that I'd feel better about *being* here. But today…today I hugged my daughter and she hugged me back, but it felt like something else was hugging me. Not someone. Some*thing*."

Mitch takes a breath and prepares to unload a story on her. She can tell by the way he starts that this is going to be a long one. He tells her everything, what happened at the meeting, and then what happened later to Darla in Josh and Marissa's rental. When it's over, Ellie takes a second to absorb everything she's been told.

"Said you wouldn't believe me." Mitch musters the best smirk he can this close to midnight.

"She's alive?"

"Yes. She's—in her words—freed."

"That's…amazing."

"I think we can *free* the girls too. But we have to get them out of here. The Mayor might find out what we've done to Darla. He might come gunning for us."

"What are we going to do?"

"Well…we have a plan. Josh's plan, really." He proceeds to tell her everything.

"Really?" she asks.

"It's the best chance we got."

Ellie swallows, finally realizing that this is it—they either fight the town that refuses to let them go or die trying. "Fuck it," she tells him. "Count me in."

Mitch oversleeps, dreams right through his alarm, but the phone ringing on the nightstand jars him loose from the weird, repeating sequence. This time around, Brianna led the live crab-eating extravaganza, and she was force-feeding the others, packing their throats full of the squirming crab shells. Mitch died in the dream, choking on the crab shells, and that's when he woke up to the incessant ringing.

"Hello?" he answers, the room sliding, swirling before him. The weird dreams always leave him feeling punch-drunk for the first ten minutes after waking.

"Mitch?" It's Darla. She sounds impatient, like something's happened.

Something bad.

"Yeah, I'm here." He checks his watch, realizes *it's time*.

"The raven is on the writing desk," she says, and then there's a soft click of Darla resting the phone back on the cradle.

*The raven is on the writing desk.*

If anyone was listening to that call, they'll know something is going down. Not exactly subtle code, but an obscure reference that will definitely leave the eavesdropper perplexed.

The important thing is the plan's in motion.

Foley—he's on his way to the diner.

And Mitch will be there.

Waiting.

# PART FOUR

## THE GOODNESS OF ART

# CHAPTER FIFTEEN

Elroy Foley enters the diner, hand on his firearm, finger already curling around the trigger, ready to free the hand cannon if the situation screams for it. The adrenaline has already kicked in, sending his heart into a stuttering rhythm, and there's no stopping it. This is it. This is primetime, what he's prepared his entire career in law enforcement for. This moment. It's time to be a hero.

He eyes the empty booths, the space behind the counter, and a sense of unease falls over him. Now, the gun comes free. Slipping into the diner, he checks both aisles, the right and left, and each is empty, vacant, free from human forms.

Somewhere in the depths of his mind a red flag is raised.

"Officer! Come quick!" a panicked voice shouts from somewhere behind the double doors that lead into the kitchen. "Help me!"

He rushes forward, feeling like an action star in every movie he's watched since he was a boy. Bruce in *Die Hard* or Sylvester in *Rambo*. Something with a high body count, something that makes him feel like a man on top of the world.

An American hero.

He lowers his shoulder and slams through the double doors, training his weapon on the first thing he sees. Darla screams, claps a hand over her chest. She looks worried and terrified and on the verge of screaming again, a sound that makes him feel like his eardrums have been perforated. Her eye leaks tears, her jaw stretching as the terror takes hold. Foley scans the area quickly, every corner, every inch, and deems it safe from any threats. He moves forward, looking for something to give him an excuse to pull the trigger.

"Where are they?" Foley asks, refusing to drop his guard. "The interlopers? You said they were here? Threatening you?"

Darla seems to struggle with a heavy breath. "They ran that way," she says, pointing to the back door with a tiny square window lit with morning sunshine. "But I got one."

"Got one?" Astonished, he squints at her. "An interloper?"

She nods. "In the walk-in."

He follows her finger to the large metal door at the end of the kitchen. Swallowing his fear, he makes his way over to the walk-in freezer, approaching the way he would a suspicious vehicle he just pulled over, one that came back with some hits after dispatch ran the plates. It's a position he's been in before *(blood on the seats, blood on the shirt)* and he has more confidence now than he's had in those previous encounters.

"In there?" he asks, feeling his heart rate accelerate. He swallows any residual doubts and moves ahead.

"Yes," she says timidly.

"All right." He confronts the freezer and knocks on the door. "This is Elroy Foley of the Lacuna's Point Police Department. I'm coming in there. I'm armed and I will fire upon you if necessary. Understood?"

No answer.

He glances back at Darla. "The fucker armed?"

She shakes her head, but the movement lacks confidence, so it looks like he's going in ready for whatever.

"Good." Foley opens the door. He's greeted by a swirling, arctic mist, one that seems to wrap around him like a seductive specter, freezing him to the bone upon contact. His body doesn't like that, the cold, and he takes a step back, reeling from the frigid touch.

Once the vapor disperses into nothing, he focuses on the threat in the freezer.

But there is nothing there.

No one.

"What the..."

Before he can piece together the puzzle at hand, turn around and confront Darla about the confusing circumstance, something connects with the back of his head. A heavy, powerful blow that draws a black curtain over his conscious mind.

Mitch taps Foley's cheek, and when that doesn't work, he has Darla hand him a water bottle. He doesn't think twice and empties the bottle over the cop's head. If this doesn't do the trick, he thinks, he might pop the punk in his mouth. Then he thinks he might do that even if he doesn't come to.

Behind him, the others stir. He looks over his shoulder and sees Ellie, her arm wrapped around her daughter, both of them shivering. And they're not alone. Darla's positioned behind them, Josh behind her, and Marissa brings up the rear. The whole crew is there (minus Kya) and they're ready to do whatever's necessary to escape this place.

Foley's eyes flutter and finally open. There's a moment of unsureness, a moment where the bastard cop doesn't recognize his surroundings. Then he realizes. And Mitch has never been happier.

"Got you, you son of a bitch," Mitch whispers through a wide smile. The satisfaction of watching Foley's upper lip tremble, the nerve within losing control, is unparalleled. "Now you're going to play by our rules."

"I'll gut you," he says, a heavy growl resting in the back of his throat, the animal within making its presence known. Mitch watches the creases in his face wiggle, twitch some. It takes him thirty seconds to realize the nerves themselves aren't causing the motion— it's something else. Whatever that thing within *actually* is.

"We don't have a lot of time," Mitch says over his shoulder. "He's already...changing."

"Changing?" Dawn asks.

"Into one of them," Marissa answers.

"I think so," Mitch says, and then turns back to his prisoner. "Isn't that right?"

"You think you can escape this place?" Foley asks, and now he's smiling. Mitch watches a red line appear across his face, like he's been scratched by a ghost. "You think the Mayor will let you? Never. Never in a million, million years."

"Yeah," Mitch says, continuing to flash his happy teeth at the bastard. "We'll see about that. Even if we don't escape, watching you die is going to be the highlight of trying."

"You think you can kill us?" Foley asks, looking to each of them. The more the man talks, the less he sounds like Elroy Foley, the cop they met on that first day. Mitch isn't so sure the cold is responsible for bringing out the entity within—more like the situation. The threat of extermination. Mitch stares into the cop's eyes, still sees they haven't changed color. The red line across his forehead has widened some and begun to dribble scarlet. "You think this cold will kill us? Fool. We were born in a place much colder than this."

His change in voice sends Mitch's skin crawling with cold bumps. He knows he can't show that he's afraid, so he keeps on the offensive. "Yeah, you might have been. But your little meat suit can't survive subzero temps forever. It's called hypothermia. But your little alien brain probably doesn't know what that is, does it?"

Foley's eyes light with excitement, like this news brings him pleasure. He opens his mouth wide enough so Mitch can see the dark cavern within. The man shakes with laughter, his whole body, and if it weren't for the awful giggle emanating from deep within, Mitch would probably assume the man's having a seizure.

"Fuck's so funny?" Mitch asks.

"We know everything of your world. Our knowledge is infinite."

"Well, you shoulda thought this one out a little better."

Mitch turns.

"Where are you going?" the Foley-Thing asks. "Our conference hasn't concluded."

"Oh, that's where you're wrong. It's done. Over. That's a wrap, Jack." Mitch hops out of the walk-in, where the others have been waiting, watching. The thing inside Foley scoots his whole body forward, and Mitch watches the cop's face split again, come apart at the seams, tear like a plastic bag holding too much weight. Antenna-like protrusions rise from the wounds, leaving behind the bloody patches of flesh, thrusting themselves out into the cold environment, leaving the safety of the warm meat-bag behind and searching for some new warmth to lie in.

Mitch doesn't give the emerging creature the opportunity. He shoots Foley two middle fingers before slamming the door shut, locking it, and sealing the alien thing inside.

A muffled screech from within unravels every one of Mitch's nerves, and he hopes that whatever has left Foley's body can't escape.

Because if it does, then they're all absolutely fucked.

Ellie watches her daughter back away and knock into a rolling cart holding some kitchen supplies. She hates the look on Dawn's face, the terror rounding out her features.

"That thing…" Dawn says, her voice wavering. "Is inside us?"

"No," Ellie says quickly, though she has no way of knowing that, and, honestly, it sounds like a complete lie even to her own ears. It's totally possible that these creatures are living inside them all, slowly taking over their bodies, breaking them down day in and day out, without them even realizing it. Ellie can't shake the story Josh told them, about his first day here, when he saw the man down by the shore inserting one of these crab-like creatures into his open abdomen. Then, of course, there are the dreams. The clock tower, the light. That special place they went to where reality seemed to have no margin to exist. Weird occurrences that helped scramble her brain up so good that she's having trouble recalling simple things, like where she was born, the names of her nephews and nieces, her daughter's birthday. Things she should know on demand have taken her ten, fifteen minutes to remember. So yes, it's possible this thing is inside them, feeding off their cells, devouring every nutrient, sucking out the essence of their souls.

They could all be hosts for these ultra-terrestrial mole crabs.

"No," Ellie says again, sounding more confident this time. "No, I don't think so, baby."

No one refutes Ellie's answer, no one dares to, but their inspecting eyes examine each other, at least allowing the possibility to breathe.

A few minutes later, the group enters the diner's main-sit down area and tries to capture their breath, control their wayward thoughts. The silence lasts longer than Ellie likes, and she wants to say something, rally the troops, but Mitch is the first one to realize they have work to do, a lot, and it won't be long before the Mayor notices something is amiss in his paradisal slice of the American Dream. Also, there's no telling how long the walk-in will hold the thing that was inside Elroy Foley.

"It all starts at that clock tower," Mitch tells them. "I think it controls everything. We only saw inside the Mayor's office, but there's more to that place." Now, he looks to Ellie. "You were there. You felt it. Like…that place is not normal. Hard to put into words, but it's almost like that office has infinite space."

Ellie did feel that, being inside. *Lacuna's Point is a place that feels much bigger than it looks.* Oh yes, it was hard to deny that fact.

"Josh," Mitch says, snapping his fingers at the kid as if to say, *You're up to bat.*

"Right," Josh says, dipping into his backpack and pulling out some reading materials he nabbed from the bookstore. "Clock towers," he says, opening up an old, worn hardcover that practically comes apart at the binding, "throughout history, provided a very important function in some societies—not just a means to tell time, but also a means to show the position of the stars and the planets. Also, they were used to call town meetings and signal prayer. In Lacuna's Point, as we all found out very early on, it signifies the bringing of the Light."

Ellie shudders just thinking about the Light, that awful whiteness. She can almost hear the soft tunes it brings in the distance, that sweet, hypnotic melody.

Josh flips to a page that depicts a clock tower with the clock portion swung open, revealing a hidden world within—an open valley with a majestic stream, a mountainous backdrop. The townspeople below are on their knees, offering their prayers to the magnificent sights their eyes are privy to. "Some cultures and villages used to believe these towers could hold supernatural abilities, that they could act as portals to other worlds or other times. Various religious groups—cults—used to make them worship these edifices and held sacrifices for them, and, in turn, they would be allowed access to the special places on the other side. Worlds that existed far beyond their dreams."

"Great," Marissa chirps, pinching a cigarette between her teeth. She hands one to Darla, who accepts it feverishly. "So we have a town full of religious fanatics that are ready to sacrifice us to some dark God." She shrugs. "That about sum it up?"

"Essentially," Josh says. "Maybe it's something else, but maybe this is how it started." He sighs, looking over to Mitch. "Mitch is right—the clock tower is our play. We need to find a way to destroy it."

"And fast," adds Mitch.

"And how the hell do we do that?" Marissa asks. "Not to be negative-fucking-Nancy, but we aren't exactly in a position to succeed. If it's true, and this whole town is possessed by those fucking alien crab creatures, then in about five minutes we're gonna have every eyeball in the town's limits looking for us." She puffs out a cloud of smoke. "Not to mention, that thing could get out. And when it does, it's going to hunt us down."

Ellie nibbles her thumbnail. "So what's the plan?"

Mitch sighs, letting Ellie know he hates the odds. "There's only six of us. Seven if you count Kya. And if what you say is true," he says to Dawn, "and they're keeping her locked up in the tower—"

"They are," Dawn confirms. "The Mayor thinks she's dangerous. I don't think the Light has taken to her like the others. Me either, though." She shrugs. "I don't feel affected at all."

Ellie leans her face on her daughter's shoulder, elated to hear that news. But she also wonders if Foley felt affected.

"Then..." Mitch says, "...we're going to have to be careful. Get her out before we do what needs to be done."

"Seven's a good number," Darla says wistfully.

"I like seven," Marissa adds. "Lucky number, right? *Seven Samurai. The Magnificent Seven.* The original, though—not the remake."

"Ah, Steve McQueen," Darla says dreamily.

"You're all getting off track," Mitch interrupts.

Josh clears his throat. "Seven deadly sins. I remember I had to know them for Catechism."

"Focus." Mitch folds his hands on his right knee. "I have a plan. But we're going to need a few things first."

"What's that?" Ellie asks anxiously.

"Well," he says, squinting at them. "How many of you have ever played the game of chess?"

Josh raises his hand. And Marissa.

"That's it?" Mitch laughs incredulously.

No one else raises their hands, and Ellie hears the creature's screeches begin to die down.

"So, in chess," Mitch continues, "you can't think solely about the move you're making. You have to think about the next move and the move after that, what your opponent is going to do with the opportunities you present them. Games aren't won on the move you're making, it's all about the move three, four moves from now."

"So," Ellie says, trying to wrap her head around Mitch's lesson. "We have to anticipate what the Mayor will do? How he'll react?"

"To our first move, yes."

"And what's our first move?" Marissa asks.

"We just made it." Mitch nods to the freezer, the dying sounds of the alien creature. "It's sitting in that freezer."

"And…" Darla says, swallowing a lump. "What is the Mayor going to do about it?"

"Well, I anticipate he'll gun for us."

"We've been careful, though," Ellie says. "I've been spending so much time with Dawn, he can't possibly know that we're involved."

"We have to assume he'll know," Mitch tells her. He turns to Dawn. "We're not the first ones to rebel against him, against Lacuna's Point. Isn't that right, Dawn?"

Dawn nods. "Yes. Kya. She did everything she could to leave. She fought, and…she almost got away. From what I know…what I've heard…it's the closest anyone's ever gotten to escaping. It really pissed off the Mayor. Like, *really*. People were actually afraid of him. Sure, they talk about him now, like he's some great leader, a beloved figurehead, but, man…those first few months…people would cower in their shoppes and homes. It was crazy."

Mitch smiles proudly. "That's my girl."

There's a moment of silence, but then a soft clicking comes from the walk-in, like the creature inside has given up and is asking for mercy, to be let out. No one rushes to answer the call.

"So, this is all well and great," Marissa says, stamping out her cigarette on the counter, intentionally missing the ashtray, which was only a few feet from her. "But clearly Kya failed—no offense—and now she's trapped like some princess in a tower in some old-ass fairy-tale, a tower we need to destroy without getting ourselves killed or taken by some magical Light—and oh yeah, by the way, there's a town-wide talent show we're all supposed to be participating in so this crazy-ass alien-god-thing can absorb our creations for food—if I'm understanding that whole aspect correctly—and…am I leaving anything out? Oh, that's right—we all might have some weird crab-creatures living inside us, so…yeah…that's a thing."

No one responds. Josh, wincing at how crazy this all sounds, scratches his scalp. Ellie feels the weight of the next few hours, what could potentially happen to them before they escape (*if* they can escape), pressing down on her shoulders.

"Again," Marissa says, sighing, "I don't want to sound all fucking negative, but things aren't exactly looking up, and I'm happy for you, Ellie." She acknowledges Ellie with a slight nod, then her eyes settle on Dawn. "I'm happy the Mayor is allowing you to see each other, but I haven't seen Rosetta since I got here and I'm starting to feel a little hopeless." She eyes Mitch as her next target. "So...my point is—do you have a fucking plan, or do you not?"

Mitch chews his tongue for a second, then says, "Yes, I have a fucking plan."

Dave Fester takes his usual sunny walk across the quad toward Ace's Place, already tasting those two eggs over easy and the freshest orange juice his tongue has ever had the pleasure of absorbing. When he gets there, he's disappointed to find the place dark, not a single light on in the joint whatsoever, and despite the dim appearance—the OPEN sign is still flipped, facing outward, letting the town know the diner is still accepting customers. At first he thinks it's just a power outage, maybe a downed line somewhere from some storm he can't remember. Come to think of it, he can't remember the last time it stormed in Lacuna's Point. Heck, has it ever? It always seems so sunny and bright out. It always seems so perfect.

*God sure does love Lacuna's Point,* he thinks.

Maybe a transformer blew. But if that's the case, wouldn't most of the town be out? Dave looks around, sees nothing of the sort. Sees other shoppes and businesses in the full swing of the morning hustle.

But not here. Not his favorite diner in the whole wide world.

Dave tries the door and finds it open. Steps inside. He's immediately hit with a strange stench, something acidic and foul, something he's not sure he's ever smelled before. Like, maybe what a landfill might smell like if it was on fire. It's almost enough to drive him away, but the mystery unfolding in Ace's Place is too great to abandon. He must know what happened here.

Must.

"Darla?" he calls, seeking out his favorite waitress. "You here, darling?"

No answer. Silence, the kind you can hear a breath in, dominates the place. Dave tunes his ear to the back, the unknown space behind the kitchen doors, and thinks he hears something that sounds like labored breathing. He creeps over to the doors, has himself a peek through the oval window.

Nothing. Empty. Just like the rest of this place. He thinks this is where his mystery train lets him off, that he should go back and grab Elroy Foley, let the town's main authority figure carry out the rest of the investigation. A trained professional. Someone who knows what they're doing, someone who can actually help.

But Dave doesn't do that, and he doesn't know why, only that it feels right to persevere and carry on with this rogue inspection. There's something fun about being in this moment, inserting himself in a dangerous adventure outside the daily routines and familiar patterns that are easy to get stuck in. The excitement causes his bladder to fill.

Doing his best not to pee himself, he pushes through the doors and heads into the kitchen that sits in frail shadows. The rustling, the breathy sound he heard earlier, is much louder now, and it's coming from the walk-in freezer. Shuffling toward the big metal enclosure, he grabs a clean knife from the cutlery block, holds it out for protection.

"Hello?" he asks the sound.

The sound gives no reply. At first. Then, after a few seconds, there's a chirping sound, like a cricket rubbing its wings together. Dave now thinks someone locked an animal in there. He knows he shouldn't continue, knows he shouldn't open the walk-in's door. Leave it alone, whatever it is. It's no business of his, and usually when someone sticks their nose in business where it doesn't belong, well, they're apt to lose that nose. That's what Dave's daddy always used to say whenever the mean bastard had him bent over his knee.

*"Let meeeeee ouuuuut."*

Dave freezes, the knife handle slipping from his numb fingers. The blade nearly lands on his toe. It misses by mere inches and clatters onto the floor. He backs away, the instinctive notion to run present but subdued by a spell of paralyzing fear. His backside knocks against the counter, and his bladder empties into his tighty-whities, soaking through the cotton and darkening the crotch of his best pair of slacks. The stain squirts down his pant leg.

*"Let meeee ouutt."*

The plea sounds more human than the first time around. It's still an unsettling rasp, the way his grandmother sounded on her death bed while she begged for a cigarette despite the condition of her shriveled and blackened lungs, and there's nothing in that voice that prompts him to listen. He stands there wasting seconds, valuable time he could be getting help. But there's something inside his soul keeping him there, something heavy, something that beckons him to stay. It feels *right* to stay. To help whatever's been locked inside.

Good citizen he is, Dave Fester feels the need to help.

"I can help you," he says, putting his hands on the metal handle, lifting it. "Hang in there, buddy!"

He slides the walk-in door to the side and reveals the truth about the person inside, and once he sets his eyes on the prisoner, he feels like he's revealed a different truth altogether—the truth about himself, about Lacuna's Point.

To his surprise, he sees Elroy Foley rising to his feet, his face open and bleeding through loose flaps of skin, as if his face was cut and stitched and now those stitches have come undone. His face is a jigsaw puzzle of torn flesh and scars and things moving, twitching beneath the surface, swimming in the facial tissue.

Dave Fester wants to scream with revulsion. But he doesn't. Because in Foley's face, he recognizes the truth within himself.

Whatever has happened to Elroy Foley is okay.

More than okay.

It's right.

# CHAPTER SIXTEEN

After an hour of strolling through the deserted town of Lacuna's Point, Wally Stanton puts his hands on his hips and takes a deep breath. Eyes examining the vine-covered exteriors of the shoppes that line the street, he lets out a gust of trapped, hot air.

"Whew," he says, wiping the summer-induced sweat from his forehead. "This place is dead with a capital D, partner."

Dan, who doesn't feel much like a partner at all, more like a puppet that Wally brings out for a show when he needs to make a quick buck, can't argue. The town is Dead. Capital D included. "No sign of Ellie. The girls. Mitch." He glances around at the empty streets. Overgrowth has weeded up through every small crack, so tall that the straw-colored shrubbery has fallen to one side, providing a natural blanket over the decayed blacktop. Some of the buildings have crumbled inward. Fallen rocks of chipped concrete have made the journey a rocky trek, and more than once has Dan almost twisted an ankle by stepping in the wrong place. He'll be happy to be far away from here. Something about the town, the dead, eerie silence the expired society provides, injects his nerves with a chilly discomfort. He's always checking over his shoulder, sensing someone watching from afar, but he knows that notion is a silly one because there's nothing here. Not anymore. Not for a long, long time.

Still…

Something *is* watching him.

He can feel it.

"No sign of anything," Wally confirms, walking toward him. "We've checked nearly every building and I don't know about you, but I'm tired of yelling at ghosts, especially since they ain't yelling back."

*Ghosts.*

He can almost feel them. A whole town of ghosts, the dead, the people who once lived here. Their dead, staring eyes, watching him from beyond this world.

"You all right there, partner?" Wally asks him. "Just catch the flu or something?"

"No," Dan tells him, and he moves down the street, flattening the overgrowth with each step.

"Where're you going?"

"Something weird about that clock tower. I can't put my finger on it."

Wally steps out from under the shadow of the building so he can peek at the clock tower in question. "I mean, it's a clock tower. Guess that's weird in and of itself."

"I don't like it. Feels...out of place."

"This whole town feels out of place, man."

"Well, yeah." Dan moves down the street, farther away from the detective. "I say we check it out. See what's inside."

"Why?"

Dan stops. Turns. "I don't know. Just a feeling."

"A hunch?"

"I think...if Ellie did come here...that's where she would have gone."

Wally squints as if Dan couldn't possibly know such a thing. But then again, he was married to her and for nearly a decade, so that has to count for something.

"All right," Wally says, giving up, shrugging off his doubts and concerns. "All right, let's have ourselves a peek. But then we're packing it in. Think we've wasted enough time today."

Dan wants to agree. But the haunting sense of a thousand eyes locking onto him won't leave him alone.

And the clock tower is where they're staring from, waiting there, wishing to be set free.

A half-hour late. *Not bad,* Ellie thinks, but she wonders how Danielle will react. In the time spent there, she's never given the woman a reason to reprimand her. She's always approached the gallery with caution, mostly because she knows Danielle is on it, knows that she's aware of Lacuna's Point, the power it holds, more so than some of the other citizens, those who toil around oblivious to the true nature of this place.

As she passes through the front door, Dawn behind her, she immediately locks eyes on Danielle Harris and the permanent lines etched in her skin that make up her perpetual RBF. She's already glancing down at her watch, and Ellie wonders how long she's been holding that pose, waiting for them. Probably longer than any normal person would.

*If she's a person at all.*

The scene at the diner keeps replaying itself over and over, the loop projecting those awful images in her mind. She can't prevent herself from experiencing that hideous creature extricating itself from Foley's skin, the monstrous being beneath emerging from its fleshy chambers, born into this frightening and terrible existence. She shudders as the images flip through her mind on repeat.

Dawn hasn't spoken much during their walk over here, save for a few *yeses* and *mm-hmms* in response to Ellie going over the plan. But now, she's the first one to speak when Danielle casts that evil-stepmother glare in their direction.

"Sorry we're late, Miss Danielle," Dawn says, taking off her sweater and tossing it on a hanger. "We were having coffee and lost track of time."

Danielle doesn't respond, only glares at them with eyes that definitely aren't human. The longer she stares in silence, the more Ellie is convinced she's part of the same species that Foley is. Or was. She doesn't know what he is now.

"It's fine," she says, lowering her wrist. She snaps her fingers and points to the back. "New pieces just came in. We need them sorted and hung. Pronto."

Dawn shakes her head. "We just got new pieces yesterday," she says. "Why another shipment? Where is all this art coming from? We don't have enough—"

"Are you really asking questions right now?" Danielle saunters out from behind the desk, her lower lip quivering. "Does it matter? Just do what you're told."

Dawn sighs. Moves to the back without another word.

Ellie wants to stand up for her, tell Danielle to take that Frappuccino sitting on her desk and fuck her own face-hole with it, but she refrains.

"The town-wide talent show is tomorrow afternoon," Danielle says. "We have a lot to showcase. A lot of talent and the Mayor won't tolerate anything short of perfection. Do you understand?"

Ellie understands. Maybe too much now. "Will there be Light?" It's a question she's heard around town these last few days, and she thinks it applies here. It's a dangerous question, and it might throw off the whole charade. Mitch warned them about acting too comfortable, too assimilated with the town and their peculiarities, but this time, the words just slipped. Ellie feels her face burn with regret.

Danielle grins. "Of course there will be Light. There will be lots of Light."

"Good." Ellie returns a smile, half-broken. "I feel like…I need it, you know? My head's been funny. Confused." She knows she could be digging herself into a greater hole, but she can't stop now.

Danielle tilts her head to the side, traces of apathy carving lines into her human mask. "Oh honey." She approaches her, hands out, and grips Ellie's arm, squeezing, trying to instill a comfort into her bones despite the icy death chill of her touch. "You have nothing to worry about. That period of confusion will pass. It always does. For everyone. The Light will come and take you away and you won't feel—"

The black bag slips over her head, cutting off her words. Behind her, Dawn pulls the drawstring tight, ratcheting the cord around her throat, closing off her airways. Danielle yelps into the hollow vacuum the bag provides and begins flailing her arms about, reaching desperately for her attacker. She's able to grip a handful of Dawn's hair and pulls her head to the side. Dawn cries out, and Ellie hears a tearing sound—like thin paper being ripped apart—and she knows Danielle has unrooted some hair from her daughter's scalp.

Ellie reacts. Doesn't think. Just…reacts. Lashing out, she boots Danielle in the stomach, deflating her lungs. She's surprised by the ferocity of her movement, and even though Danielle deserves that—or at least, the creature within does—she still feels a sliver of regret creeping in. She wishes she could take it back, resort to other means of incapacitating her, but it's much too late for that.

The woman crumbles to the ground as Dawn readjusts her grip. The black bag deflates and inflates, slowly now as the seconds pass, the air supply within getting low.

"Don't kill her," Ellie says, reminding her daughter of the plan, but Dawn doesn't seem to hear her. Ellie watches her eyes, the fear, the three lost years of her life, the realization that Danielle is a part of that missed time, a proponent of that gap she will never reclaim, and the fear suddenly bleeds from her eyes and is replaced by something else, something red. "Dawn..."

Gritting her teeth, Dawn tightens the cord, using all her strength.

"Dawn!" Ellie lunges forward, trying to pry her hands from the bag, the cord pulled so tightly that the surrounding flesh is turning blue. "Let go!"

But she doesn't. She fends off her mother, wrenching the bag, the woman's head, away from her. And then comes that terrible popping sound, the one that coincides with another twisting of the neck. The woman goes completely limp under Dawn's control.

"What have you...?" Ellie's jaw strays open. "Did you..."

Dawn lets go, allowing the woman to fall to the floor with a weighty thump. No movement. Clearly dead. Upon realizing she's taken this way too far, that her anger's gotten the best of her, three years of frustration and torment unleashed in a single mindless act, she kicks herself away from the body, skittering like a crab over to the opposite wall. Dawn starts to hyperventilate, sucking in air, acting as if her lungs are getting none of it.

A panic attack. Ellie knows them well. She slides across the floor over to her daughter, throwing an arm around her, holding her close. "I'm so sorry, baby," she says, and she's not exactly sure why she's apologizing, but this does seem like her fault. Maybe if their relationship had been better, then Dawn wouldn't have taken that secretive trip to Virginia Beach to meet that mysterious guy, never would have gotten lost in the dark labyrinth of Lacuna's Point. She tries Monday-Morning-Quarterbacking this outcome a hundred different ways, trying to relieve herself of the blame, but she can't do it. It's her fault, all right. Always has been, always will be. "God, I'm so sorry."

Dawn cries into her mother's shoulder. "I *hate* this," she says, shaking with each heavy sob. "I *hate* this place and what it's taken from me."

"Me too," Ellie says, petting the back of her head, feeling the dampness soaking through her shirt. "Me too."

As the two of them embrace each other, something moves beneath the black bag over Danielle's face.

Something pulsates.

Marissa patrols the outskirts of the amusement park near the shore, surveying the vehicles that have been parked in the lot, the ones that have never moved, not since the day she arrived. She wonders how many of the drivers had rolled into Lacuna's Point to stop for a bathroom break or to get a coffee and never left, how many of them are still here now. How many have died like Skelly, who was too old, whose talents were all used up? The cars range from vintage classics to brand-new models, and though Marissa can't tell the difference and what those models are, she continues to watch them and behind her, keeping a lookout for anything suspicious whatsoever.

She turns back to Mitch. "Hurry up, will you?"

Mitch pokes his head out of Ellie's Subaru. "Someone coming?"

Marissa scans the trees, the misty haze that's infiltrated the spaces between the shedding branches. "No, but they could be."

"I'm almost done," he says, and then dips back down, losing himself in the backseat. He continues to toss around random items, burrowing his way through the mess.

"Well, what are you looking for, man?" She toys with lighting another cigarette, but her lungs already feel like lead weights. She stops, puts the paper death stick back in the pack with its brothers and sisters.

"Just something," he calls back.

"Very specific."

"Just wait a second." And then: "Aha!" He crawls back out of the car holding a pair of headphones, Beats that look fairly new. "Wife got them for me last Christmas. Haven't used them much."

"Really? With everything going on, you want to listen to some jams?" She laughs incredulously. "Glad to see you're taking your plan very seriously."

"This is going to—"

"Can't trust you." She turns and speeds off, toward the trees, back to the town where the inevitable end awaits her, awaits them all. Where they will suffer at the claws of Lacuna's Point, become hostages under the eye of that awful force keeping them trapped there, like animals in some inhumane experiment. Mice in a maze with no exit, destined to wander endless corridors until starvation kicks in, until they are depleted of their earthly basics. Air, food, water. Until the town has taken everything they have, stripped them of their souls.

Eaten their individuality.

That's what's happened to Rosetta, wherever she is. Dead now, probably. Gone forever. And there's no one to blame but Marissa herself. She's aware of the influence she has, how her little sister always wanted to emulate her. Fucking *be* her. That kind of power, that sisterly bond, comes with immeasurable responsibility, the kind she's always taken for granted, never respected, and now look where we are. Lost. In that maze. That dark labyrinth with no exit. Rosetta's dead—she's come to terms with that, processed that information and put away the residual grief to deal with later, once she's out of here—but it's still her fault, no matter how she slices it.

*I could have stopped her. I SHOULD have.*

But she didn't. Now Rosetta—sweet, little, innocent Rosetta—will never see her parents again. Will never grow out of her rebellious teenage years. Will never go away to college. Or get a job. Will never marry the love of her life. She'll enjoy none of those things.

Because she's dead.

DEAD.

"Marissa," Mitch calls after her. He jogs to catch up. She wants to run, run far away, but there's nowhere to run to, really, even if Lacuna's Point had no invisible barrier blocking their escape. Home is a funny concept to her now. She knows where it is, of course. Knows Tempe, Arizona like the back of her hand. But when she closes her eyes to picture the front porch or the fruit-punch color of her parents' entry door, the dove-gray bedroom carpets or the marble countertops of the kitchen—there's nothing there. A blank space. A black screen. No image whatsoever. She knows these things exist, but there are no *images* to associate with the words.

It frightens her to even think of home now. How much longer will she last here? How much before she ends up lost, like Rosetta?

She thinks she'd rather slit both wrists and be done with it. In fact, she might just do that. Tonight. After Josh is asleep, resting for the big day. They'll undoubtedly fail with their plan—there's no sense in even trying. So, why not grab a boxcutter from one of the local shoppes and get the deed done? Check out of this place, once and for all. Book herself a one-way ticket to a different kind of blank space.

"I know how you feel," Mitch says after she stops walking and buries her head in her hands. She's at the edge of the trees; on the other side of them, the hotel stands tall. Beyond it, the clock tower peeks its massive head over the stretched pines, mocking her small stature with its glorious length. Daylight beams off its face, glimmering like some valuable token of time.

She wants to set the motherfucking thing on fire.

"You don't know shit," she says to him, wiping her nose with her sleeve.

"Yes, I do. You think we can't win. You're thinking of giving up."

"We're all thinking that. You don't fucking know me."

"You're right. Don't know you but for two weeks. Right?"

"Yeah. Two fucking weeks."

"Feels a lot longer than that, don't it?" There's a gentle sensitivity in his voice that she's come to appreciate. It doesn't make her want to slash her wrists any less, but it's appreciated.

Mitch walks around her so he can show her his face, the sincerity in his expression. "I know you're feeling weak and you think my plan is basically bullshit."

"Basically."

He holds up the Beats. "This can work."

"Even if we get out of here alive..." She shakes her head, tears touring down her face once again, the well seemingly endless. "I failed. Don't you get that? I couldn't save her. I'm going home to my parents' house without her, and what am I supposed to tell them? Am I supposed to tell them what happened here? What I saw? About those fucking things that act like people?"

Mitch delays, and she knows he's thinking of the best lie he can, whatever will talk her down from this ledge. "You'll think of something."

"I've never succeeded in anything except being a good older sister, and now I've failed at that."

She pushes past him. Getting the last word in is satisfying, but the need to cut herself and spill the wine that runs through her is almost overwhelming. If she doesn't find a tool to end herself soon, she might just explode.

"Wait," Mitch says, and she stops. Doesn't know why, but it's definitely the sound of his voice, the sorrow infused with the words, the *humanity* in them. "You didn't fail."

"Oh?" She rotates back to him. "And how is that?"

"You found her. When no one else could."

"She's dead."

"You don't know that, not for sure." He sighs, steps closer. "And even if she *is*, at least you'll know the truth. And this place cannot take that away from you."

The well drains again, and she wipes the slippery surface of her face with the back of her hand.

"You succeeded when no one else could," he says. "Be proud of that. And fight back against the monsters who destroyed her. Do it for Rosetta. She'd want you to. Giving up—well, you're right. I don't know you or your sister, but I doubt she'd want you to."

A ferocious, warrior-like scream rips up her throat as she drops to her knees. Mitch wraps his arms around her, the embrace providing a certain level of warmth, of comfort, but there's still more frustration to exorcise—she screams again, this time into his shoulder. The solid muscle muffles the sound. It feels good to let go of that rage. It makes the bad thoughts go away, at least for now.

She screams again, one more time, not even considering the fact that close-by ears might be listening.

When Quincy Black enters the quad, it's like time itself has been put on pause. Everyone setting up the tents and tables in preparation for tomorrow's festival has ceased doing so and turned their attention to the town's head honcho, dropping their jaws at the unexpected presence of their mysterious and fearless leader. As much as Black loves their affection and attentiveness, he doesn't want to intrude on their hustle for too long. He doesn't want to unsettle their mood, ruin their excitement for the big day. But he has no choice in the matter. It's come to his attention that he might have been overzealous in his approach to procuring new talent, and that his eagerness and greediness have caused them great potential harm. The town, he has concluded, is in great peril. There's evidence that's been brought to his attention, of course, but there's something else too. Quincy Black has his feelings, his trusty gut, and he can usually tell when something is deeply and undeniably wrong. It's an ambiance the town exudes. It's happened before, that simple alteration of *mood*, that peculiar scent of something amiss—happened three years ago, in fact—and now…it's happening again.

*The goddamn interlopers…*

Something has to be done, and fuck—the one man he's counted on to usher these outsiders' smooth transitions is currently incapacitated.

"My beloved townspeople of Lacuna's Point," he says, strolling toward the center of the quad, where the good people have abandoned their current duties so they can listen to the infinite wisdom of their gracious host. They've already begun to form a circle, leaving their chores without almost any delay at all. "Gather 'round! Come hither! We have a quick bit of news to discuss and then you can all be on your merry way. This is an emergency meeting and I thank each one of you for coming out and supporting our great cause."

Once the people's sole focus is officially on him, Black clears his throat and adjusts the bandages covering his old face. He'll need to swap them out soon for a cleaner wrap; he can feel the material softening over the leakage beneath, the coalescing of his human appearance taking much longer this time around.

"Good of you to come out to Lacuna Point's Annual Art and Talent Show Extravaganza! I have no doubt it will be our most successful celebration yet. That said, we have to take measures so the event goes off without a hitch. I want to discuss a matter with you, a very important matter—I know you're all well aware of this year's inductees, and that we've taken on more new arrivals than we ever have in the past. Perhaps I was a bit too acquisitive in my approach this year and I take full responsibility for this little misstep. The benefactor grows hungrier and hungrier each and every year, and even though my intentions come from a good place, I do think I missed the mark. In doing so, we have run the risk of rebellion against our cause. I think we can all remember three years ago, the great pain that was caused by a few of the town's new talent."

The crowd grumbles in agreement, in recognition of those scary and tumultuous times.

"A rough period for all of us. Sometimes, when people don't understand the mysterious ways of how our town operates, the benefactor and the positive symbiotic relationship that our way of life and his has formed, well…sometimes people reject what they cannot comprehend. And we have to be there for them. We have to teach them, put them in their rightful place. Make them see. Now, these particular newcomers, I feel, and I'm saddened to report this—they do not see our ways, they do not recognize the great importance of tomorrow's event, and they might be in league with nefarious forces counterproductive to our own. They may seek a way to disrupt our festivities, might find a way to destroy and ruin our celebration. They might do so violently."

Gasps all around him.

"I do not wish for them to even attempt such a thing, so what I'm asking you—my good people—is to help me gather up these individuals and bring them to me. It's very important that they remain alive, but I do understand that, in times like this, mistakes might be made, and violent problems require violent solutions, so if death is a necessary byproduct of keeping our way of life intact, then so be it. The benefactor will not be satisfied if there *are* accidents, and we will be punished appropriately, but at least we will have our town, our way of life." He stretches his lips in a proud grin, feels the bandages stick to his ruined mask of human flesh. Black watches their expressions, how easily they wilt and bend to his will. It's like convincing children to carry out a simple chore. Take out the trash or vacuum your room and you will get candy for dinner. *Contain the interlopers and you will get the Light.* "Now, we all know there is no escape from this place, so even if the interlopers try, they will fail. But that doesn't mean they can't make life very hard on us over the next year. We do not want a repeat of three years ago. We have to protect this land. We have good people in place to do exactly that, but I feel like, as a town, with our efforts combined, we can bring this potential threat to a swift conclusion without much fuss. That way we can go about our day tomorrow and enjoy the Light without any complications. So…will you help me, valued people of Lacuna's Point?"

Everyone reacts with a spell of silence. Then, someone, a frail man whose bones show through his thin skin, asks, "What about the Light?"

"Clarify," Black says, surprised that the people have not already bent their knees to him and pledged their undying devotion to the cause. That they haven't pisses him off. "What about the Light?"

"It's just…" the man continues. His name is Winfred Golden, *Fred* to most, and Quincy Black doesn't like his questioning tone, the accusation it carries. "It's just we haven't had any *good* Light in a while. We would sure like some. And the music! Haven't heard those sweet sounds, either."

"I've felt sick these last few days," a woman says, speaking up. Black's eyes dart across the collected faces before him and locate Aubrey Peters as she pokes her head up from the crowd, her timid, mousy appearance not matching her plucky intentions. "I think the Light will help. It will help save us all."

The town grumbles in agreement.

All they care about is the Light, the power it gives. It's been two weeks since their last dose, but that flash of light was nothing compared to the big transfer that happens on Arts Festival Day. Small potatoes as the saying goes.

Black holds up his hands, laughing quite a bit at their minor infraction, their sliver of disobedience. "All right, you rascals. Settle down. The Light is coming, and you will all be saved once again. Swept into the chasm of which it all creates. You will never feel better. Tip-top. But that's contingent on you bringing these folks in alive, so they can share their art with the benefactor, help produce the greatest output of Light this town has ever seen."

Aubrey Peters doesn't back down. "Hope so. Feel awfully sick lately."

Black wants to crush in her skull. "Would I lie to you, Aubrey?"

"No, sir," she answers immediately, and then shrinks back into the crowd, disappearing into the sea of worn faces.

"The Lacuna rests and when it is time for it to wake, it will give us the Light as it always does. Do not fret. This town has always operated on this unique dynamic and will continue to do so. Sometimes, the town needs extra protection from those who do not understand the ways, and this is one of those times. You must help protect it. Protect yourselves. The Lacuna."

No one seems too enthused or inclined to do so.

Black takes a deep breath. "Listen, I didn't want to have to do this, but...I think you need to hear this." He turns around, scanning the faces before him. "Where's Dave Fester at? Dave, you out there?"

Dave pushes himself through the throng, squeezing between two people near the front. "Right here, Mayor Black."

"Oh, good." Black welcomes him with an open arm, throwing it around the man's shoulder. "Dave here had a harrowing run-in with the interlopers today, didn't you, Dave?"

"Well..." Dave winces, looking like this is a line that should be carefully tiptoed. "You could say that."

"Why don't you tell us what you discovered at Ace's Place."

Dave looks on hesitantly.

"Go on now. Tell them what you found this morning."

"I...I..."

"Don't be shy. The people deserve to know the truth, what they're dealing with."

"What truth?" someone asks. Bret Callahan.

"Yeah, what's this all about, Dave?" queries Ernie Cole.

"Go on, Dave," Roberta Thomas encourages. "Tell us everything. No holding on to secrets now."

"That's right, Dave," Black says, smiling at him with his eyes. "No secrets among us. Not this town. Not Lacuna's Point. The truth is important. If we don't have truth, what do we have?"

"Well..." Dave says. His voice falters some. "Well, I went to Ace's, like every morning..."

"Speak up!" someone shouts. Black can't pinpoint where it came from.

"Go on," Black tells Dave. "Louder."

Dave clears his throat. "I went to Ace's Place!" He's shouting now. It hurts Black's ears when he raises his voice like that, but he does his best to ignore the pain. "I went there because that's what I do every morning! Best damn coffee in Lacuna's Point!"

"Hey!" shouts Benny Kaine, owner of the coffee shop over on fifth.

"Sorry, Benny. But you know it's true." Dave quickly forgets Benny and his shitty coffee and continues on. "Anywho, I went there for my morning routine and the place was deserted. I couldn't believe it. So I went inside. And I...I found something."

"Well, what the heck was it?" Gerry Elm asks what everyone's thinking. The faces around him are zoomed in on Dave and his story.

*Good,* Black thinks. *Let them know. Knowledge will drive them.*

"Don't leave us in suspense now!" someone chimes in.

"I found Officer Foley is what I found." Dave looks disturbed by this admission. "Someone locked him up in the diner's kitchen, in the freezer. But he was..."

"He was what, Dave?" Black asks calmly, patiently. The cusp of this certain truth arouses him. "What was he?"

"Well, his face was all messed up. Cut or something. He had these things growing out of them? The interlopers...they must have tortured him or something because he was in bad shape and his voice was all...I dunno...scratchy or something. Like he swallowed a bunch of glass."

"Horrible!" someone laments.

"Disgusting!" another adds.

"We need to find these sum-bitches!" someone else comments, and this announcement is followed by an enthusiastic cheer.

*Good,* Black thinks. *Now you know what's at stake.*

He turns to Dave and claps him on the shoulder, applauding his courage to speak before the town. "Thank you, Dave. I really appreciate your bravery here today. On our benefactor's behalf, I'd like to present you with a key to the town once this is all over. Once the interlopers are caught and the Arts Festival goes off without any problems."

Dave's previous face melts into one filled with absolute elation. "That...that would be an incredible honor."

A key to the town is the most prestigious award one can earn in Lacuna's Point, and with it, comes extra Light.

Black turns from Dave, facing the crowd. "I'll have you all know that Elroy Foley is recovering just fine, so there's no need to fret regarding his condition. He'll be ready to launch back into action before you can say, *sweet pumpkin pie.*"

A wave of relief washes over the crowd. Some turn to one another and shake their neighbors' hands, as if they're offering peace at Sunday mass. Even the town's priest, Father Adams, raises his hands and gives thanks to the Lord. But Black knows there is only one Lord they need to give thanks to, and that Lord is the benefactor, the true inspiration behind Lacuna's Point.

*The Lacuna itself.*

Their God, now and forever.

Black nods along as the town's well wishes and Lord-thanking tapers off.

"He'll be back on his feet in no time at all," he reiterates. "Just a quick rest and recharge. But this is why we'll need your help to handle these interlopers. They are dangerous and Officer Elroy Foley will need assistance bringing them in. He's been good to us, that Elroy, yes? He's helped us out in the past, and even though he's far from perfect, he's handled things. So…will you stand with your beloved boy in blue and do what needs to be done in order to preserve our town? Will you?"

Each townie glances at the person next to them, then shrugs.

"As long as we can have the Light!" someone shouts, and the crowd audibly agrees with that sentiment.

"Oh, you'll have the Light," Black growls. "You'll have all the Light you'll ever need."

# CHAPTER SEVENTEEN

In the chamber of the Mayor's secret quarters, Kya Green tries to remember bits of her past but finds the task extremely difficult. It's like trying to see through a thick fog, the way headlights can't cut through and only illuminate the surface. That's what she can see. The surface of her memories. And there isn't much there. Sure, she can remember her father, what he looks like—but her sisters, Brianna and Tiana, her mother—no, it's hard to visualize their faces, what they look like exactly. A few weeks ago, she forgot her mother's name. Just…forgot it. Like, it was there, somewhere, in the back of her brain, but she couldn't locate it. Weird, right? Lotta weird things are happening to Kya lately, and she knows why—it's because she's here, in the Mayor's secret room, atop this godforsaken clock tower in this fucked up town there's no escape from.

She closes her eyes once again, tries her best to remember something from her past, a specific memory, hoping that will help her remember the faces. A day at the boardwalk. The beach. A family cookout. A trip to Six Flags.

But there's nothing. Nothing she can remember specifically, vividly. She remembers these things happened but there's no visual component. Images are lost on her.

The door to the chamber opens and in steps the good Mayor, back from his speech to the town about securing the future of this place. This fucked up alternate reality.

"Good to see you, my little sweet treat," the Mayor says. "Hope you're getting along just fine."

She looks at the concrete wall she's chained to. The manacles clasped around her wrists and feet.

"Be a lot fuckin' better if you just let me go," Kya tells him.

"Yeah," he says, sighing. "Not gonna do that. And I think you know why."

"Because I'll kick you in the balls again? Not that what you have down there is balls. Who knows what your freakish inhuman ass has hanging below the belt."

Black shrugs as if whatever *is* down there is inconsequential. Then he moves across the chamber, over to Eddy's face, where the hands of time click, click away. Next to the ivory disc that holds time itself, a phonograph sits on a small table. The Mayor heads over to the device, stops, and glances back at Kya.

Kya eyes the phonograph, surveying the gold cylinder that sticks out of the box like a shiny flower, and the dark center from which the bad sounds travel. "Please don't."

"You are an interesting specimen, Kya Green," the Mayor goes on to tell her. "You're not particularly talented. Sure, your little poems are something, mildly amusing, but that's hardly enough to earn an invitation to this place. Your closeness with Dawn Brower is another something, and it does seem that spending time with the girl has rubbed some magic off on you—guilty by association as you might call it. But you yourself aren't particularly juicy enough to contribute anything worthy of keeping you around. Yet...the Lacuna wishes for you to stay despite your rebellious nature and insistent refusal to obey the laws of this place. Maybe...that in and of itself is your art, and maybe that's why the Lacuna finds you so intriguing. So tasty."

"Fuck you."

"Ah yes. Those words again. You'd think after all this time together, you'd come up with something more original."

"Okay, fuck you with a rusty spoon."

Black rolls his eyes, not amused. "You're beginning to bore me, Kya Green. Where's that zest for life? The fight? You've caused me great trouble, but I've grown to miss your defiance." He sighs, then looks down at the phonograph, toying with something on the square platform the mounted golden cylinder stems from. Shooting her a glance, he waits for her protest. But a protest is predictable, and Kya knows protesting does her no good when she's chained to a fucking wall. "I'd love to let you out again. To allow you to walk out of here, free. It brings us no pleasure to keep you here."

"My father is here," she says. "He'll get me out."

Laughter rises up the man's (thing's) throat. "That's a delightful delusion. But he will become just like everyone else who finds themselves lost in the Lacuna. Another wannabe artist that just needs the right creative push to ascend into greatness."

"This place isn't greatness."

"Oh, but it is. You're just not allowing yourself to see the bigger picture. Here, in Lacuna's Point, you can be whatever you want.

Success is guaranteed. All that is asked of you, is that you contribute."

"You steal from people," Kya says sharply. "For that *thing.*"

Black winces at the term, the accusation. "It's a positive symbiotic relationship. They surrender their art, and in return they get the Light."

"The Light is bullshit. It blinds them to the truth."

"The Light is pure cosmic energy, palatable ambrosia, and the truth is what we make it."

"You're so full of—"

"SILENCE, COW!" Black's shadow stretches across the ceiling, an all-encompassing stain that seems like it could go on forever. Once it covers the entire chamber, Black's eyes begin to glow like cat's eyes floating in the dark. It reminds her of the Cheshire Cat from *Alice in Wonderland*. "You will not speak ill of the Lacuna and its ways. This is an ancient ritual and I've spent millenniums perfecting this place, stabilizing my relationship with the Lacuna, establishing nature and order and truth. I've done things your human mind simply cannot comprehend."

She bites her tongue even though she knows she's getting the music anyway.

Black returns to the phonograph. From somewhere in the shadows next to the old music box, he pulls out an orb about the size of a Magic 8-Ball. The thing glows with a faint magenta light.

"You'll see the way soon enough, my child," Black says, touching the golden cylinder, transferring power from the orb to the phonograph, using his inhuman body as a conduit.

The music plays, discordant tunes that sound like metal scratching and breaking coupled with staticky gusts of wind. Kya screams, her mind reaching the edge of madness, leaning over and leaping off.

The room focuses, bokeh sliding back and forth until the images coalesce, become solid circles of brilliant light. He sees familiar paneling on the walls, golden ornate sconces, and the impeccable cabinetry, and when he looks up, he sees the dazzling chandelier hanging over the Mayor's office, the beautiful candles placed in each arm giving off little circles of fiery luminance.

Foley feels like a truck's run over him, and then that truck's driven another thirty feet in reverse only to run him over a second time. His face burns like someone's run razorblades down his cheeks and across the forehead. He touches the areas in question and the pain bites harder. Something crusty in those areas, and dark flakes fall into his lap.

Dried blood.

He stands up, his knees protesting the sudden movement. It's hard to put weight on them, and he ends up taking another seat.

*What the hell happened?*

The last thing he remembers is entering that diner, going into the kitchen to assist with the waitress's distressing calls, and then getting knocked in the head. He does remember waking up in the freezing cold, shivering his balls off, but even that's become a little hazy.

But something happened, had to have considering the terrible shape he's in. Like someone's gone and carved up his face, pummeled him with baseball bats.

*Interlopers.*

Yes, it's all coming back to him now. The details are moving in like fresh air through an open window of a stagnant-smelling room. Those piece of shit interlopers did this to him. He supposes it's his fault, should have nipped this situation in the bud back when he had the chance. But no—it was too mean to do that, what he really wanted to do, bust a few heads and make an example out of someone. The way the Mayor savaged Darla's eye—now *that's* how you get a point across. He'd broken that woman's ankle, sure—but that happened during the change, the coming of the Light, so that didn't drive home the point, the lesson of *don't fuck with Elroy Foley or you'll get the wrath.* He should have done something else, something extreme, something outside of that alternate reality. But then again, there would come the cries of abuse, harsh and unfair treatment, and bullshit terms like "police brutality." Pussy liberal nonsense that Elroy Foley has no time for, and thank God Lacuna's Point doesn't have too many of those assholes running around, spouting their bullshit. It's nice to live in a town free from all that leftism, Foley thinks—good God-fearin' people here, yes sir.

He should have cracked a skull or two, and knows a missed opportunity when he sees one, and that was a lob-job that Elroy Foley whiffed on big-time. Now, the town is amuck with interlopers, those who do not know the ways. People hellbent on tearing down their little community, blasphemers who spit in the face of God and wipe their asses with the American Flag.

*Teach them a lesson,* instructs that little voice within. *Get that gun out, son. Show them the truth. Like you showed them years ago but they were too blind to see reality smacking them upside their heads.*

*Like you done showed that boy.*

That boy. Yes. Him.

The street. The splotches of red that stained the asphalt. The three holes in his chest.

Standing outside the car door, smelling that bold, raw scent of some nameless metal.

It's like a dream, those images. He seems to remember them. The parades that followed. Protests. Fighting with his wife. Yes, he recalls those hectic times. Specifically his wife now. *Ex* actually. The night she spat in his face and told him she was filing for divorce. That he was the scum of the Earth, always had been, and that she would never associate herself with such filth ever again.

He wanted to hit her that night. Smack her right in her ungrateful mouth. She never complained until that one little mistake went public and blew up his entire life. Never complained once. Thinking back, he shoulda popped her one. Right in the mouth. To let her know.

*Let her know who's boss.*

Just like Daddy used to when little Elroy got out of line, the way he took him over his knee and used the belt. Just like that, but with knuckles against teeth.

He hates Debbie for leaving, hates her so bad it makes him tremble just thinking about her—and why is he thinking about her? Now, of all the times? He hasn't thought of her once over the last few years or so. So, shit—why now?

He can't say, but those memories have been there all along, sleeping beneath the surface. Like a crab, skittering across the bay under a full moon. There. Just below the waterline.

*Crab.*

Huh.

He feels something move beneath his skin. Twinge. Tweak. Crawl.

He remembers Lacuna's Point, coming here after the whole thing went down, after his face appeared on every national television news station. Well, not *coming here*. Being *invited*. *Coming* makes it sound like he stumbled upon the place, and that certainly wasn't how it went down. No, he remembers standing at the edge of a pier, maybe not far from here, maybe somewhere in Virginia Beach, looking out across the water, how the setting sun threw shades of sparkling orange at his eyes, the purple shadows that fell over the emerging night. He remembers swaying on his heels. Holding that bottle of Jack, nearly polishing off the entire thing. Everything was blurry and he also remembers that he never took a swimming lesson in his life, never dunked a toe in any pool. He remembers thinking it would be pretty easy to drown, being this drunk and having no experience in the tide. He remembers thinking this was his out from everything that would follow—nationally televised court hearings, the social media mob and their torches and pitchforks. He was already the most hated man in America (according to some bull-cocky Fox News poll) and no amount of ass-kissing or apology-making was going to change that, even if he was just doing his job, protecting and serving and upholding the law. Even if it was self-defense.

A mistake.

*Murderer.* That's what they called him. And that's what he was. *Technically.* But he didn't feel like a murderer.

"I was doing my job. Protecting people," he says to no one. Black's office is entirely empty save for shadows that seem unnaturally long in all the wrong places. Maybe he's addressing ghosts. Maybe the ghost of that kid he executed. Maybe he's here, listening, hearing his pitiful excuses.

"Kid," he says, snorting. "He was practically a man."

*He was sixteen.*

"And he was armed," Foley says, feeling sick now.

*With what? The knife they found tucked in the glove box under the car's manual? Nowhere in reach?*

The thing inside him is on the move now, squirming through him. He can feel it rooting around his brain, and now he thinks that's why his memories are suddenly clear. *It wants me to see, feel these things.*

A wave of nausea passes through him. A funny sensation ascends his throat. He turns his head and pukes on the Mayor's expensive carpet, a material that probably costs more than the Richmond Police Department paid him in severance once they canned his ass on the grounds of *improperly discharging a firearm.*

"I felt threatened." Elroy is crying now, tears falling over the self-stitched rips in his face. "I was in danger."

But the young man wasn't armed, a fact the prosecutor was so readily willing to prove.

"I thought he was..." He rocks back and forth in his chair. "I thought I saw it. Everything happened so fast and I was..." Rocking harder now, he feels his rage stewing, boiling over. "It's bullshit. They shouldn't have been uncooperative. They should have listened to me. I am the law and they should have listened! THEY SHOULD HAVE—"

*(murderer)*

*(killer)*

*(racist-cop-pig-fuck)*

"LISTENED TO ME I AM LAW!"

"Good Lordy, Elroy," Black says from the doorway. Foley never heard him enter, too caught up in his thoughts to notice. "You sure seem like you're having a fit. Christ, you puke?"

Foley ignores his question—the blasphemy too—and claps his hands together in prayer. "Oh, Black, thank God. You have to help me. I'm starting...starting to remember things."

Black winks as he scratches at a pink stain that's bled through the fabric of his headpiece. "Interesting. I assume these are unwanted memories, yeah? Of the before times?"

"You told me you'd take these things away. When I agreed to come here. You said you'd take them all away. What I'd done. The shame..."

*(racist-cop-pig-fuck)*

"So I did," Black says, moving from the door, around Foley, and standing behind his desk. He glares at Foley like he's the most pathetic sack of human flesh he's ever seen, and then leans over, pressing his glove-covered knuckles on the mahogany desktop. "But the human brain is a wondrous tool and sometimes you can't predict what it will forget, what it will remember. The Light will help—all you need is a little to make you feel less like...well, *you*." His expression hangs, begins to sour as his lips rear back like a feral canine prepared to savage the flesh of those who get too close. "But I'm also having trouble feeling sorry for you, Elroy. You've disappointed me. Again. You promised me, *promised* me you'd keep our streets safe from the interlopers and those who do not understand the ways."

"It's your fault," Foley barked back at him, his tenor surprising himself. "You brought too many this time."

"Ellll-roy," the Mayor scolds, sing-song like, as if Foley should know his excuse is invalid. "You know as well as I do that the Lacuna does what it wants—I'm merely the facilitator of its will."

"Well, tell that damn thing to calm the fuck down!" Sweat pours down Foley's face in beads the size of popcorn kernels. "It's ruining this town!" *Ruining me!* he wants to add but somehow refrains.

In an instant, Black's hand shoots out, his fingers gripping the bottom of Foley's throat. Foley thinks the creature known as Quincy Black has enough strength to rip out his esophagus like some ridiculous Kung-Fu movie. Cutting off his air supply, Black leans in, seething. The pink splotches staining the bandages mutate into shades of angry orange.

"The Lacuna's will is law, you pig-fucking psychopath." Instead of ripping, he pushes Foley away from him, sending the big cop backward, into the chair positioned in the center of the office. Foley stumbles, hits the chair, and the wooden structure breaks under his weight. Foley collapses on the floor hard, landing atop the chair's broken pieces. "You will do as it demands or I swear to the powers of the Great Verse, I will watch it reduce your soul to particles. Cosmic dust, Elroy Foley. That's all you are anyway, you and your kind. Humans are nothing more than insignificant specks of matter, taking up way too much space in the vacuums of this realm. The only reason you are alive is because you're candy to the Lacuna. And once it doesn't need you anymore, once it no longer enjoys the taste of you on its magnificent tongue, it will obliterate you, stomp you out like little bugs, and move on to the next universe it seeks to feast upon. How does that make you feel to know how truly unimportant your life is? How small you are?"

Foley wipes a spot of blood from his lips. "I don't give a shit. I just don't want to remember anything anymore. Like you promised."

"You're pathetic. A pathetic excuse of a soul and a waste of human matter."

Tears bathe his face, but he doesn't feel sadness. Only exhaustion. He wants it to end, this ongoing nightmare.

"Take care of them," Black spits. "Take care of the goddamn interlopers and end their goddamn agendas, and make Lacuna's Point a safe place again. A *great* place again. And I promise you, you can have all the Light that will fit in that fat head of yours."

"You promise? I truly won't remember? You'll make me forget it all?"

"You take care of them," Black tells him, "and the only thing you'll know is how great you are."

Black turns back to his desk. Foley didn't notice it before, but a small object draped in a black cloth rests on the right-hand corner. He doesn't know why, but the second Black reaches for it, his heart sinks like a boat with bullet holes in its bottom.

Black uncovers the object, and Foley sees what looks like a Magic 8-Ball. He almost snickers at the idea of Black shaking the damn thing and asking it a stupid question: *Will Elroy Foley save the town?*

*YES OR NO?*

Black faces him, holding the sable ball in two cupped hands. The black inside the ball tumbles, swirling like creamer dropping into a mug of dark roast. Soon, the darkness within begins to fade, draw back, and a white injection starts to swallow up the inky plumes that roil and rage. Soon, there is only white.

"Look into the Light," Black says.

And Elroy Foley does. After one quick glance, he feels better already.

"Will you do what's necessary, Elroy Foley? Will you do what the Lacuna asks of you?"

"Yes," he says, the room already diminishing, fading away on its own. Soon, there will only be that bright, white light.

That painless transfer of memories leaving him forever.

Dusk has fallen over Lacuna's Point, injecting dark swirls into the starry ceiling. Tomorrow, the sun will usher in a day of celebration, the Arts Festival where everyone showcases their talents, offers them up as a sacrifice to a deity they've never seen but very much believe in. A spiritual presence that fills all things, that maybe exists somewhere beyond the sky or the forbidden outskirts of town. Or maybe it's something less spooky, an entity that's hidden deep within themselves, locked away in the special place where we keep our deepest, darkest pieces of ourselves.

There are signs everywhere, of course. Posters announcing tomorrow's festivities. When the shoppe owners close their doors for the night, they put up signs informing the customers they will be closed tomorrow, so, that way, the whole town can enjoy the day-long party without feeling the need to wander off and browse the plethora of retail options. No distractions. Just fun. It's the best day of the year, a fact no one would argue should you bring up the topic in conversation. Best day of the year in the best town of America.

The Arts Festival.

And the best part? The end, of course. The grand finale.

The Light.

And it will shine across town, fill the streets with such an incredible warmth, such a sense of belonging and cohesiveness, that even the coldest heart will relish these positive sentiments. Furthermore, the Light brings a promise. A promise that their beloved way of life will remain intact and safe and free from the confines of an uncivilized society for another annual cycle.

Oh yes. The Light will come.

A gift from above and below.

From beyond.

It will feel good.

Bask in it, good citizen.

Mitch makes it to the art gallery in ten minutes, running the entire stretch, not looking over his shoulder to see if anyone or anything's giving chase. He's lucky no one's out and about, that the shop owners have finished closing their establishments and gone home for the day. Mitch also wants to rest up for tomorrow, but first—there's one order of business to take care of.

"What the hell's going on?" Ellie asks, greeting him at the door. As soon as he's inside, she shuts, locks the door and draws the shades. "You were supposed to be here fifteen minutes ago."

"I got caught up with Marissa and Josh. We were going over some details."

Dawn emerges from the back, her face long, as if someone has just told her she needs intense, immediate treatment to combat some malignant disease.

"What's going on?" Mitch asks, feeling a certain change in the air. *Not a good one.*

"We have a problem," Ellie answers.

"Great. What problem?"

"It was an accident," Dawn says, and now Mitch starts to panic. The plan is already a dangerous one, the type that can't afford any missteps or complications. The look on Dawn's face suggests this is a very *big* complication. "I didn't mean to."

Mitch looks from Dawn to Ellie.

Ellie shrugs. "It just…sorta happened."

Mitch can't take it anymore. "What sorta happened?"

"I killed her," Dawn admits, and then throws her hands over her face to catch the tears that come in fresh torrents.

Mitch tilts his head. "No."

Ellie nods slowly, puts her hands on her hips. "Yep. She's dead. Been dead for at least three hours now."

"Fuck."

"Yeah, I know." Ellie squints at him. "Is it really that big of a deal, though?"

Mitch leans against the counter. "I don't know, El. Maybe. Maybe not. What if these things have some kind of…collective consciousness or something?"

"You've been stuck in your own book for too long."

*She doesn't know how funny that is,* he thinks. "No, El. I'm serious. We have zero idea how these *things* operate. That was…" He was going to say *dumb,* but one glance at Dawn, the tears and the hitching sobs, and he decides against it. "All right. Let's see it. The body, I mean."

"We locked her in the back room." Ellie moves toward the back, but not without hugging her daughter and telling her it's all going to be okay.

Mitch can't really agree. He doesn't have a good feeling about this. Surely one of them will notice when Danielle doesn't come home tonight. Doesn't *report*.

He follows Ellie to the back. As soon as she opens the door, a grotesque stench slams into his nostrils.

"Oh." The odor puts him on his heels. "*Wow*."

"Yeah," Ellie says, the wild, ungodly aroma not seeming to faze her. To Mitch, it smells like someone ate expired hot dog meat and steamed cabbage, then threw up that disgusting mixture all over the place. "She started to smell almost immediately. Weird, right?"

"Weird doesn't even begin to cover it," he says, lifting his shirt above his nose, though it does nothing to block out the smell. "Where is she?"

Ellie leads them to the end of the hallway, to the backroom where they left the body. Carefully, she pushes open the door, as if there's a possibility that Danielle's corpse has reanimated.

She gasps.

"What is it?" Mitch asks. She doesn't answer. He tries to sneak around her, see what she's seeing, but she's blocking the doorway, just frozen there. "What—?"

She steps aside.

He sees it. The corpse on the ground.

"Ho. Lee. Shit," he says, and now he knows where the odor is coming from.

"She...she wasn't like that earlier," Ellie says, her eyes glued to the floor where the woman's body lies in a mess. Danielle's head is gone and the top half of her—from her shoulders to her waist—has split open like a banana peel, four rinds of meaty raw muscle and mangled bones folded back. A small river of blood has run from the butchered body across the floor and is still flowing. Chunks of burst meat and globules of skin litter the area around her. It's like a stick of weak dynamite exploded in her upper half; instead of blowing everything up, it just pushed everything inside out. She lies there like a recently hatched egg. The thing inside, whatever her corpse has given birth to, is no longer a prisoner of the womb that was her body.

Ellie begins to take one mindless step toward her, but Mitch grabs her shoulder. "Don't."

"She was…right here." Ellie shakes her head, rejecting the image before her. "No, no, this isn't right."

Dawn keeps behind the both of them, leaning against the wall.

Mitch asks her, "This normal?"

She shoots him a *what-are-you-nuts?* glance. He eases his hands into the air.

"Just asking. Seen a lot of crazy shit here."

"Look," Ellie says, pointing to the far wall. The window. The *open* window. "I think whatever escaped *her*, escaped *us*."

And that's when Mitch realizes how fucked they truly are.

The moon has pierced the black veil above and is now hanging over Lacuna's Point like a giant cheese wheel, giving luminescence to those hard-to-see places where the streetlights won't dare go. Elroy Foley stands on the bank opposite the old hotel, the place where most of the newcomers come to stay, hoping their trip here is a temporary one, a mini-vacation or a getaway they can head back home from after a few weeks of foolery and hell-raising. Foley looks up at the twenty-story structure with a sour taste in his mouth, so sickened by the mess he's found himself in that he spits, trying to rid the flavor from his tongue.

"Well, Elroy," says Dave Fester, the man who saved him from that incident at the diner. Correction: That *ambush* at the diner. He owes the man a great deal, including his life. It's the kind of payback a few beers won't cover, but a few beers might be a good start, and when this shit with the interlopers is over, hell—Elroy might just invite the guy out for a few forbidden drinks. "What's the plan?"

Foley turns to the six folks who've come to help, along with the six black hoods Mayor Black has supplied. Those creepy-ass motherfuckers remain menacing in their dark suits, and the fact they never speak a gosh-darn word is even creepier. Each is armed, whether it be with buckshot or a small-caliber pistol he's borrowed from the station's armory. Some have brought guns from home, and some have been supplied by good citizen and all-around solid friend-o, Bobby Mac. The gun shop owner has also brought something special with him, and Foley can feel himself getting giddy about the whole thing. It's almost enough to erase the nerves, the doubts concerning whether he can pull this thing off.

"We're going in there, ask them to come with us, no fussin'." If the incident at the diner is any indication, he doubts this will all go down smoothly.

"What if there is a fuss?" asks Alvin Sweaters, who owns the record shop down 9th Ave. He's holding his shotgun across his body like he would a guitar. Foley doubts the man's had any target practice—probably couldn't hit Tilda Sweeny's big ol' fanny from a step away—and the fact he's cocked, locked, and ready to unload somewhat scares Elroy. Accidents are too common in these situations, and Foley's had enough accidents over the last three years that he hardly wants to hear the word *accidents* ever again. But he pushes his concerns aside and puts stock into things going off just fine because…well, because they have to.

*If not, you're a dead man.* Black's voice. His inhuman tone, the one he uses when he's furious.

"Won't be any fuss, Sweaters," Foley tells him straight. "These people aren't armed and we are."

"Do we have permission to fire?" asks Don Trills, a young entrepreneur who owns the computer and phone medic down the road from Danielle's art gallery. "You know, if things go badly and all."

"No one fires anything unless I do first." Foley wipes his brow with the back of his hand. He's sweating something fierce, and for the first time in a long while, he doubts his body has the strength to carry out what needs to be done. *Sweet Geez Louise, I'm not even fifty yet.* He should be more than capable of handling this type of stress, but his heart and lungs and brain spout a different story.

"Yikes, Elroy," Trudy Rickmers says, examining him as if she's Doctor-fucking-Quinn Medicine Woman about to make some grim diagnosis. She's not a doctor, though, far from it—just the owner of the pet shop across town, next to the movie theater. She runs it with her wife, Ashley Howard. "You got the sweats, man."

"I'm fine," he tells her, the tone carrying *Knock-it-off* vibes. She clams up pretty quickly, and Elroy thinks he should use this newfound voice more often. "Let's go. Quicker we get this done, the sooner it's beer o'clock. Y'hear?"

The group hears, nods, save for the black hoods. They just go with the flow.

Foley has a terrible feeling in the pit of his stomach, and it sure ain't the Quesadillas he devoured at dinner.

It's a similar feeling he had once upon a time ago when he pulled over a young Black man for speeding. A night that had started out like any other but ended in gun smoke and blood and death. Tears. Regrets.

He wants to cry now.

Instead he signals the Stations of the Cross, asking Jesus to get him through tonight and tomorrow, so he can live peacefully ever after.

He wishes for the Light, all the town can give.

# CHAPTER EIGHTEEN

Josh is packing the suitcase he stole from the house, the suitcase that strangely reminds him of his father's, the one he packs every time he and mom have one of their blowouts. Unlike his old man, he's not packing clothes for a two-day getaway from the "ol' ball and chain." No, instead he's doing the opposite—he's unpacking clothes. Throwing them on the floor, tossing them on the bed. Anywhere he can so the bag is nice and empty. Because something else needs to go inside—firecrackers, M80s, whatever else that old coot stocks down at the Fireworks Emporium. The stuff the son of a bitch wouldn't sell to him. He wouldn't sell them to Marissa either, so he doesn't feel too bad about it. Obviously it's an *outsider* thing and not an age thing. If Mitch or Ellie had tried purchasing some boom-boom sticks, they'd also be denied.

But no matter. Josh got one over on him, stuffed an M80 in his pocket while the bastard was pointing to the rules and regulations of purchasing fireworks so openly displayed behind the counter. Thought he was pretty smart reading off that list, but Josh was the big victor. Well, not really—he only got away with one. But he *will* be the victor. The Emporium is closed now, and the only thing standing in his way of a whole bag full of *bang!* is a thin sheet of glass that can easily come down with a hammer. It's his last night in Lacuna's Point, so he doesn't care much about getting caught. Mitch is right—if they wanted them dead, they'd be dead by now. So what's the worst that can happen? End up like Kya? Locked alone somewhere? Josh doesn't care. This place sucks, no matter which way you slice it.

After the suitcase is empty (save for the small stick of big boom) and zipped shut, he stands up straight and tilts the bag onto the wheels.

"You look good, twerp," Marissa says, rubbing his head.

"Stop."

"You ready to do this?"

He opens his mouth to say, *Hell yeah, I am!* but now that he's thinking about it...is he? He's not so sure. Maybe this isn't the best play. Maybe just hiding out in the woods with Mitch, Ellie, and

Dawn is the better move. Just go meet them and skip the midnight robbery.

But he can't do that. They'll need those explosives. It's part of the plan.

*Vital.*

Mitch is counting on him. Ellie and Dawn.

He can't let them down.

Plus…he really does want to go home. He'd take seven-thousand screaming matches between Shawn and Sally Davis over another day in this town, with these people.

Not people.

Something else.

*Beings that stick crabs into their guts!*

*Blech.* He doesn't want to think about that. Not now. Not ever.

"You okay, sport?" Marissa asks.

"Yeah, fine."

"Let's hit the road, huh? We're supposed to be meeting Mitch and Ellie at the spot."

"Sure thing."

Before either of them can move for the door, there's a knock. Three hollow sounds, drawn out and timed perfectly apart, that cause Josh's flesh to prickle. It's as if someone has thrown *him* into a walk-in freezer, shut the door and locked him inside.

He looks to Marissa, and she peers back.

No one speaks.

The knocks come again.

Finally, he musters the guts to say, "Who is it?"

A pause. A sigh. "You know damn well who it is, short-fry."

*The cop.*

*Damn.*

"What do you want?" Marissa asks.

"Might I have a word?"

Josh panics, jumps onto his toes, rocks on his heels, itching to get out of there. They're on the seventeenth floor and he thinks barreling through the window might be preferable to letting that copper inside the room with them.

Not a cop, though, he thinks. *A monster.*

Before he can figure out how he knew they're inside, Josh says, "Go away." As if that's gonna work. "Go away and don't come back."

"Afraid I can't do that, kid. And I think you know why." A pause, a breath. Heavy. Like he's jogging as he talks. "Have it on good authority that you and your crew are up to no good. Trying to spoil things for our little life here."

"There's nothing here," Josh says, and somehow those three words feel like an admission of guilt.

He looks around, looking for somewhere to stuff the bag, the weapon inside. Under the bed? He drops to his knees, begins shoving the bulky carrier underneath the frame. It gets wedged, and then completely stuck. He can't move it another inch. "Shit!" he squeaks, struggling with the thing, praying Foley will just go away.

"You okay in there?" Foley asks.

"GO AWAY!" Josh shouts at the door.

"I'm gonna give you to the count of three, then I'm coming in. Best prepare for wrath if you don't open up."

He's heard this threat before—pops, drunk, knocking on his mother's bedroom door once she's locked him out.

"One," the cop says, and rather calmly. Calmer than his father ever uttered the word. "Two." A little change in his voice, the rage seeming to build like a roller-coaster ascending that first drop. Almost there. Almost. "Three!" The final number rips through his mouth, coming out scratching and weird, an almost inhuman ring to it.

Josh trembles.

And then there's the first kick at the door. The impact shakes the floors, the walls. The lamp on the bureau jitters a few inches closer to the edge. With the second, he hears the jamb crack like lightning striking an old tree branch. Marissa squeaks with surprise. She backs herself into the corner of the room. On the third try, Foley's foot connects squarely with the door, and the jamb completely splinters where the latch bolt sits against the striker, forcing the door inward in a hurry. The hinges squawk with the violent swing.

Foley's shadow fills the doorway.

"No," Josh mutters, still putzing with the suitcase, giving it one final rip. The effort actually works and the suitcase comes free, unplugs from under the bed frame. He sticks his hand in the open space where the zipper didn't close all the way, reaches inside, and grabs the lone explosive stick—the infamous M80—he lifted from the Fireworks Emporium. Marissa tosses him her lighter. With one heroic effort, he plucks the lighter from the air. Flicks the wheel. The orange flame dances dangerously close to the wick. "Don't come near me! I'll...I'll blow us all up!"

Calmly, Foley shuffles into the room. "Son, put that thing away before you go and blow your pecker off."

"I'm warning you!"

"So am I," he says with amusement. "I ain't kidding. Saw a kid blow off his own cock once. Nasty mess. They couldn't put the pecker back in place—what was left was too mangled, and, shit—they never found the rest of it. Gone and lived the rest of his life with this little nub for a dick. Bright side, somehow his balls survived the whole ordeal. No use for them now, of course...kinda like tits on a bull. But...shit—least he kept *some* of his manhood." He points to Josh's crotch. "You get to keep both your dick and balls if you put that lighter down."

"I'm not doing it," he says, backing himself into the heater against the far wall. Foley steps forward into the quiet light the dingy hotel room provides. The man's face is badly cut, and the Frankenstein stitch-job looks like it could give at any point. Josh swears he sees something alive in his cheeks. "I won't put it down. You'll have to kill me."

"Kid," Foley says, keeping a hand on the top of his gun, the loose grip suggesting he isn't keen on using it. "Don't be an idiot. Come on. You and your friends have to come with me. Mayor's wish is for you to remain in custody until after the Arts Festival. I don't like it any more than you do, but we have to do this and do it now."

"Fuck you, pig," he says, flicking the lighter's wheel once again. "Fuck you and go burn in hell."

"Now, now. I can tolerate a lot of things, young man, but blasphemy and naughty language from your mouth are two things I won't." His lips flick up in a twisted smile, the kind that hides something else. Pure anger, possibly. Hate. Contempt. "Now come on—give me the banger and let's stop dicking around."

The cop steps forward.

Josh puts the flame to the wick, watches the waxy string spark and glow.

Two bangs happen within seconds of each other. The first: he watches his hand disappear in a fury of blood and bone, fire and smoke. Everything from his wrist down completely disappears in a scarlet explosion, and the impact of the blow is strong enough to pick him off his feet and carry him back into the wall, a forceful shove he somehow recovers from. He's somehow still standing when he recognizes the damage of the second bang, peering down at his stomach, the small hole dead-center in his abdomen the size of a quarter. Arcs of blood squirt out like a near-defective water gun, splashing on the carpet before him.

Everything goes a little hazy before it goes dark.

"Ah, shit, kid," he hears Foley say before the shadows on the walls begin to move, leaking into his vision from the corners. Before he can pray to God, pray himself away from this awful place, the lights go out, and the last thing he sees before never waking is his parents fighting, arguing, screaming, and him leaving the house forever and realizing what a terrible mistake that was.

Foley knows it's only a matter of seconds before everyone hears and comes running to see what happened. He hopes to clean up the mess and make sure this doesn't make it back to the rest of the interlopers—killing one of them, especially the kid, is apt to make them a little less compliant, he imagines. Don't matter what truly happened. Don't matter that the kid threatened to blow them all to smithereens. Nope, they won't hear a word of that phooey.

*(killer)*

*(racist-cop-pig-fuck)*

Foley snorts while looking at the kid's crumpled form, the dead-eye stare that peers out into worlds unknown. He takes the short walk over to the cooling corpse, kneels. Shuts the kid's eyes because it bothers him, that stare, the one he's seen before. Not any easier the second time around, plus—it makes him go back to that time he'd sure like to forget.

*(killer)*

*(racist-cop-pig-fuck)*

"Oh my God," Marissa says from the corner of the room. He completely forgot she was there. Her eyes bounce from the kid over to Foley, the kid's murderer. "You fuck...you fucker, you motherfucker."

"Hey now," he says, putting his arms out like all can be explained in a few short sentences. As if the kid with a hole in his stomach is nothing more than a mother's broken vase on the dining room carpet. "He wasn't cooperating, and he threatened to kill me—kill us all."

Marissa's eyes find the gory stump that used to be a hand, flesh and bone and blood. "You butchered him." Tears fill her eyes, stream down her face.

"He did that to himself, you see? He was—"

"You fucking asshole! You butchered him! You goddamn psychopath!"

"HEY! Watch your mouth! I will not listen to—"

Marissa screams and then runs at him. He doesn't know what else to do but raise the gun at her. Beyond that, he has no clue. Without giving it much thought, he pulls the trigger. There's a loud pop—the world's largest popcorn kernel exploding to life—and the left side of Marissa's face disappears in a bloody spark. Her feet are still moving when this happens, and her momentum carries her forward a few steps. Even though half of her brains are splattered on the wall behind her, enough remains to allow some sort of cerebral communication between nerves and muscles because she continues to drift ahead, passing Foley, and stumbling down. Her head knocks against the large bureau that hosts the old-school, boxy television set, a whopping fifty-two incher.

About a minute after, the girl is lying flat on the ground, motionless. She's still breathing, but for all intents and purposes— she's dead. Foley glances up from the body trending toward corpse status and sees Dave Fester standing in the open doorway, a few of the other notable townsfolk behind him.

"Thought the Mayor wanted them alive?" Dave asks.

Foley sighs. "Not as important, these two. The others—very much so."

"We searched the rooms," Bobby Mac reports. "Nothing."

"Where'd they go?" Trudy asks no one in particular.

Foley shrugs. "Can't be far."

Bobby Mac nods to the two bodies. "What you want me to do with them?"

Leaning his head back against the wall, examining the red smears that have stained his police uniform *(racist-cop-pig-fuck)*, Foley bares a wicked grin. "You still got that C4, Bobby Mac?"

Marissa's eyes open just slightly, scoping a blurry view of the hotel room. Her body feels like she's been set on fire, a storm of flames flickering through her every muscle. She can't bring her hands to her face to see what damage has been done, but those fiery sensations feel most concentrated there. She has trouble remembering what happened five minutes ago, how she got here.

*Josh and I were…*

*Oh God…*

She looks right and left. Near the front dresser she sees a small lump—still too blurry to make out completely—and wonders if that's Josh, what's become of him.

*Dead.*

She can't help but think she'll join him soon.

Something materializes in the bleary atmosphere before her. A shape that looks oddly human and oddly familiar. Something tugs at Marissa's heart, a violent squirt of blood passing through her aorta. Whatever this presence is, she does not want to see it. The shape that shouldn't be here.

*This isn't how it was supposed to happen.*

" 'Rissa?" a small voice asks, and Marissa's heart melts down like a nuclear reactor gone haywire. " 'Rissa, it's me."

She doesn't feel tears roll down her face, but she knows she's crying. "Rosetta?" The words hurt, come out like coughing lava rocks.

"It's me, I'm here."

"Oh…fuck." It's all she can say on the subject. A part of her thinks this isn't real, that she's died, or is dying, and that this is an angel welcoming her to Heaven, and that this angel has taken the form of her lost baby sister. "Fuck."

She shudders with grief, the kind that stains the soul forever. Trying to fight through the haze of melted colors before her, she tries to imagine her sister's face, what it looks like now. What Lacuna's Point has turned her into. She's seen many horrors here in the past month, and this is one she might be thankful she can't see.

"It's okay," Rosetta says. "It's all okay now."

Rosetta is close, within reaching distance. Her sister drops to her knees, and Marissa feels Rosetta take her hands into her own. She puts her hands to her chest, against her heartbeat. But what she feels is something else. Something papery and plasticky, some sort of package her sister is wearing like a baby carrier. Marissa looks up at her sister's blurry image for clarification.

"It's okay," Rosetta says, and the more she repeats those two words, the more Marissa realizes how untrue they are. "They said if we did this, we could go home."

"D...did...what?" Marissa croaks, and by the time she releases the question, Rosetta's hand is on the move, revealing something she's been carrying this whole time. Marissa can't make it out for certain, but it looks like one of those game-show buzzers, the kind the contestants on *Jeopardy!* might use to answer in.

"Sssh," Rosetta says. "Close your eyes, sis. We're going home."

Before Marissa can respond, an electronic click sounds, but that noise only lasts a second before a bigger, greater noise conquers the world, obliterating reality.

Marissa feels something hot punch her in the face, but that's it. There's no pain. Only infinite darkness.

And wherever she goes next definitely isn't home.

"So, this plan is getting more and more screwed up, huh?" Ellie says while hustling down the street and toward the woods on the opposite end of town, the selected space to ride out the night and wait for morning. "That thing could be out here, hunting us."

"If it wanted to hunt us, I'm pretty sure we'd have seen it already," Mitch tells her, and that seems to make sense. "It's where it goes that I'm afraid of. I don't know if it can communicate with them, but...shit—it might be telling the others what happened."

They speed toward the woods and Ellie can't get her mind off Danielle, the condition of her body. That thing sprung out of her like a jack-in-a-box.

Dawn stops walking.

Ellie turns to her. "What is it?"

Mitch takes a few more steps, but he's looking back at them. "Come on. Don't stop now."

"Something's wrong," Dawn says, her face souring as if she's sipped on something unexpectedly gross. Wincing, she begins to rub her stomach, trying to smooth out whatever's causing the stoppage. "I feel...wrong."

"Dawn?" Ellie asks, moving toward her daughter, assessing the best way to comfort her. Does she hug her, pat her shoulder? Touch her at all? It's like she's forgotten how to be a mother, forgotten how to fix her kid's issues. There was once a time where, after one quick look at Dawn's face, Ellie would know exactly what to do, how to treat the situation. But now, it's like looking at an open body and being asked to remove a kidney with no knowledge of human anatomy and no tools.

*Instincts,* Ellie thinks. *None of us really know anything, parenting is all instincts.*

"What is—"

Before Ellie can complete that sentence, an explosion rocks the night. Even though the sound is coming from the center of town, she ducks for cover, uncertain that this is the last noise of its kind. Once the explosion is over, she looks up, tries to see where the blast came from.

"No..." Mitch says, ambling forward, seemingly stunned by the image his brain is receiving. "No..."

"What is it?" Ellie asks, following his gaze. Then she sees it. The hotel, the place they've been staying at since their arrival, has a giant hole near the top of it. She knows exactly what floor the explosion came from without needing to count the windows—it was *her* floor. Whoever detonated that bomb must have thought they were inside.

Angry black smoke rises toward the dark clouds above.

Mitch turns to Ellie. His eyes are glistening with tears, and at first, Ellie doesn't understand. There's no reason he should have any sentimental attachment to that place, no reason to mourn the loss of some basics that did not belong to them. Unless these are tears of joy, tears of *oh-thank-fuck-we-weren't-inside.* But they aren't happy tears. Ellie knows sadness when she sees it, and the look straining Mitch's face reminds her of the one she's seen in the mirror many times before.

"What is it?" she asks him.

"It's them," Dawn answers instead. "Josh, Marissa. They're dead."

Mitch's lips tremble. "They went to go grab a suitcase from the room. They were gonna hit the Fireworks Emporium to stock up for tomorrow. For the plan."

She thinks he'd like to add, *You'd know this if you were around more often, you stupid bitch,* but he's much too polite to say such a thing. Besides, his face is enough to inject her conscience with a heavy dose of guilt.

"Oh God," Ellie says as a spell of lightheadedness comes over her. She needs to sit down and does so on the concrete sidewalk. Some of the lights in the houses on the edge of Lacuna's Point come on. Faces appear in the windows, look up at the hotel, and watch the smoke spiral off into the sky, creating more darkness.

*Darkness creating darkness.*

"He killed them," Dawn says distantly, as if she's seeing something in the destruction that they can't. "Foley. It was him."

"How do you know?" Mitch asks her, his voice unsteady.

Dawn shakes her head. "Just do."

A chill grabs Ellie's neck.

"Okay," Mitch says, wiping away the tears, his nose on his sleeve. "Okay, we have to regroup. Make a new plan. It's okay," he coaches, himself more so than the others, Ellie thinks. "It's gonna be okay—we're going to be okay."

"Are we?" Ellie asks, doubtful.

Mitch doesn't answer that question. The strong smell of death and destruction answers for him.

From the parking lot they watch the hotel burn in a blazing glory, the top half of the structure now an inferno, the flames traveling throughout and now working their way to the lower half. A few people who were staying there are among Foley and his band of deputized citizens, along with the Mayor's black hoods, watching the fire rage, burn out of control, destroying whatever possessions they had brought with them.

"Should we look for the others?" Dave Fester asks. "The others—Bobby Mac and the rest—want to know how to proceed. If not, I'll tell them to head home and rest up."

Foley studies the fire, how it eats the building. "Tell them to sleep. Tomorrow morning, first light, tell them to be ready."

"Okay, boss. You got it."

"And, Fester?" Foley says, spinning to him.

"Yes sir?"

"You did good tonight. Didn't flinch when we needed to do what we needed to do. Never flinch, never hesitate. Remember that."

"Thank you, sir. It was my honor to serve the Mayor and the people of Lacuna's Point." His eyes smile a thousand smiles. "The Lacuna itself."

"The Light will be your reward. You'll get your fair share, what's coming to you. I promise it."

Dave bends a knee, dips his head forward. "It's truly my pleasure. Truly. Just want what's best for the town, and if..." He glances up at the hungry flames, the billowing black smoke. "If that's what we needed to do, then I'm glad to have done it."

"The Light," Foley says again, turning back to the fire, the results of his quick action in the pursuit of keeping Lacuna's Point a safe place for all. "It'll be ours."

# CHAPTER NINETEEN

Mitch shakes her awake, and she's greeted by his face, his forefinger pressed firmly against his lips. She sits up, sees Dawn is fast asleep on a bed of leaves and pine needles, towering trees all around them, moonlight slanting through the branches and shining on her beautiful face. It reminds her of when she was a kid and used to fall asleep on the couch, some Disney movie long past finished and the blue glow from the T.V.'s inactivity illuminating her face. Mitch pulls her from this memory with a nod, asking for a private word.

She gets up from the filthy ground, hoping no ticks have attached themselves to her skin, but then figures *ticks* are the least of her worries. Yawning, she follows him out, far enough so Dawn can't hear them, but not far enough so she can't see her daughter either.

"This whole thing is fucked, El, I know it," he begins, grabbing the top of his head as if his brains might burst from his skull the same way that thing ejected itself from Danielle's upper torso. "I can't believe they're dead. It's...I feel like it's my fault."

She yawns again, hardly able to keep her heavy eyes open. "Not your fault. Hey..." She grabs his shoulder. "It's...it's this town's fault. At least..." She swallows, unsure whether to say the thing she wants to say. "At least the four of us are still alive."

"Kya..."

"She's alive, Mitch. She's still your daughter. You have to believe that."

He nods, and she hopes he does believe that, because if he doesn't, then they all might be dead come tomorrow evening.

She meets his wandering gaze. "What will we do tomorrow without the others? The fireworks was our play, right?" The *play* was simple enough—create a distraction all around town while the Arts Festival (ceremony) takes place and the Lacuna spreads its filthy Light, handing out the bright source like candy on Halloween night. Mitch was certain it would work, buy him enough time to reach old Eddy and shut the thing down, destroy whatever inner workings make the clock hands run, because that was the key, and he was sure of it.

"I don't know," Mitch says. "This changes things."

"I wanted to stay here, you know." She dips her head in shame, horrified she's admitted such a thing—but it's true, every word of it. And once she starts to share, there's no stopping the truth train from pulling into the station. "I wanted to forget about leaving and just stay here because Dawn is here, and even though this town is wrong in all the worst ways, I didn't care. A part of me still doesn't, Mitch. A part of me wants to say 'fuck it,' and stay behind, with Dawn, and live out our lives in Lacuna's Point."

"El, these people are literally turning into monsters. Hell, some of them are already monsters. You'd turn you into a monster too." He sighs, the information too much for him. "You know that, El— why the hell would you want to stay knowing that life awaits you?"

Ellie pinches shut her eyes, blocking tears. "Because...the feeling I had when I first saw her after three years...I can't describe it, but...I just never want to go back and feel anything else...and this place, Mitch, *this place*—it won't ever let us go. Never. It will follow us always because it wants us—wants *them*—and it will never stop until it gets what it wants. You have to feel that too."

Mitch nods. "But this place—it's not reality. Lacuna's Point is just...just a mirage." He motions to the forest around them, the trees and the invisible barrier that lies somewhere beyond them, that force field that will make them sick if they try to trespass the known world. "None of it is real. You know that. This place is a bad dream, and fuck, El—it's time to wake up." He takes a deep breath as if he means to reset himself. "And furthermore—you're nothing to this place. Your life means nothing to this place. It's using you. You're food. A resource it wants to mine, a crop it sows and reaps. And what happens when you're all used up? Do you ever think about what happens then? Remember Skelly?"

"Isn't that what life is anyway? Doesn't the real world do the same thing? Use us? Eat us up? You make reality sound like it's that much better."

"At least we're free out there," Mitch tells her.

"Are we really, though?"

"Compared to this...of course."

"At least maybe we'll be happy here."

Mitch bites his knuckle. "El, please don't fall apart on me. I'm begging you. I can't...I can't do this alone."

"Mitch, just think about it." She swallows, imagining her life in Lacuna's Point with her daughter, working in that art gallery forever, happy. "Maybe we don't have to leave. You said it yourself—you weren't happy back home. You and Angie were fighting all the time. You weren't happy one bit."

"Wasn't happy because we lost Kya. If she's back home with us, we—"

"Kya's here, and this thing won't let her leave."

"Then I'd rather die trying to break her out," he snaps. "Look, tomorrow, we're going through with the plan—a different version of that plan, but we're going through with it."

"Did you start your book, Mitch?"

"What do you care about the book?"

"They're expecting you to read tomorrow. Aren't they?"

Mitch glowers at her. "Don't worry about that. I'm going to hand-deliver what I have to the Mayor. *Personally.*" He shakes his head. "I need you tomorrow. If this is going to work, we're going to need everything to go right, and I can't lose you to this place. It's just us now."

*Us now.*

Hearing that makes her feel hopeless.

"Yeah," she says, yawning again, wiping sleep from her eyes. "Yeah, I'm sorry. You're right. Just...this place is really scrambling my brain. Just forget what I said. Tomorrow. Tomorrow we go through with it."

He casts a dubious glance. "Yeah?"

"Yes."

"Okay, good. We'll have to figure out a new distraction, but I have some ideas. Here's what I have in mind..."

She listens but there is music playing softly somewhere in the distance. It's a sweet tune and she wants to hear it.

Forever and ever, as long as she lives.

As long as she has the Light.

Night gives way to morning, and the people of Lacuna's Point rise from their dreams, ready to start the new day, refreshed, rearing to go. Dawn Brower sits up from her makeshift bed in the woods, stretching and yawning, trying to recall the dreams she was torn from by her internal alarm clock. It was a strange dream and the more she dwells on it, the more she concentrates on the aspects of the sleep-driven vision, the more specific the images become, the sharper their clarity. She envisions a beach, sticking her toes in the sand while a giant jellyfish rests on the surface of the Atlantic. The jellyfish talked to her, told her a story of how it's come to live in the ocean, how it dropped through the clouds from someplace beyond them, and how it found a home in the water's tomb-like depths, how wonderful it was not to be on the land because under the ocean things are pure and perfect and no one can hurt the jellyfish. The jellyfish lives free in the ocean's murky depths, free from human pollution and noise, the curiosity of people, the poking and prodding that would be done to it all in the name of curiosity and scientific discovery. The jellyfish tells her she can live that way too, that the ocean is safe for her, so why not come in? Take a dip? Cover herself in the murk, the fathomless depths, and live free in the endless trenches of the Great Verse?

She dove into the waters just as she woke, the natural bath coating her sense, filling every nerve with a shot of ice—it was like stepping into the warm light of the sun on a chilly afternoon.

But the dream died right after, and now she's here, awake, in the woods, wondering what the hell the dream meant, if it meant anything at all. Maybe nothing. *Probably* nothing. But then again, she suspects it's the most important dream she's ever dreamed, and she doesn't know why.

"Sleep well?" Ellie asks, handing her a bottle of water.

"Not great."

"Me neither. At least you look like you got some."

She shrugs. "Had some weird dreams."

Her mother nods along with her rolling eyes, as if *weird dreams* is par for the course. "Do you remember when you were little? Whenever you had a bad dream, you'd pile into bed with Dad and me?"

She doesn't, not really, but nods anyway, feigning recognition. "Yeah, good times."

"You used to snuggle right between us. You'd fall back to sleep almost immediately. Out like a light, *literally*. It was impressive.

Your father and I always got a kick from that. It was like being next to us made you feel safe enough to go back to sleep, even if the nightmares were still waiting for you."

Dawn tries to remember this but has great difficulty seeing through the murk that prohibits memories from resurfacing. Her childhood is a fragmented scrapbook of short images. Many blank spaces she can't fill in and forcing herself to remember physically hurts. Even her father's face is just shadows and contours, no definable features or attributes that would separate him from any other person she's grown to know in Lacuna's Point. She does remember his name, Dan, and she thinks that's a good start. She can't say that she'll be able to remember it tomorrow or that she could have yesterday, but now that her mother is talking about him, she can at least remember that.

"Do you think he'll care if I come back?" Dawn asks. "I mean, for some reason I can't remember if he actually *liked* me."

Ellie clicks her tongue, clearly disapproving. "Honey..." She kneels and looks skeptical about touching her, but then she starts rubbing Dawn's shoulder, and for the moment everything is fine. "Of course he'll care. He's your father and he loves you. He was out there every day looking for you. *Every* day. Every minute he could."

A sting pins her eyes. "How come it's hard to remember him?"

At this, Ellie looks like she has no certain answer, but she hangs her head to the side as if she's willing to trot out a theory. "It's because of this place, I think. It does something to you, to your brain. Mixes you up. I've...I've felt it too." She kisses the crown of Dawn's head. "But once you're home, it will all come back."

"You really think so?"

She doesn't, and Dawn can tell by the way the skin around her eyes creases, the way her eyes grow cloudy with uncertainty as they try to conceal the truth. "Of course," her mother lies, but it's a necessary lie, a lie to keep her going, and Dawn doesn't hate her for it. She'd probably do the same if the roles were reversed. "Your father loves you very much. We used to text all the time on your birthday, and he'd tell me how much he misses you and how he'd pray every day that you'd turn up alive and well."

More lies, and even though Dawn knows that's not the truth, it still causes her eyes to leak sadness. "I want to see him again."

Ellie's eyes twinkle as the past flashes through her. "Yeah, me too, actually."

It's nine o'clock sharp when the tower's bell rings, alerting the town that the festival has begun and the Light will be arriving soon. The town's art is on full display and there is music playing, those talented souls strumming on guitars, beating on bongos, and blowing into oversized whistles, melodic collections of soothing sounds that come from varying distances and directions, and even though these tunes are segregated, it doesn't matter—collected, when standing in a position where a listener can absorb more of one sound or several, the music sounds just fine.

More than fine. *Perfect.*

There's food, too. Art isn't restricted to the visual and auditory senses. Taste is just as important. Baking of the highest order is on full display. Kate's Cake Shop has brought a whole booth full of delicious treats, everything from cupcakes to wedding cakes, showcasing their talents, displays and samples to drum up future sales. Baker's Dozen, the doughnut shop on 4th Street, is giving out freebies, and anyone who stops at their station cannot pass on the glazed pumpkin fritters. Girl Scouts are moving packaged cookies like they won't exist come tomorrow, and who the hell really knows—maybe they won't.

There are other art forms in attendance, photographers and filmmakers, comic book artists sharing their concept sketches along with selling a few full-page illustrations. There's so much happening on the sidewalks and on the meadow separating 1st Street from town hall that a few hours might not be enough to see everything, but the people come in droves and they come with open eyes and open hands and open mouths.

This is all fine, of course, and the Mayor is enjoying his time as he watches the town indulge from his position in the tower, observing like a hawk over a field of mice. But he knows what they're truly here for—and boy, is he going to give it to them. The Light will be here soon. The Lacuna stirs awake as he stands there, looking through Eddy's porthole, down at the ground where the good people of Lacuna's Point scurry like busied ants from hill to hill.

*The Light.*

*It will be here soon.*

"And the town will live on forever," he says aloud, not meaning to.

"What?" Kya asks from her position in the corner. She's rubbing her wrists where the steel manacle has chafed her skin.

"Nothing. Just thinking out loud."

*The Light.*

But before it arrives, there is the matter with the interlopers, the ones that remain alive. They must be dealt with, and although two of them have already been sorted—not how he wanted it to go down, and he's a bit miffed at how that travesty was handled—there are still three of them on the loose. Four if you include Darla the waitress, and he doesn't, because she's a good girl and she's told him lots of secrets. She had to if she wanted to keep her remaining eye. Foley promised he'll intercept the rest before they carry out whatever plan they've concocted (which has undoubtedly changed considering the hotel explosion), whatever they think they'll get away with—but let's face it: the man is simply a fool, and furthermore, he's unreliable. There's no way he follows through and does what needs to be done. He was a failure in real life, and he's a failure here in the world that rests between realities.

Quincy Black curses himself for trusting in Foley, putting his faith in a broken human once again. How many times he'll learn this lesson, he does not know. But it probably won't be the last. From the moment Foley was brought here, Black had concerns. These concerns were quelled by the man's take-no-guff attitude, how he'd handled himself in dealing with tough interactions in the past. How he'd kept law and order, kept his town safe from potential violent outbreaks and those who have gone against society's grain. And he'd done a pretty great job here too, until recently. Every year, new citizens become inducted, and each transitional period comes with its fair share of problems, those not wanting to comply with the rules of this new lifestyle, accept the gift that the Lacuna has bestowed upon them, but Foley has always handled them efficiently, albeit with a few missteps along the way. But...Foley is also perfect because he's a desperate man, and a man that desperate for acceptance and forgiveness—well, he'll do just about anything to obtain it. Which is his greatest strength and weakness, and Black figures he'll have to deal with the yin and yang of that very human conundrum.

Such is the way of humans.

The complexities they are.

The sorcerer steps away from his view of the town and returns to the globe sitting atop the podium in the center of the clock tower's belfry, next to the giant bell itself. He ducks under trusses and structural beams that run laterally and diagonally as he eyes the swirling black of the globe's inner contents. It's growing darker. The inky, cumulus shapes roll and turn over, the repeated act still captivating as previous renditions. When he reaches the magical sphere, he puts his hands against the glass-like surface—*glass-like* because there is no earthly name for this material—and draws from it, absorbing some of the brume through his fingers, letting its essence fill him. His eyes dance skyward as the incredible rush of emotions, the otherworldly junk now coursing through the human veins he's adopted, cleaning his soul, leaving him satiated for the time being. He lets go and pulls back from the dark orb, that resting egg ready to hatch and give birth to the new year.

The Great Reset is upon them.

The town wants the Light.

But Quincy Black thinks it's the dark that feels best.

"What is that?" Kya asks, trembling before the mystical sphere and its total glory.

Black eyes her, flashing her a sinister smile. "This is everything, my dear. This is everything."

Foley makes his way through the crowd, doing his best to keep an eye out for Mitchell Green, Ellie Brower and her daughter. It's easier to look for three than it is to spy on seven, and the fact that two have been eliminated and two (Darla and Kya) are completely tied up for the moment bodes quite well for him, or so he thinks. Black doesn't see it that way of course, but what the fuck does he know? He's not the one out here hunting rabbits. He's back in the cabin, cleaning up the joint and prepping for dinner. The weird-eyed son of a bitch doesn't know the first thing about a good hunt.

Foley remembers hunting. Actual hunting. Rabbits and deer, not human beings. Those long days spent out in the tree-cluttered hills of West Virginia with his old man, who always smelled like sweat, Busch Light, and Marlboro Reds. Those impossibly long stretches in tree stands and trekking through the forest, the vast silences between kills. The aftermath—the skinning, the gutting, the cleaning.

He looks back over his shoulder and scopes out the top of the hotel, the structure's burnt ruins. The evidence of his failure is no longer smoking. A storm came in the night and put an end to the flames, and Foley wonders where that storm came from, how it ended up in Lacuna's Point when the skies were pretty clear and showed no signs of rain.

Strange.

But not all that strange. And certainly not the strangest occurrence that's happened over the last five years.

"Hey there, Elroy!" shouts Donna Fuller, owner and operator of Baker's Dozen. Her voice nearly busts Foley's eardrums. He shakes his head, the waterlogged sensation in his ear, and then spins toward the squat, freckled woman with her hair pulled back in a neat, hairnet-covered bun. "Pumpkin fritter?"

He offers a frail smile, the best he can muster. "Sure thing, darling. Thank you very much."

"Are you excited for the Light, Elroy? Are ya?" Her spread lips put on a half-moon display of crooked-but-white teeth. She doesn't wait for him to respond since the question's more of the rhetorical sort—*of course he wants the gosh-darn Light*. "I've been so dang tired lately. And the things I'm remembering! Good Lord, I can't wait to forget them come tomorrow."

"It'll be good to wake up tomorrow with a new perspective on things, that's for sure." He takes a fritter, pops the treat into his mouth, bites down and lets the pumpkin flavor wash over his tongue. One of the best things he's ever tasted, that's for sure. "That's a good fritter. The Lacuna will be pleased with your effort, Donna. Most assuredly."

The woman crows with delight. "Welllll, thank you for saying that, Elroy! That just makes me the happiest girl in all the world!"

She leans in, looking both ways as if she's afraid of curious ears and eyes. "Any luck with those pesky interlopers?"

Foley swallows. He wonders how many of the common folks know about what's going on. How many of them truly understand.

"Don't worry," Donna says, gently slapping his shoulder. "The good Mayor told us everything. Well, *mostly* everything. We're here to help if it comes down to it. Gotta keep our town safe. Keep it pure. Ain't that right?"

"Yes, absolutely. Keep it pure."

"Well, good luck out there. I know you'll take care of them good. Just like all the others." Donna points her spatula to the top of the hotel, the charred remains looking like the top of a muffin left in the oven for too long. "Good work there."

He opts to keep his mouth closed on the subject.

"Don't worry. Tomorrow you'll forget all about it. Will be nothing but a dream. Ten years here and you kinda get used to it. The remembering, the forgetting—it all gets better *in time*." She squeals with laughter as if there's a joke in there. If there is, Foley doesn't catch it.

"You have yourself a good day, ma'am." He tips his cap to her. "And good luck with the fritters. Damn delicious they are."

She waves him goodbye, then approaches another pedestrian, prompting them with free fritters.

Foley strides off in search of his deputized few, hoping they've made progress with *their* hunts, and also hoping to avoid the Mayor's black hoods.

He doesn't know why but those things scare him more than the consequences of failing the Mayor once again.

Dawn puts the pipe wrench to the fire hydrant and pulls, hard as she can, just as Mitch demonstrated on the first two they came across. Once the valve turns, she backs off, opting to go slow because of the pressure. That's what Mitch said to do, and she knows nothing of fire hydrants and how they work, and honestly—she doesn't know what good opening them will do for the plan.

Mostly because she believes nothing will help them escape. This place isn't a town; it's a tomb.

As she rotates the valve, a sinking sensation infiltrates her stomach, like she's falling in perpetuity. Like someone dropped her from the clouds of a bottomless world. There's a part of her that wants to leave this place, put Lacuna's Point in the rearview and never step foot in this fucked up town ever again. But there's a part of her that wants no part in the escape plan, and doing things like being on the run from the law, conspiring against the Mayor and defying his ordinances, and even missions like opening fire hydrants, strike her as sinful. It makes her somewhat ill to help organize, plan, and plot against the place she's spent three long years in. Nausea grabs hold of her just thinking about living life on the other side of Lacuna's Point, back in the real world, a concept so ludicrous she almost laughs. She's torn between these two ways of thinking—be free or be here. Both seem right. Both seem wrong.

*The Light,* she thinks. *If I just have some Light, I'll forget all about it. I'll forget about everything. There will just be this, me, and now.*

There's something inside her that hungers for that bright flash of forgiveness—she can feel it working around within her, feeding off her. Her nerves, her memories, every single molecule that makes up her spiritual self, her *talent.* Every time she puts a brush on canvas she feels the thing within gorge on her production. It eats but never fills. What is it exactly, she doesn't know, but feels its presence the way one senses a shadow behind them. *A shadow inside me.* She thinks it's the same thing that escaped Foley's face, the thing that shot itself out from the upper half of Danielle's body like a rocket ship, that crab-like entity that came from the sea, though the sea, the one that rests on the other side of the town, is not the Atlantic—she doesn't know where it is or what's on the other side of it, but it surely isn't attached to the same reality that Dawn came from. It's an endless sea, she thinks, impossible to fathom the true vastness of its reach. And she thinks there are worse things than hungry crabs in that ocean.

Much worse.

Yes, she wants the Light. She wants to listen to the sweet music that plays from the clock tower while she absorbs every UV ray.

"Hey!" someone shouts at her, ripping her from her thoughts.

She glances down to see water hemorrhaging from the valve, which rests three-quarters open. The town's supply gushes, washing everything from her ankles down, soaking her socks and shoes. Then she looks up at the intruder, the person who's caught her in the devious act.

"What the hell do you think you're doing?" the man asks, walking over to her. She realizes it's Richard Bunn, owner and operator of Bunn's Books, and he doesn't look too happy with what his eyes reveal to him. "Hey...you're one of them! Hey!"

He turns and shouts back to the center of town, but before he can make his voice be heard, Mitch emerges from a nearby alley and clocks him over the head. The wrench drops the man in an instant, and he takes a violent spill on the sidewalk, crashing against the concrete, bending awkwardly on contact. His head takes the worst of it, and not long after the man lies still on the walkway, a spreading red puddle fans out beneath his cracked skull.

"Shit," Mitch says.

Dawn surveys the damage. The man begins to twitch. She pulls back and meets Mitch's eyes. "I think you killed him."

He doesn't seem too shaken by the news. "What's going to happen to him?"

She shrugs.

"That thing—those crab-things—like Foley and Danielle had...how long before they come out?"

"I don't know. No idea how it works."

"I want to kill one."

"Maybe we should go. More will come if we don't hurry."

Mitch hesitates, studying the man's face, the last flicker of light going out of his eyes. Then he faces the hydrant, watching arcs of city water flooding the street. "Was that your first?"

Dawn delays in responding, opening her mouth, moving her jaw, but unable to articulate that single word. But finally, she finds her voice. "Yes."

"All right. Your mother's close. Let's keep hitting the hydrants up the streets. There's only a few left. We won't have a lot of time before they come running out, so we have to hurry."

Dawn watches Kya's old man strut off, toward the next objective, but she finds it difficult to get her feet working. She can't help but glance down at the man's ruined human form, the cracked cranium, the ugly red spilling, staining the otherwise clean concrete. The blood fills the cracks between the slabs.

And then she swears she sees something move behind the man's eyes, his flesh.

About five minutes after Mitch Green opens his third hydrant, Quincy Black becomes aware that something is happening in his town, something bad, something he should be *reacting* to. Clutching his dark globe with both hands, he strolls across the belfry while continuing to sip on the obsidian brew within. Through his eyes he watches the good people below experience art, eat delicious treats, absorb the sweet original tunes and melodies provided, and drink from the flavorful well of this creative experience. On the surface, everything looks swell. Everything is going as planned. But he can only see the meadow, and 1$^{st}$ Street is blocking his view of the rest of the sprawling town. He can't see the streets past it, where wrong things may or may not be happening.

*Oh, it's happening.*

*Wrong things. Lots of them.*

A change enters him, souring the moment, and he looks down to see the globe change color—it's no longer filled with billowing inky formations. Instead, the crystalline sphere is now filling with pink bursting starts, twinkling in and out of the shimmering luminance held within. The new life born before his eyes startles him.

*The Lacuna.*

*It has arrived.*

*It is here and it is hungry and it will eat.*

Black bounces with joy. *And I will profit.*

Closing his eyes, he pictures the sky, the being beyond it, sitting there, just beyond the veil, that blackened-blue stretch, the star-studded expanse that caps the universe and everything it keeps beneath it. He doesn't see it moving there but knows the time has come—the ceremony will have to start soon, and the Light will be upon them.

*The Light will do what that fuckwad Elroy Foley can't.*

It will reset them. Free them from their thoughts, their wants and needs, and make them see that the town's wants and needs are truly the only things that matter.

The Lacuna's wants and needs.

Just before he can go change his bandages in preparation for the new year, a scream tears down the streets. Then another. Another. ANOTHER.

Looking out across the meadow, he squints. Sees a commotion. A crowd has gathered near the edge of the lawn, at the sidewalk.

Then he watches it happen—one of the Lacuna's children is born into the world, splitting from its host in the most violent way imaginable. There's a splash of crimson that washes into the street as the thing makes its exit, and the witnesses of this instant miracle take a step back, giving the species room to breathe.

To exist.

"Not going according to plan, is it?" his prisoner asks, and he doesn't need to turn back to see her smiling; her voice is smiling enough.

Black's body goes instantly weak, and he nearly fumbles the chthonic sphere.

# CHAPTER TWENTY

They reach what must have been the town's municipal building. Vines have crawled over the steps, making the trip up a treacherous one, but Dan seems to navigate the hazards well. The same can be said for Wally Stanton, who takes the climb two steps at a time, not wasting a single movement. Both men reach the boarded entrance in no time at all.

"Well," Wally says, examining the two-by-sixes nailed over the door. "What now?"

"We could pry it open," Dan says, running his fingers along the wood, testing the material, checking for faults.

"Uh, sure. Let's go to Home Depot and buy a pry bar, come back here and crack the bastard open." The suggestion comes dripping with sarcasm, and Dan doesn't care for it.

"Don't need a pry bar." He grips the wood close to where it's been nailed in, applies leverage by placing his foot on the frame, and then uses his entire body weight to pull back. It takes a good three attempts for the nails to loosen, but when it does, the wood rips back and comes free. Dan's able to break the other side easily this time around, and a good angle removes the makeshift barrier. He repeats the process with the others. Wally finally chips in to help, but there's an uneasiness about his approach, and Dan senses this is a task he'd rather not see finished.

"What're we doing here, Dan?" Wally removes the last timber and casts it aside.

"There's something familiar about this clock tower," he says. "Like...I've seen it before."

Wally seems stunned, and Dan can't exactly blame him. The words hardly make sense to him and he was the one who spoke them.

"Where?"

Dan shakes his head. "Dream, maybe. I don't know. I have this image in my head of Dawn standing beneath a clock tower." He glances up at the clock's dead face, the inert hands of time permanently stuck on three o'clock. "That clock tower."

"Do you know how daffy that sounds?"

Dan nods. "Oh, I know it. Which scares the shit out of me." Dan stares at the door. "But it feels right. Doesn't it?"

Wally glares at him. Dan senses a force at work here in the dead town of Lacuna's Point, and that Wally feels it too.

Wally undoes the strap on his holster. "Okay, let's go inside."

"What're you doing with that?"

"Just makes me feel safer, all right." Wally motions for Dan to step back so he can lead the way. "On the count of three."

"Three," Dan says, and then pushes through the door. The hinges croak like a midnight bog. The second the barrier is open, a smell escapes, powering both men back a few feet. It's a death smell, one of decomposing things—wood, but flesh and meat too, the kind long past maggot season. Dan thinks this is the worst thing he's ever smelled, and working on the farm the past couple of years, he's smelled some terrible things. Nothing stacks up to this, and he tucks his nose behind the collar of his shirt, which does virtually nothing except make him feel somewhat better about breathing in potentially harmful gases. He pokes his head back into the entrance, hoping that time and exposure will take care of the stench.

When Wally brings out his flashlight and shines the light in the room, Dan feels his heart miss a few beats.

"What in God's name?" Wally scans the walls, the floor of this entry foyer.

The place is covered in bones.

Human bones.

Joyce Eggelston is the first one to see Harley O'Rourke go down in the puddle. When her eyes adjust to the sight, she sees it's not just a puddle that caused Harley to slip—it's a flood. Well, not a real flood, not like the flood in Genesis, the one Noah sailed on, but there are at least three inches of water in the gutter and it's not moving anywhere. The sewers must have backed up, Joyce thinks, otherwise this water would be beneath them, and, so—where did it come from? It stormed briefly the night before but surely there have been harsher storms that haven't caused the streets and sidewalks to fill with water.

She hears liquid rushing from somewhere close and then looks down 1st Street to see a fire hydrant spraying an endless discharge of water out across the street and the sidewalk, wetting everything in sight. She frets because the water is nearing the shoppes' front doors, and the amount of damage the flood could cause is catastrophic. She doesn't want to even think about it, even though she doesn't have a single stake in any business in Lacuna's Point, has only lived here a little over a year now, and—

Does she live here? She can't remember exactly where her house is, but it seems it's not in Lacuna's Point. Somewhere else? She has no idea.

*The hotel,* she thinks, *you're staying at that hotel because of Freddy.*

Freddy. Her boyfriend. Well, *ex*-boyfriend, really. Maybe. She doesn't know. She hasn't spoken with Fredrick Alexander Sterling since that fight…a year ago? That can't be. Can't be a year. Has it been that long? Huh. Fancy that. She's been here a year already and hasn't looked back. She wonders if she still has that job at the bank, working as a teller. She should probably get back to that. Or not. Maybe she should just stay here. Forever? That sounds good. Maybe it's the Light that's making her confused, and if she just sees the Light, that blinding flash, everything will make more sense to her.

Yes, she thinks. *That's probably all I need.*

But how come she hasn't thought about home in Bakersfield, Georgia in so long? It doesn't feel right but she can't dwell on those things now, not with Harley O'Rourke down for a ten count and bleeding out. He's not moving, not twitching like they do in the movies and the doctor shows on television, and—holy shit, he's slumped down in the water, the small waves entering his airways via his nose. If she doesn't do something, the man will certainly die. And she's not the only one to notice what's happened—Peggy Howard and Tim Baxter have come to see what they can do to help, but Joyce gets the feeling there's nothing that *can* be done. Because Harley is dead.

That's right. No longer alive, gone forever.

But still—she expects him to spring back up like one of those inflatable punching clowns her brother had when they were kids. She expects that, but that isn't what she gets, not exactly. Not at all, actually.

Once Peggy and Tim kneel in the water next to him, Harley starts to convulse (finally, those doctor shows got it right, after all), violent shakes that cause quite a stir among the approaching collection of witnesses. Some step away, the shock of the situation causing them to do so hurriedly, and some cover their mouths, muffling their audible gasps. Joyce does a bit of both but mostly remains close to where she was, ankle-deep in the surging water.

"What's happening to him?" Peggy asks Tim, and Tim has no clue but he's trying his best to keep Harley where he is, holding him above the water line and protecting him from the aggressive quake that's attacking his body. He tilts the man's head back while probing his mouth, making sure the tongue is free and clear from getting in the way of his gnashing teeth.

Frothy foam bubbles between his lips, and a volcanic eruption of spittle and oral discharges like liquified toothpaste follow. Harley's body begins to spasm harder now, trembling so violently that Tim is forced to drop him back into the water and back away to protect himself from the thrashing limbs. He stands next to Peggy and Joyce, the three looking on, practically the whole crowd of festival attendees standing behind them, and watches as something punches through Harley's chest in a great burst, fragments of flesh and bone shooting skyward. Next, Harley's whole body begins to split, a fissure running vertically from his forehead down into his groin, and he opens like a walnut shell, soupy scarlet sludge merging with the water below. From the ruins of Harley's body, a crab-like creature the size of an expensive designer handbag emerges, surveying its audience with two beady eyes, snapping at them with the two massive pinchers on the end of its arms. It darts away from its human womb and skitters into the water, moving hastily in no particular direction.

Joyce can barely believe what she's witnessed, and she thinks this is something she's seen before, perhaps in a dream; she thinks she might even be dreaming now. She almost laughs at the absurdity of this scene. Pinches her forearm to wake up, but no such luck. This isn't a dream. This is reality.

Or some alternate form of it.

As the sea-bug disappears behind some bushes and skitters off into the town's labyrinth of buildings and shoppes, Joyce drifts toward the cake stand where the girls behind the table watched the whole thing go down with awe and morbid fascination. They barely pay any attention to her, still focused on the unreal thing they've just witnessed, not until she picks up the big knife used to slice through the thickest of wedding cakes.

One of the girls turns to Joyce and asks, "Hey, what're you doing with that?" The girls seem genuinely concerned.

And maybe they should be. Because right now, there's an idea in Joyce's head and it's so powerful, so pure, that she cannot shake it. She seems to think that whatever happened to Harley O'Rourke can happen to her too, and that it would be a good thing.

*A great thing.*

"I'm going to be free," Joyce responds dreamily. "I'm going to wake up."

She drives the knife into both eyes as the girls scream into her face, as the whole town screams when others start dropping to the earth, the water. As they start to convulse with violent revelations.

As they wake.

Mitch rounds 6th Street, the hydrant behind him spewing forth its watery guts into the avenue. He tosses the wrench into the gutter and watches the tool hit the sewer grate with a splash. The plan has worked so far; the sewers backing up are expected but not a permanent issue for the town. He knows they'll get on with fixing the flooded streets soon, but that buys them time. Time he needs to get to the clock tower, to do what needs to be done.

*Find Kya.*

*Get out of there.*

Meanwhile, he hopes Ellie has pulled herself together and is on her way to a safe place until he's ready for her.

Charging down the street, toward the meadow where the Arts Festival should be in full swing, he hears someone's anguished cries ripping down the street, heading his way. Cautiously, he changes course, curious of the sounds and what could be causing them.

He moves to the end of the street, knowing he might not like what he sees around the bend. When he gets there, his heart nosedives.

*Holy shit.*

At least a dozen people flop around the shallow water that's flooded part of the meadow, their bodies shaking and flailing, their joints twisting and bending in ways that don't seem anatomically possible. Their mouths open and smoke billows out from their facial orifices, like soft misty ghosts leaving their earthly shells, the flooding streets having some unintended cataclysmic effect on them. This was meant to be a distraction, nothing more, but it seems the people of Lacuna's Point—the creatures that have taken up residence inside their bodies—have other plans.

The water is doing it, whatever *it* is, and it's drawing them out of their fleshy housing units.

The ghost smoke continues to pour out of them, and Mitch wonders if he's looking into a human soul leaving the body. It's an odd thought, but once he has it, he can't think of anything else, and those wisps of vapor leaking from their noses, mouths, and ears can't possibly be anything else.

Mitch sees one of the crab-like beings slip through a victim's open mouth. He recoils, hiding behind a small half-wall that borders a small bed of flowers. The alien crab pinches the air, snapping its bloody pinchers, and then leaves the human island, hopping into the flood. Mitch watches with fascination as the creature skitters along the surface, riding the river down to the meadow. He follows it, wondering exactly where it's going, what it intends to do with its newfound freedom. He makes sure not to get too close, not to tip the thing off. Reaching 1st Street, he peers over the brick half-wall that separates the sidewalk from the meadow, watching the alien crustacean skitter up the bank, searching for something in particular—a new human.

Mitch doesn't piece it together until about three seconds before the crab finds a new host. A woman standing behind a table, overstocked with cupcakes and cookies, notices the thing much too late, and even if she had seen it coming, there was nothing she could do. The thing launches itself in the air, aiming at her abdomen. In a few quick slashes, it makes good work of her belly, ripping the flesh and creating a sizable slit to squeeze into. There's almost no protest from the woman, and after the crab is done with its task and is safely inside her stomach, she begins to hold the ragged, bleeding opening with both hands in the most loving way, like a future mother proudly showing off her baby bump.

Mitch can't believe what he's seeing but knows this—he doesn't want to see any more of it. To his left, down the street, he sees more citizens writhing around in the flooded road, fog rising from them, pinchers and blue carapaces peeking out from whatever exit they can find or make.

*Create.*

Mitch wants to create. Create a fucking exit out of here.

More crustaceans leave their hosts in a violent wave of extrication, shedding their human clothes and fleeing via the water, toward the meadow where warm refuge awaits.

Mitch grabs the walkie-talkie attached to his hip. "Ellie?"

She comes back almost immediately with, "Yes?"

"Where are you?"

"Meeting up with Dawn on 10th. Why?"

"I need you to listen to me and listen carefully."

"What? What is it?"

Mitch swallows, wondering how he's going to explain this, if he should even try. "I need you to forget about the plan. I need you to take Dawn and start running. As far away from here as possible. However far the town will let you, but—for fuck's sake don't look back. And don't *come* back. No matter what."

"Mitch, what—"

"Ellie—trust me. Just do it. Just run. Something is happening here, and I think it's best if you and Dawn are just far, far away from it."

He watches another victim's lower jaw crack open, the flesh of his cheeks ripping as the crab within forces its way out. The man's body jolts with the onset of death. The crab leaves the body, scampers up the hill, and finds a man with a newspaper tucked under his arm, selecting this guy to be his neck skin suit. The crab leaps into the air with such surprising grace that Mitch can't look anywhere else; he's truly captivated by this remarkable process and thinks he could watch it a hundred times over. As he watches, he notices there are a few seconds where the host wrestles with the transformation, but that's it. After the claws do their dirty work and carve an entry point, the crab dips inside the red refuge and claims dominion over the human flesh. After that, the man smiles like the alien presence has filled him with a sense of purpose. As if he's discovered the true meaning of his existence.

Mitch tears himself away from the chilling display. "Do you hear me, Ellie? I said *run.*"

"I hear you," Ellie says, and it sounds like she's crying. "Where are you going?"

"I'm going to the goddamn clock tower. I'm going to get Kya, and I'm going to stop him. The Mayor."

"Okay..." Sniffles. Tears. Mitch can't help but think this is the last time he'll ever speak with Ellie Brower again. "And Mitch?"

He sneaks around the half-wall to the other side, planning to take the long way around the meadow, around the back of the buildings to keep himself out of the town's all-seeing eyes.

"Yeah, El?"

"Thank you. For everything." She whimpers softly. "For coming with me. For believing."

"Just get your daughter somewhere safe and don't worry about that stuff now. We'll talk later." That last part feels like such a lie, and he knows that she knows it too.

He shuts off the walkie-talkie, and heads toward almost certain death.

When Ellie turns off the walkie-talkie, she can't stop the flow of tears from leaving her eyes, the sobs causing her every muscle to hitch and pull. She looks to her daughter, who's also wearing a mask of tears, the grim situation working its way into her as well. They look to the streets, the results of their work gushing and flowing and turning the paved streets into shallow rivers. Work that was supposed to help them achieve victory, but after listening to the defeat in Mitch's voice, Ellie doesn't think there's any way around the inevitable—*you are never going to leave this place.*

*At least, not alive.*

"Thank you, missy," Foley says, snatching the walkie-talkie from her jittery hands.

Ellie looks around at the faces of the six men who've boxed her in, ugly faces that stretch with smug, victorious smiles and eyes that wish her to meet some violent, grisly end. The same eyes that probably watched Josh and Marissa meet their doom with absolute glee. The same faces that will smile when Darla—wherever she is—pays in full for her transgressions against the Mayor.

She doesn't know how the next few minutes will play out, but she can almost taste the blood in her mouth, the wet, musky flavor of her earthy tomb.

"Fuck you," she spits.

"Not nice," Foley responds, wagging his finger. "Told you—I don't like naughty language. It's unbecoming and it makes you sound uneducated. Plus, it insults our great town. Ain't that right?" he asks his deputized crew.

Ellie hasn't noticed the little gold stars pinned to their chests until just now, a realization that causes her to chuckle despite the bleak state of things. The stars remind her of when she used to teach third grade and how she had a board with each student's name on it—the gold stars were put there when the students did something good, something praise-worthy. She can't help but laugh at the irony.

"Something funny, ma'am?" Foley asks, looking over his glasses.

"Just realizing how pathetic you all are," she says, corralling her laughter. She immediately changes her tune, the sting of sad tears attacking her eyes once again. "What happens now?"

"Well," Foley says, scratching his nearly ruined face. Ellie notices that the Frankenstein-monster-stitch-job is coming undone, pus and other gross fluids squeezing through the loose flaps of skin. The thick, disgusting discharge is enough to toy with her gag reflex, and she wants to vomit all over them. "I've been thinking about that, missy. Been thinking long and hard about what to do with you. The Mayor—he wants to see the both of you, keep you until the Light comes, make sure you accept it without any complications. The Light will do the both of you some good, methinks. Helped me. Helped with the ugly thoughts in my head, so I'm sure as heck-fire it will do the same for you."

"I don't have any ugly thoughts," Ellie quips.

"Sure you do, darling. We all got ugly thoughts. It's why we need to accept the Light."

The others agree, nodding and vocalizing their support with piggish grunts.

Ellie looks to Dawn, surveying her face, the confusion building, pushing her eyebrows farther up her forehead. "I'm sorry, Dawn."

Dawn looks to her mother but doesn't speak.

"I'm sorry," Ellie continues, "that I pushed you away."

"Mom…" Dawn's face breaks, her shoulders heaving as misery runs its blade through her soul.

"I pushed you away. I was too strict and I…I just should have been a better mother. Should have listened to you more, shouldn't have…" She gulps, and it feels like there's an apple lodged at the base of her throat. "Should have made you want to come talk to me about things, you know? Like boys…and—"

"Okay," Foley says, grabbing her arm. "That's about all the *Days of Our Lives* drama hour I can handle for one day, so let's get a move on, shall we?" He nods at the others, no one in particular. "Grab them and let's get going."

Two folks step forward, reaching for one of Dawn's arms.

Ellie directs a stiff finger at them, toggling between each target. "Don't you lay a finger on her."

They laugh, small guffaws that claw away at Ellie's last nerve. When they don't listen, she balls her hands into fists and takes a step forward.

"I said, get—"

The pain barely registers, but the world dims and she knows something's happened to her, something bad. She blinks and she's on her knees now, her head level with everyone's hips, staring at a bleary, shadowed version of Lacuna's Point. Something wet coats the back of her head, and she puts two fingers on the surging sting. Bringing blood before her eyes, the pain blooms across her skull. She cranes her head and sees a smiling Foley standing behind her. He's holding out the butt of his gun, showing off the hard surface that busted her scalp. There're a few fresh droplets of blood on the surface, dripping.

"Woman, I asked you politely. Now you gone and made me do something I regret."

Ellie doubts he has any regrets.

She turns away from him, back toward Dawn and her captors. "I said," she rasps, finding it difficult to breathe and speak at the same time. "Get your hands off…"

She crawls toward them on all fours. Each movement is followed by the dreadful sound of Foley's boot hitting the sidewalk.

"Darling, I think we need to work on your listenin' skills." She feels her hair pull tight, and she's jerked back so hard that something pops in her neck, an audible crick. Chin skyward, she cries out as a lightning bolt of pain streaks down her spine. "Get up," he growls into her ear, and she feels his hot breath, smells carrion. Between his fumes and the grotesque infection leaking from his wounds, she wants to vomit right there, and gags just thinking about it.

He hoists her up on her feet. Foley marches her forward, and Ellie plants her feet on the ground, resisting the cop's direction. She feels his anger flare as he shoves her forward, but it's only enough to move her a few steps.

He glares at her, nostrils expanding. "You're not making this easy on me, toots. You know that?"

She knows that.

"Let her go." Ellie nods in Dawn's direction. "Let her go and I'll stay. Willingly. Forever. The Mayor doesn't need both of us." She doesn't know that, not really, and for all she *does* know, Dawn is the *only* one the Mayor wants.

"Actually, he does." Foley motions for his henchmen to take over.

Two brutes grab Ellie's arm, begin dragging her back. She looks up to see two of the black hoods in control of her now. "NO!" she shouts, and then begins flailing around, slapping the air wildly, trying to claw at the black fabric concealing their identities, the monstrous features beneath. "GET AWAY FROM HER!"

The black hoods parry her attacks with ease.

Foley storms forward and knocks her on the head again, and this time she sees it coming. Powerless to avoid it, but she still sees it coming. The impact connects above her left eyebrow and drives her head back, causing an intense burn to zip down her spine.

"Stop acting like a bitch and get moving." Foley bites his lip and stomps his foot. "There you go, making me use the naughty words again." He unholsters his gun, directing the barrel at her forehead. Presses it between her eyes. "Act out again, and I'll kill you myself."

She doesn't budge.

"I said MOVE!" Rosy splotches bud on his cheeks, around his eyes, like a cartoon character unexpectedly eating a hot pepper. "MOVE!"

Ellie remains where she is, in the clutches of the two black hoods, flashing Foley a defiant *fuck-you* smile.

"I'm gonna ask you once, and then—"

"What will you do with me?" Ellie asks, shrugging as if she doesn't care, and this point—she doesn't. Whatever fate the man chooses, so be it. "I asked you a question. What will you do if I don't comply?"

She's repulsed by the way the flaps of flesh move when he speaks. "I'm going to fucking kill you."

At this, she chuckles, which surprises even her. "Made you use the naughty words again," she says, almost dreamily, as if she's finally discovered the secret of this place. That it truly is a dream world, and all she needs to do is wake up.

And the best way to wake up from a bad dream?

*Die. You die.*

"Run," she says, looking at Foley, though the words aren't meant for him.

"Yo, boss," one of them says, "I think the floozy is damaged goods."

Foley doesn't respond, but he does wiggle a schoolteacher's finger at her.

"Run," she repeats, and then rips one arm free. She goes immediately for the gun in front of her, and she's surprised when it doesn't go off, surprised her brains haven't shot up into the air in a cloudy, crimson mist. One hand holds the barrel, but one hand isn't enough, and the black hoods collaborate on prying her fingers off the metal death cannon. One of them makes the mistake and puts a hand on her head, fingers dangling too close to her mouth. Ellie doesn't pass on the opportunity to dish out some pain and chomps down on the gloved finger, biting until she hears blood squelch and the pressure against the bone begins to hurt her teeth. The black hood actually screams, a muffled outburst that's oddly human.

She quickly loses what little control she had, feels her fingers slipping off the clean metal surface. "DAWN! RUN! NOW!"

There's a loud bang and her whole body jumps, her hands instinctively pulling back and covering her face, as if that's going to protect her, keep her safe. She expects to feel a swell of pain sweep through her, but it doesn't come. She's relieved to be spared from this agony, but the relief quickly dries up when she looks down at her gut and sees a gaping, bloody hole just above her right hip.

As if the pain was waiting for her to notice the wound, it rushes through her at once, filling her every nerve. The unbearable wave of anguish crashes down on her, and she sinks to her knees.

She looks up at Foley. Gunsmoke billows up before his angry grimace.

He pulls the trigger again. There's a sound, the loudest one she's ever heard, and it's the last sound she'll ever hear.

The pain gets no worse. A quick vision of the sky moving all-too-quickly flashes past, and the endless dark follows her into eternity.

Dawn freezes. She can't help it. She expects herself to scream, to cry, to do something other than stare as her mother's head snaps back, a violent burst of blood and brains spraying into the air above her, but she does nothing save for watching the madness unfold. Her mother's body hits the pavement with no restraint, collapsing like a doll onto a child's floor. She expects to see her body move, some tiny interaction with the world, but there is nothing. Ellie Brower remains still. Cold. Dead.

Dawn gasps. Suddenly a thousand childhood memories come flooding back to her. Memories of Ellie walking her to the bus stop and seeing her off to school. Ellie helping with homework. Dawn helping her with house chores. The two of them at stores, shopping for clothes and shoes. Not all the memories are fond ones. Bad ones seep in too. The fighting, the yelling. The screaming, the threats of kicking Dawn out of the house, permanently, once she's eighteen. The breaking of glass things. There's a lot to unpack and Dawn has no time to do so now since Foley and his men have already gotten over her mother's demise and have started walking toward her.

She glances down at her mother's unmoving form, wishing they had more time. It isn't fair to end it like this. She knows she should listen to her mom's last words, her last wishes, but she finds herself drifting over to the corpse and kneeling. She plants a kiss on her forehead and apologizes as many times as she can, both silently and audibly, before the crew comes over and rips her away from the last interaction she'll ever have with Ellie Brower. She wasn't a perfect mother, but she was a good one, and Dawn remembers this now.

She combs her fingers over her mother's open eyes, closing them.

Hands hook under Dawn's arms, lifting her away.

She goes kicking and screaming, but it's no use.

Ellie Brower fades into the distance, and Dawn knows that's the last time she'll ever see her again, in the flesh.

At least she has the memories to keep her warm and oh-so-human.

Mitch sneaks around the buildings undetected, managing to escape the beady black eyes of the crab-creatures running amok throughout the town. He makes his way down the back alley behind the diner, trying to keep focus, but he can't help himself and peers inside. One glance through the diner's window and he stops. Sees Darla—what's left of her—resting on the counter like an order that's ready-to-go. She's on her back, and her entire midsection has been opened, the gory crater exposing a messy assembly of butchered organs that no longer serve any purpose because the operator is dead. The crab that had made its exit is nowhere to be seen, but evidence of his hasty exit is apparent—red splatter coating the counter and walls like spilled paint. Darla's one remaining eye is stuck open, staring directly in Mitch's direction. *It's all your fault,* that one good eye says, and Mitch shakes his head, cursing the Mayor, the town, and everything Lacuna's Point stands for.

He avoids further distractions and keeps moving, his thoughts running a thousand miles a minute. He wonders if Ellie and Dawn were able to escape or if they've suffered a similar fate. *Shouldn't have left them. That was fucking stupid,* he scolds himself, but he's also aware the women are smart and capable of surviving on their own. Ellie in particular. She's a survivor. She's gotten through the last three years virtually alone, having no one to share the burden of losing Dawn with after Dan left. As rough as things have been between Mitch and Angie, at least they've had each other to lean on. Some kind of support.

The clock tower's base is in view now, and he makes for it, but before he can get out from under the shadows of the diner and the two adjoining shoppes next to it, a figure appears at the end of the alley, a smiling figure, one he recognizes.

It's Bobby Mac, the gun-loving neckbeard. Mitch doesn't know for sure, but he's pretty sure he had something to do with the explosion that took place at the hotel.

As if Bobby Mac can read his thoughts, he says, "Yeah, that's right. I helped kill your friends. I mean, Foley—he did the work. I just destroyed the evidence." The bastard pretends to wash his hands, as if this absolves him of all his sins. As if blowing Josh and Marissa to flakes of ash means the whole thing never happened at all. "Now, where you going, boy?" Teeth appear through the mess of hair around his mouth. "The Mayor's looking for you. Tells us you have a story to read him."

There's something off about his voice now, but Mitch can't place it.

"Well, that's actually great, because I was just on the way to see him."

"That right?"

"That's right."

"Well," he says as something swims beneath the flesh of his face, an undulating wave that sweeps across his left cheek. The skin stretches, something poking its way to the surface. "You won't mind if I escort you, you know, just to make sure you get there all right?"

"I know the way."

"I know you know the way." A sinister laugh gurgles in his throat. "But I'm gonna walk you anyway."

Mitch doesn't see much choice in the matter. And there's no use provoking the gun-carrying cracker anyway. "Fine by me."

And so he walks. Toward the stairs that lead up city hall. Toward the tower holding the town, his daughter, and time itself hostage, under watchful, knowing eyes.

# CHAPTER TWENTY-ONE

It takes him ten minutes to adjust to the smell, and "adjust" is hardly the right word. More like, "able to suffer through it." Dan, shirt up over his nose, steps into the room underneath the clock tower, the tomb for dozens, maybe a hundred, dead bodies.

"What the hell is this?" asks Wally Stanton, looking over the pile of skeletons, his complexion blanching.

"Thought you could tell me," Dan says. "Looks like a tomb."

He walks over to the spiral staircase that leads to the top of the tower and places a foot on the bottom stair.

Wally stops him. "You don't know how sturdy that thing is."

He's not wrong. Dan tests the bottom rung, stomping on it, and the whole staircase shakes like it's one missing bolt away from collapsing. Glancing up, he realizes it won't be a quick journey to the top, and if the stairs do fail him, it's a long drop down.

"I think I'll take my chances," Dan tells him, and he doesn't know why. He has no reason to wander up that way, no evidence to suggest that what he'll find up there—if anything—will be of any use to the case or finding his ex-wife.

"Why?" Wally asks, his brow fixed with an equal blend of confusion and concern.

Dan wishes he could explain better—or, at all, really—but he offers Wally this: "I think there's something up there."

"What?" Wally ambles over and tries to look up past the spiraling railing comprised of old, rusted iron, the kind that flakes off and leaves orange stains on the skin. "What do you see? I don't see anything but shadows and dust."

It's true—there's nothing there but the dark and floating dust mites. But it's the feeling Dan gets when he puts his foot on the bottom step. The lure of *needing* to know what's up there, at the top, inside the clock tower's head. He's surprised Wally doesn't feel it too.

"You don't see it?" Dan asks, pointing. "Something moved up there."

"I'm calling for backup," Wally informs him, stepping away. "Do *not* go up there, Brower. I'm serious. Don't do it."

"Okay."

As soon as Wally places the call and turns his back, Dan takes the steps, two at a time, continuing to ignore the nauseating stench occupying every square inch of breathable air, and Wally's plea to, "Turn the fuck around this second."

The parade marches toward old Eddy, and Dawn Brower leads the way, feeling like an A-list celebrity being escorted to a big event down a red carpet. The presence of the men behind her fill her with harrowing thoughts, that whatever waits for her in the Mayor's office is something similar to the treatment her mother just received—death.

But then again—maybe not. The Mayor's used her over and over again, making her paint things, *offerings* for whatever cosmic master Quincy Black obeys. Dawn serves a purpose here. She's needed. Or so she's been told.

As they round 1st Street, the arts festival comes into view, the entire scope of the celebration sprawled out before them, only it's much different from what Dawn remembers. Fewer people. And when her eyes follow the trails of blood that streak down the small hill that slopes toward the street, she almost shrieks. Bodies, several, lie face down in the small lake that's taken over the pavement. The water has risen to the top of the wheels of a few parked cars. Dawn focuses on the bodies, their mutilated states, ripped open and split down the center, like costumes after a Halloween party, no longer needed and thrown hastily aside. Her gaze connects with a dead man's death stare, his jaw snapped open at a seemingly impossible angle, the opening of his oral cavity wide enough to stuff several fists in. A perfect size for an oversized crab to skitter through.

"Well, I'll be damned," says Foley, surveying the massacre. Some of the people who survived the first wave of attacks cower under their tables of food and art, their faces scrunched with fear and general disgust. "Looks like we missed the party."

A few of the deputized men snicker at this; the black hoods continue their silent partnership. Someone bumps into Dawn, urging her to move along and make a wide berth around the carnage.

Dawn follows the path to the steps of town hall and stops before mounting them. She doesn't think she has the energy to make it to the top. As she debates giving up, lying down and dying right there, one of the deputies gets handsy, shoves her up the first step.

"Hey!" she barks through her teeth, and she's fully prepared to turn and swing at the man's jaw.

"Hay is for horses," Foley says, stepping between them. "Move along, little lady. The Mayor is waiting and it's best not to make him wait long. You've disobeyed the oath you've taken and he's not very patient with defectors."

"I didn't defect," she says, almost pleading, and hating the sound of her own voice.

"That's up to him to decide." Foley points up the stairs, smiling. *Enjoying* this game.

Outnumbered, she knows fighting won't get her anywhere. It will only make things harder on her, and she needs to be more strategic with her approach. She smiles at him and goes along with his demands.

"What happened to your friends down there?" she asks, nodding at the savaged bodies opened like cocoons for vicious butterflies.

Foley looks over his shoulder, and then returns to her just as quickly. "They've been reborn. No big deal. Happens every year."

The man's face pulsates with the promise of also being *reborn*.

"What are you people?" she asks, trembling now. Trembling because she really doesn't want to know the answer to that question.

"You'll know soon enough once you give yourself over to the Light," Foley tells her with a smile. "Because deep down, you're one of us, too."

Mitch knows he has the element of surprise on his side, and that Bobby Mac won't see it coming if he acts quickly enough. When they reach the top of the first set of stairs and his feet are firmly planted on the landing, he spins and shoves Bobby as hard as he can. The gunshot goes off in a booming explosion, popping several holes in the wall behind him. The force of the push is enough to lift the pear-shaped man off his feet, and when he lands, he's thrown off-balance, goes down hard, his head crashing on one of the steps. Bobby's eyes flicker, toying with entry into an unconscious world, and Mitch knows he has the golden opportunity to finish the job. He sprints down the stairs, catching up with Bobby before his near-lifeless body reaches the bottom step.

Kicking the gun away from his grasp, Mitch notices there's still life in his eyes.

Bobby opens his mouth, but Mitch doesn't allow the words to form. He brings his fist down on Bobby's teeth, feels the hardness break away under the force of his knuckles. He doesn't stop after one punch. Fist after fist lands on their targets, and when he finally does stop—from exhaustion and nothing else—he lifts himself up and stands over Bobby's ruined face, which now looks like a Jack-O-Lantern left out well past the first week of November, deflated and misshapen. His eyes have already grown swollen knots. Mitch doesn't think he's killed Bobby Mac, but he's gotten him pretty close to death's edge.

Mitch doesn't feel too bad about it. What's done is done, and he has an appointment with the Mayor. He grabs the man's shotgun, then heads up the stairs.

When he reaches the top, he looks down at Bobby Mac one last time.

A seizure controls his body, his limbs flailing about like one of those roadside inflatables shouting out a good used car deal. Smoke pours out of the man's ears, nose, and mouth. Then his face begins to extend outward, something inside puncturing the flesh, the tips of some bloody claw forcing its way out. Mitch sees a single crab claw breach the surface, dripping with blood, a fog of luminous mist folding over it.

Mitch suddenly feels the need to hurry things along, and runs down the hall, toward the Mayor's chamber that sits below the spiraling staircase that leads to the top of the clock tower.

Dawn feels everything she's ever known melt away inside of her. She feels like this is information she's known the entire time, that she's slowly transitioning into something else, something more than human, but whatever it is, she can't know completely. Every morning she finds herself in front of the mirror brushing her teeth, noticing something different about herself; an extra line in her face here, a dimple that wasn't previously present a week ago, a change in the color of her hair that wasn't done intentionally with some store-bought dye. No, these little changes have happened over the course of the last three years and they've come in small strokes like any great piece of artwork. No great painting was ever accomplished in one sitting, but rather spread out and worked on meticulously until the artist's true vision is fully formed. Months. Years. Decades. It's different for each piece, the same way the Light has infected some residents immediately, while others it takes much, much longer. But it's all worth it in the end, she supposes.

*The art's always worth it.*

She understands this now. Looking into Foley's hate-filled glare, she knows everything he does, because they are colors from the same palette.

"I'm not going in there," Dawn says, standing up to Foley.

Foley continues to bore into her. " 'Scuse me?"

"Not going in there," Dawn repeats, more defiantly this time. "The Mayor can go fuck himself."

Foley winces, bites down on his lower lip. "Well, little lady. I think you need to be taught a pretty good lesson."

"Fuck your lessons," Dawn spits. "Fuck you and fuck this stupid town."

"My, my. So much gusto I can hardly contain myself." He unholsters his weapon and points the gun directly at her forehead. "Move. Along."

"Shoot me, you fuckin' pig. Just like you did my mother."

He glares at her, cheeks quivering with rage. "Fuck you call me?"

One of the deputies puts a hand on Foley's shoulder as if that's going to calm him, but Foley simply shrugs it off.

"I said," Dawn says, stepping toward the gun, allowing the barrel to press against her forehead. "You're a fucking *pig*. Oink, oink, motherfucker."

She expects the bullet to speed through her head and clear a path for eternal darkness, but instead, Foley shoots out one gloved hand and wraps his fingers around her throat. Hoisting her onto the tips of her toes, he keeps the metal firmly pressed against her head, hard enough to leave an indentation behind.

"You fucking people," he says, blinking, and clearly hating her for making him utter another obscenity. "You think you can just come in here, do and say whatever you want without any consequences?"

"The Mayor wants her alive," one of the deputies reminds him. "You've already wasted the others—he won't be pleased if this one dies."

Foley glares sideways, then allows Dawn to stand once again. Smacking his hands, she breaks away.

"You're lucky," Foley says to her, gripping her head and rotating her so she can face the door. "But you won't always have protection. Remember, everyone is expendable. Replaceable. There're a thousand folks out there who can doodle like you. A million." She feels his eyes on the back of her head. "Even purty ones like yourself."

He shoves her forward.

The pig is in control, and she can smell the bacon.

When Mitch slips into the Mayor's office, he's surprised to find it empty. It seems so long since he was here. Two weeks ago feels like two years, but the place hasn't changed since that initial visit. The small library on the west wall is still overflowing with books that look like they've never been read, and the mahogany desk still fills the space at the head of the room, the matching bureau behind it displaying a bottle of merlot and two glasses that have never hosted human lips.

In the far right corner of the room, he spots the spiral staircase. He wishes he knew enough about guns to check to make sure he has one shot left, but he doesn't know the first thing other than *point* and *pull the trigger*.

He makes for the stairs. When he reaches the first step, he looks up, all the way to the top, and it's an intimidating distance to the belfry. In the distance, he sees something flickering, like candlelight. He wants to call to his daughter, to make sure she's still alive, that she's actually up there and not dead, and that his journey north will be worth something. If nothing else, taking out the Mayor will be a worthy reward.

He moves stealthily up the stairs, taking his time, but halfway up, he wonders how much time he has and if the noise of his footsteps will give up his position. If the Mayor already knows he's coming. He has to, right? And if he knows, and he's there, waiting, will he be afraid? Will the weapon in Mitch's hand do anything or will the round simply bounce off his chest like Superman? Is the thing that calls itself the Mayor immortal?

These thoughts plague him and not for the first time. Thinking of Kya, he muses over her safety, if pushing the action is putting her life in more danger.

*I can save her.*

*I can strike a bargain.*

It's his last plan. He knows the Mayor wants what's inside him, that book, that novel he's been meaning to write, that piece of art the Mayor wants on his shelf, wants to hand over to the thing that drives Lacuna's Point. That's his bargaining chip. The novel for his daughter's freedom.

But that's a last resort. That's only if the bullet bounces off Quincy Black's face.

He manages one step before a familiar voice starts barking in his ear. *If she dies, you might as well not even come home,* his wife says, soon-to-be-ex if things continue to trend the way they have. Even if he brings Kya home—what will that change?

Before Mitch knows it, he's reached the top of the stairs, his calves and quads letting him know he's out of shape. When he rises from that final step and plants his feet on the plywood-laden floor of the belfry, he sees the Mayor's back, the man (the thing) facing the semi-transparent shield of the town's giant timekeeper.

"Da...Dad?" a small voice croaks from somewhere close. "Dad, is that you?"

Mitch looks and sees his baby girl in the corner of the belfry, chained to the wall. She looks a lot thinner than she had two weeks ago when he saw her briefly, nearly emaciated now. She looks like she's been crying. Splotches of dirt and grime stain her shirt, her jeans. Her hair is wild and looks like it hasn't been brushed in ages.

Mitch nearly chokes on the sadness building in the bottom of his throat. He fights the urge to run over there and rip the chains from the walls.

"You know," the Mayor says, keeping his back to him, "when the first sign of life entered the universe, it was a speck floating across a starless void. Insignificant to the Great Verse as it were, but now, endless eons later, it is everything to it. Life. So very much of it out there. In ways you cannot possibly fathom."

Mitch pumps the shotgun just like in the movies.

"And I see you've come here with the intention of ending mine." The Mayor turns now, showing off his face, the hideous features he's kept under wraps until this moment. The skin is jelly-like, somewhat translucent, a slimy mask that reveals some misshapen skeleton beneath. His eyes are polluted with a deep red haze, bloodshot clouds that float around their obsidian centers. Half an ear is missing. His nose looks broken, twisted slightly to the left as if someone clocked him with a hammer. The top of his skull has very little hair on it, some lengthy clumps here and there, and Mitch assumes the creature's face is the victim of an unfortunate burn.

None of these features look impeccably human.

"What the hell are you?" Mitch asks, aiming the gun at him.

"I suppose there's an answer to that. I suppose there's even a good one."

"Well, you better start talking before this gun talks for the both of us."

This amuses Quincy Black, and he lets loose a small chuckle. "You humans do love your violence, oh how you crave it."

"You want to talk about violence? How about what that animal did to Josh and Marissa?"

"That was a mistake and not our intention. For that, we're sorry."

"What about my daughter?" He nods at Kya. "What about her?" Fighting off the tears, he toys with the idea of just pulling the trigger and ending this one way or the other. "Are you sorry about that?"

"Again, not our intent. We don't like to chain our artists up, but sometimes, difficult people can have an effect on those around them, and they need to be kept separated from the pack. It's a delicate ecosystem in Lacuna's Point. I'm sure you won't understand but—"

"I don't understand what the hell is happening. What is this…this Lacuna? What does it want with us?" He growls. "Where is the fucking thing?"

Black smiles. "It's on its way. Very close by now. Just waking as we speak. And when he gets here, it will be just like every year—

he will take what he wants, feed on the artistic offerings of this place, and when he's done and the festival is over, back into hibernation he will go. And a bright Light will spread over the town, resetting things to how they usually are. And Lacuna's Point will carry on as it usually does, existing, pumping out its art and cookies and cakes and music, and all the other things that our culture thrives on, that good ol' Americana."

"What are you talking about, man?"

Black flashes that devil-you-know grin. "You ever see a piece of art in the décor section of your favorite store and wonder where it comes from—who's painted such a wondrous collection of colors and images? How about the cupcakes at your favorite supermarket? They get them from somewhere—sometimes it will say made in 'Fulton, Massachusetts' or 'Davenport, Texas.' But that's where they go after it leaves places like Lacuna's Point. Oh, yes. Did you think Lacuna's Point is the only place like this? No, no. There are dozens and dozens of communities like this, dedicated to the magnificent process of creation. Some of the best books and screenplays have been made in places like Lacuna's Point. There's something about being in the presence of other creatives that really brings out the best in us, no?"

"You're full of shit. You talk a good game, but…but that can't be true."

"Which part? The fact that there are other communities exactly like this one, communes hidden in the gap between two worlds, or that they simply exist virtually unknown to the masses?"

"Yes. Both. I don't know."

"You are naïve, Mitchell Green. Maybe even stupid. But you've seen it firsthand. People go missing in America all the time. Some of those people are never found. Where do you think they go?"

Mitch hates the smile the thing wears. He adjusts his aim after letting the barrel dip some. "Like I said—you talk a good game, but now it ends."

"I don't think so. We have much to discuss, you and me. For example, let's talk about that novel you've been working on. Today was the deadline to see some progress, and I can speak on behalf of the Lacuna when I say, novels are very juicy. Very tasty. Especially personal ones, novels that really dig into the soul of a person, you know? So…" The Mayor sidesteps from his position and goes to a small podium, where a round object rests by its lonesome. Mitch can't help but compare the thing to a Magic Eight-Ball, the kind he and his friends used to toy with when they were kids. The ball is black, but it's not an Eight-Ball. Magic, maybe, but nothing you'd drop in the center of a pool rack. A prismatic glow emanates from the center of it, casting wave-like light on the belfry's angled ceiling. "You've been here for two weeks. I suppose you have *some* progress. Let's have it. Read it for me."

"You want it?"

Quincy Black grins with his eyes, like a wolf before a lamb's slaughter.

"Okay," Mitch says, digging into his back pocket. He pulls out a single piece of paper, tosses the crumpled ball across the belfry.

It tumbles, lands near Black's left foot. The Mayor bends over, scoops it up, untangles it, and then proceeds to read the words silently. "What is this?" he asks, after his eyes comb over every letter.

"It's the start of the novel."

"A paragraph. Two weeks, you've only produced one paragraph."

"It's a good goddamn paragraph." Mitch sees he's struck a chord.

"You've been working on it," Black says, as if trying to convince himself that this is true. "I've had eyes watching you, and they've reported that—"

"Been working on it. That's all I got."

Black pockets the paper and stretches his neck, left and right, the bones cracking, sounding much louder in the belfry's acoustics. "No matter. The Lacuna has enough this year. There's already so much talent. A few chapters would have been nice, but I have a feeling you will work harder on it in the coming year. I guarantee it. Because I will be watching you, Mitchell Green. Every day, and I will chain you to the goddamn wall if I have to, force you to put pen to paper, draw the ideas out of you even if I have to reach into your soul and squeeze every creative droplet from your pathetic muse!" By the end of this declaration, he's growling. "You need to write that novel. The Lacuna will drink every word of it, and in return, it will grant you the best life one could have—pure happiness, day in and day out. You and Kya can live here, together, and enjoy nothing but the best of what America has to offer. Doesn't that sound…perfect?"

Mitch glowers at him. He doesn't forget about the shotgun, *can't* because it feels impossibly heavy now. "What about the rest of my family? My wife, my other kids?"

The Mayor shrugs as if no barrier can stop them. "They can come, or...like most people...you will forget everything that's happened before Lacuna's Point. The past has no influence here. *Time* has no bearings."

"This is crazy, the craziest bullshit I've ever heard."

"Some of the craziest things end up being true. As a writer, you should know that some truths are far more believable than the zaniest fiction."

"And what do *you* get out of this whole thing?"

"I get," Black says, looking down at the ball resting in the cup he's made with his hands. "I get the leftovers. The extra-juicy stuff."

"That thing important to you?"

"This?" he asks with a smile, and it's a dark smile, his teeth stained like he's been sucking on licorice. "This is one of seven in all the Great Verse, and it is mine. *Alllllll* mine. I've crossed oceans and deserts and unfathomable worlds just to procure one. It's the most precious thing I own. The most precious thing anyone can ever own."

"Well..." Mitch aims at the black ball, "kiss that shit goodbye, motherfucker." He fires off a round, but Black must have sensed it coming, because, in a blink, he's standing ten feet away from the spot Mitch was aiming for. "Naughty, naughty, Mitchie-my-bitchie. If my math checks out, that leaves you with only two shots left, at most, and there are about six men on their way up here, excluding my black hoods, each of them armed and very dangerous. So you best keep them because..." He turns his finger into a gun, dropping his thumb like a hammer. "You're gonna need them, partner."

"I want to take Kya..." His eyes shift to his daughter, his heart breaking seeing her in this condition. "...and Dawn and Ellie. And I want out. Just let us go. You don't need us and our art. You have a whole town of people that are willing to die, to be food for this thing."

"Dying...yes," Black says, nodding, inviting Mitch to take a look out the porthole with a sweep of his arm. "Seems the eggs hatched a little early this year. And, well, we'll need to restock the pond. That's the thing about the process—the Light—humans can only absorb so much of it before they're all used up. Skelly was a huge loss to us this year. Big loss. The Lacuna really enjoyed the tunes he produced. His music was legendary in these parts. Pity he passed, but all creativity has a shelf-life, and his had come to pass."

Mitch grimaces as he recalls the images of the man's body splitting apart. "Those things coming out of those people…what are they?"

Amused, Mayor Black winks at his guest. "Children of the Lacuna."

"Children…" Mitch tips the crown of his head toward Kya. "Is she…"

"A carrier?" Black picks at an oozing wound on his chin. "Gosh, Mitchie, I really don't know the answer. Contrary to what you might think, I don't have all the answers, nor do I care to interfere with the Lacuna and its life cycle. All I know is its desires—people, their abilities to create—and that I've provided a place for it to feed. In return, we get the Light, I get my magic, and the rest, as one might say, is history. Beyond that, I could care less what it does, could care less about these interdimensional creatures that inhabit the human bodies. I just call them the Children, and that works for me. It would do you well not to worry too much about it. It's just a side effect of living in Lacuna's Point."

"A side effect…" Mitch adjusts his aim once again, lining up the barrel with the grotesque face before him. "There's going to be a side effect for getting in my way, Mr. Mayor. Now, let us go, or I'm going to shoot you and anyone else in my way until we're outta here."

"Like I said," Black says, his one hand gliding over the surface of the magic orb, "two rounds, right? Use them wisely."

# CHAPTER TWENTY-TWO

About halfway up, a rung gives out from under him, and Dan's foot punches through, causing him to fall forward. The entire staircase moves, rattles, messes with his equilibrium, bringing him a tough spell of vertigo. He hears rusted metal hitting the floor below him and hopes Wally wasn't in the way of the fallen debris.

"Are you okay up there?" Wally shouts, his voice echoing in the narrow chamber.

"Fine!" he calls down, pushing himself back up to his feet.

"*Now* will you come down?"

Dan peers up. Almost there. He can almost see the belfry at the top, the giant bell that rests in the center of the tower's uppermost compartment, daylight soaking through the clock's semi-transparent face. At least when he gets there he'll have some natural light and not whatever dim luminance his almost-dead phone provides. He glances down at the bottom of the tower and can't see anything but grainy shadows. Somewhere down there, Wally lets go of an impatient, *I'm totally over this* sigh.

"No," Dan says, taking the next step cautiously. "I'm almost there."

"Damn it, Brower. Are you kidding me?"

"Stay down there then!"

"You know I damn well can't!"

He hears Wally put a foot on the first step, and immediately wants to tell the detective not to bother, that the combined weight of the two men might overload the staircase and bring it crashing down. But who is he to tell the detective how to do his job?

*No one*, he thinks. *Just a farmer.*

*A husband.*

*An ex-husband.*

*A father, and future father.*

Dan pushes ahead, ignoring every creak and crick the staircase makes, the pressure of their footsteps testing the durability of this relic. Soon after, he reaches the top, looks down into the shadows below and sees Wally down there, his shape delicately placing feet on the flat platforms, holding the railings with both hands for added safety. At this rate Dan will have inspected the tower's chamber and come back down before Wally makes it halfway up.

*Useless,* he almost says aloud, but doesn't. And that's mostly because the first thing he sees upon entering the belfry—besides the nonoperational bell—has left him completely speechless.

The human suitcase has been opened, and that human suitcase once had a name, and his name was Bobby Mac.

Foley examines the mutilated corpse of a man he considered a friend—or, as good a friend the nature of his duties to the town could afford. He runs his eyes over the way the body came apart, split from belly to neck, the ribs splayed open, entrails thrown across the carpet like someone opened one of those party streamer air cannons and the man's guts were all inside. It's a gory sight, but nothing Foley hasn't seen before.

Foley kisses the cross hanging from his neck and then rises up, facing his crew and their prisoner. "Well, he's dead. Nothing's gonna bring him back."

"What...what happened to him?" asks Hank Treadaway. He looks much like the others—scared beyond his wits. Nervously, the man tugs on his denim cap which proudly displays the Confederate flag.

"What the hell does it look like, Treadaway?" He points to Bobby's bloody husk. "Little fella inside wanted out and got out. Wish he'd done so a little more cleanly—hell of a mess to clean up, and, well, I really liked Bobby Mac. Good Christian, him."

Hank doesn't seem to like that answer, his face full of more questions, each one seeming to fight for the right to come out first. "Is that...gonna happen to us?"

"Well, I suppose it might. Best to stay safe and be on the lookout. The Lord's Light is coming, y'all. No need to fret. We'll all be saved soon. Just gotta get these interlopers on the right path." He shoots them all a glance, even the black hoods standing in the background like statues. "Y'hear?"

No one says they don't.

"Come on." Foley waves the gang over, inviting them to side-step this nightmare and head up the stairs, toward the belfry, where Quincy Black awaits their presence. "We got work to do."

"Tell me more," Dawn says, speaking up.

"What now?" Foley asks, surprised by the girl's mouthiness given the situation. "Say what?"

"I want to hear about the Light."

Foley thinks this might be a ruse. "Well, the Light comes from God, ma'am." He puffs out his chest, hoping this intimidating tactic will make her think twice about whatever nonsense she's up to. "You do believe in God, don't you? Our Shepard of the Light?"

"Well," Dawn says, licking her lips. "Of course."

"Good. Then if you're good with God, then you shall receive the Light and receive it well." He stares at her, slightly amused by the face she's making. Then her eyes find the ceiling. And her face changes.

Foley looks up. "What the—"

Before he can finish that thought, a white object zips down from the ceiling and latches onto Hank Treadaway's head. The creature, about the size of a small football, slashes down with its claws, stripping away bits of Treadaway's face, peeling back layers and layers of flesh as it tries to create an opening wide enough to slip into, and Foley thinks the thing's approach is all wrong. A bad approach isn't enough to stop it from trying though, and a gash opens along Treadaway's cheek, spilling freshets of red. Treadaway screams, though the sound is abruptly cut short due to the creature seizing the opportunity to squeeze inside the narrow tunnel that makes up the man's esophagus. The surrounding men—even the black hoods—leave their posts to help Treadaway, trying to stop the crab-creature's unauthorized entry. Foley is surprised by the reaction himself—to his knowledge, these creatures want nothing more than a warm sack to hide in, at least that's his interpretation. The men struggle with the crab, wrestling with it, getting out of the way of its fierce pinchers, dodging each quick strike. Treadaway's face has become a mask of blood, more red visible than skin. Foley wonders how long this will go on, how long before the thing wins out, and as he does so, an incredible swell of pain enters his body from below his belt. He hunches over, gripping his gonads as a deep, intense pain burns its way across his entire groin. The pain spreads into his stomach and down his legs. His vision blurs, but when he turns to face the source of the agony, he can still make out the girl standing before him, a smile plastered to her face.

A smile he wants to cut off with a sharp knife. Slowly. So she hurts.

"You…bitch," he says, and then something heavy hits the side of his head, revealing a total darkness he never knew existed.

Dawn is surprised she's been able to conceal the pipe wrench for the entire trek, but it seems like these idiots underestimated her, never once checking her pants for weapons of any kind. It's a lucky oversight, for which she thanks whatever god is watching over them, an act she finds quite humorous given the state of things, the true horror in charge of Lacuna's Point.

As the rest of Foley's clan struggles with the albino crab, trying to pry the thing from their pal's face, Dawn uses the golden opportunity to take another swing. Foley's skull dents like a car door after a minor collision. There's no blood, no breakage of skin—just an ugly-looking indentation on his dome. Once he's lying on his side, his eyes rolling back, Dawn gets moving.

She ignores the black hoods, the two figures shifting their focus onto her. Bolting for the spiral staircase that leads all the way up, she doesn't look back.

Overhead, the world grumbles, a stretching, vibrating sound he can't ignore. Mitch's eyes find the ceiling. The sound rolls like thunder above, almost natural, but Mitch's gut tells him this is the opposite of natural.

"Heeeee's heeeeere," Black sing-songs. The ball resting on his palms begins to fill with white smoke, the blackness it previously held fading, giving way to the awesome display of heavenly light. "The Light will be here soon."

"Drop the fucking eight-ball," Mitch instructs, aiming the gun again.

"You can't hurt me *or* the Glass of Light. So go ahead—waste your last shots."

Mitch wants to test the theory again, but thinks Black isn't lying. Both of them seem truly impervious against the weapons of mankind.

"Come with me, Mitchell," Black utters, his voice changing, growing more guttural. "Open your eyes to the Light."

"Fuck you."

Black closes his eyes, draws a deep breath. The swirling white vapor within the Glass continues to dominate the dark half, and soon the black will be conquered, and the white will stand victorious. Within ten seconds, Black opens his eyes and stares up at the ceiling. "I can see him. He is coming. Oh, yes, what a joyous occasion. You should really lend yourself to the Light, Mitchell. Let it fill you. Let it flow through thy bones, infiltrate your very core, allow it to numb your fears and insecurities. Allow all that human suffering you cling to fall away. Bury those detestable pieces of yourself. Accept the Light, Mitchell, and become one with the Lacuna. Let it drink and feed on your abilities, nourish itself from the fruits of your gardens. Your reward will be everlasting perfection in the Lacuna's very own reality. You will become one with the town and its glory, never having to worry about—"

The shotgun booms. The round plugs Black's chest, driving him against Eddy's number VI, nearly dropping him through the tight egress between the clock's face and the attic's framing. The orb falls to the ground, rolls across the attic's floor in Mitch's direction.

He feels compelled to rush forward and pick it up, though every fiber of his body is telling him not to, no way, don't dare touch the thing that's not meant for human hands.

"NO!" bellows Black, his face warping and twisting, as if holding the magical sphere was keeping everything intact from his neck up. "NO! DON'T YOU DARE FUCKING TOUCH IT!" His voice is too loud for any human voice to match, and Mitch's eardrums begin to bother him, a dull pain seeping into the center of his skull. That's when he remembers he still has the Beats in his back pocket. "DON'T YOU DARE!"

But before Black can collect himself, rebound from the impact, Mitch is already gunning for the orb, sliding across the wood on his knees, not caring if the rough surface tears him up. Within seconds, the gun is in his lap and the orb is in his hands, fingers gripped around the smooth, glass-like surface.

"What have you done?" Black says, his features melting away, more of the humanoid appearance bleeding, liquefying, turning into a wet clay amalgamation of dripping flesh and blood, fluids that hold no human significance. Mitch wonders if he'll ever see what Quincy Black's true form looks like, and figures it's probably something his human eyes aren't meant to see. Something his mind can't perceive.

Mitch plugs the Beats into his ears, whips out his iPhone, hits the music app, and listens as his wedding song plays—"Earth Angel" by Chuck Berry and the Starlighters—silencing the ear-splitting cries and head-thumping screams from the beast before him.

And then, Black makes for him, lashing out, bony and unnaturally-long fingers outstretched, reaching for the orb that's snug between Mitch's steady hands. Mitch begs for the man-thing to get closer, to *try* to take the ball away from him. He promises he's got a little something for him, a little something Black might not be expecting.

But when Black gets there, Mitch doesn't have the power to react. Instead, Black wraps his cadaverous fingers around the orb, taking up space on the object that Mitch can't cover.

There's an explosion of Light, a wide starburst of milky radiance that spreads across the belfry's whole, dousing the walls, the ceiling, the bell, the clock, and the occupants within, showering them in a divine glow of sparkling shine.

And that's all Mitch can see now.

Before it takes him, he wonders if he'll ever see anything else again.

Dawn hears the blast and picks up the pace, dashing past the Mayor's office door, slamming it shut behind her and sealing out the awful sounds of the crab-creature shearing its way into Treadaways's body, the shouts of the townsfolk opposing this heinous act.

Once inside, she collects her breath, just for a second before sprinting over to the opposite end of the room where the spiral staircase waits—the only exit, it seems, is up, and Dawn knows that's exactly where her best friend is being kept, exactly where Kya's dad should be, saving her ass.

Saving them both.

Thinking of Mitch Green makes her think of her mother, how she wishes she had ten more seconds with her, enough time to apologize for everything she's ever done, apologize for getting herself lost in this fucked-up place, this labyrinth of lies.

A bang sounds off, and the door to Black's office is nearly lifted off its hinges. Dawn freezes, glances back, and waits a spell. Just when she thinks it's safe, the door shudders again, accompanied by a thunderous boom, and the jamb splits, splinters, spewing shards of wood on the ground before it. A gap wide enough for something to slip through opens up, and Dawn sees a human arm covered in blood and pinkish fluids, viscous and chunky, poke on through, its hand blindly searching for the door handle.

*Foley,* she thinks, and her heart plummets.

Gooey sweat drips onto the brass knob as the man's fingers locate its target. A slimy puddle collects on the floor as the hand grabs, turns, and releases the door from its shut position.

Dawn darts for the steps.

Foley pokes his face inside the room, though the thing resting atop its neck is hardly a face now. More like a folded assembly of human features and something else, something *alien.* Hollowed eyes, deflated muscle tissue, and strips of skin dangling like melted cheese from an oven grate.

Dawn has no time to scream.

Instead, she ascends the stairs without looking back or down.

The thing follows.

# CHAPTER TWENTY-THREE

*The Light fades, dies down, and is replaced by a soft lilac glow. Behind him, his feet stand on some dusty, rocky plain, clearly far and away from the clock tower's belfry, clearly in some other space and time. He's holding the glass orb. Across from him stands Quincy Black, though the image he projects is a far cry away from the vaguely human appearance he's been disguised as this whole time— now, he looks like an old, withered warlock, long silvery hair resting on his shoulders, his forehead and cheeks a patchwork of cracked skin. Sunken black suns for eyes sit so far inside his head that Mitch wonders how he can see at all. The eyes glint with some iridescent shine, greenish and animalistic, reminding Mitch of the possums he catches snacking in the outdoor garbage cans back home. He doesn't know why but the man's nudity, his frail, bony form, and the coarse white hair grown all around the private places, is the least concerning thing about his appearance.*

*Black snarls with delight, revealing blackened kernels for teeth.*

*"What's so fucking funny?" Mitch says, looking out across the lavender moonscape of this foreign land, beyond Black's figure. The world doesn't look as barren as he previously noted, at least not when he takes a good look at the shrouded horizon, the dark shadows and mountain peaks poking up, jagged cutouts in the dusty, purple glow of the atmosphere. The sky is cloudless above him but hidden in that same hazy blur. Flashes of lightning pepper the surface in white sparks, quick strikes hidden deep within the smog, creating pure white blinks that go off like a paparazzi party.*

*And beyond this...something floats. Up there. In the sky. Beyond the single cloud that seems to act as the barrier between here and the stratosphere. That massive shape begins to materialize, drifting among the strange cosmos like a blimp over a football stadium.*

*Swimming, Mitch thinks, the shape is swimming.*

*The shadow is bigger than any blimp, however. It's about the size of a football field, and the godlike being is undulating in such a way that Mitch can't even pinpoint the thing's definable shape. The gargantuan creature's girth, its totality, surprises him, even though his mind has already somewhat unlocked, changed his perspective* of reality. The surreal image before him stretches his ability to believe in unnatural things, and when he focuses on Quincy Black, the thing he's become, he knows this is not a trick of the mind or some cerebral breakdown he's suffered—no, it's real, and he's been temporarily transported into some alternate space or time, some vacuum in the universe kept separate from the one he used to know.

The Lacuna.

That's what this is.

The monster glides over him, sailing across those endless, cloudy skies. Then, unexpectedly, the shape begins to dart back and forth like a fish snapping up food flakes. The agility this entity exhibits confounds Mitch, shaking him to his core; a thing that size shouldn't be able to fling itself with such quickness, swim in the murk above with such grace, but it does, shooting its frame toward the bursts of lightning, collecting, feeding on those blinding flashes. The pattern becomes apparent with this second glance, and Mitch stares up in awe as the true terror behind Lacuna's Point surfs and eats, eats and surfs, holding dominion over everything below and beyond this awful realm.

Mitch wonders what's taking place in town, if the Light has appeared, the all-encompassing spark that folds over their eyes, blinding them and taking away their pain, their memories, and any semblance of their former selves, slowly stripping away their individuality and converting them into mindless servants for this truly unnamable monster. And for those strong enough to reject the influence of this great transaction, he wonders how their minds process these revelations, how consciously aware they are of what's happening behind the great veil that goes by the name of Lacuna's Point.

Mitch can see the talented folks, what their efforts have been turned into—Light for The Lacuna. Their abilities stolen, offered up as gifts for a hungry, higher power, the beast that preys on their light, love, and ultimate happiness, until they are purged of this wealthy stock and there is no more creative drive left, the wells of their originality drained, dried up, forced to exist in mediocrity, destined to produce nothing but dreck for the rest of their uninspired lives.

"Watch it feed," Black says, turning those hollow eyes to the sky, relishing the feast unfolding before them. The enormous shape that looks a bit like a jellyfish continues to zip back and forth, soaking up the Light, and the Light disappears like lightning bugs fading to darkness on hot summer nights. As the feeding drags on, Mitch notices the clouds are beginning to part, revealing the true dark nature of the universe over them. "Watch it devour, take on this beautiful and bountiful banquet of souls."

"Make it stop," Mitch says, feeling the energy of the orb filter through him. He gets an idea that maybe his soul is at risk, as if (by standing here on this other plane) the thing above is absorbing some of him, sucking out his energy and allowing the transfer to ascend the cosmos. "I said make it stop."

"But why?" Black asks. "Why stop? You can feel it, can't you? That transfer of power pouring into you, filling your soul, giving you an endless supply of not just imaginative thought—but hope too, the necessary drive for all creative beings. Hope is short in your homeworld—there's simply not enough to go around. Hope is the war within all people, a war most will never win, but you can, Mitchie Green. Ohhhhh, you can have all the hope you want in Lacuna's Point, and that hope will accelerate you and make your dreams come true. You can live the life you've always wanted. Be respected by your neighbors, be recognized for your accomplishments—be loved. That's what's missing from your life, isn't it? Love? You need it, of course you do—all humans need love and care—you are fragile creatures, after all. But that's not a problem here, in Lacuna's Point—here, all are loved. All can hope and dream, and all can see the Light."

"It's not real."

"What isn't? This?" The ancient magician scans the barrens, the sky above. "This realm is very real. It's the world behind the world, the gap between realities where only gods can roam. The world you know—this 'reality' you speak of—is nothing more than a curtain dropped over your eyes to keep you from experiencing the other worlds—like this one. The Lacuna. The space between."

"No...no, this is a trick."

"Reality is the trick, friend. The greatest trick the universe has ever constructed, has ever bestowed upon the human mind. Wake up my little Nemo—you've been living in a dream your entire life—a life filled without love and hope and the tools necessary to do what *you've been built to do—to create something meaningful, something that can and will inspire others to do the same."*

*"No."*

*"Yes."*

*"You're a liar," Mitch says, feeling like someone knocked the wind out of him with a battering ram. "This is not real."*

*"Since the day you stepped foot in Lacuna's Point, your creative drive has taken off like a rocket ship exploding toward the stars. You know it, I know it—there's no sense keeping secrets from yourself." He glances down at the orb, the white beams shining up between their fingers. "I can see into you, Mitchell Green. Your pain. Your woes. Your insecurities. Your crippling self-doubt. These things that damper your creative force. Let go of them. For yourself, for the world. The people need your art, your stories, the truths they expel. Let them have it. Let the Lacuna and the Light it provides give you the strength to carry out your greatest achievements. Let the writing flow from the Light through your fingertips. Let it—"*

*"NO!" Mitch shoves him back, but Black doesn't release the orb. He believes no matter how hard he pushes him, how much strength is behind the act, that Black is forever tethered to the object and— here—no force will dislodge him. "Get away from me. Take me back! TAKE ME BACK!"*

*A wavy smile runs across Black's face, showing those decayed morsels dotting his gums. "Never. You are one with the Lacuna now. And this place shall be your home. Forever."*

*Before Mitch can tell him to fuck himself, a funny thing happens, one he can't quite wrap his mind around. A sharp red line appears at the top of Black's forehead near the scalp and runs down the front of his face, splitting his skin, halving his face. Black's expression crumbles with worry, this sudden cosmetic alteration quite the shocker. His lips tremble as the mysterious dissection of flesh concludes.*

*"What is this?" Black asks.*

*And before either can answer, the two flaps of skin fold back, revealing the bloody combination of rotting, maggot-infested muscle and the knobby malformed skull beneath it.*

When Dawn clambers into the attic, she immediately sees Mitch and the Mayor holding the orb, jockeying for control of the object that's spraying out a considerable amount of bright, blinding light. Fighting through the shiny streaks, Dawn can make out the pair's eyes, noticing both sets are completely whited out like they've been possessed by some unearthly invader. She moves farther into the attic, putting distance between the opening and the sounds coming from below, the creatures and whatever Elroy Foley has changed into. The things bounding up the shaky, brittle spiral staircase.

"Dawn?" a small voice asks, and Dawn's attention turns to the corner of the belfry where Kya is resting on the ground. Metal manacles clamp her wrists and ankles, attached to galvanized chains, thick enough to give the average bolt cutter a real issue. "Dawn, is that you?" The girl sounds loopy, like she's been fed cough syrup on an empty stomach and has spent the time since staving off the coma-like sleep that follows.

"It's me," Dawn says, and rushes over to her, bypassing the Mayor and Mitch, dropping to her knees. "It's me, Ki, it's me." She runs her hands over her friend's body, making sure no mortal wounds have inflicted her. Kya's in pretty good shape save for her mind, which may or may not completely collapse in the coming moments. "I'm going to get you out of here. Is there a..." Dawn glances down at the manacles. "A key?"

Kya's head lolls, her eyelids fluttering wildly. "Pocket."

"Whose pocket?"

Kya lifts her arm, directing one finger toward the target—the Mayor. Black's head is cocked back, his eyes staring into worlds beyond this one, and Dawn knows what she has to do. She wishes she had a knife—that way she could run the blade across the bastard's throat after she gets the key, kill two birds with one stone. But she doesn't have a knife. She has nothing but her fists and wits, both of which will only take her so far.

Especially if Foley shows up.

*When* he shows up.

"I'll be right back," Dawn tells her, and then dashes over to the Mayor's side, stopping a few feet away so she can take the last few steps cautiously. Spying the man's jacket pocket, she sees the top of the skeleton key poking out. Without giving it much thought, she digs her hands into the crevice, gently closes her fingers around the curved metal, and frees the key. Gradually retracting her hand, she ensures she doesn't disturb the Mayor from whatever spell he's been put under. Next, Dawn slinks back over to her oldest, best friend, and sticks the key directly in the keyhole of the first manacle. Pops both sets with an audible click.

Free, Kya rubs her wrist. She's still out of it, hardly quick to her feet, but Dawn helps her.

"Dad?" she says, noticing her father, his altered state. She leaves Dawn's side, begins shuffling across the room, and Dawn does nothing to stop her.

At first.

It takes a second for her to realize she's intruding on something. The two men—though the Mayor's new (inhuman) face resembles the grotesque mask of some cheesy Halloween costume—are locked in some cosmic staring contest, and Dawn gets the impression that this is a party Kya shouldn't break up.

"Don't," Dawn whispers.

"He's in trouble," Kya says, soft trails of tears traveling down her cheeks. "We need to help…"

Dawn remembers something; she's been up here, in the Mayor's private quarters, many times before, when she was being reprimanded for breaking the town's rules, being forced to spend long hours here, painting and carrying out (what she always thought was) meaningless art projects. There's a box. Close. Not more than a dozen footsteps away, tucked in a corner of the belfry. A box that holds numerous art supplies, tools of all kinds.

She speeds in that direction, no longer caring if the Mayor wakes up from his odd nap, locating the small cluster of cardboard boxes. Once there, she begins to rifle through them, tearing and ripping and throwing out everything she can until she finds what she needs. Baking sheets and musical instruments, tools taken, stripped from the people who once came to Lacuna's Point, their sole possessions replaced by inferior versions, all fall to the floor in a glorious clatter. She heaves a harmonica over her shoulder, and the second it leaves her fingertips, she finds what she's looking for—something she can use to protect herself. It's not much, hardly a thing at all—but it's something.

Exhuming the small scalpel that was tucked in an apron buried beneath some brushes and color palettes, she glances back over her shoulder and watches Kya lay her hands on her father, attempting to separate him from the source of light that has grown dangerously bright. One quick glance directly into the glow and Dawn can't see anything but white for at least fifteen seconds.

Once she regains her sight, Dawn—scalpel in hand and ready to do damage to anyone who dares cross her—sees something emerge from the stairs. It's Foley of course, and he's wearing several of the ugly crab-things on his clothing, the malformed monsters clinging to him as if he's the net that scooped them out of the bay. A pair leech to his dead-gray flesh, digging their claws beneath his skin, shoveling pinches of meat into their greedy little mouths, growing fat from the nutrients their host provides.

Dawn yelps, though she doesn't mean to—the sight is too much for her. She means to avoid the approaching man-thing, the hideous figure making its way to the stair's summit, entering the changed atmosphere of the belfry, but her vocal outburst attracts Foley's eyes, which have clouded over, making him look even less human. Something slithers out of his mouth, and to Dawn, it looks like a snake, something black, reptilian, but then she realizes it's the man's tongue, just his tongue, as gross as that is. The dark muscle leaves behind a thick motor-oil stain across his lips and chin.

Dawn spins toward Kya. "Kya!"

Kya's head snaps toward her, her eyes wide with terror and desperation. Dawn holds the scalpel and tosses it to her friend, her best friend, the best damn friend a girl could ask for. Kya snatches the tool from the air with surprising deftness, especially considering her weakened state. But between the two of them, Kya was always the athlete, so the quick grab doesn't totally bowl Dawn over.

Kya steadies herself, holds the blade to her eyes as if examining the sharpness of the tip, and Dawn knows that she knows what must be done. As Kya turns to the Mayor, Dawn turns to Foley.

Foley's head sits crooked to one side. Like maybe he's suffered a stroke, and for all the man's been through, that wouldn't surprise her. The dark void of his mouth moves and stirs, the shadows within coming alive and drawing breath, hoarse whispers, inarticulate and garbled, spewing forth a pungent odor, black liquids that spill out in watery dumps. He has one foot in the attic, the other on the final stair, and that's when Dawn decides it's time to make her move. She kicks out her foot, the flat surface of her toes landing squarely on his chest. She's summoned enough force to send the man's shoulders arching back, but not quite enough to throw him off balance.

The leeching crabs on his flesh, those rotund critters, continue to hang on, biting and sucking, depleting the cop of life's necessary nutrients, the muscle that packs his bones noticeably shrinking. Foley's skin loses its pallor, and he's become ghost-white in the projecting lights the orb's thrown against the belfry's shadows.

Foley opens his mouth, trying to articulate some coherent thought, but it appears—in addition to his muscle and pigmentation—his thoughts have also bled from him. No sound emanates from the man's vocal cords, and he reaches out like a walking corpse in search of human brains. It doesn't take much for Dawn to motivate herself; she makes another attempt to defend the belfry from his presence. She aims with the tip of her toes this time, kicking the bastard in the chin, snapping his head back like a Pez dispenser in the angry hands of some maniac kid. This time, the force is enough for him to lose his balance, and he topples over, falling down on his back, tumbling down the spiral staircase.

With a rush of adrenaline, she flips over onto her stomach and faces Kya, who has drawn a vertical laceration down the middle of the Mayor's face. The blood begins to pour from the cut, running down his face in speedy rivulets. Then, his human eyes return, the white glaze that was hiding them shrinking at once.

"You naughty girls." A thin smile spills across his face. "Time to let the Lacuna feast on your bones..."

*Mitch watches Black's face split down the middle, blood streaming from the wound, turning the elder's face into a mask of gleaming red lines. Since realizing that something has interfered with this special moment, his eyes have changed, lost some of their luminance, the iridescent quality gone—but also still there, swimming somewhere in the murky waters of his mind.*

*"I'm going to kill both of them," says Black, grinning at Mitch. "I wonder how the ground dust of their bones will taste on my tongue." His tongue probes the air as if sampling such delights.*

*"Leave them be," Mitch says. "You lay a finger on—"*

*"You've made your choice, Mitchie. You now have to deal with the consequences."*

*Mitch blinks, and Black is gone.*

*He's alone now. In the Lacuna, that giant godlike jellyfish sailing the sky over him, clouds rolling like waves come ashore. Some of the cumulus formations fade to nothing, revealing a stretch of endless dark universe, and instead of stars, there are eyes, an incalculable number, that blink and stare, blink and stare, and Mitch can feel their hatred penetrate the depths of his soul, investigating his thoughts, his truths, whatever those might be.*

*Mitch feels a touch of madness taking him and doubts his mind can handle much more of this. He thinks this is where he'll die.*

*He's fully prepared to succumb to that great, final moment in time. In life.*

Kya watches the left side of the Mayor's face peel back like some cheap latex mask that hasn't cured yet, hasn't stuck to its subject quite right. It hangs off the side, revealing the bloody, chaotic mess of muscle and tissue, tumorous knots that live just beneath the surface of the Mayor's human costume. It turns her stomach, and she wants to vomit, but there's no time. The Mayor has turned from the glowing orb, abandoning the spread of Light, and is now facing her, his perfect white dentures showing despite the copious amounts of red leaking into his mouth.

"Come here you little cunt," he says, reaching out with both hands, and she notices his fingers have stretched, the flesh and bones elongating like good taffy, and his nails have grown considerably long and pointed. "Come to your new Daddy…your new God."

"Kya!" Dawn screams, and Kya looks over just in time to see the thing Elroy Foley has become take her neck, those hideous creatures entrenched in his flesh now leaving their host and jumping on hers like fleas finding the first available fur-body. "Help!"

Kya holds out the scalpel as Quincy Black approaches, those elongated inhuman fingers searching for soft, warm muscles to sink into. She slashes the air between them, but Black doesn't flinch.

Doesn't blink. He keeps moving, almost hovering over the ground as he closes the gap.

"Don't worry, Kya," he says, his voice different, more guttural. Every syllable dripping with sinister inflections. "I'll make it hurt, every second, and those seconds will last an eternity. Your own personal Lacuna of pain."

"Fuck you, you piece of shit!"

She lunges at him, scalpel out, driving the tip directly toward his right eye. There's a sharp squelch and an agonizing howl once she works the sharp point deep into the socket. Not deep enough to kill, but deep enough to deal some serious damage. She retracts the scalpel and goes for the other eye, but that attempt is blocked by Black's forearm.

"Kya!" Dawn screams again, and Kya looks over to see her friend being devoured by the thing that's shed Officer Elroy Foley like a snake leaving its old skin behind. Foley's mouth drops open impossibly wide, his jaw so broken that the skin around his lips has split and torn like an old T-shirt stretched beyond its limits, and there's a big, black mass emerging from the center of it, something that looks like a giant caterpillar, a long, doughy body, and the prolegs are reaching out, extending from its human cave, looking for purchase on Dawn's flesh.

The distraction gives Black the opportunity to reach her. He grabs her throat and hoists her up, throwing her against the rafters, pinning her to the long wooden beam that fortifies the roof. Everything goes immediately dim, even the abundance of Light escaping the magical orb, the one her father is still holding, losing himself further and further into the white abyss that glows, that seeps out and infects everything it touches.

She thinks this is it, this is how it ends, this is how she finally dies. After three years, the torment is over, and she can finally move on.

She closes her eyes and waits for Death to clamber down from its dark throne and claim her.

Then, she hears someone say, "Hey, Black?"

Through the dim haze of the room, she squints, looking at her father. He's still holding the orb, the Light still shooting out of it in glorious waves, but he's no longer captivated, entranced by its hypnotic powers.

He's staring at Quincy Black.

And he's grinning.

The belfry begins to shake, a lot, so much she can feel Black losing his balance, swaying to one side and then the other.

She doesn't know if the vibrations are coming from below or above, but either way, its presence is godlike.

A purple light floods the room, beaming down from the heavens that have suddenly appeared where the ceiling used to be—and it feels like oblivion coming to claim whatever's left of her fractured soul.

# CHAPTER TWENTY-FOUR

Staring into the radiant purple glow before him, Dan Brower doesn't believe he's ever seen anything more beautiful in his life. The tiny orb, no bigger than a golf ball, emits a lavender shine that fans out in holographic streams, bathing the walls of the clock tower's belfry in this majestic hue. He finds himself drawn to it, much like a moth to a glowing lantern. Before he knows it, he's completely captivated, fixed on the object and its unearthly shine, drawn to the mysteries that might lie inside this violet world.

"Brower?" Wally asks, finally catching up. Much too invested in the light, Dan doesn't bother acknowledging him. "Brower, what—"

The light shines brighter, peeling back every shadow, revealing each beam and truss, every naked material the attic offers.

"Stand back," Dan warns him. "Something is happening."

And something is.

The entire world begins to quake.

The clock tower's ceiling and roof are completely gone now, the top half of the clock itself disappearing in the newly formed realm that's taken over the sky. It's the place that Mitchell Green has just come from, that purple world with the jellyfish-like monstrosity cruising across the eye-littered cosmos. The Lacuna has come, it is here, and everyone in the room can now see into its vast and endless surface, behold the wonders no human eyes have ever set upon.

Mitch smiles at Black, the man who currently has his daughter pinned to the ...well, the ceiling was there, now it's been eaten by this new world. He's hoisting her into the air, the magenta haze that's filtering down into the attic. He's facing Mitch, looking none too pleased about seeing him again, and Mitch notices there's something gravely wrong with his face; whatever human mask it had tried to replicate is now gone, peeled back, disclosing the hideous makeup of fat boils and tumorous growths beneath. Mitch ignores the grotesque nature of this evil being, the power-hungry monster who will stop at nothing to get what he wants, who will continue to lure and drag people into a town most would never want to step foot in ever again if they only knew what *he* knew, if they only knew a fraction of the truth. Mitch smiles, knowing he's got the good Mayor exactly where he wants him.

"What are you so fucking happy about, Mitchie-my-bitchie?" shouts the Mayor. He points a gnarled, bony finger at him from across the attic. "You've lost! The Lacuna has come! Oh, what a joyous occasion for you! The truths you shall now know!"

"I don't think this is going down how you think it's going down," Mitch says with confidence. He glances up, watching the shadow-thing glide across the purple murk, the foggy veil now separating and losing some of its smokiness. Within seconds, Mitch—and the rest of them—can see the God's true form, the face of the Lacuna, the thing that sleeps and eats and sleeps again. The thing that dreams and causes the minds around it to dream too. The thing that will undoubtedly cause many ongoing nightmares for Mitchell Green, should he be so lucky to escape what's coming next.

Mitch nods. "Quincy Black—see you in Hell, motherfucker."

From the sky, large tentacles drop down like a combat chopper's rappel. The alien extensions hit the floor and flop around, trying to gain traction on the foreign terrain, and once they realize the nature of this earthly bottom, they turn their attention on the task at hand.

"What did you do?" Black asks, and his focus has shifted away from Kya now—in fact, he's lowering her. Her feet reach the plywood below. He's still gripping her neck, an act that continues to supply Mitch's veins with hot lava, disgust circling every inch of him, but he's able to control the murderous rage for now. At least she's back on the ground, one step closer to freedom. "You…" Black says, those sunken eyes twinkling with realized doubt. "You…fuck! WHAT DID YOU DO?"

Mitch answers by continuing to keep quiet and smiling at him. Black finally lets go of Kya's throat, turns completely, and storms across the room, looking up at the thing he's been feeding for the last seventy human years or so—though Mitch believes it's much longer.

Black's sunken eyes fill with light, and maybe it's *the* Light, the very same source that seems to power the town and keep the people from revolting, from escaping.

Black screeches, "YOU WILL NOT—" but he doesn't finish that thought. Instead, a fallen tentacle coils around his left leg, squeezing him tightly like a boa securing its next meal. Then, the tentacle pulls, tripping Black, forcing him forward, onto his face. The magical wanderer hits the ground with a driving blow, the impact strong enough to make the plywood jump, revolt against the nails that pin the board to the framework. Lethargically, Black's head lolls to the side, and he arches his brow as if he wants to make one last plea, one final deal to prevent what's happening from actually happening. But he can't speak. That spectral light fades from his eyes, leaving them dark and cold, barren like much of the landscape he's destined to become a prisoner of. And then, like that, Mitch Green can tell the bastard to fuck himself one last time before the tentacles collect around him, wrapping them in their powerful, slimy extensions, and then hoist him up, airborne, into the spectacular alien skies of the Lacuna, toward the hungry gargantuan that patrols the eye-studded spaces of unreality.

"HELP!"

Kya is able to take her first full breath when she hears her friend cry out for assistance. Her eyes dart across the room and she sees Dawn fending off the monstrosity that Foley's become. He's trying to drag her back down the stairs, those football-sized crabs continuing to dig at her flesh, searching for ways inside.

Mitch runs over to the stairs and reaches out, grabbing Dawn's hand, taking it and pulling her. But Foley is determined to tow her back down. He's wrestling with her other arm, and it seems like he has twice the strength Mitch has, especially now that he's recuperating from that trip across the stars to that other plane.

He has both hands on her now but allows one of them to leave Dawn so he can punch Foley in the face, a face that has been reduced to a bleeding sheet of raw, pus-leaky muscle. The cop's head knocks back, and Kya hears bones crackling along with the alignment-altering snap of the man's spine, the whiplash causing him to arch in the most unnatural of ways. His body is decomposing and weak, fragile in almost every way, and Kya wonders if one more pop will put him down for the count. Just when her father rears back with his fist, another tentacle whips down from the sky and slithers around both Dawn and Foley. The two are lifted up as if they just jumped into a chamber with zero gravity. Then they're planted in the center of the belfry, near the bell itself, and dropped onto the floor. There, the two bodies separate. The crabs fall from Dawn's body, and the second they hit the plywood, they seek out the shadowy spaces the attic has to offer, seeking refuge from the eldritch beast that rules the spaces above this world. But it's no use. There's no shadow this monster won't find, and several more cables of alien flesh drop from the purple shroud, curling around its prey—the crabs—and yanking them skyward.

Foley makes one last attempt to corral Dawn, and his badly disfigured hands, missing pockets of flesh and displaying fingers bent in grotesque directions, are able to grip her ankle. Another tentacle comes for him, snaking around his waist and lifting him into the air. But one comes for Dawn too, and, in a blink, Kya watches her friend's feet leave the plywood, her body falling in reverse, the purple haze claiming her. Elroy Foley grips Dawn's ankle, clutching and dragging her up into the misty atmosphere.

"NO!" Kya shouts and jumps from where she's standing, reaching out and gripping her hands. Dawn shouts back and takes Kya's hands, and Mitch comes running over to help. There's a split second when Kya thinks this is the last time she'll ever look her best friend in the eye, that her arms can't handle the game of tug-and-war for long, that they'll pop right out of her sockets, but she manages to hold on just long enough for another fleshy rope to fall from that cloudy expanse. She watches it slip around Foley's throat like a noose, making several revolutions, covering every inch of decaying flesh from his shoulders to his chin. The tentacle tightens its hold, and Foley's eyes burst in their sockets, splashing the back of Dawn's pants with vitreous goo. Then, the cop's grip begins to slip. Loosens completely. Foley's mouth works its way open as if there's some final word to be spoken, but alas, there is not. The man goes fully limp, losing complete control over his extremities, and his body slips away and slides upward, toward the sky, toward the God, into the belly of the Lacuna, lost forever beyond the stars and the endless horrors that await him there.

The three survivors of this attack fall to the floor. All at once, they turn their attention to the ceiling that is not there, the purple reveal of that other place. In the light, clouds fold over the sky, the jellyfish God, and everything gets grainy as the purple wash begins to deepen, darken, fade away into the distance. In a few blinks, the clock tower's roof and ceiling reappear, and it's like the past twenty minutes or so never actually happened.

There's still some purple light filtering down into the room, and Kya looks to her side, sees the magical orb that Quincy Black once possessed, held so dearly.

She grabs it.

"What are you doing?" her father asks.

"I don't know..." And it's true. She doesn't. But there's something inside of the thing that calls to her, that makes her hold it, that forces her to gaze into that soft magenta glow. "I can see..."

In that instant, a crack appears near the clock tower's face, matching the same hue of the orb's glow, that lilac stain so boldly presented only moments earlier. And she sees a hand reaching through it. A face.

"Dad?" Dawn says, her entire body trembling.

Dan Brower looks confused, and then, even more so, terrified of his discovery. "What...Dawn?"

"Dawn, wait," Mitch says, holding her back. "How do we know it's really him?"

"Mitch," he says, dumbfounded. "Holy shit—Mitch, it's you. Kya? *Holy shit.*"

"What do you see?" another man asks from somewhere behind Dan.

Dan turns and says, "I found them! I found them!" Then, to the three: "Guys, hurry up. I don't know how long this will stay open, but...it's the strangest thing. I can *feel* it closing." He winces as if the doorway is a heavy load he cannot hold forever. "Hurry," he says again, nearly breathless.

Dawn doesn't hesitate and sprints forward, rushing toward that purple crevice.

Kya and her father exchange glances. Shrug. Before they follow, Kya grabs her father's wrist. "I missed you so much, Dad."

Tears in his eyes, he nods. "Yeah, I missed you too, baby."

"I want to go home."

He hugs her, and she's never felt better in all her life. "Let's go home."

Dan hugs his daughter close and, overcome with emotion, begins to sob in a way he never has before. He can't believe the moment is real, can't believe that after three years he can finally hold her again, can finally reconnect with that special love previously lost. There aren't a lot of ways to describe this feeling, and if asked in the future, he doubts he'll articulate what it truly feels like. But if he has to try, he would say it feels like the day she was born, only three of four times that because she was never lost then. Only found.

And now she's found again.

"Having real trouble understanding this," Wally says once they're all outside by the unmarked cruiser, far enough from the abandoned clock tower, close enough to the outskirts of the dead town so that they all feel safe.

Mitch doesn't think he'll ever feel safe, knowing that even the ghost of Lacuna's Point still remains intact and standing, able to be rediscovered. He wonders what will happen to the town, the other side of it, now that it's lost its leaders. Then he decides he doesn't really care, that he hopes it all falls into the endless void of that great beyond.

"Why don't we table the questions, Wally," Dan suggests. "I'm sure everyone is tired and hungry and needs some time to...*process* things."

"What did we see, Brower?" The nervousness in Wally's words is evident. He clearly saw something on the other side of that purple glow, something he caught a glimpse of and shouldn't have, and now that madness exists within him. It'll start out as doubt, Mitch thinks, but it's a doubt that will rest there forever and could transform into something more, something possibly dangerous.

"I saw some people who were kidnapped," Dan says. "Taken to this abandoned town."

Dawn nods. "Yeah, it was that cop that took us. Or at least…he pretended to be one." She hangs her head, sniffling. "And he killed my mother."

"Good Lord," Wally says, wrestling with his belt as he arches back. "What'd this fella look like?" He takes out a notepad, starts scribbling in it.

Mitch sighs. "He had the most inhuman eyes I've ever seen in another person. In fact, I don't think this maniac was very human at all. He was a complete monster."

Wally swallows. "And this fella, this kidnapper—he still alive?"

"Doubt it," Mitch answers, and that's the last thing he has to say on the subject, until he's forced to later in some official capacity. But by that time, the three of them will work out a better story, one that will stick. One that will make more sense than the truth.

Because the truth—no one will ever believe.

Mitch hardly believes it himself and he was there.

# TWO WEEKS LATER

She's in the bathroom, staring at the mirror image longer than most people would care to look at themselves—not for the first time since coming home—and she's wondering if today is the day. Kya's felt it coming on for some time now, at least over the last four days, and every day she feels those sensitive sensations in the pit of her stomach, she's positive she's getting closer. Now, she's sure it will happen today. Dawn has felt it coming on too, and the girls have been texting each other almost every hour to see if there've been any significant changes.

Just when she thinks her instincts are wrong, she feels that swimming sensation resurface. Like a rush of adrenaline or an irregular heartbeat, that quick flutter in her belly. She puts both hands on the vanity and leans over the sink, opening her mouth and preparing for the thing that she's sure will happen. Continuing to stare at herself, not sure why she wants to subject her eyes to the upcoming horror, she braces for it.

It rises up her throat, a slow ascent. Crawling almost. Kya feels every movement, every step. She almost chokes when the thing lingers near her gag reflex, and that's when she starts to heave, her whole body lurching, helping the thing inside make its earthly exit. She sees that milky-white shell reach the edge of her lips, the big pincher protruding between her teeth. It fights to stay inside, pinching her cheeks and tongue, trying to grip on and stave off the ejection. Once she has a better view of the crab, she grips the fucker with both hands and pries the thing from her lips, carefully opening the pinchers so it won't rip her up. The extraction provides her with instant relief, like tearing off a Band-aid that's taken a pretty good hold. After the successful maneuver, she drops the albino crab into the sink, watches it struggle and squirm languidly, as if being introduced to this new climate has taken a toll on its body. Belly-up, the crab kicks its legs and pinchers, all ten attachments wriggling in unison. It fights to adapt, but she knows the truth far quicker than the crab does—it will die here. It would die anywhere that's not in that place between places, a place like Lacuna's Point.

As she watches its movements grow feeble, her phone rings.

"Did it happen?" Dawn answers as soon as she hears Kya pick up. "Did it happen for you too?"

"Yes."

"Oh," Dawn says, breathing a sharp sigh of relief. Within seconds, Dawn is crying, like when she called four years prior to say she was accepted to Georgetown too, and that their adolescent plans were finally coming to fruition. Different situation, different tears. But same Dawn. Same *them*.

Same relief.

"I'm going to stomp the fucker and then flush the remains," Kya tells her, watching the crab cycle through its last attempt to acclimate.

Dawn staunches the flow of tears long enough to say, "Do it." And then: "Ki? It's really over now, isn't it?"

Kya peers into the mirror, feeling more like herself than she ever has. "Yes. Yes, it is."

After she hangs up, she plops the dead-ish creature on the tile floor, brings her foot down several times, several forceful stomps until there's nothing left but fractured white shards and lumpy deposits of booger-green guts. Then she flushes the remains, watches them disappear down into the toilet's watery swirl.

Then she remembers—there's something else she needs to do, something she probably should have done already. Inside her pocket, she retrieves the other thing—the orb from Lacuna's Point.

The magical sphere she lifted from the clock tower, old Eddy.

Only here, it's the size of a marble, not a Magic Eight-Ball. Perfect for flushing.

And she does.

The second flush takes the sphere into the plastic labyrinth of the plumbing system.

Never to be seen again.

Never to be remembered.

Kya Green closes her eyes and cries the kind of tears she's never cried before.

*"THE END"*

Mitch types those two words—the two most beautiful words in any writer's arsenal—in the document and then sits back, stares at the screen for longer than probably necessary, but he doesn't care.

After six weeks of working non-stop, exploring every idea and plot point, he's finally done it.

He's finished his novel.

His eyes well. It's been a long journey. He's relieved, but a part of him will miss it, those little precious minutes of the creation process that you can't relive until you make something else. But the first will always be special. Even if the writing isn't the best. Even if he'll get better with more practice. Even if not all the ideas coalesce on the first go-around. Fact is, he's finished, and finishing is worthy of the biggest celebrations.

He presses print and waits for the machine to spit out all two hundred and twenty-one pages, about a hundred-thousand words. Once it's finished, he tucks the pages under his arm and heads downstairs.

Angie's in the kitchen, making her evening cocktail.

"I finished," he says, placing the manuscript on the counter.

She smiles at him. "Congratulations."

"Thanks," he says. "It's just a rough draft. You know. Needs work. Plus, I have this other idea that's been bugging me, so...I might start on that right away. I dunno."

"What will you do with that one?"

He sighs. "Someone wants to take a look at it, so...I'll probably give it to them. See what happens, though." He shrugs. *No big deal.* "This is just a trunk novel."

"Trunk novel?"

"One that sits in the trunk, never to be read by the masses." He smiles. "Because it's so bad."

"Ah."

They stare at each other, waiting for the other to know what to say next.

Then Angie says, "Well, I can make you a drink. You big author you."

Lips curling, he flashes his teeth. "Yeah, I'd love that."

She goes for the cabinet and he grabs her, putting his arms around her and pulling her close. He kisses her, more passionately than he has in a long time, probably not since their wedding day.

"Where'd that come from?" she asks, and her eyes genuinely seem like they want to know. It's the first time in a long time she's looked at him that way—with so much attention.

"I love you, Angie Green."

"I love you, too."

"No, but I really do. And I'm not just saying that. I truly, truly love you."

They kiss again, and it's better than the one before it.

"I know I haven't been the best husband these last few years. But things are going to change. *I'm* going to change. Okay? I promise."

"Okay."

"And now that I got this novel out of me, I feel like I can move on from that weird place in my life. Does that make sense?"

"Not to me. But if it does to you, then I guess that's all that matters."

"I love you."

"Love you, too."

Another kiss. Warm, wet, and homey.

She makes them drinks.

Later, before Mitch leaves to go upstairs to bed, Angie says, "Mitch? I never really thanked you for bringing our baby home."

He nods. "Thank you for giving us something to come home to."

The next morning, as soon as the sun appears over the horizon, Mitch Green kisses his sleeping wife goodbye and heads downstairs, grabs the manuscript off the counter, and makes for the car in the driveway. He then proceeds to drive five and a half hours from New Jersey to Virginia without stopping, not even to pee. He avoids his morning cup of coffee specifically for this reason.

He parks in the dead lot near the outskirts of Lacuna's Point, deciding to walk to the clock tower. It hasn't changed in the six weeks since he's last been here, with the exception of the police's caution tape around the front door. But that's no issue because he isn't going inside, has no intention of doing so. He doesn't even want to go near it, but a promise is a promise, a deal is a deal, and Mitch Green doesn't think he should tempt the gods by going back on their accord.

He bounds the steps of the municipal building, the manuscript tucked neatly under his left arm, his concentration never leaving that moonlike face of the giant timekeeper. He examines the dead hands that will never move again, and he tries to recall his time spent on the other side. It's weird; six weeks and his memory is hazy, full of holes and gaps, like an old broken dream. He doesn't regret not remembering every awful detail of his time there, and it's enough to recall only some of the bad things that happened. But like all dreamworlds, he thinks that—in time—the memories will dwindle down, and it will become hard to recall a single image of that alien space.

It doesn't matter. He's come to finish the thing and get out of there. Never return again.

He leaves the manuscript on the landing, about ten feet from Eddy's entrance. Before he turns his back, he thinks he senses someone on the other side of the door. A presence, though not exactly a maleficent one.

A haunted feeling spikes down his spine, motivating him to spin around, and he practically runs back to the car.

Once there, he looks at the clock tower one last time. On the steps, where he left his first completed manuscript, is a figure, one he recognizes immediately. It's Ellie Brower, and she's standing tall. Smiling. The manuscript is in her hands. She gives him a curt nod that seems nothing more than an acknowledgment of the transaction, though he believes there's a thank you buried inside there somewhere. Least, that's what he tells himself.

He nods back.

Then she turns, heads back inside, disappearing behind the door where the rest of Lacuna's Point's specters have gathered to marvel over their new offering.

Mitch shakes his head, gets back in his car, drives home, and, as he does so, the memories of Lacuna's Point fade and fade, and by the time he pulls into his driveway, he's forgotten where he was that morning.

But he thinks it's time to grab coffee and get started on that book he's always wanted to write.

# TURN THE PAGE

POP'S SHOP looks like any other gas station/convenience store combo, though it has this certain undeniable backwoods charm, and Bill Rubin heads inside to pay for the full tank he's just pumped. He greets the man behind the counter with a smirk and a twenty spot.

"Beautiful day, isn't it?" Bill says.

"Hmm," Pop (presumably) says with a grunt. The old man has the personality of a disinterested hound in its golden years, and Bill thinks that the customer service industry probably isn't the right place for him. But Bill guesses at eighty years old (or however old he is) the business has taken its toll, worn him down into the curmudgeonly form before him.

"Say, you ever hear of a place called 'Lacuna's Point?' " Bill asks, getting to the meat of this conversation, the reason he paid in cash rather than swiping his card at the pump. "Heard it's not too far from here, but we're having some trouble locating it. It's not on any map, that's for sure."

"We?" Pop nods out the window. "You mean, you and those assholes with all that camera equipment?"

Bill turns, looks to his crew. "Yeah, we're shooting a documentary."

"A docu-what-now?" Pop glares at him as if the term's offensive to country folk.

"A documentary? You know. A movie. But it's investigative journalism. It's based on those people who went missing around this area. A few years ago, those two girls were found. Said some psycho dressed up as a cop and kidnapped them. Talked about a place called Lacuna's Point. But...no one can seem to find it. Which is weird, right?"

Pop nods. *Weird, all right.*

"Now there's all these blog posts," Bill continues, "and people are claiming they've been there and have seen the clock tower that—"

"Son," Pop says, scratching his stubble. "You ain't making a lick of goddamn sense."

"Oh," Bill says, his mood souring at once. "Sorry. I guess I'll just go, then." He turns for the door, gets five steps, and then hears Pop clear his throat.

"You know," the old man says, "on second thought—I have seen that clock tower. It's been in this one old town that's been abandoned for—hell, going on eighty-plus years now. Ain't nothing there now but old, abandoned buildings. Shit, don't even know if the town has a name."

"You've seen it? Lacuna's Point?"

The old man shrugs, traces of a grin bleeding through. "I've seen the clock tower in passing, that's about all."

Excitedly, Bill asks, "Do you know, like, where exactly?"

Pop nods, that smile stretching farther. "I'll draw you a map."

# AUTHOR'S NOTE

The bulk of this novel was written in early 2020 when so much was happening around the world and in the United States. It's interesting how much real-life horror made its way into this novel, and I can't say it was a completely conscious effort. I'm very proud of how this one turned out, and I hope you enjoyed your trip to *Lacuna's Point*. Some of you may recognize the Mayor from another work of mine—if you did, what a prize for you. If you didn't—well, keep searching. You never know where he'll pop up.

I'd like to thank a couple of early beta readers who provided some feedback: Janine Pipe (author, filmmaker, producer, and the hardest-working person I've maybe ever met) for being the first to put eyes on an early version of this manuscript, and Deb (my favorite Scares That Care neighbor!) for her keen eye on a later draft.

I could easily fill up a few pages with *thank you*s, but I feel like I already used up enough paper with this book. I do want to thank a few more people who helped bring this novel to life in one way or another. Andrew at DarkLit Press for saying "yes" to *Lacuna's Point* in the first place. It's not easy to commit to publishing a 120,000+-word novel (especially in the small press business) but Andrew championed this from the second I sent it, and I don't think I've ever met a more dedicated EIC; his constant hustle and marketing insights have been invaluable, and I'm lucky he took a chance on me and this novel—thank you, sir. Also, shout out to my film/tv agent Karmen Wells for believing in my work and making this last year or so an exciting one. Much love to my wife, Ashley, for her continued support while I travel to other worlds for a few hours each day—none of this would be possible without her love and encouragement. And finally, my son, Jack, who continues to shape my understanding of the world in new ways each and every day. Love you both to the stars and back.

TM
11.29.2022

# A NOTE FROM DARKLIT PRESS

All of us at DarkLit Press want to thank you for taking the time to read this book. Words cannot describe how grateful we are knowing that you spent your valuable time and hard-earned money on our publication. We appreciate any and all feedback from readers, good or bad. Reviews are extremely helpful for indie authors and small businesses (like us). We hope you'll take a moment to share your thoughts on Goodreads and/or BookBub.

You can also find us on all the major social platforms including Facebook, Instagram, and Twitter. Our horror community newsletter comes jam-packed with giveaways, free or deeply discounted books, deals on apparel, writing opportunities, and insights from genre enthusiasts.

## VISIT OUR LITTLE-FREE-LIBRARY OF HORRORS!

# About the Author

Tim Meyer dwells in a dark cave near the Jersey Shore. He's an author of over fifteen novels and novellas, including Malignant Summer, The Switch House, Dead Daughters, Limbs, and many other titles. His screenplay adaptation for The Switch House has won two finalist awards (Semifinalist, ScreenCraft Horror Competition 2020 & Semifinalist, Filmmatic Horror Screenplay Awards 5). He exists on coffee and IPAs.

You can visit him at timmeyerwrites.com.

# CONTENT WARNINGS

VIOLENCE

GORE

PROFANITY

RACISM

# DARKLIT
## PRESS